Love in a Warm Climate

Love

in

A Warm Climate

Helena Frith Powell

GIBSON SQUARE

First published in 2011 by Gibson Square Books

www.gibsonsquare.com

ISBN: 978-1906142773

Printed by Clays, Bungay.

To my girlfriends, most of whom are not French.

Love in a Warm Climate

Rule 1

Be careful where you put your (matching) underwear

The French Art of Having Affairs

"Since when did you start wearing a bra?" I ask my husband as he walks into our bedroom.

This is not typical of our Sunday afternoon conversations, which on any other Sunday might include a discussion about crap articles in the Sunday papers, his latest round of golf (possibly worse than the articles), what to have for dinner or whether or not the children should have a puppy.

But today is different.

Ten minutes ago, dutiful wife that I am, I started to repack his black Mulberry leather bag, a Christmas present from me last year. He is still commuting back to England for work while I stay in our lovely new home in France. Only Nick has clearly been doing more than just working.

Unpacking the bag I found socks, crumpled shirts, boxer shorts; all the usual stuff. I rummaged around to reach the last few bits. Then I touched something that felt somehow unexpected. It felt like lace and silk. I took it out. It was a bra. And it was not for me. Unless he bought it for me eight years and three breastfeeding children ago and just forgot to hand it over.

I dropped it as if it had burned me. It lay there on our blue and white patchwork bedspread, as real as everything else in the room but totally out of place. I wanted to scream, but the sound stuck in my throat, as if someone was trying to throttle me.

I tried to breathe deeply and calm down. Just because there was a bra in his bag didn't necessarily mean he had been shagging its owner. There might be another, perfectly reasonable, explanation. He might be a cross-dresser. Would that be better or worse?

Or maybe it was a joke. Nick had just been on a business trip to New York. Perhaps one of the other traders thought it would be a good wheeze to liven up his homecoming. But if that were the case, they would have chosen something slightly more garish. A red lace number with tassels, perhaps? Or maybe black PVC in size quadruple D. But not the cream lace and silk item with a delicate floral pattern lying on our bed, which is the kind of bra you buy for a woman you actually like, as well as want to shag.

I picked it up again and turned it over a couple of times. It was a B-cup. It looked new. The label said La Perla. My best friend Sarah has underwear from La Perla; she is the fashion editor of a glossy magazine so gets sent it for free. I picked up some La Perla knickers up once when I strayed into the posh underwear section of Peter Jones. They were over £100, which is more than I would usually spend on a fridge. When the sales assistant asked if she could help me I was worried she might charge me just to hold them.

"So why are you carrying a bra in your bag?"

"Ah," says my husband and stops dead in his tracks as he spots the bra in my hand. There follows one of those silences that are more noisy than quiet.

"Ah … I'm sorry I forgot to tell you I'm a cross-dresser but I only do it on Sundays and I am getting help'?" I try.

Nick laughs uneasily and tries to flash that cheeky Irish grin of his that never fails to charm people. It's failing now, however.

"It's not mine," he begins.

"You surprise me," I respond, adding. "And I suppose that's supposed to make me feel better."

"I can explain. You see; it's like this."

He walks towards me slowly across the wooden floor. I can see he is trying to buy time before he comes up with a good enough excuse for the bra in the bag.

"Is this one of your famous Irish jokes?" I ask. "The one about the Scottish bloke, the English bloke and the… er, expensive bra?"

"No, Soph, I'll level with you. I've been seeing someone, but really it meant nothing. Honest."

Dear God. Has he been reading *The Bastard's Book of Tired Old Clichés*?

"Who is she?" I demand. "Clearly not a French woman or she

would have left her knickers in there as well; one is no good without the other as any self-respecting French woman will tell you."

At least if she is French then I can ruin her week by confiscating one half of her matching underwear set.

"She's French, from Paris. She's called Cécile," he replies. "She's one of our most important clients. I can't explain how it happened, but it started with work meetings and then she insisted we go out one evening and…."

He trails off.

"And?" I prompt. "And when you told her all about me and your three young children she said 'what a lovely bunch they sound. Please take this bra home for them?'"

He sighs. I see the fight go out of those gorgeous green Irish eyes. He has that look he had when Liverpool scored against Chelsea in the 90th minute of the FA Cup Final.

"Oh Soph, she just seemed so determined and to want me so much, in the end I just gave in. Pathetic I know, and there's no excuse, and I am truly sorry. I suppose I was flattered."

Yes, he most definitely has been reading *The Bastard's Book of Tired Old Clichés.*

Daisy the cat comes in and starts rubbing up against his legs; bloody feline traitor. Does she know the French aren't big on cat rescue homes? God, I'm angry. Not with Daisy, she doesn't know any better, but with him, and with this French bitch.

"And how long has this liaison been going on?" I ask, rather impressed with myself that I can come up with such a long word in my darkest hour.

"I met her about five months ago," he sighs.

"You've been seeing her for five MONTHS?" I leap from our bed in shock.

I can't bloody believe it. He's been betraying us all for all that time, the total shit. Now I'm not angry, I'm furious, added to which I feel like the most stupid woman alive. How could I not have noticed?

"Well, not really seeing, more, well, sleeping with. It's more a sex thing Soph, really, but it's you I love."

"If it's me you love what are you doing shagging some flat-chested floozy?"

"Well, you don't seem to want to sleep with me."

"It's not that I don't want to," I shriek. "It's just that I'm so bloody tired. In case you hadn't noticed we have three small children and I've just been knackered for years."

I want to punch him but instead, much to my fury, I start to cry, more from rage than anything else. And the more I cry, the angrier I am at myself. Whatever happened to dignity in crisis?

The injustice of it all makes me angrier by the minute. We have been together for ten years, we have had three children and now I am no longer the right bra size. I slump back down onto our bed.

"Sweetheart," he says, and starts walking towards me again.

Sweetheart? I put my hand up to stop him. "I think you'd better just go," I say.

Nick looks amazed. "Soph, darling, don't be silly, we can get through this storm in a B-cup."

I glare at him. There are times when his humour can take my

mind off anything. This is definitely not one of those times.

"Seriously," he goes on, sitting next to me on our bed, our beautiful mahogany sleigh bed; a romantic wedding present from his parents and my mother and whichever one of her five husbands she was married to at the time. The bed where all our children have been conceived, where I have breastfed and nurtured them, the bed they crawl into when they need comforting and sleep in as a special treat when they're not well. I never imagined I would be sitting on it with Nick discussing his lover's bra.

"I thought moving here would be the end of it. I really wanted to make a fresh start. I know you're knackered, you've been brilliant, you've looked after everyone so well; you really don't deserve this. I'm so sorry Soph, I really am. But let's be honest, you hardly notice I'm around. The last time you were the one to start sex was probably before Edward was born, which is…."

"I know how long ago it was," I snap at him. It was five years ago. Have I really not initiated sex for FIVE YEARS? I try to think but I can't focus. Surely that can't be the case. What about his birthday?

"You didn't even initiate sex on my birthday," he says. He has an annoying habit of reading my mind.

I can't fight back. The walls seem to be moving backwards and forwards. I feel like I'm watching myself in a film. I wish someone would rewind it and take me back to the bit where I see the bag and I decide to let the faithless bastard unpack it himself. Even though I don't know he's a faithless bastard.

He takes my hand.

"Please Soph, I made a stupid mistake, she doesn't mean anything to me. Please give me another chance. I promise I'll stop seeing her."

Yeah, right, I think. "Fuck off Nick," I say. "I hate you." How trite; but somehow nothing else comes to mind. And it pretty much says it all.

Looking at him, imagining him with someone else, I feel sick. I remove my hand from his. The thought of him with another woman is wrong, it's repulsive, it's … not fair.

"Come on Soph, we can work at this, don't you think? It's worth it for the sake of the children."

"And what about for our sake?" I ask. "Is it worth it for our sake?"

Nick sighs and gets up from the bed. He walks around the room for what seems like an age. He looks out of the French windows across the vineyards. I can't begin to imagine what he's thinking. I sit there like a nervous schoolgirl in the headmaster's office waiting for Nick to determine the future of our marriage. He broke it so either he has to fix it or it's over.

I can hardly allow the thought that it could be over to enter my head. How can it be? We have three lovely children, twin girls and a boy, and ten years of marriage behind us. And a cat, two peacocks plus a stray dog. And we've just moved to a new life in France. This is not an ideal time to be splitting up.

Rather as your life is said to flash before your eyes when you've had an accident, I see our past: our first date, the little black dress I wore, the kiss goodnight, the butterflies I used to feel every time I thought about him, our first romantic weekend in Paris, meeting Nick's parents and knowing somehow I would come back to that house outside Dublin often, his proposal in Hyde Park, our beautiful wedding, the twins, Edward, the move to France and then what? The film stops there.

Finally he comes back and stands in front of me. He runs his fingers through his dark hair, something he does when he's either nervous or trying to look good. I assume it's not the latter.

"To be honest Soph, sometimes I feel like we're no longer a couple," he begins slowly. "We're just two people who happen to live in the same house."

"I don't see you making a huge effort to change things," I retort, getting more bitter by the second. "I mean when did you last do something romantic, like buy ME a bra? Oh no, you save that sort of chivalry for your slutty girlfriend. Well why don't you just run off with her? I hope you and her perfectly small breasts live happily ever after. But don't expect the children and me to be around when she chucks you out and finds another floppy-haired Irish lover boy to tickle her French fancy."

Nick looks like I've slapped him. "Oh fine, just hurl abuse. Look, I didn't mean for the Cécile thing to happen and I'm not trying to justify it but I guess if I had been happy at home I wouldn't have been looking for anything else. I suppose what I'm trying to say is, it's all very well shutting up shop, but then don't expect your customers to hang around."

"Shutting up shop? This isn't Tescos we're talking about; I'm not open 24 hours and you certainly won't be getting a loyalty card."

"Fact is you're not open any hours," he snaps back. "Do you have any idea how nice it has been over the past few months to hang out with a woman who lusts after me and can think of nothing nicer than giving me a blow-job? Have you any idea what a contrast that is to the woman waiting for me at home who practically cringes when I touch her and for whom sex has just become another household chore?"

In front of us on the floor lies the bra, which I threw there in a hissy fit, hoping it would spontaneously combust. It hasn't, but I feel that I might.

Suddenly, Edward our son bursts into the room, followed by the twins Charlotte and Emily.

"Daddy, quick, you have to come," they all shout at once, vying to be the first with the news. "Frank and Lampard are having a fight."

Nick rushes off to deal with the animal crisis and I stand up, preparing to follow downstairs mechanically. The bra lies in front of me. I pick it up and wonder for a moment what to do with it. Should I use it to make a voodoo doll? Flush it down the loo? Not with French plumbing. Wear it on my head as a sign of protest? I throw it into the wardrobe. Then I walk downstairs.

I feel like a zombie, or rather like a zombie with a terrible hangover who's been hit over the head with a cricket bat. But the children need to be fed and put to bed. It's Sunday today and they have their first day of French school tomorrow. I put on some water for some pasta and get out a ready-made sauce. I don't have the brainpower to come up with anything else.

On autopilot I start grating Parmesan like my life depends on it. All of my mind is taken up with the extraordinary news that Nick has been unfaithful to me, that it's been going on for five months, that she's called Cécile and has small breasts.

After ten minutes or, quite possibly, ten hours – I have no grasp on time – they all come charging back inside. I realise I haven't stopped grating. We have enough grated Parmesan to fill one of MY bras. Anyone for cheese with some pasta sprinkled on top?

"Frank and Lampard are fine," says Nick. "They were playing or possibly mating. Whatever it was, they're friends now."

Great, so now we have gay peacocks. We sit down to dinner. I don't eat anything and Nick and I don't speak to each other, but the children don't seem to notice. They chat and argue and behave like they normally do, totally oblivious to the parental drama. Nick eats a couple of mouthfuls of food and when the kids have finished he takes them off to the bath.

After fifteen minutes he comes back to tell me they're all getting into their pyjamas. He stands nervously at the door, unsure whether to come in or not.

"Soph?" he says.

I stop clearing away and look at him. "I think if it had been a one-night-stand, Nick, it might have been different," I start shakily. "But yours is a proper relationship; it's been going on for several months, for God's sake. I don't think there's any point in you staying around here, you're obviously happier elsewhere."

There is no other option, I can't see how we can just go back to being Nick and Sophie after this. His infidelity is there and it always will be, like an unpaid debt. Or like someone else's bra in my wardrobe.

I walk past him upstairs to say goodnight to our children. He doesn't try to stop me.

"Hey baby," I say to Edward, my usual way of greeting him as I walk into his bedroom.

"Hey mummy," comes his usual response. I lean over him and breathe in his newly bathed squeaky clean five-year-old smell. If I could bottle that I could make a fortune. I kiss the girls goodnight. They go through the usual ritual of making me come back when I have kissed them goodnight so they can kiss me goodnight. I can see them hiding torches under their pillows, ready for nighttime chatting as soon as I have gone, but I let it slide for once.

I pass our bedroom where Nick is repacking THE bag. Briefly, I consider hiding a pair of my smalls in there, but the thought turns to ash as I remember that everything in my knicker drawer, rather like me, has seen better days.

As soon as I get back to the kitchen I start shaking all over. I go to put the kettle on, an instinctive reaction in times of crisis; I'm not sure I could eat or drink anything at all. Still, it feels better to keep moving.

I hear Nick walk upstairs to kiss the children goodnight and then come back downstairs.

"Soph?" He walks gingerly back into the kitchen but keeps his distance from me. Maybe he's worried I might have the bread knife hidden in my leggings. Actually they're so tight he'd easily spot it. Have I really become a woman who wears badly-fitting leggings? Have I sunk so low? Is this all my fault?

"Look, you have every right to be furious; I have been a total prat and I'm sorry. I didn't mean for this to happen, but it did. Please give me another chance?"

I don't look at him. I can't bear to. I can almost feel him contemplating walking towards me and taking me in his arms and making everything all right again. Half of me wishes he would, but instead he sighs.

"Soph?"

"Get lost," I reply.

"Please?"

I turn around to face him. "Nick, I just need you to go, I need to think, I'm too confused. Please just get out of here."

He looks at the ground, takes a deep breath as if he is about to launch into some 'please forgive me I'm Irish and genetically predisposed to infidelity' speech, but instead he whispers goodbye and walks away.

It seems incredible that a couple of short hours ago I was happily married, or at least I thought I was happily married. Now all of a sudden I am not. A bit like thinking you are a size 12 and realizing once you've tried the dress on that you are, at best, a size 14. Which is one of the reasons it is important to shop often. Unlike scales, clothes sizes cannot be ignored.

I hear him shut the front door and walk down the gravel path towards his hire car. Ironically, if anything I thought I was the one who was dissatisfied. I was the desperate housewife longing for something else, but not really bothered enough to find it, nor in fact even sure what it was. Things were never really bad enough for me to find out. As I said, I thought we were happy.

Not in an ecstatic passionate way, a let's-have-sex-in-the-morning (yuck, heaven forbid) kind of way. But the way most married couples are happy, going on from one day to the next, coping with kids, work, money worries and occasionally finding each other again and not being irritated by a tone of voice or the way someone butters their toast or flops into a chair on top of the cat or the millions of other little things that can turn marriage into drudgery and, when things are bad, warp lust into something simmering just below loathing.

I walk out onto the terrace. Our fish fountain is working away steadily, indifferent to the drama going on in the house. I normally love the sound of the water gently cascading from the fish's mouth to the basin below – it's soothing as a sleeping child's breath. But right now I wish it would shut up. The moon is rising over the vineyards. It's a beautiful peaceful evening but I feel totally and utterly depressed. Is there enough Calpol in the house for an overdose, I wonder?

The thought of Calpol reminds me there are three little people who need me, all safely tucked up in their beds upstairs, totally unaware of what has happened and of how their lives might be about to change forever. I sit down on the edge of the fountain, weakened by the thought of it all. As well as the children there's the vineyard, a house, a dog and a treacherous, petite black cat. Talking of which, the faithless creature has come out and is rubbing against my legs. I lift her up and put her on my lap.

"Any more nonsense from you and I'll throw you in the fountain, along with your feckless Irish friend," I say sternly.

She looks up at me then pushes her little head onto my arm, telling me she needs to be stroked and loved.

"I know how you feel, Daisy," I whisper, and I start to cry.

But I have to pull myself together. I have to be strong. I am about to become a single parent in a foreign country.

Rule 2

Affairs are a way to liven up a dull marriage

The French Art of Having Affairs

The reason I will always remember Christmas 2008 is not because my mother's husband was arrested for money laundering and carted off to prison just before pudding, but because it was the first time Nick mentioned moving to France.

Harry was my mother's fifth husband, so by then she had got used to losing them. After the police showed up, the talk was of nothing else but Dirty Harry (as he was dubbed even before the brandy butter had melted) and his laundry. But later on, when we were sitting in front of the fire, Nick changed the subject from police brutality (I mean imagine arresting a man on Christmas Day?) to our future.

"I think we should move to France," he said, handing me a

glass of brandy.

"What?" I almost choked on my drink. "Because of the police? Have you been laundering money too?"

"No," he laughed. "It has nothing to do with that."

He leaned closer to me. "I'm serious Soph. I've always wanted to live there, ever since I went to St Tropez as an eighteen-year-old and fell in love with a French girl on the beach."

"I don't expect she'll still be there," I replied, settling into my chair.

There are some things that seem insignificant but in fact end up changing your life. Like the time I just missed a number 36, started chatting to someone at the bus stop and ended up with my first (and last) job, at Drake's Hotel in London. Or the day my uncle gave me a copy of *Wuthering Heights* when I was sixteen. A life-long obsession with the Brontës was born, resulting in me calling our twin girls Charlotte and Emily. I did briefly think about calling our son Branwell after their opium-addict brother, but was afraid it might be tempting fate. So I called him Edward. How many opium addicts called Edward do you know?

And some things pretend to be significant but turn out to be an anti-climax, and don't change your life at all. Like losing your virginity. The most significant thing about the whole event for me was how disappointing it was. Or turning eighteen; you think somehow you will wake up more mature and sophisticated with a clear idea of what you want to do with the rest of your life. I almost expected my features to change in some small way. But I woke up, looked in the mirror and realised that I was still the same girl. The same girl with the same spot I'd had on my forehead the day before. Only it was bigger.

Our move to France started as something seemingly insignificant that might never happen then turned into reality and a new life.

Nick had long been harbouring a secret dream to sell up in London, ditch his job in the City and run a vineyard – probably along with half the commuters on his early-morning tube to the City. There's nothing quite like a smelly armpit in your face to make you dream about being anywhere else, and a vineyard in France is as good a place as any.

Then about three years ago his parents bought him a membership to The Sunday Times Wine Club and he went on a wine tour of Burgundy. He came back full of enthusiasm about the life of the wine-makers, the climate, the landscape and of course the wine. He developed a rather irritating habit of swilling wine around his glass before drinking it and after a few glasses would start to talk about owning his own vineyard.

I assumed it was a phase he would grow out of because he's not one for unfeasible schemes. He is reliable and sensible. The kind of guy people refer to as a rock. He likes football, cricket, rugby… in fact practically every sport.

He is nice to his parents and rarely impulsive, which is one of the things that first attracted me to him. I grew up with a mother whose second name was impulsive, her first being wild, so I longed for stability and normality. To me, being normal seemed impossibly exotic. I came home from school one day when I was about ten to find my mother reading a book on nihilism and smoking a joint.

"Why can't you bake cakes like normal mothers?" I demanded.

The following day there was a brick masquerading as a cake on the kitchen table; I was amazed it could withstand the weight of it. And there was a most terrible smell of burning all around the house. My mother was standing proudly next to the cake wearing a tea-towel around her waist. After that I let her get on with her nihilism, whatever that is.

So while other girls looked for excitement from their boyfriends, someone to whisk them off their feet and surprise them with outlandish gestures or mad-cap behaviour, I just wanted someone who would appreciate the importance of an Aga and who could stop me from turning into my mother. Obviously he had to be handsome and good in bed as well. And preferably Irish with green eyes and floppy dark hair. But impulsive and wild? No thanks.

Nick is that stable person. He is the kind of man who always goes to the gate to board the plane at the first call while I am still spraying myself with Eau Dynamisante at the duty-free Clarins counter. He has been supporting the same football team (Chelsea) since he was four years old. I didn't dare be too late down the aisle on our wedding day because I knew he would be at least half an hour early. For his stag night there was no chance Nick would be whisked off to Majorca by his pals and end up shaven-headed and semi-naked in a local jail: it was held a cautious ten days before we were married and his brother, who is also his best friend, was in charge of organising it, thus ensuring Nick would come out unscathed and floppy-haired for the big day.

So I didn't take his plans about France too seriously. I suppose I just thought it was all too unrealistic and impulsive. I mean everyone talks about moving to France and living the good life, but very few people actually do it. It's just like everyone always talks about drinking less and getting fit. Or reading *War and Peace* before they die.

I assumed Nick was basically just too sensible to up sticks and move to France. Although secretly I wished he would. To me, France meant glamour, good wines, irresistible cheeses and everything that is good in life. But it was a dream; I couldn't imagine how my favourite childhood holiday destination could ever become a place where we could live. It was a bit like drinking champagne every day.

The dream all started to become more real in January when Tom, a work colleague of Nick's, upped and left to live in Limousin. Up until then, Nick was an armchair émigré, with or without a glass of brandy. After Tom moved, he began to look at the French idea really seriously. If Tom could make his dream reality, then so could he.

"Blimey Soph, he's even more boring than I am," joked Nick. "If he can do it, then so can we."

Rather in the same way that I developed an interest in sport soon after I met Nick, I thought it would be better to join in the French dream than be excluded. So I started reading guidebooks with titles like *Life Begins at Calais* and *How to Realise your French Dream*. I read and learnt all about the ins and outs of buying a house in France, about how important it is to make friends with your local mayor and about the perineal re-training women are put through as a matter of course after childbirth. Shame I missed out on that one. I half wondered whether seven years after giving birth to twins was too late to begin. I can see the reality TV show now: *The Pelvic Floor Factor* – squeeze your way to success.

I read *Madame Bovary* and *Bonjour tristesse*. I watched incomprehensible French films like *Jules et Jim* and pictured myself looking glamorous in a large hat by the sea while my children made sandcastles that resembled Versailles while wearing chic stripy long-sleeved T-shirts from Petit Bateau.

I quickly became what people call a francophile. I even started having French lessons on Wednesday lunchtimes at Linguarama on Clapham High Street, with a rather pinched-looking woman from Toulon called Valérie who had perfectly manicured nails and a constantly sore throat, probably from correcting my excruciatingly bad French accent. If someone had told me when I was at school how appallingly difficult French was to learn as an adult, I think I would have paid much more attention. One of the things that spurred me on was the thought that if we managed to move and make this dream a reality, my children would never have to go through the humiliating experience of mastering the French language when you're at an age when your mouth simply won't bend enough to make the right sounds any more.

Nick was like a happy schoolboy.

"It's nice to see you so excited about something that doesn't involve a ball and men wearing shorts," I said to him.

"I could say the same about you," he joked.

His face lit every time we talked about moving to France. We spent hours making plans. We sat up until late into the night drinking wine, talking about what sort of life we would have, what sort of wine we would make, how we would cope with the move, what to do with the cat.

"She has to have a piece of paper from the vet to certify that she hasn't got worms or fleas before they will let her in," I told Nick one evening.

"As if French cats don't have either," he said.

"Maybe the French will introduce a similar rule for English women going to live there," I said. "Making sure they are pencil thin and wearing matching underwear. According to this book Sarah gave me about finding my inner French woman, they won't be seen dead in non-matching underwear."

It was like we were having another baby – one less fattening and hopefully less painful but certainly as expensive. Nick had found a quotation in a wine book that read "The only way to end up with a small fortune from making wine is to start with a large fortune". But we were not going to make money; we were going to change our lives.

"We could have peacocks, Soph," Nick said. We were wine tasting at the time – our new hobby and one so much more practical than other hobbies as it is easily done in the comfort of your own home so you don't have to risk getting arrested for drunk driving.

I felt like a woman in the throes of a new romance. I looked at my stable and predictable husband in a whole new light. He was no longer Nick of the dreary job and pin-striped suit. He was Nick the brave, Nick the conqueror of new territories, our leader into a new adventure surrounded by vineyards and peacocks.

"I can't wait. How many peacocks shall we have?"

"First we have to have a realistic strategy," said Nick, who had obviously not tasted enough wine.

"I agree," I replied, although I was really thinking it would all be fine once we got there and we shouldn't panic too much.

But we did our maths on the inside cover of one of my guidebooks in Charlotte's pink marker pen. The plan was this: once we had found a vineyard and house, we would sell our house in Clapham, use what we needed for a deposit on the property, get a mortgage for the rest and use the remaining capital to buy machinery, invest in the business and live on until we started to generate an income. Nick calculated that if we bought a vineyard of around 15 hectares in size, depending on the local appellation rules (how many bottles you can produce and so forth) we should be able to produce around 100,000 bottles a year.

"If we sell them at around three euros a bottle we will have a turnover of 300,000 euros," he said, jotting down the numbers as we chatted. "Around 200,000 of that will go on costs, leaving a profit of about 100,000."

Nick would carry on commuting to his job in the City, living in London during the week with his brother to save on rent until the first harvest in September the year after we moved. Then we could use his two bonuses to invest in the business. Once the wine was ready to sell he would leave and work full-time with our business.

All this planning took place in February. Nick's moving to France full-time seemed a long way away. But he would come out at weekends and holidays, and also once the office was set up would try to work one or two days a week from France, providing they could hook him up with the software from the London office. We would also employ someone a couple of days a week to work in the vineyards.

Meanwhile, I would be in charge of not only overseeing the vineyards when he wasn't there but also marketing the wine using my contacts in the hotel business and new ones I would build up. I would get a database of restaurants and bars to target. I might even have business meetings again, I would be part of the working world once more after spending the last seven years looking after the twins and Edward. It was an exciting but slightly scary thought. What was it like out there nowadays? When I thought about it I felt a little like a woman who was suddenly being thrown back onto the dating scene after years in a stable relationship. Would the punters respect me in the morning? After all, what did we know about making wine?

"Soph, you'll be fine," Nick reassured me. "You've given birth to twins, nothing can be more difficult than that."

We started looking seriously at places where we could buy a vineyard. Nick quickly ruled out Burgundy and Bordeaux; they were far too expensive. We would have to look elsewhere. We narrowed our search to the biggest wine-producing region in the world; the Languedoc region of southern France, an area spanning hundreds of miles between Provence and Spain.

On our first visit, in April this year, I was immediately captivated by the landscape. It was like someone had taken everything that is beautiful about France and put it into one place. The light was the thing that I noticed first. It was one of those crisp, clear spring days, with just a hint of the warmth to come in the sun. The sky was a shade of bright blue I don't think I have ever seen before. It was exhilarating to look at. I read somewhere that the light is so beautiful because of the lack of pollution. It was so clear and sharp and seemed to give the landscape such beautifully defined contours.

We drove from the airport towards our hotel in a small town called Marseillan.

"'Some say Marseillan is like St Tropez used to be before Brigitte Bardot decided to take her bra off and made it famous,'" I read out loud from my guidebook while Nick drove. "'The port is one of the nicest places in France to sip a glass of wine or simply stroll watching the boats come and go.' Maybe we should buy somewhere near there," I suggested.

"It sounds lovely," said Nick. "But properties near the coast are much more expensive."

I gazed out of the window at the countryside. It was as if the motorway was the only evidence of modern man. The rest was bright green vineyards with pretty stone houses. In the distance I could see medieval villages on top of hills. I longed to explore them all. I felt like a kid in a sweet shop desperate to get out there and experience it all.

We drove down a road next to a long deserted beach, stopped the car and walked onto the sand. We even took our shoes off.

The sand was cool but not uncomfortably cold. It felt great to be so close to nature, having just stepped off a plane from grimy London that morning. We walked for about an hour just looking at the sea with its endless colours and movement.

Nick took my hand. "We must bring the kids here. I can imagine Emily doing cartwheels on the sand and Edward kicking a football."

"And Charlotte bossing them about," I laughed.

"Amazing that they put up with it. I mean Edward I can understand, he is so much younger, but Emily was only a minute behind her," he said.

"I agree," I said. "They do rebel sometimes, although not for long. They seem to have got used to the benign dictatorship. I think it makes them feel quite secure."

We stopped to watch a dog paddle in the sea. Nick put his arms around me and hugged me.

"This is such a good idea for us all," he said, stroking my hair.

I hugged him back and was surprised by the intensity of the moment. It reminded me of our early days together, before the children and the daily grind turned us into Mr and Mrs Average. I could almost detect the kind of spark I used to feel and hadn't felt for years, an intense feeling of anticipation and pleasure deep inside I had lost somewhere along the way. I was sure then that France was our future. I felt like an excited teenager on her first date. It was all going to be fine. I loved my husband, he loved me, and soon we would be living in this beautiful place. For the first time in several months I was just where I wanted to be.

After our walk we headed back to the car and drove to the

hotel in Marseillan. The guidebook had not exaggerated. It was one of the prettiest places I had ever been to; there wasn't a brick out of place, and even a rundown old barn close to the hotel was charming in its shabby chic decay.

"You've got to hand it to the French," said Nick as we sat eating oysters for lunch on the quay looking out over the water. "They may not have won many battles and they can't play cricket, but they know how to live."

"Do you remember the Ile de Ré?" I asked.

"Of course I do, our honeymoon" he smiled. "It rained every day. We nicknamed it the Ile de Rain. Why?"

"I was just thinking that it would be nice to get back to that feeling we had for each other then," I said feeling myself blushing slightly; we rarely talked about our feelings. "You know, how close we were, always talking, always, well it didn't matter that it rained the entire two weeks and I just think that…."

"I agree," he interrupted me. "But with normal life and kids and responsibilities all that kind of stuff suffers."

"So what are you saying? That we just give up?" I was hurt that I had broached the subject of being closer to each other and it seemed to me he was rejecting the idea. Had he not felt the same spark I did on the beach? Why did he have to be so sensible?

His face softened. "Of course not, Soph. No, we never give up. I just don't think we should beat ourselves up over the fact that we're not pouncing on each other every few minutes any more. That's all. Shall we get the bill? We've a lot of exploring to do this afternoon."

He beckoned to the waiter and for twenty-four oysters we paid about the same amount we would have paid for half a dozen in London. Yet another good reason to move to France.

That afternoon we ventured inland through tree-lined avenues with views over hills covered with small oak trees, through deep gorges and chestnut hills as far as the Black Mountains, where the climate and lifestyle are totally different to those on the coast. It was like another world. Close to the mountains there are goats, sheep and even cows; the lack of grass closer to the sea would make it impossible for them to live there. We decided we would like to buy our vineyard somewhere between the two, so we could have the best of both.

The landscape across the Languedoc may be diverse but one thing remains constant: the vineyards. They are everywhere. It is impossible to drive for more than a few kilometres without seeing one. They are various shapes and sizes; some on hills, others flat, some tidy with neat rows of vines just starting to bloom, their fresh green leaves almost translucent in the afternoon sun, others with weeds growing freely. Some vines are tall and thin, others short and trestled in rows.

To me they made the landscape seem exotic and full of promise. We stopped to take a closer look at a vineyard close to a town called Montagnac. There were about fifty rows of vines in perfect lines following the gentle slope of the vineyard. The grapes were just starting to grow and the leaves were bright green, some of the newer ones the colour of a salamander, almost fluorescent. In the distance on the top of a hill was a building next to a tall tower, giving the impression that the main part of the church had been separated from the steeple. A large cypress tree grew nearby. It was hard to imagine a prettier view. There was a rose bush planted at the end of every third row of vines.

"How romantic," I said. "Maybe the wine-maker planted them for his wife?"

Nick laughed. "It's a nice idea, but in reality this is something a lot of wine-makers do because the health of the rose bush is a good indicator of the health of the vines, rather like a canary in a coal mine who warns of a gas leak by keeling over."

"When we have vineyards, will you plant yellow roses?" I asked. They had been my favourite since I wept when Daniel Day Lewis gave them to Michelle Pfeiffer in *The Age of Innocence*. I imagined Nick and I walking around the vineyards checking on the vines and smelling the roses before heading home to an aperitif on a sun-bathed terrace.

"Of course, darling," he said, hugging me. "Any colour you like."

We walked onto a small track leading towards the hills. It felt so good to be out in the fresh air, moving and breathing deeply. We passed a field of olive trees; ten rows with seven olive trees in each one, more or less in a straight line. There was tall grass growing between them, mixed with white daisies, poppies, yellow sweet clover and forget-me-nots. The flowers and grass swayed in the gentle breeze. To one side of the field were mountains covered with thick green foliage and to the other the lane we were walking on, which led to the nearby village. There was a small stone hut in one corner of the field. I imagined the person who looks after the trees must spend his days gazing at the perfect views around him. The whole scene was so serene and pretty, I tried my hardest to imprint it on my mind and cursed the fact that I had left the camera in the car.

We made three trips to the region after that first visit but it took a while to find our dream house. I suppose that's the problem with a dream: you have an image of what you want and not much lives up to it. We were shown places that are wrong for one of many reasons. Either they were modern and ugly, and like most British house-hunters in France we were after 'old stone'. Or they were next to a motorway (not great if you want your kids to grow to be adults) or next to a kennel full of barking dogs (not ideal for a good night's sleep, which I find hard enough to get without added variables).

My friend Sarah is mad about yoga and meditation and says you need to visualise things that you want. I met Sarah on my first day at university. She was standing in front of me in the matriculation queue and turned around and raised her eyebrows during a particularly condescending speech by the principal. We have seen each other practically every week since that day. She must visualise a lot of shoes. I have hardly ever seen her in the same pair twice.

In the visualisation of my ideal home I saw flowers. When I was a little girl my mother and one of her more tolerable husbands took me on holiday to a house in the Savoie. The little farmhouse was surrounded by mountains and close to a lake. It was one of the happiest holidays of my childhood that was otherwise rather interrupted by my mother's constant remarrying, relocating and attempts at baking. The house was old stone, and one of the things I loved about it was its abundance of flowers. Roses grew up the old stone walls; there were yellow ones, red ones, pink ones and white ones. Wild flowers grew in the grass. Daisies were planted in pots all over the stone steps and wisteria framed the house on all fronts. There were irises, petunias and even sunflowers. Each flower had its own scent, and I spent hours gazing at them and inhaling their sweetness. The owner was apparently mad about gardening and planted flowers to celebrate his wife and children's birthdays every year.

One night I dreamt of a house surrounded by roses. They grew inside and out. They intrigued me, but when I tried to go into the house the thorns grew into monster thorns and created a barrier. I tried to force my way in and found blood on my hands.

That was the night before our final house-hunting trip. The dream was the culmination of my worst ever week in London.

I was out for a drink with my friends Sarah, Carla and Lucy one evening. Carla is a recent addition to the group, a mum I met at school who is Italian. She has three children too. Lucy is another friend from university. She is the sort of woman I would usually avoid; she has that kind of easy perfection that makes you want to curl up in a ball and die. But she is also one of the nicest people I have ever met, so we are still friends. She works in publishing and lives with her investment banker husband and two children on the posh side of the river. Her husband is called Perfect Patrick. Or at least he was Perfect Patrick until he lost his job and Lucy became the sole provider. Not so perfect any more.

Up until that evening, I hadn't really realised that anyone else would notice the extent of my post-children decline. I felt invisible, I suppose -- something that I think happens to a lot of women when they have children, age and put on weight. The latter two in my opinion being a direct consequence of the first one.

We went to Drake's, the London hotel I used to run before I had the babies. We were having a lovely time, chatting, bitching about old college friends and enemies, comparing nail varnishes (I, for once, had some on; Sarah of course had the latest colour, which was yellow for no other reason, I concluded, than that was the only colour no woman had at home and hence was profitable for the sellers of nail varnish. It looked terrible.) Lucy was telling us about her latest Booker prize nominee, Carla was about to embark on an affair with her tennis coach, and Sarah had just been assigned to help with the re-launch of a magazine that was being overseen by the CEO of the publishing company she works for, so we had a lot to talk about.

There were two men sitting at the bar who sent over a waitress with four glasses of champagne. We didn't want to be interrupted because were having a lovely time together, so we sent it back. One of the men, who had obviously had too much to drink, stumbled over to tell us how rude we were to refuse his generous gesture.

"And it's not like you're anything special," he slurred. "Look at you," he added, pointing at me, "with your mummy breasts."

"Yeah," his friend joined in laughing. "The phrase 'beached whale' comes to mind."

I was wearing quite a low-cut top, which I had thought was fairly attractive when I put it on at home. Okay, so I know I am not Elle McPherson, but I'm hardly what Sarah calls "boilingly ugly" either. Suddenly I felt terribly exposed and unattractive – a feeling that has not really left me since. Luckily I still knew the security guard at the hotel and he threw the men out for me – not before Lucy, who studied Law when we were at university, had threatened to sue them for defamation and disturbing the peace.

But even that didn't help my self-esteem or restore any pride I might once have had in my 'mummy breasts'. In fact, I wondered how much luck Lucy would have suing for defamation; they were pretty mumsy-like.

The following day I was mugged on my way from Sainsbury's to my car, in broad daylight. Someone just bashed into me and grabbed hold of my handbag; it all happened so quickly I didn't stand a chance. It was like a gust of wind arrived and suddenly I was standing there without my bag. I felt like such a fool. I have always imagined I would be one of those brave victims of crime you read about in the paper. I envisioned headlines like 'Mother of twins and toddler beats renowned thug (later to be unveiled as serial killer and mass rapist as well as solely responsible for climate change and just about every other ill in the world) into submission with can of baked beans' and a picture of me proudly holding a dented can of baked beans with the children smiling benignly next to me. This would then lead to huge endorsements from Heinz, which I could use to surgically reduce my breasts. And free baked beans for life. But instead I just froze.

I wasn't hurt, but since then I haven't really felt safe in

London; I am just always waiting for the next disaster. And our area of south London seems to be getting worse, not better. Only last week a young man was gunned down in a drive-by shooting. Just the phrase drive-by shooting would have seemed ridiculous ten years ago, like you were describing New York or somewhere miles away that you only ever see on TV. And it's not just the violence; the whole place is in dire need of a makeover. There is graffiti all over the place, boarded-up shops, houses that look uninhabitable. Why has all this only started to hit me in the last couple of years? Maybe when we first moved there, before we were married, we were so excited to own a home we didn't even notice the decay around us. But I don't think it's that I'm convinced that while some parts of London have become more gentrified, our neighbourhood has gone downhill. Rather like my 'mummy breasts'.

Rule 3

Pick a lover who has as much to lose as you do

The French Art of Having Affairs

After the ritual humiliation of getting through airport security, we boarded our flight to Montpellier. This was always going to be our last trip over for a while; we couldn't afford to keep coming back and forth. If it didn't work out we had decided to leave it until after Christmas, although we had originally hoped to move during the Christmas holidays. I figured Christmas is so stressful anyway – would a small change of country, lifestyle and home make it any worse? And it would be satisfying to feel we had achieved the dream Nick first mentioned by the fire on Christmas Day a year before.

I looked out of the window. This was our fourth trip so I recognised where I was. When it lands, the plane does a kind of swoop over pink flamingos and water before it approaches the runway at Montpellier Airport. We disembarked into a different world to grey old Stansted. It was a bright, sunny and warm day, despite being late October.

Nick almost fell down the steps of the plane checking his BlackBerry. I thought he was checking work messages, but since the bra-in-bag incident, I now suspect he was responding to some sexy text from the French mistress. Maybe she was hoping I would find the text messages and got fed up with waiting for me to do so, which is why she planted the bra. One of the downsides to picking an unmarried lover is that they are likely to hope you're going to get caught out.

The road from the airport was pale in the early morning sun and there was not much traffic.

"I can't get over the fact that even the motorway is beautiful," I said to Nick. "I'm sure it's a good sign when they plant flowers and trees in the middle of the road."

Nick laughed. "Yes, a sign that the people here pay too much tax."

I ignored him; nothing could spoil my enjoyment. There were stunning views either side of the motorway of vineyards and mountains, and olive trees planted down the middle, mixed with oleander, some of which were still in flower. It was amazing how obvious the seasons are there compared with London. It was so autumnal; the leaves were turning from green to copper and were much less abundant than they had been on our last trip. The sun was lower and the shadows longer, but there was still real warmth in the air.

We arrived in Pézenas about an hour after landing. We had based our search from Pézenas for three reasons: one, we loved the town with its beautiful old stone buildings, bustling Saturday market and cobbled streets. Two, there are no less than twenty estate agents there. And three it is between the beach and the mountains, which is exactly where we wanted to be.

"It seems to me that French estate agents are either extremely stupid or stubborn or very possibly both," I said to Nick over lunch. "It doesn't matter how many times we explain what it is we are after, we have been shown one hopeless property after another hopeless property. Why should today be any different?"

We were in a little bistro at the edge of the Place du 14 Juillet, where we had enjoyed a steak and *frites* in the October sunshine.

Nick shook his head. "Maybe it won't be, but we have to keep trying."

"In an ideal world, would you rather order another bottle of wine, or go looking at unsuitable properties?" I asked him.

"In an ideal world I would spend the afternoon looking at suitable properties," replied my sensible husband, bless him.

I smiled. "Yes, but the chances are they will show us nothing we like. And it is so lovely here. And we probably won't come back until next year, so I vote for whiling the afternoon away with another bottle of rosé. What do you think?"

"It's a nice idea, Soph. But while I am not sure we will find anything this afternoon if we go, I know for sure we won't if we stay here."

"No you don't. Remember me and the number 36 bus? That man over there might be a *vigneron* on the verge of a nervous breakdown desperate to sell his beautiful château for a knock-down price to the first person that asks him," I said, pointing to a man in a beret sitting a few tables away drinking a white drink that I guessed was Pernod rather than milk.

"Go and ask him," said Nick, laughing. "But ask the waiter for the bill as well, just in case he's not. Remember, French women rarely drink more than one glass of wine – what was that Coco Chanel quote you read to me the other night from a magazine?"

"Elegance is refusal," I replied in a silly French accent. "But I'm not a French woman. You can tell I'm not because I have just eaten lunch. And it's a book, not a magazine. Sarah gave it to me. It's going to help me to find my inner French woman."

The more I read of that, the less sure I am that I have an inner French woman. They are all about seduction, slimness, perfectly manicured nails and matching underwear. None of which apply to me. In fact, Sarah is more suited to all that. She probably thought I needed the book more than she did.

"And you'll never get the chance to be French either if we stay here all afternoon. Come on, let's go," said Nick, calling for the bill.

We left the restaurant and headed north of Pézenas towards the mountains. We were early for our meeting, of course. When the agent showed up he first showed us a tiny bungalow with several hectares of vineyards outside a town called Lamalou-les-Bains. He was the smallest man I have ever seen, about the same size as the twins, and came from Essex. The house was no good; it looked more like a caravan than a home, and we would have to knock it down and start again. The land was lovely, at the base of a mountain range with uninterrupted views over miles of unspoiled countryside, but the town itself was quite sinister, with more people in wheelchairs than on foot, and those that were on foot walking with crutches. It's the kind of place that makes you feel young and healthy, even after a long lunch and a bottle of wine.

"Why is everyone ill here?" I asked. "Is there something wrong with the water?"

The agent laughed. "No, Lamalou is where the French send their war veterans. There is even an expression, 'going to Lamalou', which means you are getting ill."

"Not the worst place to end up," I said.

"Where are you going next?" asked the shortest man in the world, as we walked to our hire car.

"Oh, some place over near Boujan," said Nick, sounding as if he'd lost the will to live.

"That's the one you'll buy," replied the miniature estate agent.

"How do you know?" I asked.

"I just do," he said, tapping his nose, which I noticed not for the first time, was preposterously large for his face and body.

Rule 4

Stay interested in your spouse and family

The French Art of Having Affairs

We met the next agent at a bar in a village called Hérépian with a busy high street and large fountain. He was Dutch and unusually tall. Is no one a normal size around here? He was also early. Nick ought to live in one of those Northern European countries; everyone is on the same time as him. We got into his car because he said the house was hard to find. I liked the sound of that.

As we drove towards the hills, our spirits lifted. I think we both felt more comfortable closer to the hills where the landscape is less arid and there are fewer tourists. It feels more like a real place, like the kind of place we can make a home and raise our family.

We were on a beautiful winding road through tree-covered

hills. To our right in the distance was a mountain range that, our agent told us, is called the Espinouse. The mountains were a mixture of colours in the afternoon sun, ranging from deep green to purple to shades of blue.

"Assuming there's not a housing estate around the corner, this could be very exciting," said Nick, turning round from the front seat of the grey Berlingo van and squeezing my hand.

"What?" yelled Mr Vorst, the agent, nearly driving us all into the ditch. He was deaf in his right ear, so every time someone spoke he turned around to listen with his left ear, leaving his car to navigate the road by itself.

We came off the mountain road and turned into another road lined with plane trees. It curved gently ahead of us like a crescent moon. I was dying to see what was around the corner.

"Wouldn't you just love to drive along here every day?" I said to Nick. Either side of the road were vineyards with rows of neatly planted vines. We were alone on the road; there seemed to be hardly any traffic at all in this part of France. When we got around the corner I could see a village in the distance on top of a hill. It was one of those places one might see on the motorway as one drove to a Club Med hotel in Provence and think 'What a dreamy place, I wonder who lives there?'

"That's Boujan," said the agent, pointing at it. "The nearest village to the house."

We arrived a few minutes later. It was a small, sleepy village that consisted of the same things as just about every other small village in France; a bar, a *boulangerie* selling everything from *pain au chocolat* to chewing gum, a Hôtel de Ville, a chemist, a church, a war memorial and a primary school.

There was a compact square in front of the Hôtel de Ville where some men were playing *boules* – just about the only sport, along with darts, that Nick has never shown any interest in. But even he was carried away by the idyllic scene.

"I might take up *boules*," he mouthed at me silently, so the agent wouldn't drive into the ditch. I nodded and smiled. Moving to France is one thing, but *boules* really is pushing things. At the time, of course, I was unaware he had taken up the other French national sport of having affairs. I suppose as this was October he must have been two months into the liaison by then. But he hadn't really changed much at home, in fact he seemed a bit more cheerful and I thought his focus was on the move to France, not moving in on some French bird.

The village was like a dream village. In the main square there was a plane tree in each corner.

"They provide shade in the hot summer months," explained Mr Vorst.

In the middle there was a stone hexagonal fountain with a stone column in the centre. On two opposite sides of the column were two spouts shaped like snakes from which cool clear water poured. On top was a flower arrangement that had red, pink, yellow, white and blue flowers that must have been in baskets, but it was so abundant it looked as if they were growing from the fountain itself.

We walked over to the fountain and drank some of the clear, cool water.

"The water comes from the mountains," said Mr Vorst,

pointing to them. It tasted cold and fresh and a little earthy.

Across the road from the square the stone church tower was bright in the afternoon sunlight. The bells rang four times signalling the hour. We walked over to the war memorial, an obelisk-shaped statue with a brass soldier perched on top of it. *A la mémoire des enfants de la commune de Boujan morts pour la France 1914-1918* read the inscription. There were about thirty names carved into the stone; I read some of them, imagining the young men who had their whole lives in front of them and the mothers and lovers who must have mourned them: Hippolyte Pierron, Joseph Courtois, Ernest de Sade, Marcellin Bartin. Underneath there was a smaller section dedicated to the Second World War. Around the bottom of the memorial were small colourful flowers. Wooden boxes of colourful plants lined the square and the streets as well. Even the bar, La Petite Auberge with its rather dilapidated exterior and old-fashioned yellow faded sign headed *Consommations Choisies* and listing drinks in pre-war writing like *Bière Pression le demi* and *Café Noir la tasse,* had hanging baskets of bright flowers.

"Maybe they're gearing up for the France in Bloom competition," I said to Nick. "Did you know that a third of French villages enter it every year?"

He looked at me as if I had finally lost the plot.

I longed from that moment to be part of the life they lived here, even if it did mean that Nick took up *boules.* This was not just because of the way it looked, though, but because there was an atmosphere of community here. It reminded me of the England of my childhood that I would like my children to grow up in but that no longer exists, where the pace of life is slow and there is a real sense of community, somewhere people still care enough to keep an eye out for other people's kids and there isn't just CCTV watching. This was a place we would all be safe in, a place in which they could be children without fear. In London I daren't let them out of my sight for a second, the papers are endlessly full of horror stories of abductions of children and people being stabbed for doing nothing more than walking down the road at the wrong time.

We went back to the car and drove through the village, past a bus stop where a group of women wearing slippers sat chatting under a giant painted Dubonnet poster slowly being erased by time and the elements. They stopped their talking and looked up as we drove past. They didn't really look like they were actually waiting for a bus. Sure enough, I saw another elderly lady walking from her house with a fold-up chair to join them. She too stopped to stare at the unknown car.

"Imagine living in a place where a car you don't recognise constitutes an event," I said to Nick. "I think I would rather get to like it."

Nick nodded. "It sure beats the drive-by shooting that makes for an event round our way."

We drove down another tree-lined road towards what was to become our new home. Close to it was a château that looked more like a mini-Versailles than a Languedoc wine grower's home. It was absolutely magnificent, with turrets and towers and a long avenue of cypress trees leading up to it. I imagined the inhabitants must be terribly glamorous, and might possibly even wear 17th-century clothes.

"That is the Château de Boujan," the agent told us. "Their land adjoins the land of Sainte Claire, but they have around thirty hectares, whereas you have only sixteen. They used to be one property. Back in the last century it was boom time for the wine makers of the Languedoc because they were able to produce six to eight times as much as their counterparts in northern France due to the climate here, so a lot of these flamboyant châteaux were built. Château de Boujan is still very much a working vineyard but the owners of Sainte Claire have not maintained the vineyard so there is a lot of catching up to do. But they tell me it is excellent *terroir*. This part of the region used to be covered by seawater. The vineyards here are built on a former coral reef. Fossilised coral is very good for vines because it drains well and vines hate to have wet feet. It is perhaps the only vineyard in the world with such a unique *terroir*."

I looked at Nick questioningly. "That means the land you grow the vines on," he explained. "Some experts say they can taste the soil or *terroir* in the wine."

We drove on past the château. The tree-lined road turned into a dust track that ended about 150 metres on at a small roundabout with a fountain in the middle. When I say fountain, it was more of a trickle of water, forcing its way through years of foliage and bright green moss that had grown over a simple stone pillar with a pattern around the top that was barely visible, but it was charming. We got out of the car and looked up at the house. My heart skipped a beat. I had what the French call a *coup de coeur*. My nipples stood on end. It was similar to the feeling my Italian friend Carla described when she first met her new tennis coach.

"Is this normal?" I whispered to Nick. "Is it possible to fall in love at first sight with a house?"

The object of my newfound love was Sainte Claire, a French farmhouse and one of the prettiest places I have ever seen. My first impression of it was that I didn't really care what was inside; I just never wanted to leave. I stood and gazed at it in awe. The château next door was all very splendid, but this was a *home*.

The house itself was large, with three floors. The façade was whitewashed limestone. The windows were all closed with shutters painted blue. On many of them the paint was peeling off, yet somehow that didn't make it look scruffy but in fact added to the charm. The roof was old tiles and there were three chimneys. On the middle floor there were some French doors leading onto a balcony that I longed to stand on and admire the view from. There were plants growing at various heights up the limestone façade; wisteria, roses and jasmine.

It was almost as if the house had been painted in the position it sat in, nestled in front of the hills, with views all around, each one prettier than the next.

"We are in the foothills of the Cévennes Mountains here," said the agent.

I looked around me and breathed in the air. It was scented with thyme and lavender. As I inhaled I felt as though it was rejuvenating me, filling me with the goodness of the Languedoc and rinsing out all that London filth and stress.

An avenue of olive trees led to the garden and the hedgerows were full of flowers: poppies, wild gladioli, daisies. I even spotted a bunch of capers growing wild on the wall of the house.

"They'll come in useful for spaghetti alla puttanesca," I told Nick.

Not that I've ever made spaghetti alla puttanesca. I always forget to buy the capers.

We walked up the four steps leading to the front door. I immediately imagined the children racing up to be the first one in.

I smiled at the thought of the children. "I can't wait to tell them about this place," I said to Nick. "It is just what we've been imagining."

In fact it was far better than anything I had been imagining – one of those rare moments in life when the reality is better than the fantasy.

"The house has not been lived in for almost a year," explained Mr Vorst. "When Madame Gréco died the family argued about what to do with it. In France you cannot disinherit your children so all her five children inherited a portion each and couldn't agree on selling it or keeping it, as is more than often the case with these old properties. Eventually the lawyers got involved and the decision to sell was taken. Meanwhile none of them were allowed to use it, so it is very dusty and obviously like all old houses there is some work to be done, but it is in fundamentally good shape, the fittings are excellent."

I looked at Nick to see if I could gauge what he was thinking. In the unlikely event that he hated it I'm not sure what I would have done. He gave me a short nod, which I translated to 'Yes, Soph, I know it is fabulous but if you don't stop grinning like a

Cheshire cat on heat the price will double before we even get inside the door.'

Mr Vorst opened the shutters and unlocked the front door with a key that looked like the one Mary Lennox used to unlock the secret garden in one of my all-time favourite books. He pushed the door open and immediately we felt cold air coming out from the house.

"These houses are designed to stay cool," he told us. "The walls are thick and there are shutters on all the windows. In the summer, people shut them during the day to keep the sun out."

We were in an entrance hall with large beige flagstones on the floor. On either side were walls with doors leading off into rooms. The agent walked into a room on the left and opened all the shutters. Light flooded in. It was the kitchen that was located in the extension we had seen from the outside.

I could already see that it was a lovely house, that it had been loved and just needed a bit of attention. The kitchen didn't look at all bad for somewhere that hadn't been used for several months. There was a large flue at one end where the cooker must have stood. Several spiders had set up home there; they scuttled away, shocked into flight by the light. The sink was below the window, with a view over the vines.

I started imagining shelves filled with over-sized jars where I would store everything from walnuts to cranberries. No matter that I never did in London – this house was going to be a new beginning. I might not find my inner French woman, but my inner domestic goddess was raring to get out.

"I love this kitchen," I told Nick. "The children's chicken

nuggets and chips days are numbered."

"They always show the kitchen first," said Nick. "Kitchens apparently sell houses."

"Oh, I thought estate agents did," I replied under my breath. "You'd better not be trying to put me off; it's too late for that."

"They will leave the table and chairs," said Mr Vorst, pointing at a large round oak table and matching chairs. "You are lucky; some people even take the light bulbs. There is a small fireplace in here too." He pointed at a steel door in one of the beams that when opened revealed a little oven – perfect, he said, for wood-fired pizzas, whatever they are. "Madame Gréco's children have divided up what they want, heaven knows how, and anything you see left here is included in the price. That also includes the barrels and machinery in the *cave*."

"The what?" I asked.

"The *cave*," said Nick. "It's the winery, where the wine is made and aged. Can we go on?"

I was keen to linger in the kitchen cooking imaginary feasts for the children, but we walked out into the hall and crossed over to the sitting room.

"It's quite small," said Nick.

"That's because it hasn't got any furniture in it," I protested, walking over to the window to touch the marble windowsill. I loved the fact that everything seemed so solid and well made. "Rooms always look smaller when they're unfurnished."

If we had been sitting down I think Nick would have kicked me in the shins. Instead he shot me one of those looks I have grown to hate over the years. It's his 'Oh, how could you be so stupid, Sophie? I really am getting angry' look. And in that phrase I am always Sophie, not Soph, so I know I'm in trouble. It reminds me of being told off at school and makes me feel about seven years old. It is usually followed by an LIC (lecture in car).

A tour of the dining room next door followed. I kept my mouth shut, half sulking and half worried. I really didn't want an LIC. Mr Vorst would probably drive us into the ditch.

Then came the sitting room, which had a vast fireplace in it – proof, I guessed, that it must get cold here. I imagined us all snuggling around it in our pyjamas with cups of Horlicks playing card games, and wondered if by next Christmas we would be leaving brandy for Father Christmas here. Even Nick couldn't hide the fact that he was impressed with the fireplace, or maybe that look was more dread at the thought of chopping logs big enough to fit in it?

We climbed the stone staircase and onto the first floor, the agent going on ahead to open the shutters. Each opened shutter revealed another part of the house. The stairs were broad and worn smooth but looked like they would last at least another five hundred years. I loved the feeling of space; I could stretch out both my arms and still not touch the walls.

We walked into the master bedroom. This is where Madame Gréco had her boudoir, bathroom and dressing room. The floors here were wooden, giving it a warmer feel than downstairs. There was a large Victorian bath on a raised platform at one end of the bedroom and a double sink.

"I can't believe it, I've always longed for a Victorian bath," I whispered to Nick, unable to contain my excitement any longer.

I had to stop myself from jumping up and down on the spot.

We opened the large shutters in the middle of the room and walked out onto the balcony. Mr Vorst was fiddling around with something inside so Nick came and stood next to me.

"This view reminds me of a postcard," he said. "Just look at the vineyards. I think I can see more shades of green than there are in Ireland."

He was right. There was everything from the bright grass to the olive trees to the oak and the plane trees lining the road that leads to the village and the cypress trees leading up to Château de Boujan. There were vineyards in every direction, perfectly planted rows of vines with leaves on the cusp of turning from green to autumnal bronze and red. They seemed to be a couple of weeks behind those closer to the sea. The lines of the vines led to the mountains in the distance, inviting me to walk between them towards the deep green hills.

I noticed a perfect rose bush growing from a chipped blue ceramic pot. It had worked its way up the soft light stone and looked like it was part of the masonry. It had wax-like petals that at the tips were almost black, the red was so intense.

The plant was about three feet higher than me. I asked Nick to take a picture of me in front of it. An Alsatian dog wandered past the house beneath us and Nick took a picture of him too.

"He's beautiful," said Nick. "Where is he from?"

I sensed that Nick was keen to adopt an animal before we even bought the house. He grew up with lots of dogs in the countryside and misses not having them. I had vetoed a dog in London. Partly because I think it would be cruel to have a dog cooped up all day but also because I don't know anyone who has one who doesn't find walking them a chore. Apart from my friend Carla, the one who is having an affair with her tennis coach. She uses the walks as an excuse to call him.

When we had coffee mornings together, she told the rest of the amazed mothers all about her trysts; in the car, at the tennis club, even in her own broom cupboard.

"Has your tennis got any better?" I asked her once.

"No darling, I gave up tennis when I discovered sex. I found I was much more talented at it and I never lost. Surely you realise that tennis coaches are not really there to teach you to play tennis?"

She didn't seem remotely ashamed or even worried that her husband would find out.

"You can't eat the same pasta sauce every night," she says in her thick Italian accent, flicking her long black hair, when we question the wisdom of serial infidelity. I guess you can't if you're Italian. Personally I had rather gone off pasta sauce in any flavour. I thought it must be hormonal. But maybe Sainte Claire with its wild capers and France with its oysters would prove inspirational.

"I think the dog lived here. The foreman next door at the château has been looking after him," said Mr Vorst. "I will show you the other bedroom on this floor."

"How many bedrooms are there in total?" asked Nick.

"There are four," answered Mr Vorst. "It is not an overly large property but there is a barn that could be converted if you needed more living space. It is already semi-habitable, it is where the grape-pickers used to stay during the harvest."

I was about to say to Nick that a barn would be perfect for the girls when they are older. They could be self-sufficient there and play loud pop music and dye their hair green without bothering us. As long as it wasn't French pop music, obviously. There have to be some limits. But I decided to keep it for when we were alone. More arguments to convince him Sainte Claire was the only place for us.

We went up to the top of the house, where there were two large bedrooms, each with a small attic-style window at the front and a larger one at the side. There was a bathroom in the middle of them both, with doors joining it from each one. I was already seeing bunk beds in the slightly larger room for the girls and getting butterflies.

Apparently the key to buying the right house is being able to see yourself living there. I could see myself there very clearly, as well as my entire family and all my friends. Lucy would fit right in; she would waft from room to room wearing some floaty diaphanous creation and carrying an intellectual book. Sarah would be curled up on the sofa, her blonde hair tied up in a ponytail, reading the latest copy of *Vogue*. Carla would be in the *cave* with the wine-maker, assuming we had one. Or out looking for one if we didn't.

As we walked downstairs, Nick whispered to me to stop grinning and squeezed my hand. I took the hand squeeze as a sign that he loved it as much as I did. My butterflies intensified. I was sure Mr Vorst could hear my heart beating.

We walked outside into the bright sun, providing a stark

contrast to the cool interior. The agent walked us around the house to a terrace on the other side of the kitchen.

"Look at the marble table," I said to Nick. "Great for breakfast."

The agent seemed to have miraculously regained his hearing.

"The marble table and chairs are included in the sale," he said smiling. "And look at the fountain. The basin is probably big enough to swim in on a warm day."

"Yes," said Nick. "But it's empty. How can we be sure it works?"

We walked towards it. An over-sized, vertical fish made of stone was the spout. I could see where the water would burst out of its mouth and imagine cooling off underneath it on a hot day.

"All the electrics are in order," said the agent, as if he were quoting straight from the 'How to Sell a House on the Spot' manual.

I was sure he couldn't possibly know whether they were or not, but I didn't care. We could always fix the fountain. I was in love. I was like a young girl who had just met her dream boy. Small details about his electrical circuits or lack of them were unlikely to put me off.

The terrace looked out over rows of vines leading to the mountains in the distance. It was now almost five o'clock, approaching my favourite time of day, when the shadows lengthen and the sun caresses you with its dying rays. And you know a drink is not far off.

"Take a walk to the vineyard," said Mr Vorst. Nick and I wandered off alone.

"I love it, love it, love it," I repeated as quietly as I could.

"I know," said Nick. "But try not to show it quite so blatantly. We still need to negotiate a good deal here, the asking price is high for the amount of land involved."

The vines were about one metre tall. The grapes were still on them – Mr Vorst had explained that they weren't harvested this year.

"There are weeds all around but the vines look healthy," said Nick, bending over to inspect a bunch of grapes. I did the same.

"Amazing to think they turn into wine," I said to Nick, holding a bunch of grapes in my hand.

He laughed. "Soph, they don't just turn into wine, we have to make them into wine. There's a whole process…." He was about to tell me about it when his BlackBerry started wailing and he wandered off with it stuck to his ear, a more and more regular occurrence over the past couple of months. Funny that.

I was left alone in the vineyard. There were rose bushes at the end of some of the lines of vines, both yellow and red. I thought about where we might be a year from now if we bought Sainte Claire. We would have harvested the grapes, either by hand or machine if we could afford to rent a machine, we would have bottled the wine and we would be trying to sell it. We would have pruned the vines, sprayed them to protect them from disease, weeded around the base and trellised them. It seemed a lot to achieve in one year but I was longing to give it a go. I was longing to make a life here for all of us, to live off the land, to go back to nature and get away from tarmac, crime and traffic wardens who seem to multiply every week like hordes of locusts, as well as the rude men with bad taste in breasts and handbags (why would you otherwise mug a woman carrying an old Marks & Spencer special?).

I saw Nick walking back towards me. I might once have thought this was a pipedream, but by now I was all for it now and even grateful to him for coming up with it.

"The estate is at the boundary where the appellations of Faugères and Saint-Chinian meet. Monsieur Gréco was with Saint-Chinian," Mr Vorst joined us, "a respected and popular appellation. When Monsieur Gréco was alive he used to work the vineyard and did well out of it. When he died Madame Gréco just sold the grapes to a local *négociant* who sold them on to other wine makers or the local wine cooperative."

In the vineyards we were standing was a little stone hut, which I guessed was where the workers would stop for lunch. It had a tiled roof and a jasmine plant growing up the walls. It was like something from a scene in a dreamy, hazy French film with no discernible plot.

"Any minute now Gérard Depardieu is going to lumber past swigging a bottle of red wine and chewing on a baguette," I said nudging Nick.

"I hope Emmanuelle Béart is with him," he laughed.

We walked down a dusty track that Mr Vorst told us was often used as a *boules* pitch. The *cave* or winery was between the house and the vineyards, opposite a barn used to house the grape-pickers during harvest time. It was a whitewashed building and the most chaotic thing about the property. Inside bits of broken machinery lay around and there were bottles all over the place. I couldn't imagine how it would ever be cleaned up. But Nick looked ecstatic.

"What a mess," I said.

"It's marvellous," said Nick under his breath. "Look at these *foudres*; they must be over one hundred years old. This is like walking into wine-making history."

There was a row of around twenty huge oak casks along both walls. They were on their sides.

"Once the wine juice is squeezed it is pumped up into the casks through the top and then left for a year or so to take on the taste of the oak as it ages," Nick explained.

"Well, it's great they're all here," I said.

"Not on a practical level," said Nick, suddenly coming into his own. "Nowadays everyone uses stainless steel or concrete so they can control the amount of oxygen that gets to the wine and also it's easier to reduce the temperature; which is essential if you want to avoid the wine turning to vinegar. We'll have to invest in some of those. And some peacocks of course."

I was so happy to hear him say it. Not that I could see how anyone could fail to be charmed by Sainte Claire but I needed to be sure that Nick could see himself there as strongly as I could.

We walked back out into the early-evening sunshine. I had the sensation that nothing had changed for generations. The view to the mountains was the same, the vines, the roses and the beautiful stone house and barn. It felt secure and peaceful.

"I wish I had a Tardis and could just transport the family, the furniture and Daisy right this minute," I said to Nick.

I was reluctant to leave as we walked back towards the house and to the agent's Berlingo van. Before I got in the car I took one last look up at the rose on my balcony and said a silent prayer that we would be back soon, crossing my toes and fingers as I did so. The agent went around closing all the shutters again. I said a silent prayer that next time they were opened it would be by us and that we would be here to stay.

We drove back with the agent to his office in silence, partly for fear of endangering our lives but also overwhelmed with a sense of how important it was for us to buy the house, how it encapsulated our whole French dream, how it was the one real chance we had to turn our dream into reality.

We sat down in his office. "The asking price is €850,000. They had an offer," he told us looking through some papers, "of €790,000, which they have rejected. But I know they are keen to sell before the end of year for tax reasons."

"If we were to offer €10,000 more than that, do you think they would accept?" asked Nick.

The agent leaned back in his chair, which reclined under his weight. At one stage I thought we'd lost him, but he bounced back. "I can ask."

He called the lawyers representing the feuding French family. I had terrible butterflies. I tried to breathe deeply, to squeeze all my nerves into my toes and not look too desperate. Mr Vorst jabbered away in very fast French. Neither Nick nor I were any the wiser as to the outcome of the conversation when he finally put the phone down.

"They will call me," said the agent. "As soon as I have some news I will call you."

"But did they sound optimistic?" I asked.

Mr Vorst smiled and leaned back in his chair again. "Lawyers rarely sound optimistic," he said to the ceiling. "There is nothing more you can do, I will call you the minute I hear anything."

Nick and I left his office and walked towards our hotel.

"It is amazing that all this has happened in a day," said Nick. "This morning seems like a lifetime ago. We left London at nine o'clock not knowing that we would end up seeing the house of our dreams today and that our lives could change forever."

By the time we had eaten dinner we had both checked and re-checked our mobile phone signals about forty times.

That night I veered between euphoria and desperation; one minute I thought 'Why wouldn't we get the house? We're offering a good price and they're keen to sell'. Then I would think, 'One of the siblings will decide they don't want to sell and so the whole thing will just collapse'.

"I mean why would you want to sell such an incredible place?" I said out loud to no one in particular at three in the morning. "It must be one of the most beautiful houses in France."

I listened to Nick breathing peacefully, which made me feel safe. This was the biggest thing we had done together since saying 'I do' and having three children, two of them at once. It was a huge adventure and we needed to make it work.

Miraculously, I fell asleep again almost straight away despite my panic attack. When I woke up in the morning, I took this as a sign that the international conspiracy to keep me awake had not reached France – yet another good reason to move there.

But I left the promised land with a heavy heart the following morning since there had been no call from the agent. As we boarded the plane, I wondered if I would ever walk through the vineyards at Sainte Claire again. Not only could I see myself being happy there – I couldn't see myself being happy anywhere else.

Rule 5

It is better to be unfaithful than to be faithful without wanting to be — Brigitte Bardot

The French Art of Having Affairs

"Mummy, where's Daddy?" There is a voice coming from somewhere asking a question I cannot answer. I know I need to react but I can't seem to open my eyes.

"Mummy, Eddie took my fairy dress and says he is going to wear it to his first day at school," another voice joins it. "Tell him he can't; he's a boy, and anyway it's my dress."

"You wear my flip-flop tops." The first voice is back. I'm longing to see what's going on and to know what a flip-flop top is.

"Your flip-flops stupid, they're called flip-flops," says the disgruntled owner of the fairy dress.

Why can't I open my eyes? It feels like something dark is forcing them closed. Have I gone blind overnight? Is it possible to lose both one's husband and one's eyesight in a few short hours? Has God blinded me for visualising my husband's mistress being publicly exposed as a home-breaker and having her head shaved by booing crowds in the Place du 14 Juillet as I am awarded the Légion d'Honneur for services to the French wine industry?

"Mummy, wake up and listen," bellows a third voice. "You have to get up, it's morning time. It's light outside. We're supposed to be starting school today."

I sit up, feeling dazed and disorientated.

"Mummy, why are you wearing a scarf around your eyes?" asks one of my children.

Of course, the reason I can't open my eyes is that I have a lavender-scented bean-bag tied over them with a leopard-print scarf. I couldn't sleep because of the bright moonlight forcing its way into the bedroom through the rickety old shutters. Or was it more to do with the fact that my husband of ten years and the father of the three little people currently clambering on top of me admitted to an affair last night with a French woman called Cécile?

I unwind the leopard-print scarf and bean-bag from around my head.

"Mummy, you don't look very good," says Emily, head to one

side, before putting her thumb in her mouth. I almost burst into tears at the sight of the three of them, all in their pyjamas, beautiful with blond tousled early-morning hair, looking up at me expectantly. Emily already has her cat's ears on. She was given them for Christmas a year ago and never goes anywhere without them. I have got so used to seeing them they almost seem to be a part of her, but I wonder what the French will make of her eccentricity.

"That's not very nice," says Charlotte, adding with the brutal honesty of a child, "but it is true."

"Mummy looks like a fairy," says Edward, climbing closer to give me a hug. I clasp him to me greedily. Obviously this morning I am more vulnerable than most mornings, but poor Edward's first words were 'det away' because I have always smothered him with hugs and kisses.

"I look like a fairy too," he continues, wriggling free from my arms. "Where's Daddy?" he adds, looking around the room while doing an unsteady twirl on the bed to show me the fairy dress at its best. I wonder for a brief moment if I can pretend their father is hiding to avoid telling them the truth. But they would soon run out of places to look in our bedroom-cum-open-plan bathroom.

"Edward," I say looking at him and stroking his blond hair. I am about to utter my first sentence as a single mother. It has to be just right. This is one of those moments they might never forget, like the first time they ride a bike or wear a school uniform. I have to make it as painless as possible for them.

But how do I explain that their father has gone? I just can't do it to them. This must be what it's like when you have to tell people someone is dead. There they are, all innocent and unknowing, and you're just about to shatter their world. I can't shatter their world – not yet anyway, not before a cup of tea.

So instead of telling Edward that his father is probably with a small-breasted woman called Cécile, I tell him he can't go to school in Charlotte's fairy dress. This probably has a more immediate effect on him than the other news would have had.

"Why not? I love it," he wails, keeling over on the bed, looking dangerously close to having a tantrum or at least bashing himself on the headboard.

"Because your teacher might not like it." I know they don't go for school uniforms in France, but a fairy dress might be pushing it. "And you look a bit, well, a bit like a girl and you might get teased."

Edward sits up. "I look like a girl?" he asks.

"Yes," I say, stroking his hair again. "I'm sorry to say you do."

"Yuk. I hate girls," he says looking disconsolately at his fairy dress.

Charlotte looks around the room. "Is Daddy downstairs in the shower?"

"No, Daddy has gone to London," I say, making an effort not to betray anything in my voice. "He had to leave for work early."

"But he was supposed to be here for our first day at school," wails Emily. "It's not fair."

"I know, I know," I say consolingly. "I'm afraid he had to go back to work urgently. But as a special treat you can have *pain au chocolat* for breakfast. A French breakfast for my French schoolchildren."

If anything can console Emily it is chocolate.

"Yipppeee!" she yells. Didn't take her long to get over the absence of her father. Maybe I should eat some chocolate too and hope for the best?

"Last one to get dressed is a rotten banana," yells Charlotte, running towards the door. I watch them. Charlotte is a smaller version of me, or at least the me I used to be before I became a mummy with a tummy; Emily is more like my mother: a total rebel. She'll be reading books on nihilism before she's ten. Or possibly even writing them.

Half of me feels like lying down and going back to sleep. So what if I'm the rotten banana? I can't muster the energy to do anything at all. I'm exhausted. My brain feels as messy as a ball of wool that's been dragged around the house for several hours by an over-excited Daisy. The thought of getting dressed, even getting up, fills me with despair.

I wonder where Nick is now. Probably already back with Cécile. She could be tying his tie for him as I lie here wondering how the hell my marriage ended. Hopefully she'll accidentally strangle him.

What am I supposed to do? I need to think about our future, about moving back home, packing everything up again (lucky I didn't throw away those £8 collapsible boxes), finding a house, taking the children out of school, finding them another school. I wonder where I put Simon the removal man's number. I didn't think I'd ever need it again, let alone two weeks into our new life. The list of things to do is endless and horrible. I don't want to dwell on any of it now; it makes me feel physically sick. But I can't possibly stay here alone with no job and rely on Nick the faithless bastard for handouts.

I think back to how excited we were when Mr Vorst called us to tell us our offer had been accepted. I had the feeling of a whole new world opening up. And now of course it is already closing.

In the distance either Frank or Lampard screeches. Nick bought them from an aviary near Montpellier a few days after we moved here. They roam around the estate looking elegant and squawking occasionally. It feels like they have been here forever, like they belong to the house and land.

I love the sound they make: it's an aristocratic sound, the sort of sound you only ever hear in England when you're on a visit to some stately home. Whenever I see our peacocks wandering around regally I'm reminded of the TV show *Brideshead Revisited*. But where is Jeremy Irons when I need him?

I get up and walk out onto the terrace. It is a chilly January morning. There is no frost but a light mist hangs over the vineyards and the sun is just beginning to wake up. It seems inconceivable that Nick could risk his family and all this: Frank and Lampard, Sainte Claire, our new life, our vineyards, everything he's dreamed about for so long, just for a good sex life. I need to understand why. I feel utterly confused and abandoned. How the hell did this happen?

I turn to my rose. "Maybe this is just one of those moments of madness?" I ask it. "Maybe he will wake up today and realise the huge mistake he's made." Then I decide that talking to a flower may be considered a moment of madness in itself. You can only get away with that if you're next in line to the throne.

How long does a moment of madness normally last? Is it a kind of mid-life crisis? Maybe it had been building up for months. Did Nick think the move to France would answer all his problems, dispel his dissatisfaction, and then find it didn't? Or did he realise that the only thing that could satisfy him was Cécile and her self-waxing legs?

Of course I don't know that they're self-waxing, but I assume she didn't get my husband to stick around for so long by wrapping hirsute pegs around him. I walk back inside and over to the mirror. I lift up my nightie and look down at my own legs. Yep, they're predictably hairy.

Is he right? Have I really let myself go? I need to call Sarah, I need to talk to someone. Last night I just couldn't face anything, but today I need to work out what to do.

A scream from the kitchen stops my rêverie. I run downstairs and find Edward trying to wrestle Emily's precious Peter Rabbit bowl, a sixth birthday present from her best friend at school in England, from her.

"Sit in your place, Edward," I say, taking the bowl from him. If I'm going to be a single parent there's going to have to be a policy of zero tolerance around here. "Girls, lay the table."

"Why does he get to do nothing?" moans Charlotte.

"Because he's only five and he doesn't get to do nothing, he's going to help me clear the table."

The twins think about rebelling but I give them one of my 'don't even think about it' looks so they get out bowls, plates and cups. They put one in Nick's place.

"Not there, silly," says Charlotte to Emily. "He's gone to London to work."

"He didn't say goodbye," says Emily before putting her thumb back in her mouth.

"He asked me to say goodbye and give you all a kiss," I lie. Why am I protecting the bastard? Actually I'm not, I'm protecting them.

I leave the room, partly to get dressed but partly so they can't see that I am about to start crying again. Maybe I should hold off telling them. He was always going to be away during the week and even some weekends, so as far as they are concerned nothing has really changed. Right now I'm so unsure of what will happen. Maybe in a few weeks I will be able to forgive him? Or maybe he won't want to come back at all after a few weeks of the full Cécile treatment.

I pull my nightie over my head and resume my investigation of myself in the full-length mirror. How could he leave all this behind? The breasts that have seen better days, the nipples that never really recovered from breast-feeding, the knees with an inexplicably useless layer of skin just above them that seems to have arrived from nowhere, the unwaxed legs and bikini line, the out-of-shape arms, the buttocks that are at the other end of pert. And I haven't even started on my face.

Sophie Reed, née Cunningham, mother of three, thirty-six years old, saggy, sad and single. And a sex-free zone. What happened to my libido? Nick was right to complain about that. It's not like I'm not aware of the issue myself. My sex drive is like one of those 80s pop stars that you used to be so familiar with but who then just vanished off the face of the earth. When I was trying to get pregnant I was keen on it, then while I was pregnant I liked it – my whole body was somehow on heightened alert.

But after that my libido turned into Adam Ant and my husband had an affair. How long did it take? I suppose since Edward I have totally lost interest in Nick and any sex life with him. It's almost as if the love I used to have for the father has been transferred to our son. Not in any sexual way of course, but all my affection and adoration. I could spend hours gazing at Edward, but I never really notice Nick any more. Or if I do notice him, it's because he's done something to annoy me like not putting his clothes in the laundry basket or nicked the bit of the paper I wanted to read. When did it all change?

There was a time though when he was everything to me, when I adored him and he adored me. Is this all my fault? Should I have made more of an effort to be sexy and seductive and lost the baby weight and had my hair dyed blonder and done all those things high-maintenance yummy mummies do? I suppose it never occurred to me that he would go off me. I have always been pretty, and vaguely thin, and attractive. Boys always liked me. Up until now that is. I still look OK, but I am no longer thin. My weight gain has been insidious: it has happened without me noticing, each baby leaving its marks in the form a few kilos. I don't look after myself like I used to. I never have facials, I hardly ever paint my nails, I have forgotten where to buy leg wax and don't even think about matching underwear even though I now live in the land where it is practically obligatory. I have become the second lowest priority on my list, just above my husband.

I drag a brush through my hair; it is still thick, blonde and long, so at least I have that going for me. Thankfully alopecia hasn't set in. Yet. I did read somewhere that you can lose your hair from shock or go grey overnight. I guess if that were going to happen it would have done so already. But maybe the shock of Nick's infidelity hasn't reached my hair follicles yet.

I still can't believe it. Nick and infidelity. Those words just don't fit together. My solid, dependable, Irish rock of a husband has slept with another woman. He has betrayed me, betrayed all of us. And the worst of it is that I only had two weeks to enjoy this French dream before it happened. I can't believe my new life, that started with the New Year, is already over.

"Mummy, quick, come here, quick, quick." Thankfully I can drag myself away from assessing my own state of decay as all three children are shouting from the kitchen again. I run from the bedroom, throwing my nightie back on as I do so in case the postman decides to show up carrying a large package.

"What is it?" I gasp, expecting to find an axe murderer in the house or at least some blood somewhere. But they are all staring at the television.

"Your boyfriend's on TV again," says Emily, pointing at the screen.

I look at the small television I have had since I owned my first flat in Fulham and that now sits on the counter in our French kitchen and is fully hooked up to Sky (obligatory for any Chelsea fan moving abroad). Classical music blares out from it. A familiar figure is in the middle of the screen, wearing black trousers and a white shirt. His hair is back-lit, making it look even more wild and curly than it normally is. He is staring intently at me with sparkling blue eyes. It is Johnny Fray, someone I met at work and who has since become a huge film star.

Emily is wrong: he was never my boyfriend. But he might as well have been, I never forgot him. I knew him for almost two years and lusted after him for even longer.

The first day I met him was the day he came for a job interview at Drake's, the hotel I was working at. He looked me in the eyes and smiled. Two thoughts came into my head almost at the same time. The first one was "Oh my god, his eyes are the most incredible blue I have ever seen". The second was "Why did I pick today to wear these trousers that make me look like a maiden aunt and forget my lip gloss?"

He started telling me about drama school where he was studying at the time.

"What sorts of things do you study at drama school?" I asked him.

"Today we learnt all about how to kiss without really kissing," he said. "What they call 'on-screen kissing'."

"Oh? Any tips?"

"I wouldn't have thought as a hotel manager you would ever need to fake a kiss," he laughed. "But I'd be happy to show you if you like."

"That's not part of the job description," I replied, ignoring his flirtatious tone, trying my best to sound professional and not give away that what I was really thinking was how I wanted to run my fingers through his thick black hair and try any kind of kiss with him at all.

He started work the following night and fitted in right away. The clients loved him, especially the women: he was attractive, efficient and good-natured. Even Lady Butterdish, the hotel's notoriously difficult and grumpy owner, was mesmerised. She was actually called Lady de Buerre, but Johnny Fray nick-named her Butterdish because he knew it would annoy her if she ever found out and also because it made everyone else laugh.

One time I overheard Lady Butterdish invite him to spend a weekend on her yacht in St Tropez. I was so relieved when I heard he had said no.

I started to look forward to his shifts and hated it when he wasn't there. Every time I saw him I liked him more. I think one of the major things that attracted me to him was his drive and ambition. I had never seen anyone work so hard, even if this was just his way of making some extra cash. And of course his looks: he reminded me of Heathcliff from *Wuthering Heights* – dark and swarthy, with a mass of black curly hair.

Johnny was tall, about six foot two, and well-built. But he had the most delicate hands, like a pianist's – small with long elegant fingers. Sometimes I had to stop myself looking at them and wondering what they would feel like over my body.

But it wasn't just his looks that I liked. He was also an amazingly kind person. I remember once when I gave up smoking we went into a newsagent's together so I could buy a packet of chewing-gum to take my mind off the cigarettes. Johnny took the whole box from its stand and bought it for me in a typically generous and flamboyant gesture. And he was more mature than other men of his age. His parents had both died when he was just six years old and that was probably partly why he was so determined to do well in life, he had no one to look after him.

Looking back on it now it seems insane that nothing really happened between us. There was so much obvious attraction there and yet it was almost like every time we got close, something got in the way. One week we were out for a drink after work, alone for the first time in several weeks. We had just settled down for a drink when my phone rang. It was my mother, frantic because husband number four had been caught with his secretary in the boardroom doing more than going through the books.

Another time it was Lucy on the phone in a state of despair because Perfect Patrick (her then crush at law school and now husband) had a girlfriend back home, and, what was worse, her mother was French. "How can I compete with a French woman?" she wailed. "Even Kate Moss couldn't compete with a French woman – look what happened to Johnny Depp."

"Patrick is not Johnny Depp and she's only half French," I consoled her, wondering what, if anything, was ever going to happen with my own version of Johnny Depp.

Then a third time (lucky for some but not for us) we finally kissed.

It was about a year after he started at Drake's. We were moving a table in the restaurant together. We had a hen party of twenty coming for dinner and needed to put two of our biggest tables together. At one stage we let go at the same time because it was so heavy. We stared at each other. I had such terrible butterflies I could hardly breathe. There was no one else in the restaurant.

Johnny walked towards me. I kept looking at him, half in panic, half in joy. I was frozen to the spot. He stood opposite me, looking down at me. He smiled, cupped my face in his hands and kissed me. It was probably the most memorable kiss of my life. He gently leant down to touch my lips with his. Tentatively at first and then with more determination. I felt dizzy. My whole body seemed to float. I sometimes think about the significant things I will remember on my deathbed – walking down the aisle, the first moment I held the twins, my first (and only) pair of Manolo Blahniks (50% at the Selfridge's sale), Nick proposing – and I still think that kiss would be right up there.

After a minute or so he let me go.

"I'm guessing that was a real kiss?" I asked, struggling to find my voice.

Johnny laughed. "Yes. But as you said, it's not in the job spec."

"Oh forget the job spec," I said, lifting my face towards his, smiling. "Kiss me again."

"Hardly the kind of attitude I expect from one of my most promising and certainly my youngest managers."

Her voice cut through our intimacy like a knife through butter. Johnny and I sprang apart. It was Lady Butterdish herself, looking like the witch from *The Lion, the Witch and the Wardrobe* in a cream white fur coat and black stiletto boots that almost certainly cost more than my annual salary each.

"Both of you, to my office," she commanded and stormed off.

We obeyed orders and followed her. She started with me and

made Johnny wait outside. I knew what was coming. I had the 'I'm so disappointed in you' speech and the 'I trusted you despite your age and inexperience' lecture.

"If you are here to seduce the staff, Sophie, then I think we had better terminate our agreement," she concluded. "Either you are serious about this job or you're serious about him. You can't have both."

I was a girl at the beginning of her career. Lady Butterdish could have made sure I never worked in London again. So what did I do? I lied to her, of course. I lied to save myself. I behaved like a coward.

"Of course the job means more to me," I said, practically choking on my words. "He's only a waiter."

"Sensible girl," smiled Lady Butterdish. "I am pleased to hear that. You'll go far. Now send him in."

I was planning to wink at Johnny, to smile to give him some sign that I did care and that everything would be all right. But when I opened the door to let him in, he had already gone.

He didn't show up for work the next day, or ever again. He didn't answer my calls. I once went to RADA to see if I could spot him leaving or arriving. I did see him, laughing and chatting with a pretty dark-haired girl. I gave up after that.

Six months after he left, I met Nick.

"Johnny Fray stars in Peak TV's brand new adaptation of *Jane Eyre*, starting Friday at 8 o'clock," says a moody-sounding voiceover. I feel something move in the pit of my stomach but can't really identify it. Could it be hunger? I haven't eaten since Nick left. No, the thought of food makes me feel sick. I gaze at the TV. So now he's going to play Rochester, my other all-time crush? A man who looks like Heathcliff playing Mr Rochester. You couldn't make it up.

"Can we watch?" asks Charlotte. "Please? Johnny would like us to."

They love Johnny. They only met him once, but he made a lasting impression on them. Partly because he took such an interest in them, but also because he gave them £20 each to spend on whatever they wanted. Edward bought a pair of Spiderman shoes that flash when you walk (very useful if I ever lose him in a dark room), Charlotte bought a huge furry dog and called it Johnny, and Emily bought two DVDs: *High School Musical* and *The Sound of Music*.

We ran into Johnny when I took the children to stay with my mother in Devon last summer. We went for a pub-lunch in a small beautiful Exmoor village called Bampton. It was one of those rare British summer days that brings everyone outside. I spotted him as soon as we sat down in the garden with our food although I hadn't seen him for more than fifteen years. My heart was thumping so hard I was worried everyone around us would hear it.

He was with a whole gang of people who were all laughing at his jokes and gazing at him adoringly. He hadn't changed at all. The unruly hair was the same, the ubiquitous cigarette was lit. But I suppose I would have recognised him from the television even if I hadn't known him. Since I knew him and we had that kiss he had won an Oscar, which led to several TV shows and A-list celebrity status.

He walked over to us as soon as he saw me. "Cunningham," he said. He had always called me by my surname. "Still as lovely as ever. How are you, girl?"

"Fine thanks," I said, shaking all over. It was so strange to see him after so long. I wondered briefly if his first thought was 'Oh my God, she's got so fat'. If it was, it didn't show – he stared at me with total affection.

"How are you? Well, I mean I know how you are – rich and famous." I added, rather embarrassed.

"Yes, not bad for 'just a waiter,'" he said, smiling. I was catapulted back to that meeting with Lady Butterdish.

"Johnny, I didn't mean it, you know…."

"Cunningham, don't be silly," he said interrupting me by putting his hands on my shoulders. I felt my knees buckle slightly as he touched me. "We were young and silly and you did what you had to do to keep your job. Do you mind if I join you?"

"Of course not," I said. It was so good to see him. He still looked great; he didn't look a day older and his eyes were just as mesmerising.

He turned to my mother. "Hello Mrs Cunningham, how lovely to see you again. Last time I saw you was at Drake's at Sophie's birthday, wasn't it? You haven't aged a day."

"Thank you," said my mother, looking terribly chuffed. Like most women, she actually believes people when they tell her she hasn't aged in twenty years.

"And are these your children?" he said turning to me.

"Yes, this is Charlotte, Emily and Edward," I said gesturing to the children, who all, rather miraculously, stood up, smiled and said hello. I was terribly proud of them. Nothing like a real live film star to make them pay attention.

"Good Yorkshire names," he grinned. "I'm a very old friend of your mother," he told them. "Life throws at you many things, but very few friends. In fact, I fancied her. But I was too ugly for her." He pulled a stupid face that made them all laugh.

"You're only ugly when you pull faces," said Emily. "Otherwise you're not."

She was right. Actually he looked better than most people do even when he was pulling a silly face.

"Thank you, miss," said Johnny. "You'll be a good friend and you'll have good friends. Look after them – life throws at you many things but few true friends." As he spoke he turned to me and took my hand.

"I've never forgotten your kindness to me all those years ago in London, giving me that job when I had no experience at all," he said quietly, almost as if he were referring to the intimacy we had shared. For some reason it made me blush.

"Your mother is a wonderful person," he told the children. "I loved her when I was a boy."

"Why didn't you get married with each other?" asked Edward. "Was she your darling?"

"Maybe because you smoke," Emily interrupted him, briefly removing her thumb from her mouth. "Mummy hates smoking."

Johnny laughed and thankfully didn't tell them that in those days I used to smoke as well.

He spent the afternoon with us, charming my mother and the children, who then didn't stop talking about him for the rest of the holiday. As he sat chatting with us people would come up and ask for his autograph. It was a bit like hanging out with, well, a film star.

He charmed me too; age had mellowed him slightly and made him more mysterious. And there's nothing like a few millions and celebrity status to make a man more attractive. But more than any of that was the way he kept looking at me, with a mixture of curiosity and affection. And the memory of that kiss.

*

"We'll see," I tell Emily who is tugging on my waistband and looking at me pleadingly.
"It's on terribly late."

"And Daddy might not like it," says Emily. "He doesn't like Johnny like we do."

"That's because he's Mummy's boyfriend and they kissed on the lips," says Edward dancing around me. "Kissing on the lips, kissing on the lips," he chants.

"Edward, stop it now. He is not my boyfriend," I say sternly, crossing my fingers behind my back. "I have never kissed him on the lips, he is an extremely old friend and Daddy is just teasing when he says he's my boyfriend."

"When I'm grown up, I'd like a boyfriend like Johnny," says Emily.

"Why?" asks Charlotte. "He smokes, you know."

"Well, apart from the smoking I mean. But he's rich and famous and on telly and that's nice."

"Come on," I say, "we need to get to school. Emily do you really need to wear your cat's ears?"

"But I can't hear without them," she protests. "And I have to learn French today."

I decide to let it go and try another time; there is enough going on today. At least Edward is not wearing ballet kit.

We decide to walk to school. It means walking through the vineyards of our next-door neighbour, but I can't see that he'd mind – it's not as if we're standing on any plants, as the vines are still just small sticks, but even if they were in bloom there are tracks between them. It is a crisp January morning and the air is cold enough to make your nipples stand on end – unless, like mine, they have lost the habit. There's not a cloud in the sky. Wolfie the dog, who as the agent said, seems to live at the house, follows us, but at a safe distance. He was obviously badly treated by someone; he seems really scared of people. The only person he goes anywhere near is Nick. I guess I will feed him now – maybe that will help him to grow to trust me as well.

We are all kitted out with hats and gloves and scarves, Emily of course with her cat's ears on top of her hat. "Knitting with one needle, that girl," Nick would say if he were here.

I can never get over just how much clutter one needs, especially when there are three children involved. And just where do all those missing gloves and socks go? Are they all partying together, making more odd socks in accessory heaven?

There are already a few people standing at the school gates waiting for them to open when we get there. The school is made up of two small buildings: one for the kindergarten section and the other for the primary school. I recognise the yellow walls from the website, which has a lopsided photograph where you can just about make out the fact that it is a building and there is a playground around it. There are drawings in the windows of animals, trees and vines, obviously by the children. It is much smaller than the school they went to in London.

My mobile phone rings. It is Nick.

"How are you?" he asks.

"Fine," I say, not wanting to give anything away to the children. "Just fine. Do you want to speak to the young French scholars?"

He talks to each in turn wishing them good luck. Edward hands me the phone back.

"Let's talk later," I say. "I need to focus on the kids." I hang up before he has a chance to say anything that might make me cry again.

"Are you the new girl?" says a voice behind me as we wait for the school gates to open.

I say yes, more out of surprise than anything else. The voice is English and belongs to a man wearing a light pink shirt, with big brown eyes and a mop of blond hair.

"Hi, I'm Peter," he says, leaning forward to kiss me on the cheek three times. Can't this man count? "We kiss three times down here," he explains. "Twice is Parisian. They hate the Parisians here."

"Right," I say. "Good to know. Do you, er, live here?"

"Yes darling, have done for two years. This is Amelia, our daughter. She's seven." He gestures towards an Asian-looking girl wearing a Hello Kitty Alice band and pink dungarees.

"Oh that's great," I say. "My girls are seven too. Maybe she can help them settle in." I look around for Charlotte and Emily. They are already chatting to a girl with masses of blonde hair wearing a tie-dye dress. They are speaking English.

"Hey, I thought we were supposed to be in France?" I joke.

"This is our new friend," says Emily. "She is going to translate for us."

"I could do with one of those," I say turning back to Peter. "I have to go to the social security office this afternoon. Does your wife live here too?" I ask.

He starts laughing. Amelia saunters off to join the others.

"Darling I AM the wife," he says, taking hold of my hand and patting it. "My other half is Phil. We adopted Amelia from Vietnam when she was a baby. We both worked in advertising in London and decided enough was enough. No more rat race, no more rush-hour tubes or fear of crime. So here we are!"

"Oh God I'm so sorry, how stupid of me," I bluster.

"Don't give it a second thought. It's an easy mistake to make. It's not as if I'm wearing my gay pride T-shirt. Anyway, what brings you here? Someone told me you're going to make wine?"

"Yes, that's the plan, although it will be a slow start. Nick, my husband is going to keep working in London for the next few months…." I trot out that line as if it is still true. What else can I do? I can hardly tell Peter that only one of us around here has a husband and it's not me.

"Oh, you poor thing," he says, once again patting my hand. Now that he's told me he's gay it seems perfectly obvious. "Well, if you ever need anything, I'm your girl!" he says, sounding like Jack Lemon in *Some Like it Hot*. "By the way, I've got my shopping hat on today. Anything you need from town?"

"No, thanks, that's sweet of you. Where do you go?"

"Carrefour in Pézenas, it's the best place around, and then of course Pézenas market on a Saturday for all the fresh stuff. Must dash, see you this afternoon for the school pick-up."

The bell rings and we say goodbye. I walk the girls to their bit of the school and watch proudly as they stand in line wearing their matching jeans, dresses and ponytails. I am not one of those mothers with twins who insist on dressing them the same to confuse the rest of the world, and actually Charlotte and Emily are non-identical twins so are easy to tell apart, and of course Emily has her additional ears. But today I thought it might be useful to show a united front. I changed schools when I was little more times than I care to remember and I would have loved to have had a twin with me. There is nothing quite as scary and lonely as that feeling of walking into a school playground not knowing anyone or having a clue where anything is. But the girls seem totally unaffected by all this newness and march into school with great confidence, chatting and smiling all the way.

They barely notice me say good bye. I walk with Edward to the nursery section of the school, the *maternelle*.

The nursery mothers are already assembled. I look at them. They are not a glamorous bunch; most look to be housewives or wine growers and they are not all pencil thin, thank God. One of them stands out; she has blonde ringlets and is very pretty. But I'm relieved to conclude that the mum-upmanship I so loathed in

London is not going to be an issue. There people would look at the label on your jeans before they look at your face. And there is no worse start to the day than feeling dowdy and worthless in comparison with other thinner, richer and more fashion-conscious mothers. Here it is clear that no one cares if your jeans come from the local market or Prada. In fact they'd probably think you were deranged to spend enough on a pair of jeans to buy you a whole new wardrobe in downtown Béziers.

Edward's new teacher Magali is waiting for him along with her classroom assistant Sylvie. I have read about Magali on the school's website, which says she has been working at the school for ten years. She doesn't look older than twenty. Maybe she went straight from nursery school into teaching.

"*Bonjour Madame Reed,*" she says smiling. "*Et bonjour Edouard, comment ca va? Bienvenue à l'école de Boujan.*" She shakes my hand and says something that makes Sylvie laugh. Edward looks dubious. I'm not surprised; I can't understand what she's saying either. Sylvie looks like the stricter one; maybe they have a 'good cop bad cop' routine going. They would need to do something to control the thirty or so toddlers I see fighting their way into the classroom.

I am always in awe of people who actually chose this career. 'What do you want to do when you grow up?' 'Be surrounded by screaming excitable and disobedient children whom I will calm down enough to teach to read.' Yep, sounds good.

"*Bonjour,*" I begin. Oh help. What the hell do I say next? Edward seems more confident than I am; he starts to walk towards her. She leans down to greet him then takes his hand and starts walking towards the classroom. This is all going swimmingly.

She turns and nods as if to say 'that's all' like Meryl Streep in *The Devil Wears Prada*. I walk back towards home. Have I really just left my three children in a foreign school? How callous it sounds. But there is no other way; I can hardly sit in their classrooms making sure they're all right. Although it might be good for my French grammar.

Sarah says the best way to learn a language is to take a lover whose native tongue (no pun intended) is the one you want to learn.

"I learnt Spanish in three weeks," she told me proudly before we moved here. "And it would have been less if we hadn't spent so much time having sex."

If I were planning on staying, I might consider it.

I walk back through my neighbour's vineyard towards home. There are worse school runs, I reflect, as I see Wolfie come out from the ditch to join me at a distance and the mountains ahead.

I am just thinking about starting to sand down the shutters before I paint them with the new olive-green colour I've chosen to make the house easier to sell, when I am almost deafened by an almighty bang. It comes from nowhere. The shock makes me jump up in the air. I look around me, terrified. It can't be thunder – there's not a cloud in the sky.

A split-second passes and then it happens again. I crouch behind a bush. This time there is no doubt as to what it is. It's a gun. Who the hell is shooting at me? And why?

My first thought is that I have been hit. I look down, dreading to see where I am bleeding from. I can't feel anything; my whole body is shaking. The faces of the children pass through my mind and I scream out loud.

"*Qu'est-ce que vous faites ici Madame ?*" says a voice. A rather unattractive man wearing far too many layers of dirty clothes carrying a rifle is standing above me. He looks like Baldrick on a bad hair day.

I am still too stunned to speak (let alone in French) and far from convinced that I am still alive. Is this what happens when you die? There is no pain: just a man in a cloth-cap with dodgy teeth. I scramble to my feet and try to explain that someone just tried to kill me.

"*C'est une propriété privée ici. Vous n'avez pas le droit de vous promener.*" he tells me, pointing his rifle in my general direction. "You have not the right," he repeats in English when he sees I am not responding to French. I leap away from him.

"*Not the right?*" I yell. Who the hell does this man think he is? Anger is now taking over as I realise I am alive and not bleeding to death and that this is the man who shot at me. "You haven't got the right to go around shooting at innocent people, what the hell were you thinking of, you could have killed me."

I'm not sure how much he understands but it feels good to shout. Hell, it feels good to be alive.

"*Vous n'êtes pas de Paris?*" he asks.

Am I from Paris? I translate the phrase in my head. What the hell has that got to do with anything?

"*Non.*" I say, remembering that should he try to kiss me, I need to kiss him three times. Happily he doesn't.

"*Hmm. Bien. But anyway, you have not the right to walk on le terrain of M. de Sard.*"

He throws his rifle over his shoulder and walks away. Great, I think: as well as matching underwear I'm going to have to invest in a matching bullet-proof vest.

Rule 6

Be breathtaking, be sexy; but above all be discreet

The French Art of Having Affairs

After my near-death experience with the man in the cloth cap, I decide to collect the children for lunch in the car. The school bell rings and the assembled mothers walk in. I see the blonde pretty lady from earlier and hear another mother say hello to her and call her Audrey. As we file into the *maternelle* section, Sylvie calls out the name of the child whose mother has arrived. She spots me and calls out "Edouard." Soon after he trots out looking fine. No scars, no tears and no ripped clothes, no accusing stares. Phew.

"How was it, darling?" I ask as we walk out into the playground to collect the girls.

"There's an English boy there called Sky," he says. "You know like the sky. The others are all French."

"Is he nice?"

"Yes, he is. Better than Charles. He's French and he thinks he's Spiderman. And he's not Spiderman, I am."

The girls join us. "Mummy, we have a new friend called Cloud," says Emily, hugging me.

"Oh, any relation to Sky?" I ask as a joke.

"Yes, it's her brother, he's in the *maternelle* section. Cloud's mummy is really thin and pretty and works in TV. You'll meet her soon."

"Can't wait," I say, rolling my eyes. "How was your first day, darling?" I turn to Charlotte.

"Good, it was hard to understand everything but Cloud helped us both translate, she sat between us, and the teacher is really nice, he's a man called M. Chabour. I can even spell his name in French now; listen."

"So can I," shrieks Emily and they both start spelling and yelling.

"Calm down, first Charlotte then you Emily. It was Charlotte's idea."

By the time we get home even Edward knows how to spell his name in French.

This is my first day as a French mother. Well, not really a French mother, but a mother doing things the French way, which includes bringing your children home at midday for a proper lunch. I have prepared a healthy and nutritious lunch of chicken breasts, runner beans and mash. Predictably, they hardly eat any of it, preferring instead to finish off the *pain au chocolat* from breakfast, which of course I won't let them do.

"This is beauty food," I say pointing at a runner bean, sounding like an Avon Lady on a hard sell. "This food will make you grow. Chocolate won't."

No reaction.

"Ok, here's the deal. Ten runner beans each, five mouthfuls of mash and three of chicken. Then you can have a *pain au chocolat.*"

"No," says Charlotte. "Seven, three and one of chicken."

"Eight, four and two," I insist, although it is against my policy to negotiate with terrorists.

They look at each other and nod. "Deal," says their leader, Charlotte.

I wonder how many French mothers have to go through this kind of thing every day at midday. I get the feeling that it's not very many. French children seem incredibly well behaved; they are always sitting in restaurants for meals that go on for longer than some marriages without so much as a twitch of dissatisfaction. Maybe it's in the genes.

Getting into the car after lunch I spot my would-be assassin. I decide to confront him and ask him in broken French what his problem is with us walking through the vineyards.

"*Oui, madame, mais vous comprenez....*" he begins.

"No, you see that's just the problem, I don't '*comprenez*' in the slightest. Why can't we just walk across the vineyard? It's not doing any harm to anyone. We're not walking on the vines or damaging anything, and it saves us 15 minutes each way, which when you add it all up is an hour a day I could be spending doing any number of more useful things than avoiding this vineyard."

I already hate old M. de Sard, the owner. I don't actually know that M. de Sard is old, having never met him, but it seems to me only an old person could be so stubborn and irrational. My cleaning lady Agnès tells me that he lives between the family apartment near the Opéra in Paris, a vast château near Avignon and his more modest (but still huge) château next to mine. But, it seems, despite spending only about three days a year here, he has sent instructions that the children and I are on no account to be given permission to cross his land on our way to school. The only thing between our house and the village school is his land. Avoiding his land means a huge detour, which on a school-run morning we don't have time for. And I didn't move to the middle of nowhere in France to get in my car every minute where there is a school walking distance away.

Gilles, as the dreaded foreman is called, repeats his mantra.

"You no go on land, *c'est interdit.*"

"What does *interdit* mean?" I ask the girls.

"Forbidden," all three children answer at the same time. Obviously that's one of the first words you learn at French school.

"What should be *interdit* is trying to shoot people who are innocently walking across land that happens to be in their way," I snap. I ask him in my basic French when his lord and master is due to come back.

"*Oh la la,*" he says shrugging his shoulders. I am stunned. They actually SAY that? I thought that was just a cliché, some sort of joke perpetuated by the French Tourist Board. He'll be donning a beret and picking up a snail to munch on any second.

"*Je n'en sais rien,*" he says.

I guess that means 'I don't know and I don't care'.

"Well, when he does come back, could you please ask him to call me or come and see me? I want to sort this out. Come along children," I snap, wagging my finger in his general direction until I notice my nails are shamefully un-manicured. I put them away in case he decides to report me to the French style police.

At the school gates, the children's new friends are already gathered.

"Mummy, this is Calypso," says Charlotte dragging me running towards a thin and attractive woman with long dark hair. "Cloud's mummy."

For some reason I am reminded of being a child, with my mother trying to set me up with other children – something I always hated.

"How do you do?" says the woman, who is wearing a similar tie-dye outfit to the one I saw her daughter wearing earlier, only in yellow. I read somewhere that yellow is the most unflattering colour you can wear, but she seems to look good in it. Mind you, she is the kind of person who would look good wearing a bin-liner, or even a yellow tie-dyed dress.

"I'm Calypso Hampton."

"Hello," I say shaking her outstretched hand. "I'm Sophie."

"Good to meet you, Sophie. Don't look so nervous," she laughs. "It's not compulsory to be friends with me. I hate the idea that just because you come from the same country as someone you have to be friends, don't you?"

I smile and agree and immediately want to be friends with her.

'How are you finding things?" she asks.

I can't tell her the truth; it might put her off me for life. "I find the whole French language thing very difficult," I say. "A few days ago in a café I asked for some butter and ended up with two beers."

She laughs. "I once told Cloud's teacher that Cloud had lice in her horses," she said. "The difference between *chevaux* and *cheveux* is totally imperceptible to me. I mean, for us hair is hair and a horse is a horse. Much more sensible. I think they do it just to confuse us foreigners. Do you know that in France your class is obvious not so much by your accent but your command of the language? For example if you use a liaison between two words ending in vowels, you're considered posh."

I can't even think of two French words ending in vowels, let alone a liaison – whatever that is. But I just nod and say "how interesting". I don't know how she sounds in French, but Calypso sounds very posh to me in English.

"Must dash," she says. "Let's arrange a play-date soon, the kids all seem to be getting on well. The little English mafia."

I laugh and nod. "Yes, it's lovely that they have made friends so quickly. I was a bit worried."

"Oh don't worry, it really is a lovely place to live, we're all very friendly." She waves and goes off.

I think to myself that there's probably not much point in my making friends, or even arguing about walking on M. de Sard's land, when we won't be here for much longer. Although at the very least I would like the children to do one term in a French school, which will mean they are miles ahead when they go back to England.

England... Soon I will have to get used to the weather again, used to that relentless greyness, the drizzle, the children's muddy feet. That's one of the most incredible things about living here; there's no mud. Mud has become a thing of the past; the wellies, which back home were out every day, haven't even been unpacked.

On the way back from school I call Sarah. As I dial her number, I wonder how she'll react; she's always got on well with Nick. She'll probably tell me to do a couple of sun salutations, breathe deeply and hope he comes back.

"Hi sweetpea, it's me," I say.

"Hi my darling, how are you?"

"Not good. Nick has another woman."

There is a crash.

"Sarah?"

"Oh God, sorry Soph, I was in downward dog and I dropped the phone. What the fuck is going on?"

"He's gone; he's got some woman called Cécile from Paris. They've been having an affair for about five months, I found out yesterday. I'm in shock."

"Bloody hell. What a bastard. Who is she? Have you told the children?"

"She's a client, apparently. And no, I haven't said anything yet."

"How did you find out?"

"I found one of her bras in his luggage."

"Shit, shit, shit. How indiscreet. What the hell are you going to do? Will you stay over there?"

"No, I don't think I can," I say. "I mean what would I do? It's not like I can find a job and we're going to need money."

"What do you mean what can you do? Run the frigging vineyard, like you went out there to do."

"But I don't know anything about wine," I protest.

"Neither did your husband, unless you count drinking it as previous experience. But that didn't stop him. You were going to market it, weren't you?"

"Yes."

"Well, now you'll just have to do the other bits too. How hard can it be? Millions of people all over the world grow vines and make wine out of them, even Australians."

Sarah's last boyfriend was Australian and he chucked her and moved in with his male yoga instructor. She is still quite bitter.

"Can't you get your mysterious French château-owning neighbour to help?"

"No, he's hateful. He won't even let us walk on his blessed land. Oh Sarah, I just don't think I've got the energy. Where the hell do I begin? I don't know the first thing about it. I wouldn't even know when to pick the damn things. In fact I wouldn't even know how to pick them."

"Don't be silly," says Sarah. "If you can find out how to make a bomb on the Internet, then I'm sure there is some information about running a vineyard. Soph, you can't just give up and come back. What the hell would you do here?"

"Find a job I guess, and somewhere to live."

"If you think being a single parent in a lovely house in France is tough, then try it in South London. Not that I know anything about being a single parent, but I see them Soph, and they look stressed. You don't need to come home. Nick the faithless bastard will have to support you all to some extent, so take advantage of that and get the vineyard up and running."

"Oh Sarah, I just can't face anything, I feel so alone. But enough about me – how are you?"

"Oh for God's sake, Soph, stop being so thoughtful. I'm fine of course – more than fine actually. I'll tell you when I see you."

"When will that be do you think? Not that I am desperate. Well actually, to be honest, I am."

"I'm looking on the Internet for a ticket right now, Montpellier isn't it?"

I nod.

"Hello? You still there?"

"Sorry, yes, I forgot I had to speak, I was nodding." The tears have started again.

"Soph darling, I can't imagine what you're going through, but you need to be strong. Are you eating?"

"Hell no, I can't face a thing. Mind you I could do with losing some weight; it's probably my fat thighs that drove him into Cécile's lissome arms."

"Loathsome more like," says Sarah. "But losing weight and getting yourself in shape is a good thing to do at a time like this, it makes you stronger, you feel empowered. I'll email you my fifteen-minute toning yoga workout now and run you through it when I get there. It's great for your abs, bum and all flabby bits. You'll be in shape within a month. And there's that book I gave you about finding your inner French woman."

"Thanks, but right now I just feel like curling up and dying to be honest, with or without matching underwear."

"Oh my darling, I'm so sorry."

"It's not your fault."

"I know, sweetpea. You'll have to tell the children, you know," she adds gravely.

"What do I say?"

"You tell them that Daddy has decided to go and live in England."

"I can't, they'll feel totally rejected and abandoned. Can't I just tell them that he's gone there for work?"

"I don't know. You really need to talk to him about that. Call him. I'll let you know what time my flight gets there. I probably won't be able to leave until tomorrow. I'll have to square it with Cruella de Ville first. I'll rent a car, so don't worry about collecting me. What do you want from Blighty?"

I try to think of something I am missing, apart from self-waxing legs. "No, just some girlie time," I say. "Thanks Sarah."

I spend most of the afternoon on my bed, alternating between sleeping and fretting. I am exhausted from the events of last night but can't seem to switch off. I look at my clock every ten minutes, worried I will fall asleep and miss the school pick-up. At 4.15 I get up and go to collect the kids.

On our way back from school, I reflect that it is now almost twenty-four hours since I found Cécile's bra in my husband's luggage and so far I have done nothing at all in terms of making decisions, breaking the news to anyone except Sarah or even considering what to do with Frank and Lampard. Maybe they could transfer to old M. de Sard's land? As long as they don't walk through the vineyards, that is.

But never mind the peacocks, I think; I am doing a great impression of an ostrich – except that my thighs are much fatter.

I wonder how Nick's feeling. Nick has that very male ability to move on extremely quickly. Just about the only time I ever saw him upset for more than an hour was when Chelsea lost the Champions League on goal difference to Manchester United. That was always what I thought was one of the great things about him: his optimism and *joie de vivre*, as they call it down my way.

He's one of those people who always sees the silver lining as opposed to the cloud. I imagine he would have taken being dumped in France quite well. Onwards and upwards, he would have said, leaping out of bed to face the day. Whereas there is just no way I can even imagine moving on at all. I feel like a truck stuck in the mud (except there is no mud here): my wheels are spinning but I'm not getting anywhere.

I watch the children on the way home, playing tigers, crouching and pouncing and growling at each other. It's the kind of thing I used to play, but I was always alone. My parents divorced when I was a toddler, and although my mother remarried more often than most people change their cars, she never had any more children. I always wanted to give my own kids the happy carefree childhood I didn't have. And until the bra-in-the-bag incident, it never occurred to me that I would do anything else.

When she gets here, Sarah will tell me that this is a good

opportunity to find another man, or even rekindle an old acquaintance, like Johnny Fray. But where will I begin? And who knows what murky secrets lurk in the depths of unknown men? A friend of mine ended up unwittingly dating a man who had murdered his wife. She only started to realise when she went to his cottage in the Wiltshire countryside, which was a total mess – in stark contrast to him, who was always well turned out.

"I've been away a long time," he told her by way of explanation. Then he offered to show her his "special" place in the woods. Alarm bells started ringing and she rushed off, citing a somehow-forgotten appointment at the hairdresser's at 9pm on a Friday evening.

When she got home she Googled him, and sure enough, he *had* been away for a long time: twelve years to be precise, for chopping up his missus in little bits and burying her in the woods. In a really "special" place.

I am thirty-six, so any man I meet is around that scary mid-life kind of age where strange things start to happen, even if they are not wife-murderers. Nick, for example, last year, started to listen to hard rock.

"It makes me feel alive," he would say when I asked him about it.

It makes me feel like throwing the stereo out of the window, but he insisted it was good for your neural pathways, those things that keep your brain active and young – apparently the more you have, the less likely you are to get Alzheimer's. In the interests of my neural pathways, I put up with it, but I still hated it.

So there's one upside to Nick going off with another woman,

I conclude as my three tigers run into the house: I will never have to listen to Led Zeppelin again.

They run past a robust-looking woman with a disapproving look on her face and a strange shade of red hair that I have noticed is extremely popular round these parts, waiting for me at my door.

"Madame Reed," she says, pronouncing the Reed with a rolling r and endless e's, so it sounds like weeeeeed, before launching into a diatribe in colloquial French. I think it has something to do with the fact that I didn't buy the right cleaning products, but with my cleaning lady Agnès I am never too sure. The only surety is that she will grumble and sweat and huff and puff a lot.

"*Bonjour* Agnès," I smile. "*Il fait beau, n'est-ce pas?*" I am trying a tactic that involves always being positive and happy when I see her, as an experiment to see if I can shake her dogged pessimism. And that includes being Miss Jolly even just after my husband has left me for another woman.

Agnès shakes her head and says, "It won't last", while wiping beads of sweat from her face.

"Are you well?" I try again, grinning inanely. My cheek muscles are beginning to hurt. I can hear the bell in the small chapel ringing. This is one of the children's favourite pastimes; ringing the bell, calling the faithful (or more like unfaithful in our case) to prayer.

"Oh Madame, how can a person be well at my age and in this country?" she laments in her own rather strange mixture of French and English and possibly a third language as yet totally unknown to man. "I have arthritis, and a bad knee and a sore shoulder. You know Madame," she leans closer to me conspiratorially: "I am over sixty. A person shouldn't have to work at my age, but I need the money, Pierre's pension is terrible even if his life was ruined by the war with Algeria. You give your life for your country and what do you get back?"

She says all this extremely slowly to be sure I understand, even the English bits, then makes a zero shape with her hand and spits out: "*Rien, rien du tout.*"

I try to nod understandingly resisting the urgent desire to wipe what I am sure is a little of Agnès's saliva from my cheek.

"And there's no point in declaring what you earn," she tells me. "You may as well not work; they just come and take it away."

The French talk a lot about 'them', an omnipotent, malevolent force with the capacity to ruin your life within seconds, rather like the Germans during the war. There is a saying here, *Pour vivre heureux, vivons cachés*: to be happy you need to be hidden. How anything can hide with her hair colour is beyond me, but maybe that's why Agnès is always so miserable. Anyway, she can't be more miserable than I am right now. Maybe I could shut her up by starting to cry again and explaining what's happened. But of course I don't. I behave in a very English way and apologise.

"*Je suis désolée*, Agnès," I say, wishing she would go away. Then she starts to tell me about the cleaning products I should be buying. I explain with the help of a pen and a piece of paper upon which I write the words shopping list that it would be easier if she would write down what she needs and then I can be sure to get it next time I go to Carrefour, the nearest supermarket.

"*Non, non,* Madame Weeeeeed." Agnès throws up her arms in despair, sending the broom flying (she refuses to use the Hoover). "*C'est trop cher. Intermarché à Bédarieux, c'est beaucoup mieux.*"

I nod and agree and wonder how I ended up with the world's bossiest and grumpiest cleaning lady. Normally I am more sympathetic, but today I am all out of sympathy.

Eventually I get away and try to muster the energy to think of what to cook for the children for dinner. I still can't face eating, I feel on the verge of either crying or throwing up all the time. My mind is buzzing with images of Nick and Cécile, although of course I've no idea what she looks like. I try to work out exactly when it began. What did they talk about? Are they together now? What are they doing? All these questions are burning holes in my brain.

Dinner is about as relaxing as sitting in a traffic jam knowing you're going to miss your flight to the dream holiday you've been saving up for for ten years. The children behave as badly as is possible. They argue with each other about everything; from where to sit to who lays the table to who can stroke Daisy the cat. They are so busy trying to kill each other that they hardly eat my lovingly prepared macaroni cheese with ham.

I wonder if they've picked up on my mood and are unsettled in some way. But then I remember that they often behave this badly. Life in London for Nick must be blissfully quiet in comparison.

"Mummy, Emily's a nulatic." Charlotte comes running into

the kitchen from the bathroom where I have sent them all to get ready for bed while I wash up. "She's put water everywhere."

"A lunatic," I correct her.

"Come on," she says impatiently. I walk behind her, already dreading the mess I am going to be faced with as soon as I get into the bathroom. And now that Nick has gone there's only me here to deal with it.

Emily is playing slides in the bath, which consists of standing up at one end and hurling herself towards the other. Edward is squealing with delight as she whizzes past him, but is wisely not trying it himself. Charlotte is right: the girl is a nulatic.

"Emily, stop," I command. This has no effect whatsoever. Emily whizzes down again, splashing water everywhere. Edward giggles wildly and starts doing the same thing. Charlotte stands next to me commanding that they "listen to mummy".

My mother's child-rearing theory is this: as long as they're not causing themselves or anyone else harm, let them be. I survey the situation. They are not causing anyone or anything harm (except maybe the bathroom), but frankly, if I'm going to cope with this single mother lark, I'm going to have to take control. My mother's theory is all very well with only one daughter, but when you have three children, and a nulatic among them, you need to be stricter.

"Emily and Edward, STOP IT NOW," I yell. Still no reaction. What the hell do I do, short of grabbing them and hurling them out of the bath? Drastic measures are required. I focus on the shower, the one static thing among the water and the flying children. I bend my right leg and place my foot on my left inside thigh, then lift my arms over my head and breathe. A perfect tree pose. Sarah would be proud of me. Emily immediately stops.

"What are you doing mummy? You look strange."

"Not as strange as you will look with even less teeth when you do yourself in sliding around the bath," I say, staring straight ahead of me. "Now both of you get out and let's get into our pyjamas."

Emily and Edward leave the bath slowly, watching me in total silence as they grab a towel each from the towel rail. Slowly I put my right leg down.

"That's better," I say, very pleased with my new Zen childcare method. I might even write a book about it – once I've mastered another yoga pose, that is. "Charlotte, you choose the book tonight."

After the book, they start acting up again. "Go to bed," I yell at them. Ms Zen yogi has retreated to her ashram. "Just go to bed, it's enough now." I tell myself to breathe deeply, calmly, remind myself that I am going to have to get used to dealing with them on my own. But why do they have to be so infuriating about going to bed? It's not like they've never done it before. They know it's bedtime. They know they have school in the morning. But they come up with a hundred reasons to do anything but turning in, from not having the right teddy to needing a pee to not being tired.

"I don't care if you're not tired," I tell Edward. "Just lie down and close your eyes."

"I can't," he says.

"Try," I say.

"I tried," he says.

"Count sheep," I tell him.

"Where?" he asks, sitting up and looking around the room.

"No, in your head, pretend to count sheep in a field and then you'll go to sleep," I explain.

"That's just silly," he replies. He has a point.

Eventually I leave him with my ipod on listening to Take That, which seems to work better than the sheep. The girls finally promise to go to sleep if they can cycle to school in the morning. I listen at their door. Silence. That could just be a bluff, but by now I'm too exhausted to care.

I take the phone, go upstairs to our bedroom and sit on the bed. It has started to rain. I can hear it pelting down. When the wind catches it, it crashes against the French windows in my room.

The phone in my hand rings, making me drop it. What if it's Nick? The way I'm feeling tonight, I might just ask him to come home. The thought of him coming home makes me cry again.

The phone rings on. I look at the caller display. It is Nick. I suppose to speak to the kids again to see how school went.

I leave it and collapse on the bed in a heap. I feel like I'm never going to be able to stop crying. My whole body convulses with pain and anger and desperation. If only something could make this go away. I just can't stand it. My whole life is falling apart and I have no one to turn to.

Daisy joins me on the bed and starts to purr. She has a calming effect on me and I am finally able to breathe and control my sobbing. The phone rings again. But it isn't Nick, this time –

it's my mother.

"Hello darling, how are you?" she asks.

I start crying as soon as I hear her voice. By the time I am able to tell her that Nick has left, she is almost hysterical, thinking one of the children has had a dreadful accident.

"Oh, thank God," she says.

"Thank God?" I wail. "My husband is having an affair and that's your reaction?"

"Well it's not as if anyone has died," she responds. "When did you last have sex?"

"Mother!" Her question shocks me so much I stop bawling.

"Oh don't be such a prude, Sophie. When?"

I can't remember. Reluctantly I tell her so.

"Well there's your answer," she says. "What man is going to hang around with a frigid wife? You girls are all the same nowadays, as soon as you've had your children you think that's the end of it. It's a recipe for disaster."

Why is everyone around me so obsessed with sex?

"So now it's my fault the bastard has walked out on us?"

"Not entirely darling, but you have to understand that sex is crucial to men, they can't live without it. And obviously this other woman is providing it a lot more often than 'I can't remember.' I'll come and see you soon darling, don't worry, everything will be fine. He'll come back, he loves the children. And the house. Are you going to stay? What are you going to do?"

"I will probably sell it, but don't come out, I can cope, thanks anyway." The last thing I need is my mother pitching up telling me I should have more sex and trying to cook. "I'll be fine. Let's talk over the weekend."

"Are you sure you're okay, darling? Shall I come out and help you?"

"No, I'm fine thanks, really."

"Be brave, something will turn up."

We say goodbye and I lie back on the bed.

I can't stand it any longer. Why is it up to me to tell the children and deal with everything? I suppose he *has* tried to call, but still, he's the bastard who caused all this trouble. I hate him for it, I hate him for turning my world upside down, for ruining my children's happy childhood, for making me feel like a pile of worthless shit. I have to talk to him though. We need to make some decisions.

My hand is shaking as I lift the phone to my ear. I feel almost sick with fear. Will some giggling woman answer the phone? It goes straight on to his answer machine. I hear his voice and I feel a pang of longing. What's he doing, I wonder. Who is he with? Cécile and her self-waxing legs, I suppose. I hang up without leaving a message and lie back on the bed, feeling horribly lonely.

The rain must have stopped. In the distance I can hear Frank and Lampard crowing at each other. For the first time ever I wish they'd shut up. I reach for my lavender-scented eye bag. My brain is still whirring and I can't sleep.

I think about our life in France so far. We've only just started to really settle in, to find out all the lovely things there are to do around here. The first week we arrived we drove down to a small town on the coast. We parked next to a lighthouse and went for a long walk along the beach. Nick and Edward ran ahead, passing a rugby ball to each other, while the girls made sandcastles. Emily must have done a hundred cartwheels. I even managed a couple of handstands – something I haven't done for years. It was windy but the sun was warm and Emily went in the sea up to her knees.

"Not a bad life, eh?" Nick said, running past me with Edward. Now I wonder if he meant that or if he was longing to be with someone else. I just don't believe he is only having an affair for the sex. How come it has lasted so many months if that were the case? And he wouldn't have risked everything just for that; he's not that base, or that sex-crazed. Or is he?

I lie awake for hours thinking about our last year together, looking for signs of exactly when Nick went off me or lied to me to be with her. I wonder if I'll ever sleep again.

I sense the sun begin to rise from behind my lavender-scented bean-bag and then I doze off. The next thing I know it is well after seven o'clock and my husband's mistress is on the phone.

Rule 7

Know your enemy

The French Art of Having Affairs

"Hello, this is Cécile," she says in an infuriatingly sexy French accent. "Nick's...." There is a pause as she searches for the right word. "Friend."

I almost fall out of bed. For a moment I think I must be dreaming. I couldn't have been more amazed if it had been Brad Pitt on my mobile phone telling me he's dumped Angelina and their mini-crèche and wants to run away with me to Guatemala. What on earth is she doing calling me? Does she want her bra back?

"Sorry to trouble you, but I thought you should know that Nick has been in an accident."

"What?" I sit bolt upright in bed. What's happened to him? When I wished death and destruction on him for cheating on me, I didn't actually mean it. I still love him; he's still the father of my children.

"He's okay," she says quickly. "He'll be fine."

"What happened?" I ask.

There's a moment's silence.

"He had a bad reaction to something he ate and passed out cold," she says. "I'm in the hospital now. He hasn't come round yet, but they say his condition is stable. I'll call you as soon as I have any more news. I just wanted to let you know."

"Thank you," I say. But actually, what the hell do I have to thank her for? "To be honest, I'm not feeling terribly sympathetic, as you can imagine. But I guess I should tell the children their father is ill."

Cécile doesn't speak.

I clear my throat. "Yes, our children," I go on. "Nick and I have three children. Two lovely twin girls aged seven, Emily and Charlotte, and a little blond boy called Edward, aged five. Just in case he forgot to mention them to you. Or maybe he was so wrapped up in whatever it is you two do that he forgot he is a father of three."

"I did know," she says quietly. Then it sounds like she's sobbing. Good, I think: let her do the crying for a change.

"You say he had a reaction to something he ate?" I ask calmly. "But Nick's not allergic to anything as far as I know. What was it?"

"Viiiaaggrraaaa," weeps Cécile.

Okay, so now I do want him dead.

Rule 8

Falling in love (or even lust) keeps you young

The French Art of Having Affairs

Sarah arrives the next afternoon in a taxi from the airport. She has our university friend Lucy with her. I start crying as soon as I see them both. Partly because I am so touched that they both made the effort, but mainly because I feel so terribly sorry for myself, for the stupid cuckolded woman they have come to console. How did I get into this state?

So Nick's mistress and I had a bit of a chat. She said she would keep me posted on his progress and even tried to apologise for running off with him.

"I'm sorry," she said. "I didn't plan for this to happen."

"You didn't plan to run off with my husband, or to put your bra in my bag?" I asked her.

"Neither, I mean, well, the bra was an honest mistake. It was in his bag and I didn't take it out."

So just because she didn't actually plot the whole thing from beginning to end she exonerates herself from blame. Typical scheming French woman.

"Well, we all know the effect just leaving it had," I say. "And you can't pretend it's not what you wanted." Then I said goodbye. I figured there wasn't much more to say. I certainly wasn't going to give her my blessing.

The children run out to greet Sarah and Lucy. We take the bags into the house.

"Daddy's living in London," Emily informs them. I have told them that Daddy is on a big work project and we're going to take care of everything here until he gets back.

"We're in charge of everything," adds Charlotte as we walk outside again, sweeping her arm across the landscape, the vineyards and the outbuildings.

"Aren't you clever?" says Lucy hugging them all. "And what is Mummy's job?"

"She does the washing and the cooking," says Edward.

"Lucky her," says Sarah. "Will you show us around?"

Sarah takes my hand and squeezes it. The children run ahead of us explaining what everything is. Frank and Lampard barely look up from last night's rice as we walk past.

"That's Frank and Lampard," explains Edward. "Like the Chelsea player."

"Did Daddy choose those names?" asks Lucy laughing.

"Yes," I say, adding quietly, "I was thinking of renaming them

Traitorous and Bastard but thought that might be a bit unfair on the poor creatures."

Sarah looks at me. "Soph, you just can't do bitterness, it's not you."

"So what do I do?"

"You rise above it," she replies.

"Yes, like a peacock," adds Lucy.

"Can they even fly?" I ask, laughing.

"Who cares?" answers Lucy. "They look good."

We walk on towards the *cave*. It is a chilly January day but according to Lucy it's much brighter and warmer than the one they left behind in London.

"How is our school?" Emily asks her. "Have you seen any of our friends? What about our house?"

"I don't know, darling," she replies. "I haven't been there. Do you miss it?"

Emily thinks for a moment and adjusts her cat's ears. "Well I do, but I like it here much better. I like our big house and garden and it's usually sunny."

"It's much better here," says Charlotte. "We can even cycle to school."

"Except Daddy's not here," adds Emily.

"That's true," says Charlotte. "But he'll come back."

Thankfully neither of my friends, the girls' godmothers, thinks this is the right time to set the record straight.

I feel ashamed as I nod and agree with the girls that Daddy will be back then change the subject as quickly as possible.

"And you've made lots of friends, haven't you?" I prompt.

All three are desperate to tell Sarah and Lucy about Sky and Cloud. As usual, Charlotte gets there first and it all ends in tears, but Sarah asks Emily to show her around the house, and Edward tells me about his friend Sky, uninterrupted for once as his sisters are otherwise engaged, as we walk around the garden in the late-afternoon sunlight.

*

"So, what does she sound like?" Sarah asks, curling up on Emily's Barbie beanbag. The kids are in bed and we are sitting in front of the fire in the sitting room. I've just told them about the Viagra incident. Lucy is shocked and absolutely horrified – in fact she seems more stunned by Nick's Viagra binge than his affair with Cécile.

"Well, I've never spoken to a French husband-stealing small-breasted scheming…."

"Don't hold back," interrupts Sarah. "Give it to us straight, gal."

I take a breath. "She sounds like Emmanuelle Béart," I say.

"I hope she doesn't look like Emmanuelle Béart," says Lucy.

"I don't know what she looks like, but I'm guessing she is not unattractive."

"The bastard," says Sarah reaching over to hug me. "Are you OK?"

"Terrible. In shock really. I mean I know things weren't perfect, but to go off and HAVE AN AFFAIR… I mean, it's quite a radical thing to do."

"Why do you think he did it?" asks Lucy.

I sigh. "Well, according to Nick he was seduced, and happy to be seduced. Apparently I don't show much interest in him."

The other two are silent.

"Well," I continue. "I guess he has a point." I wait for them to deny it. "Do you think he has a point?"

"Of course he doesn't, the Irish swine," Sarah leaps to my defence. "But it's probably fair to say that you weren't jumping on him every two minutes."

"But who does?" I ask. "I hate to break it to you all but after a few years of marriage and kids, that kind of passion is no longer there. It just goes. I still love Nick, I just don't lust after him any more, and because of that he's gone off with someone who does. It hardly seems fair. What are we supposed to do? Pretend that we want to pounce on our husbands even when we would so much rather go to sleep?"

"That would be one way to deal with it," says Sarah. "You know there are very few times when I don't envy you both, being married with kids. Okay, well, until two days ago," she shoots me a compassionate glance. "But when I hear that passion disappears I wonder whether I'm not better off single."

Lucy sighs.

"I don't know what you've got to sigh about," I say. "You've got Perfect Patrick. He's not likely to go off and have an affair, is he?"

Lucy shakes her head. "No, but mainly because he can't afford it."

"Oh Lucy I'm so sorry. Has he still not got a job? How is he handling it?"

"Not great. Patrick has always been a winner. He's just not used to being rejected. It's almost like he's in denial. He isn't really getting on with anything. It's been two months now. I feel like I'm spying on him, but every time I walk past his computer to see what he's up to, he's on some stupid website called amIhot.com? I want to strangle him."

"AmIhot.com? What the hell is that?" Sarah has almost fallen off her beanbag laughing. "Sorry, I shouldn't laugh," she adds when she sees Lucy's face. I'm trying hard not to giggle too.

Lucy smiles. "Okay, okay, I know, and I would be laughing too, if it wasn't my husband. It's a website where you put your picture up and people vote as to whether you're hot or not."

"We so HAVE to try that," says Sarah.

"We're too old," I say. "I'm sure it's geared to hot sixteen-year-olds, not thirty-somethings."

"So is he hot?"

"Who?"

"Perfect Patrick. Surely he put himself up there?" Sarah asks.

Lucy giggles. "I didn't check. I feel so bad about him. I mean it wasn't anything he did, it was just a last-in first-out kind of thing, and the credit crunch has affected everyone. But I was never cut out for this sole-provider role and it's making me really bitter."

"It's not your fault he lost his job," I interrupt.

Lucy blushes.

"What is it, Lucy?"

Silence.

"There's more isn't there?"

She nods slowly. We wait.

"Well, really not much more. I mean it's totally and utterly so ridiculous, I don't even know why I'm telling you." She crosses her arms and gets that stubborn look she used to get when she didn't want to lend us her clothes at university.

"Telling us WHAT?" shrieks Sarah. "Lucy, have you been having an affair?"

Lucy blushes again and looks indignant. "No, I have most certainly not been having an affair," she protests.

"So what is going on?" I ask.

Lucy takes a deep breath and then a sip of wine. In fact she takes three sips of wine, all very quickly.

"I'm in lust. I mean lust I have never, ever felt before, lust that overwhelms me every day like a gale-force wind. It's terrible. And totally exhilarating. Not to mention anti-ageing, I feel like a sixteen-year-old again."

Sarah and I are amazed. Lucy never talks about lust. We weren't even sure she knew what it was. For her sex was always something practical, not hot – just something that was a rather irritating part of her otherwise perfect life.

"So who or what is this gale-force wind?" asks Sarah.

Lucy sighs and shivers pleasurably. "He's called Josh." She blushes as she says the name out loud and then adds, "Joshua."

"Where does he come from? How did you meet him?" we bombard her.

"This needs another bottle of wine," I say. "Don't start until I get back. Promise not a word…." I race into the kitchen and grab a bottle of red and the corkscrew. I get back to silence. Very suspicious.

"What did she say?" I demand.

"Nothing. We didn't even breathe," says Sarah. "Now open the frigging bottle and let's hear about hot Josh."

I pour Lucy a glass of wine. She curls her long legs underneath her on the sofa and shakes her head. Her long blonde hair dances around her shoulders.

"This is the first time I have ever talked about him, and I'm getting butterflies. You're going to think I'm so stupid."

"Did you meet him on amIhot.com?" I ask.

Lucy laughs. "No. It's worse. Actually, I met him in my bathroom."

"God, I hope you were wearing something!" says Sarah.

"I was, luckily, wearing my silk cream dressing gown and not looking too bad. I was getting ready to go out to dinner so had my make-up on. Josh had just arrived from a transatlantic flight and Patrick was showing him to the guest room. He stopped off to wash his hands in the children's bathroom and that's where we met. I walked in to get my tweezers that I'd left there after removing a splinter from Antonia's foot earlier and he was standing by the sink. He looked up at me and that was it. It was like a lightning bolt went right through me, I know that is a total cliché and if I read that line in a book I would cut it, but oh my God!"

She shrieks, and I have never heard Lucy shriek before, apart from when she found out she'd got a First in her finals. "I finally know what all that lust at first sight nonsense is all about. It was literally like something clicked inside me, it was like I had a physical reaction to him."

"Wow, how amazing," says Sarah. "It sounds like me and Christian Louboutins."

"What did he say?" I ask. "Did he have the same reaction to you?"

Lucy blushes. "When we touched it was like an electric shock passed between us. There is no way he didn't feel it, I could see it in his face, I don't think that strong a physical response is actually possible unless the other person feels it too."

"I agree. So then what happened? When was this? Have you progressed from hand shaking?" I say, pouring us all some more wine.

Lucy gets up and starts pacing around the room. "This was a week ago and I am being driven MAD," she says. "I literally lie there at night next to Patrick and think about Joshua in the spare room and I can't sleep for excitement. I am LONGING to sneak out of our bed, tiptoe down the hall and go in there. It's absurd. I mean I'm a happily married woman with two children, I work in publishing, I read law, I'm level headed. What's happening to me?"

She stops and looks at us as if we have the answer.

"Look Lucy, it's just one of those things, probably brought on my Patrick's behaviour at the moment. It will pass," Sarah begins. "We all have crushes."

"Not on twenty-three-year-olds," says Lucy, flopping onto the sofa again.

"He's twenty-three?" Now it's Sarah's turn to leap up. "Bloody hell Luce, good effort!"

"What is a twenty-three-year-old doing in your house?" I ask.

"Can you believe he's the younger brother of Patrick's best friend from college in the US? He's renting our spare room, which we have had to let to get some cash in. We've been entrusted with this young, preppy, gorgeous Californian. Apparently we first met when he was sixteen. He was just a boy, I didn't even register him. But now, oh help... I can't stop thinking about... ripping all his clothes off and fucking him until I collapse."

"God, Lucy, I've never heard you talk like this before," I gasp.

"I've never heard myself talk like this before either! Half of me hates it, but the other half feels so ALIVE."

"Has anything happened? Have you actually pounced on him?"

"No, of course not. There's been lots of chat – well, flirting, I suppose."

"Details, please," Sarah interrupts.

Lucy smiles broadly. "The first time I knew he liked me was about two days after he arrived. We were having breakfast, leafing through the Sunday papers. Patrick and the kids were in the garden. I was pretending to read an article but I was so acutely aware of his presence that I could hardly see the paper, let alone breathe. He is so gorgeous. You remember Brad Pitt before the beard and the right-on attitude, when he still looked like a young Robert Redford? Well, that's Josh, and his body, oh my God, what is it about Americans and all that working out? Why were we born in England where all the men think it's okay to go through life pigeon-chested? He has the MOST amazing body, well from what I can imagine through the shirt…."

She pauses for breath. "Anyway there we were reading the papers and there was some story about an amazing necklace that once belonged to Wallis Simpson being sold at auction and he commented on it and said how lovely I would look wearing it and I said 'where on earth would I wear a necklace like that?' and joked that I might wear it while I was gardening. And he looked me right in the eyes and said: 'Would you wear just that?', and I was too stunned to speak and he kept my gaze and went on 'because if you ever did, I'd very much like to be there'."

Both Sarah and I shriek. "I can't believe he said that," says Sarah. "It's like a film."

"What I couldn't get over was his confidence, how he just kept looking at me. It was incredible. I'm having palpitations just remembering it," she says, fanning herself with her hand.

"So then what happened?"

"Nothing. Antonia or Tom, I can't remember which, came running in after a drink or something and the spell was broken. But I swear I couldn't eat a thing for the rest of the day. I was almost floating, I had butterflies inside and wings on the outside. All night I replayed the scene in my mind and wondered what would have happened if the others had been out and I had leant over the table and grabbed him."

"Why not try it?" suggests Sarah.

"Well, mainly because I'm married with two children, but also because there is still a small chance that all this is in my fevered imagination and that he might call the police, followed by his parents, and have me arrested."

We both scoff at this idea; the young man is clearly very taken with Lucy, and who can blame him? She is a classic English rose, reminiscent of a young Julie Christie.

"How long is he renting your spare room for?"

"Until he finds a flat, which I'm hoping will take a very long time indeed."

"It's such a shame that I'm going to leave this place," I say. "We could have got him over for the harvest. It would have been a perfect excuse."

"You're not leaving this heavenly place are you?" says Lucy, putting her hand on mine. "Why?"

"I can't see how I can manage all alone," I say. "But please, let's not go there tonight, I'm having such fun losing myself in your lives, I really don't want to think about my dreary situation. Give me more gossip."

"That's all from me I'm afraid," says Lucy. "I'm just a bundle of lust, and I have no idea how I'm going to get over it, or…."

"Under him," Sarah interrupts.

"Well, something's got to happen or I might just EXPLODE."

"Poor Perfect Patrick," I say. "Do you think he suspects anything?"

Lucy takes a sip of wine and nods. "Yes, he most definitely does. The other evening when we went to bed he told me that when he had come home from the shops he had had this strange vision of me and Josh up against the kitchen door, kissing passionately."

"Did you say, 'Oh, that's odd, the thought had never struck me?'" I ask.

Lucy laughs. "Luckily it was dark in the bedroom and I said, 'How bizarre, what on earth made you think that?'. And he said it just popped into his head and that he asked himself whether or not he would have minded if he had seen us kissing."

"And what was the answer?"

"The answer was yes, he would mind."

"Seems a tad unsporting," says Sarah.

"I agree," chuckles Lucy. "You'd think he might just let it slide, for once." Then she sighs. "But he is pretty perfect really, and I don't want to hurt him. I guess Josh will leave and that will be the end of it. It will probably be for the best."

"Poor Lucy," I say. "Always the sensible one, and now, for the first time, you're in the kind of hairy-bottomed scrape Sarah normally gets into. And she's sitting there looking saintly."

There is a sudden glint in Sarah's eye that I recognise. "Oh no," I groan. "I should have known better. Okay, out with it."

Sarah stands up, relishing her moment in the spotlight. "Well, while Lucy has been longing for the arms of a younger man, I have been lusting for the arms of an older one."

"Is he married?" I ask, rather bitterly.

Sarah sighs. "Yes, he is, of course, and I KNOW you don't approve but...."

"Well, having been on the receiving end of an affair, I know how miserable it is," I say.

"I'm sorry," says Sarah. "It was insensitive of me." She pauses. "Shall I stop?"

"No," we both yell.

"As long as it's not our husbands we don't really mind," I say. "Actually, you're a bit late for mine anyway, and if you could take Lucy's off for an afternoon she would probably thank you."

"Whose husband is he?"

"I've never met her, I don't really know anything about her, but he, well, I met him at work."

"Name? Age? Rank?" I demand.

"His name is Miles, he's around 55, I guess, I haven't really asked, and he's the CEO."

"Bloody hell, go straight to the top, why don't you?" I splutter.

"Your very own Mr Big," adds Lucy.

"I prefer the name Mr Enormous," sighs Sarah happily.

"Is he?"

"Well I don't know. Yet. But I intend to find out."

Sarah tops up our wine glasses. It's amazing how quickly wine evaporates when you're talking about men.

"Tell us more," I say.

"It started as a kind of joke really. I mean, I knew he is the CEO, of course, so I knew who he was but hadn't had much to do with him. Then one day he emailed me asking for my advice on the re-launch of one of the magazines, you remember? And I thought 'why not try to have a bit of a flirt, it can't do your career any harm'. So I sent a vaguely cheeky reply and 'ping', within seconds he'd come back with an equally cheeky reply and the email exchange ended with us going out to lunch to discuss things the following week."

"How long ago was this and where did you go?"

"This was about a month ago and we went to the Oxo Tower, in his chauffeur-driven car."

"Like you do," I interrupt.

"Exactly, and we had the most amazing time, everyone treated him like he was the Prime Minister, and he is kind of regal and elegant, tall and slim and well spoken, and he was so interesting, he's done so much, he started off as a war correspondent and has been all over the place. He was so interested in me as well, asking me all sorts of questions. I don't' know if it's his age but he just makes me feel so special, like a princess. Now of course I am totally and utterly hooked."

"What happened after the lunch?"

"We have seen each other four times since then. The night before last we went for a drink in a wine bar near his house. Our knees touched under the table and I thought I was going to faint; my whole body shuddered with lust. We talked about work and we agree about just about everything. 'A true meeting of the mind,' I said. 'But not of the body?' he asked. I went bright red because I have been thinking of nothing else since that first lunch. When we left we snogged under a tree on a street corner, like a couple of school kids. Ridiculous."

"What was it like?"

Sarah leans back in the beanbag and sighs. "It was like honey gently melting in my mouth. He was so bloody good. I kept remembering something that lesbian we knew years ago said. You remember Lizzy the lessie – you know the one I mean?"

"Yes, or lessie the Lizzy as we used to call her."

"Right, that's the one. Well, she once told me women make much better kissers. That they are so much better at snogging because they don't pile in like a ferret down a rabbit-hole. I reckon Miles kisses like a woman: sensitively, gently, expertly and sexily. There's none of that 'shove your tongue in as far and as fast as you can' nonsense. Oh it was HEAVEN. I could have gone on kissing for hours."

"And now what?"

Sarah sighs. "Now of course I want the main course. We'll just have to see I guess. I don't know whether he does this sort of thing a lot or what he wants or even what he thinks. He really doesn't give anything away. And I am totally gone on him."

"Power is the great aphrodisiac," says Lucy.

"What?" we both exclaim.

"Henry Kissinger. He said that power is the great aphrodisiac," she explains. "It's not just his honey-coated tongue you're turned on by, it's his position."

"But the rest sounds pretty good too," I add.

Sarah grins. "It is so good, I had no idea hanging out with an older man could be so… gratifying. And he makes me feel so young; it's so much cheaper and more practical than anti-ageing serums."

"So what's next?" I repeat.

"More of the same I hope," smiles Sarah. "I have no desire to marry him and I don't even want a promotion, I'm just using him for sex."

"He's probably delighted," says Lucy. "A no-strings-attached snogger ready for action whenever he wants it."

"It kind of suits us both." Sarah looks rather irritated. "Why does there always have to be more? Can't that be enough?"

"I think it can, for a while," I answer. "But it's human, and especially female, nature to want to progress, to develop and move forward." My head is starting to spin with the wine and suddenly I feel very tired. I'm not sure I'm up for a philosophical discussion.

"I've never felt anything close to the lust you're going on about in bed with anyone," says Lucy. "Where did my life go so wrong?"

"What?" screeches Sarah. "Then you definitely need to find a way to shag Josh. Maybe he's the first man you've met with the right chemistry for you. You know Perfect Patrick is the man for you long-term, we all know that. But as long as he doesn't find out, would a small sexual experiment really be that awful? I mean the French are at it all the time, and their divorce rate is lower than ours."

Lucy sighs. "I think I'm just too English to jump Josh. And right now, too tired. I'm off to bed. We must continue this discussion tomorrow."

We all traipse upstairs. Sarah is sharing my bed and Lucy is in the spare room. Sarah and I lie and whisper about the evening's revelations like a couple of schoolgirls.

I wake up in the middle of the night and smile. I'm so glad my friends are here with me. I'm feeling about a million times happier than I have the last two nights. They have been such a tonic, a thousand times better than anti-depressants.

That said, I do fall back to sleep wondering if it is strictly fair that Sarah has her older man and Lucy has her younger man, when I have no man at all.

Rule 9

Mystery plays a large part in any successful affair

The French Art of Having Affairs

"Mummy's doing yogo, mummy's doing yogo," chants Edward, climbing on me as I attempt Sarah's yoga routine. It took fifteen minutes when she was here bossing me through it, but things have taken a turn for the worse. So far it's taken me about twenty and I haven't even finished the sun salutations. I guess we didn't have the added distraction of a five-year-old who thinks I am a horse.

"What animal don't we done yet?" he asks as I pant beneath him, trying to work out how best to do a sun salutation without injuring my passenger.

"We didn't do the cat," I reply.

"Miaow," says Edward.

Cécile's call was a month ago. I didn't tell the children about Nick being hospitalised. And as I suspected, there was no need to. Once the Viagra was out of his system he was fine. He called to tell me so, and to talk to the kids, he was extremely sheepish and I would like to say that I was very mature and didn't take advantage of his rather humiliating situation but frankly when the man you trusted and thought you were going to spend the rest of your life with runs off with a French woman and then starts popping Viagra, he's fair game. I felt stronger than after any previous conversation with him since the split. Not that we've had THE conversation about the future, I still feel too raw for that.

I can't think what I feel about it all. I don't even know if I still love him. His deceit has deadened my feelings for him in a way. I don't feel great, of course. I still cry at times, but at least I don't cry every other minute and I feel less pain.

I am also busy organising our future and working on my body, not necessarily in that order. It's amazing how quickly your body starts to feel better when you start exercising, I can't believe I waited so long to get on with it. I lived for years with an annoying voice going round in my head that said 'I must do some exercise'. Now that voice has gone and thanks to my inability to muster up an appetite for food and Sarah's yoga routine, which she drummed into me over the four days she was here, I can actually detect muscles in my thighs. And Sarah says that not only does yoga tone your muscles, it actually helps you to lose weight because it balances your metabolism through the breathing and reducing your stress levels. Apparently when you're stressed your body seizes up and holds on to food. As if things aren't bad enough. It's amazing really because I was always under the impression that to lose weight you had to run around getting horribly out of breath, which I suppose is why I never did it before. There is still a long way to go, but at least I have made a start.

Today I have a potential buyer coming to see the house. I haven't mentioned that to the children either. They have settled well into school and life here; they like it. They like the weather, the freedom to roam around outside, their friends. I really like it. In fact I love it.

I have made friends too – well, I have Calypso, but it's a start. And even Wolfie the dog is starting to acknowledge me. The other day Audrey, the snooty pretty French woman with ringlets, said hello, but I doubt we will become bosom buddies. French women don't really do friendship, according to the book Sarah gave me. They are too busy trying to shag each other's husbands.

But even with the snooty French women I am happy here. It is now early February. In the mornings for the past few days the ground has been covered with a light frost, making the ripples of earth in the vineyards look like someone has sprinkled glitter all over them. The air is so fresh, cold and clean it makes you feel good just to breathe it. I am mortified at the thought of taking the children back to polluted London.

I just can't see how I can possibly make wine. I hardly know one end of a vine from another. It's all very well Sarah saying I should look on the Internet, but I don't think becoming a *vigneronne* is really what I need right now, along with losing my husband. I have some help in the form of Colette, who Calypso suggested could come and do some work while Nick is still in London.

I can see her now, my *vigneronne*, stomping off towards the winery on her mobile phone. She looks angry. But it occurs to me that Colette never really looks anything but angry. She now works for me one day a week, pruning, preparing the vines for the summer, cleaning the *cave*, doing all the jobs I do but twice as fast. She is also teaching me my new trade.

Colette has an incredible electric pruning gadget that peeps like a trapped mouse every time it cuts a branch. I had thought that maybe next year I would invest in some for me. Although I guess even without that machine Colette would be twice as fast as me.

"You need to decide what bits you are going to prune on the next vine as you are pruning the current one," she told me in one of our rare conversations.

As a mother of three, multitasking is one thing I can do. I could practically make toast with my feet as I carried the twins on either hip. But when it comes to vines, I'm a one-trick woman.

Colette is one of those women you just don't mess with, so I have asked her to ask next door's foreman to stop trying to kill me. She said she would take care of it; he used to be her father-in-law. I'm not sure how old she is; she could be anywhere between thirty and fifty. I would never dare to ask her, but she is not like the French women I have been reading about, apart from the fact that she is thin and she smokes. She is about my height, five foot nine, with straggly brown hair that she bunches up in a brown clip that looks like it has flowers painted on it with TipEx. She ties a red and white squared scarf over her head when she works. She wears denim dungarees every day and when her arms are exposed I can see a tattoo or two lurking. I have yet to decipher what they depict. But I am guessing there's not a tweetie-bird or a big red heart; Colette seems like a bit of a rock chick to me.

She wears a lot of silver jewellery – necklaces and rings – and seems to be able to work in the vines without them bothering her. She has an attractive face, with bright hazel eyes and big lips, but has obviously exposed herself to a lot of sun and has a few of those wrinkles around her mouth that smokers often have. I have never seen her wear make-up but Nick would say she would "scrub up well", which I think makes women sound like a muddy beetroot but he would insist is not meant to.

But even with Colette to help, I am not in a position to run a vineyard. What I need is security and a reliable way to support the children and myself. So I asked my mother if we can stay with her for a few weeks before I find somewhere to live and a job in London. London is the only place I can think about living, I want to be close to my friends. But where to work? Where is my CV? It won't so much be a question of dusting it off as starting again. Or maybe I should just call Lady Butterdish and go back to Drake's. It won't be the same without Johnny, though.

Living with my mother is not my idea of fun. Heaven knows what man she has lurking around at the moment; they're normally dreadful. The last one had a toupee, and that was the best thing about him. I will put the children into school in her village in Devon for the moment, but when I get a job in London we'll have to move again. It's all so unsettling.

I move onto my back to do the yoga 'sit-ups' Sarah has told me will totally flatten my baby-ravaged stomach. I'm meant to lift my legs up off the floor, holding them straight, and then slowly let them down again, controlling them. I'm meant to do one for every one of my years, so that's thirty-six. I can barely manage four. Not for the first time in my thirties, I wish I were twenty again.

From the kitchen I can hear the advertisement for *Jane Eyre* come on again. Emily and Charlotte yell at me to come and see my "boyfriend", but I will not be distracted from my sit-ups, in case I ever see him or anyone like him in the flesh. Sarah has made me promise to do the routine every day for at least forty days. After that, she tells me, it becomes a habit. I can't imagine this ever becoming a habit that I'd want, but I keep going.

Edward runs into the kitchen to join the girls and leaves me to my agonising leg lifts, which are at least easier without him on top of me. Happily my phone rings, so I am now able to focus on Lucy, who is calling, instead of the pain in my lower abs.

"I just had to tell someone," she breathes into the phone. "Patrick is going to Frankfurt for a job interview, thank God – I mean in more ways than one. I am sooooo angry – last week I had to sell my car, can you imagine? My precious black Range Rover with cream leather seats. I mean there is only so much a woman can stand."

"I understand Lucy, but you also need to slightly think about your family and…. Well, I mean look what happened to Nick and me because of lust."

"Oh bugger it. Soph, can't you just agree with me? I've never done anything reckless in my life. You and Sarah are always telling me how boring I am. Here's my chance to catch you up. Talking of which I saw our very own femme fatale last night. She seems very happy."

"Why wouldn't she? He's got lots of dosh, and he's amazing," I say, struggling not to let the sound of my efforts on the abs come through in my voice. "What's not to like?"

"Well, he's married, but she seems so Zen about it, I mean she really genuinely doesn't seem to mind. Maybe the fact that he's married adds to his air of mystery. She says her seduction plan is progressing well and she hopes to report full consummation of the relationship before the month is out."

I groan and release my legs to the floor with a crash.

"And," she goes on, "she says she loves her privacy and time to do what she wants when he's not around. She seems really content for the first time in years. Maybe an affair isn't always a bad thing?"

"As any self-respecting French woman will tell you," I say. "Or Frenchman come to that."

Lucy is on a roll. "I mean, if I actually release some of my anger at Patrick as well as my pent-up lust for Josh, then maybe it will be the saving of our marriage and not the other way round? Maybe this is what our marriage needs?"

Trust Lucy to try to intellectualise a quick shag.

"But what if you really like it, and have to come back for more? I mean, where does it all end, Luce? What if he falls madly in love with you once you've had your fun and starts threatening to tell Patrick and ruin your life?"

"I have considered that, but I just don't think he's the type. He is so laidback and in control of himself, I can't imagine him ever doing anything stupid."

"Well, I guess there's only one way to find out. When does Patrick go to Frankfurt?"

"On Sunday. And he'll be back Monday evening. I have arranged to have a reading day at home on Monday when the kids are at school, and made sure Josh knows that. We'll just have to see if he decides to stay at home too. Oh God, please let him stay at home. Oh help Soph, am I really evil?"

I laugh. "Lucy, no one could ever call you evil"

Lucy sighs. "Sarah says that what Patrick doesn't know won't hurt him. I guess that's the key eh? That's how a French woman would do it. She would just get on with it and then pretend it never happened. Is that possible do you think?"

"I suppose it depends on how much fun it was," I say. "Keep me posted, I want to hear everything. I'll be thinking of you."

I drive the children to school because of the rain. This is not rain in that normal drizzly English way but the kind of rain that you could use as a power shower. Just getting to the car we are all soaked through. I hope Wolfie has found somewhere to shelter; he seems to prefer our *terroir* to next door's, even if he won't come into the house. Daisy is under the kitchen table looking horrified.

I actually look forward to taking the kids to school, even when we have to drive. It is such a stress-free experience compared to

London. We drive down the lane that leads to the smarter avenue, which goes past the Château de Boujan.

"They've got a big house," says Emily every time we drive past.

Then we get to the road that goes through the village of Boujan and turn right and the school is just there. There are never any problems with a parking place, the teachers are all at the gate to greet us, the forty or so well-behaved children file in well before the bell rings at 9am. Most days I get them home for lunch. They leave at midday and are due back between 1.20 and 1.30, leaving just enough time to enjoy them before getting fed up with them again as they start bickering.

"Kiss, Mummy," says Emily at the gate. She veers between love and hate with me; either she wants to kiss me or she stomps off in a furious strop. Charlotte is more consistent – it's always a quick "Bye Mummy" with her as she runs in. She has a gang of three friends waiting for her every day. It reminds me of myself with Sarah, Carla and Lucy. Instead she has Cloud, Calypso's daughter, a girl called Maud, who is the daughter of the attractive ringleted lady Audrey, and a rather plump, friendly dark-haired girl called Clémence.

Clémence always seems so happy to see me and says "*Bonjour* Sophie" in a sweet little sing-song voice. I love hearing my name in French; it sounds so sexy and sophisticated. Now all I need to do is get the body, the matching underwear and the French accent to match. Along with the lover. At least now I have *le droit*, as the French would say. Actually they always have the right to a lover, according to whatever law it is they abide by. But I would need to get my legs industrially waxed first.

Once the children have gone, I get back in the car. I turn the radio to my favourite radio station, *Nostalgie*, which plays songs I used to dance to and now only sing along to.

Today that Bonnie Tyler song comes on, 'Lost in France'. I listen to the words: 'I was lost in France. In the fields the birds were singing. I was lost in France and the day was just beginning'.

Suddenly I am weeping. I feel so lonely, not alone. I feel vulnerable and scared. I have no one to turn to. Of course I have Sarah and Lucy, but they're in London and busy either having passionate sex or planning to.

I lean against the steering wheel. I can barely control the convulsions going through my body. My whole world is falling apart, my husband has fallen in love with another woman, it's pouring with rain and Bonnie Tyler is enjoying a revival; can things get any worse?

"Sophie, quick, drive, help me!" It seems they can get worse. Suddenly Calypso is sitting next to me, feverishly locking the door, dripping wet and panicked.

"What's wrong?" I say, although surely that's something she should be asking me, since I'm hunched over the steering wheel weeping.

"Just drive, please," she implores me. "I'll explain later."

I start the engine. "Where do you want to go?"

"Anywhere, just out of here," she looks around her in fear. "But quickly."

I drive out of the village, almost running over the village idiot as I go. This is a man who thinks it's a good idea to sway around the middle of the road asking for cigarettes. Someone should tell him smoking is bad for you.

We drive south on the road towards the coast. Calypso visibly relaxes the further away we get from Boujan.

"That was a close shave," she says, leaning back in her seat. "I reckon he'd have caught me if it hadn't been for you. It's the wind with the rain that brings it on; it brings up the sand from the Sahara."

"Who? Brings on what?" I say, wondering when I can stop driving in the opposite direction I want to go in. "What on earth is going on?"

"It's my husband Tim," she says. "He suffers from Gulf War Syndrome. I didn't mention it before because I hoped he was better, seemed silly to bore you with it. Also you might have thought I was a lunatic. But about once a year he grabs our shotgun and tries to kill me. It's a shame but there it is."

Bloody hell. I thought my husband was irritating.

"So how bad is it?" I ask her. "I mean how close has he actually got to shooting you?"

Calypso laughs nervously and runs her thin hands through her blonde hair. I notice she has lots of silver rings on practically every finger. "I've been lucky so far. I can normally sense it, the weather, his mood and so on."

"Is he getting help for it?"

"He was back home, but here it's more difficult. They don't really recognise Gulf War Syndrome, rather in the same way they don't recognise dyslexia."

"They don't recognise dyslexia? That's shocking."

"Look, there are some shocking things about the French, but then there are some crazy things about us too. And you must admit life here is grand."

Just her use of the word grand reminds me of Nick. I swallow hard.

"Yes, I agree," I say. "It is grand. Do you think you'll ever go back to England?"

Calypso snorts. "Not likely. After three years here it's hard to imagine. Back to what? Back to grey weather and grumpy people. Or is it the other way round? Not really much of an incentive."

She has a point. I guess that is what I'm heading to. How depressing.

"Why did you move out here?" I ask her, and realise how little I know about my new friend.

"Tim got an army sick pension and I was made redundant from Channel Four so we had a bit of a nest-egg. We decided to make a break while the kids were still young enough and make a fresh start. I have always wanted to live in France, ever since I was 15 and read *Bonjour tristesse*, you know, by Françoise Sagan."

I do know. It's one of the books I read before moving out here; and the author is the woman who came out with the immortal line Nick is fond of quoting, "A dress makes no sense unless it inspires men to take it off you."

Why is it that when you least want to think about someone there are reminders everywhere? He'll be on telly next. The selfish bastard.

"How are you settling in?" asks Calypso. "Have you made any other friends here yet?"

"Audrey said hello to me the other day," I tell her.

"Wow, I'm impressed. She normally only talks to men," she laughs. "Watch out for your husband with her – she's a classic French woman, her main hobby is seduction. In fact, it might be her only hobby."

I don't tell her that my husband has already been stolen by a French hussy.

"So I guess she doesn't have many friends?" I say instead.

"Well, she's from Paris so she's already at a disadvantage. They loathe Parisians here. But no, I don't think she has many friends, at least not among the other women. Although they are probably used to it and possibly up to the same thing as well. The baker, for example, is having an affair with his wife's best friend."

"How do you know all this? I always heard the French rural community was notoriously hard to infiltrate."

Calypso smiles. "You just need a good mole," she says, and then adds; "I think it's safe to go back now. By the time we get there, Tim will have calmed down."

I go all the way around the next roundabout and back towards Boujan. It is still pouring with rain, which won't make the house any easier to sell, I reflect gloomily.

Calypso shows me the way to her house. I insist on walking her in to make sure everything is all right. They live in a modern cottage close to the school – nothing as charming as Sainte Claire but a nice size with a pool and a lovely view of the Château de Boujan. At least it would be a lovely view if you could see through the endless rain.

Once inside, Calypso gets a text from Tim. She shows it to

me. "Sorry, am in bar having coffee, all calm again," it reads.

"Poor man," I say. "It must be a bit like being a werewolf or a vampire."

Calypso laughs. "Sadly that dark secret is all he has in common with Edward Cullen," she says. "See you at school later on? Thanks so much for everything, you're a darling."

"Don't mention it, yes, I'll be there," I say.

I get back in my car and try to remember what I was supposed to do with my morning before it was hi-jacked.

Welcome to the quiet life in the south of France. Since I moved here, my husband and I have split up, I have been chased by a beret-wearing Frenchman carrying a gun, and my only friend's husband has tried to murder her. I turn on the radio again. At least Bonnie Tyler has shut up.

Rule 10

Remember that nothing has to last forever, or even for an afternoon

The French Art of Having Affairs

The people that might want to buy our home are from Sussex. She is vast, he is painfully thin. The semi-deaf agent told me on the phone that they want to set up a pottery school at Sainte Claire.

I ask them how they decided on this part of France.

"It's nice and convenient from the airport," Mrs Spratt tells me breathlessly as she heaves her frame up the stairs. I should hang out with this woman more often – I feel as lithe as Kate Moss. Bugger the yoga. "And we like the countryside, so pretty with the vines and the olive trees and the lavender."

"Why are you selling, if you don't mind my asking?" asks Mr Spratt.

I don't mind him asking but I'm not going to tell him the truth.

"My husband has just been made a great job offer and so we want to go back to England," I lie. "It's such a shame, we love it here, but he has to be there full-time."

I show them into my bedroom.

"Oooh, how lovely," says Mrs Spratt. "What a beautiful bath."

I'd be amazed if she'd fit into it but don't mention that.

"Yes," I say, sounding like an article from *Hello* magazine.

"This is the room that really made me fall in love with the place. I have always wanted a bedroom and bathroom in one, and the balcony is just heavenly."

We walk onto the balcony. I expect sighs of ecstasy or at least some comment on the totally awe-inspiring view that still makes me gasp every time I look at it. It is now late March and spring has set in. The greens are vivid and the smell of fresh thyme is everywhere. The château to the right of the view looks imposing and stately in the afternoon sun, and the vineyards, which I have been pruning despite the uncertainty over our future, are neat and pretty, with the leaves just starting to make an appearance, transforming them from candelabras to living, breathing plants.

I resist the temptation to say hello to my rose in case they think I'm a loony and run screaming from the property. The potential buyers are as silent as the rose. I look at them, imaging them not appreciating the view for years to come while I sit through Sunday lunch with yet another of my mother's unsuitable husbands. It's not fair. Bloody Nick. But then maybe they are just trying to seem unenthusiastic to get a good price.

"We'll be in touch, dear," says Mrs Spratt conspiratorially, before squeezing her way back into their rented yellow Peugeot. They drive away, almost running over Lampard, or maybe Frank, on their way out.

I go back into the house to get a cup of tea. I feel the need for something warm and comforting. I walk into the sitting room. The first thing I see is our wedding photo on the bookcase. Nick is tall and slim with his floppy hair and a cheeky smile. He looked extremely handsome that day.

While a lot of my friends were having dramatic affairs with married men or tempestuous relationships, Nick and I settled very quickly into a comfortable and seemingly secure coupledom. That never bothered me; I have never been the drama queen type, in desperate need of constant highs and lows. I was happy planning our weekends in the country and our quiet nights in. From quite early on I was convinced that we would end up together. There really didn't seem any option. Where do you go when you have found someone who suits you so perfectly? Anyone else would be a let-down. Looking back on it, maybe we were *too* comfortable too early on. Maybe the spice we lacked is the spice he has now found with Cécile. I guess by some standards we didn't do badly, after all, we lasted over ten years.

Not that I didn't like sex: with Nick I loved it, in the beginning. We did little else for the first three years – I assume like most young couples. In fact, we used to try to work out the amount of times we'd made love; it was impossible, it ran into the thousands.

"If you put a pebble in a jar for every time you get a blow-job before you're married and you take one out every time you get one after you're married, the jar will still be half-full by the time you die," Nick used to joke.

I swore I would never become one of those women. I loved sex and would always want to have sex with him, wouldn't I? Why on earth would I change?

We used to laugh about a friend of Nick's from school whose wedding we went to early on in our relationship. She had been a sex-crazed lunatic up until the wedding but, as soon as she had the ring on her finger, stopped. We swore we would never become like that. I have to admit that although it has taken longer, I have become the kind of woman I promised I never would.

I blamed a lot of my apathy and lack of passion on the babies, but the twins are now seven and Edward is five. Surely it was time to find each other again? To start pouncing on each other and ripping each other's clothes off? But the only time I ever felt like ripping his clothes off was when they needed washing.

Maybe it's like this for everyone who has been married for a few years. I've read articles about spicing up your love-life, full of helpful hints such as, "Dress up in sexy underwear". Yeah, right. After seven years of sleepless nights, the first thing I want to do as soon as the kids are in bed is prance around in a thong telling my husband he is sexiest man on the planet. Apart from anything else I'm not sure I could even get a thong past my thigh at the moment.

It was unfair, really, because Nick kept his side of the bargain – he earned enough money to keep us, he looked after us, he paid the mortgage. I suppose I should have been happy to sleep with him now and again. But I wasn't and I hated myself for it. I just didn't really fancy him any more.

Sarah says it's all Darwinian. "You've had your babies with him. Biologically there is no reason to have sex with Nick any more, so your lust for him has died," she told me.

Can you imagine explaining that one? No longer would the excuse be "Sorry darling, not tonight I've got a headache," but "Sorry darling, I've got a Darwinian evolution issue".

I first met Nick while I was working at Drake's. He lived around the corner and often popped in for a drink on his way home. Sometimes he was with friends but other times he would bring a book and sit at the bar with his glass of wine, reading and looking around. The reception girls noticed him before I did. One of them even tried to join him for a drink when she went off duty but had no luck. "The Classics Man," they nicknamed him, on account of the amount of books he read.

I noticed one day he showed up carrying a copy of *Anna Karenina*. "A little light reading?" I joked when he passed me in reception.

He smiled and told me he was trying to read all the Russian classics before he was thirty. "My favourite uncle said a man should achieve three things before that age; reading the Russian classics was one of them," he said.

His voice was deep and smooth; his accent mellow Irish. I loved the way he sounded. I could imagine listening to him for hours. I had always been in love with the idea of an Irish man, possibly a result of reading Yeats as a teenager.

"What were the other two?" I asked.

I could swear he blushed. "Oh I don't think I know you well enough to tell you that," he laughed, and then he added "yet" before he went to sit down at his usual place.

I was intrigued. It wasn't every day an Irish intellectual with floppy hair crossed my path. Most crucially, he was also the first person who had taken my mind off Johnny.

It was about two weeks after our short conversation that he approached me. As he was leaving one evening, book in hand, he walked up to the reception desk, said good evening and handed me an envelope.

Inside was a postcard of a Degas painting called *The Dance Class*. It is one of my favourite paintings. My mother took me to the Musée d'Orsay in Paris to see it when I was little, and after that I dreamed of being a ballet dancer. I longed to be one of the girls in the picture wearing a beautiful ballet dress, rehearsing my pirouettes and leaps.

"I know from your colleagues that you are called Sophie and that you like ballet," he had written on the card. "There are only so many more evenings I can afford in your gorgeous bar. Will you come to the ballet with me next week please?"

He had written down his mobile number. I was stunned. The Classics Man had been coming to Drake's to see me? Not that I lacked confidence, but it just never occurred to me that anyone would make such an effort. My initial joy was slightly tempered by the nagging suspicion that he might be a psychotic stalker. I phoned Sarah for advice.

"Is he a looker?" she asked.

"Yes."

"Well then, there are worse ways to die."

I asked my mother too. "Call him," she told me. "Talk to him. You'll be able to tell soon enough if he's a loonie."

This is a woman who has married five loonies, but I took her advice anyway and called Nick.

He sounded happy, sweet and sexily Irish. I agreed to meet him the following week to go to a production of *Romeo and Juliet* at the Royal Opera House. We met at Covent Garden tube station. I had agonised about what to wear for days. Obviously, as we were going to the ballet I needed to be properly dressed. But I didn't want to look like a frigid maiden aunt or, even worse, like I'd made too much of an effort. Finally I settled on the thing millions of women before and after me have opted for in similar situations, a little black dress.

"You look lovely," said Nick who was there waiting for me when I arrived, carrying a red rose.

"Thanks. It's only a little black dress I've had for ages," I replied, then wanted to kick myself. Why was I so bad at just taking a compliment?

Nick smiled and handed me the rose.

A month later he took me to Paris for the weekend to celebrate my birthday in May. I had never felt so spoiled in my life. We stayed in a groovy little hotel, south of the Place Pigalle in Paris's equivalent of Soho.

We wandered around the bustling streets of Paris arm in arm, ate in intimate little bistros and even went up the Eiffel Tower. I say 'even' because I have a pathological fear of heights and had never been up the tower before. On my school trip to Paris I was the only one who stayed below as the rest of the class squeezed into the lift and went up to the top level to admire the views. I sat on the grass practically shaking at the thought of it. But with Nick I managed it. It took a while but he gently coaxed me to the top and I looked at the view from the safety of his arms. I knew then that this man was very special to me.

A year and a half after our first date, we got married. I was twenty-seven and Nick was twenty-nine.

But for me the feeling we had on our honeymoon has gone. I mean the lust bit, of course. And I thought he felt the same. I was amazed a couple of months ago, the night of the 'mummy breasts' incident, when I tried in vain to squeeze into the little black dress I wore on our first date. Yes, I know it was a totally mad idea, but I am often gripped by moods of inexplicable and unfounded optimism. Nick was watching me.

"You know I still want to get that dress off you as much as I did the first time I saw it," he said. "Remember that Sagan quote? 'A dress makes no sense unless it inspires men to want to take it off you'".

"You may have to cut it off me," I half-joked. "It seems to be stuck."

I couldn't understand why I didn't feel the same way. I felt really guilty that I didn't. I was hoping, Darwin allowing, that I would find my libido in France, the country of seduction and affairs. My plan had been to shake off this apathy and turn my husband into my lover again. Of course I had not bargained on Cécile pitching up. I can't believe she was already on the scene when he was ogling me in that black dress. Did I leave it too late to re-kindle our relationship? If I'm really honest was it just a plan, like a New Year's Resolution one never keeps?

My story with Nick couldn't be simpler. Boy meets girl. Boy likes girl even more than he likes Chelsea FC. Girl likes boy. Girl starts to watch football. Boy and girl get married. Twins arrive. Everyone very happy. Son arrives. More joy. Family moves to France. Boy likes another girl more. Girl devastated.

I look at our wedding picture again. I really was a lot slimmer than I am now. No wonder. I starved myself for weeks before the big day, following that well-known "eat nothing and if you feel faint have a sip of water" diet. My dress was simple but surprisingly elegant considering I started off hankering after a meringue that would make me look like a princess. It was ivory, off the shoulder, A-line in shape. My blonde hair was slightly curled (I was going for the Kim Basinger look in *LA Confidential*), and hung loosely down around my shoulders. My brown eyes were looking straight at the camera, full of hope. Next to me Nick stood, smiling into the camera. He had his arm around his wife of five minutes, half proprietary, half-affectionate. He looked so confident and sure of himself. I looked so happy, my hand resting on his shoulder.

I wonder how many thousands of couples end up looking back at their wedding photo with regret and bitterness, for what reason?

Do I now regret marrying Nick? No, of course not, since I

have the children. Life without Nick I suppose I can get used to, but I can't imagine wanting to go on living without them. I wonder how he can.

Sarah says he's beaver-struck. This rather charming phrase means that he can think of nothing apart from what lies between Cécile's legs.

"It melts their brains," she told me in an email yesterday. "I've seen it happen hundreds of times. They're no longer thinking straight and they do the most stupid and unimaginable things."

I suppose at least he makes the effort to call and talk to the kids almost every day. They are thankfully not asking too many questions, he was always going to be working from London so they expected him to be away a lot, and to save money he was only going to come home a couple of weekends a month before the vineyards got busy.

Do I regret moving to France? Despite what has happened, I have really enjoyed living here – loved being somewhere different, loved eating lunch outside in winter, adored the markets, the fresh food, and the beautiful language, even if it is totally incomprehensible, especially the way they speak it down here with the Midi twang. But my French has improved by about one hundred and fifty per cent in the two months we've been here – I'm not sure how much my lessons with Valérie helped but watching television and listening to the radio have made a huge difference. Every time I drive anywhere, I listen to all-talk shows such as 'France Culture' or 'France-Inter'. The first few times I understood practically nothing, but slowly I began to distinguish words and the great thing is they repeat the news every fifteen minutes so you can often get what you missed the first time.

I love my home, with its stone steps that make me feel like the queen of the castle every time I walk up them. I love the way the thousands of footsteps that have walked up and down them have made them dip slightly in the middle, like stones under a waterfall.

The early-morning sun is glistening on the olive leaves. I love being here, love the fresh air, the lack of people, my deep red rose plant on the balcony, the view from my balcony across my vineyards and the Château de Boujan to my right. The track to the left in between the two Sauvignon Blanc vineyards that leads to the plane-tree lined road along the boundary of the château land and then on to the village in the distance.

But instead of the confidence I had when we moved here, the anticipation of a new life for us, I feel out of my depth. I still don't think I can cope all alone; the house is too big, the vineyards are a mystery, and the language is still fairly impenetrable. How could I even have thought about running a vineyard? A bit of pruning is all very well, but how do I go from here to making wine? Sarah is mad; she's impulsive and has no fear. Which is great in some ways, but doesn't work when you've got three children to look after.

The children, my little ones, are going to be so upset. They love their school and Edward even has a best friend. At home he was always alone in the playground, pretending to be Spiderman. Now he has two little friends, Charles (pronounced in a rather sexy French way, Charle, making him sound like some kind of exotic chocolate mousse) and Sky, whom he jumps around with.

How will they cope with going back? How much will they miss it? I feel like the wicked witch of the west packing them all back to England.

Talking of the children, I have to collect them from school. I'm late so I decide to drive. I'm just about to get in the car when my mobile phone rings. I wonder if it's Nick and if he's calling to find out what my plans are. We have talked a bit but I really haven't felt like telling him much, after all he created this mess, how I get us out of it is my business. I answer the phone. It's not him; it's my partially deaf estate agent.

"Mrs Reed, I have some very good news," he says. Yeah right. Good news for him and his seven and a half per cent. "Pending permission for their campsite, Mr and Mrs Spratt would like to make you an offer for the house and land of €775,000, which I know is less than you paid for it, but I think in the current market it's a fair offer."

I don't respond.

"Especially considering the weakness of the pound," he goes on.

I still can't think of anything to say. That should give me enough to buy a semi-detached house in one of the dodgier parts of London, I calculate.

I look back towards the house; it has just started to rain, and the rain and the sun are battling it out. The sun has come out behind the house, creating a halo effect around it with a rainbow just in front of it. The soft rain-drops falling make it look like one of those magical castles in a child's toy, one of those things you shake and the snow flies around it.

I feel a desperate pang of loss and sorrow as I tell him I will accept their offer. He sounds delighted and tells me he'll be up in the morning with the *compromis de vente*.

I stand by the car for a minute wondering what I've done. I haven't even asked Nick what he wants to do, he'll probably be relieved I've managed to find a buyer so quickly – some places are on the market for several months.

Wolfie comes and stands at my side. Now and again he flicks up his head to nuzzle my hand. I feel guilty and miserable. I have betrayed his hard-won trust.

Rule 11

Lip-gloss is part of the armour you need to go into battle

The French Art of Having Affairs

So how to tell the children we're moving? We are all in the sitting room playing cards and waiting for Johnny's new TV show to start. They are being incredibly sweet. We are having a lovely evening; they ate a dinner of fresh asparagus, gorgeous olive bread and goat's cheese outside in the sun. They have already adopted the local habit of dipping their goat's cheese in olive oil and a touch of salt. I love watching them get used to eating the French way – another reason I am dreading going back home to England where the culture of food is nowhere near as important.

I still can't eat much and am living off coffee and fat reserves.

I should write a diet book; the *Lose your Husband and your Midriff Diet*. Funnily enough, my world may be falling apart but my body hasn't felt this good in years. I have lost five kilos so far and am toning up thanks to Sarah's exercises. I can now manage twenty leg lifts before I feel like spontaneously combusting, and then I fight my way through the remaining sixteen. I have become hooked on her little routine and it's amazing how much difference it makes. Though I am dreading my birthday when I have to add yet another leg-lift.

I told Sarah this on the phone the other day.

"There, you see," she replied. "Every cloud has a silver lining. Soon you'll find some sexy Frenchman who will just adore the new you and bring you to multiple orgasm within seconds of meeting him."

A nice idea, but unlikely. Funnily enough, finding another man is hardly top of my 'to do' list.

Sarah was also full of the news of multiple orgasms of her own. She and Mr Enormous had been out for dinner the evening before and ended up back at her flat afterwards.

"Oh my God, Soph, if I thought his kissing was good, well, you cannot IMAGINE how unbelievable his oral technique was."

"His oral what? It sounds like you're talking about some kind of swimming stroke."

"The way he, you know, down there…. Arrrggghhhhhhh it was incredible, totally and utterly amazing, I must have had 15 orgasms in an hour, and we haven't even had sex yet. Oh Soph I think I could seriously fall in love with this guy."

"That's what worries me," I said. "What happens next? Where

does this move on to?"

"More orgasms?"

Just as I settle down to play snap with the kids my phone rings, it's Nick. Once he's talked to them all I take the phone and walk out on to the terrace.

"Hello?"

"Hi Soph," says Nick. "How are things?"

"More importantly, Mr Viagra, how are you?"

"Oh don't. If only you knew." He sounds suddenly very tired.

"Knew what?"

"Doesn't matter, you'd never believe me."

"You're probably right, I wouldn't."

"Anyway, I'm good, thanks."

You're not good, you're an evil bastard is on the tip of my tongue but instead I say. "I guess we need to have a chat about the future?"

"Yes."

"And your thoughts are…?" I suddenly realise I'm delving into my pocket to get out my lip-gloss as we talk. What's wrong with me? He can't even see me. Still, it makes me feel better.

"Soph to be honest I just don't know. I feel terrible about all this and terrible about the kids. Shit, I never thought it would come to this."

Maybe, like Sarah, he just thought it would come to a lot of orgasms.

"Well, it has. Believe me if I could avoid disrupting their lives I would, but I don't see how I can stay on at Sainte Claire, running the vineyard and doing everything. Added to which, I don't want to have to rely on you for a living. Or anything else for that matter. So I've accepted an offer on the house."

I can hear him gulp all the way from London.

"I understand Soph, but you know I'll do what's right."

"Do I?"

"Of course," he says vehemently. "I've been a prat but I won't see the kids suffer any more than they have to, or you."

"Well, that's a comfort," I tell him, although the only thing that would truly be a comfort would be to have him weeping and begging to come back. "Bye Nick, I'll keep you posted on our plans."

I walk back in to the sitting room and we start our game. Edward keeps saying 'snap' every time which drives the girls mad, but I find it quite endearing. I guess that's indicative of our relationship dynamic; I find him angelic and sweet and they want to murder him.

"Quiet," says Charlotte. "It's starting." We stop playing Snap and focus on the TV screen.

The music begins and Johnny appears, looking rakish. Before *Jane Eyre* starts they show a film about Johnny's life. They show pictures of the small council house he grew up in, his parents, who died in a car crash when he was a boy, the aunt and uncle who brought him up, and then they show clips, starting with the first TV role he landed, playing a disgruntled young man in Blackpool, and ending with his Oscar-nominated performances in two films and then his latest role as the brooding Mr Rochester. It really is a rags to riches story; someone should make a film of it.

He does look dashing in his Mr Rochester kit with his long curly hair. The female lead is pretty. I wonder if they're an item. A part of me still regrets that we never got together.

"He won't love her, Mummy, will he?" says Emily after the show is finished. "He loves you."

I laugh. "I don't think that's true."

"Yes it is, he told us so."

"Oh I think he was just being dramatic," I say.

"What's gramatic?" asks Edward.

"Dramatic," I correct him. "It means you say things to get a reaction, they're not necessarily true."

"Well, I don't think he was being…." Emily can't remember the word so resorts to her favourite one: "Whatever. I think he loves you. I hope Daddy won't mind. He won't like you having a boyfriend."

Now would be a good time to tell them. To just come out with it and say "Guess what, Daddy won't mind at all because he's got a girlfriend". But I chicken out and take them upstairs for a bath.

Whenever Nick was away on business or working late in London, we would all get ready for bed together. It was a ritual that I loved. I loved being with them, getting all clean and cosy with them. I would have a bath with the children, and then we'd all get into our pyjamas and get onto my bed, where we'd either read a book or watch a film. There is nothing quite as lovely as newly bathed children, all fresh and rosy-cheeked from the bath, tired but not over-tired, and ready for a story.

Tonight we reinstate that old favourite ritual. I run a hot bath and put some lavender oil into it. The smell of the lavender spreads throughout the room, making me feel calmer than I have done in days. This is just the kind of evening my raw nerves need. A calm, cosy evening with the children and an early night before I face tomorrow, when I will sign away the house and our new life.

I go to bed shortly after the children do, but sleep badly. I have dreams about Johnny mixed up with the house here and boxes of belongings tumbling all over the place and the children crying, coupled with memories of my parents' split-up, my father's silent grief, my mother's histrionics.

I am woken up at four in the morning by Emily, who tells me there is a 'meanie fly' in her room before going back to sleep next to me. I am left awake, feeling totally unsafe, insecure and lost. I don't want my children to go through the trauma I went through as a child. I suppose Nick and I will be mature about it – more reasonable perhaps than my parents were. My last memory of them together is walking across Hyde Park one day when I was about four years old. They were arguing. I tried to put their hands together. My father accepted the gesture but my mother rejected his hand. I never saw him again.

I lie there fretting about our future and the reality of going from this to a semi-detached in a grey suburb from which I will have to commute to central London every day. The children will wear their house key around their necks and try to avoid getting stabbed on their way home from school. I think about what is left for me in England, now that my husband has opted for a life with Cécile and her perfect sex drive.

And I think about that couple from Sussex living in my house and living the life I so longed for and dreamed about for so long. I think about the children missing out on the chance to speak flawless French and having the experience of living somewhere else, knowing another culture and being justifiably able to support a national football team that sometimes wins things. I think about the vines, now neatly pruned and waiting to be sprayed before it starts to rain so they won't get mildew and rot.

I fall into a fretful sleep and wake at seven with a phrase from Johnny's TV programme going round in my head. I don't know where it came from, but suddenly there it is, like the bright neon light that hangs over the Boujan bar. At one stage on the show someone asked him what he attributed his success to.

"Belief in myself and hard work," he replied. "With those two things you can achieve anything".

He's right. Of course you can do anything. He went from a council house in Leeds to meeting the Queen (I saw the picture in *Hello!*, she was at the première of one of his films).

So if Johnny can do anything, why can't I? At first the thought makes me laugh and I respond with an automatic 'Don't be silly' to myself, roll over and try to go back to sleep without disturbing Emily. But the thought won't go away. I sit up in bed. Actually, why not? Is it sillier to think you can run a vineyard with no previous experience or think you can become a film star when you are an orphan from a council house? Why shouldn't I run a vineyard? Plenty of people do. Even Australians, as Sarah points out.

Maybe I can make a life here for us all. Maybe there is no need to run away. I can do it. I may not be able to hang on to my husband but I can hang on to the life I want for me and my children. I can learn to drive a tractor. And I will just have to make friends with old M. de Sard when he finally pitches up, and maybe borrow some of his workers if I need to, and some of his expertise.

I leap out of bed feeling more energetic and happier than I have since before I found Cécile's bra. I almost feel like running upstairs and waking the children to share the good news with them, but luckily I hadn't told them I was planning to drag them back to soggy old England in the first place.

I go out onto my balcony and look at my rose, my view, and my vines, soon to become exquisite wine, sold in all the best restaurants in London. The sun is already up and shining, ready to inspire me. This feels so right. For the first time in days I feel like I know what I want, although I've still got to work out how to do it.

"We're going to make it," I tell my rose confidently.

I go inside to get the phone. The deaf agent will be happily printing out the *compromis de vente* any time now. I have to stop him. I call him on his mobile from my terrace.

"Please tell them I said no," I tell him sternly.

"What? Who is this?" He sounds a little sleepy.

"It's Mrs Reed from Sainte Claire. Please tell those people that I've changed my mind."

"Mrs Reed, I'm not sure they are willing to increase their offer," says my agent patiently.

"No, you don't understand," I reply as Wolfie runs by

underneath the balcony, looking up at me briefly and wagging his tail before vanishing around the corner. "Sainte Claire is no longer for sale. We're staying."

Rule 12

Always be prepared, your next lover could be just around the corner

The French Art of Having Affairs

"What do you mean you haven't had a lover since you were married?" asks my new French friend Audrey. "What's wrong with you?"

I look down at my body for signs of any obvious physical malfunctions.

"Well, nothing. I mean, once you're married, you're supposed to stay faithful, you know, forsaking all others and all that?"

Audrey throws her head back and laughs. The lonely alcoholic at the bar nursing his Pernod turns to see where the noise is coming from. Not much happens in Boujan's bar. There is a dog that wanders up and down the length of it like a condemned prisoner in a cell, and said alcoholic will occasionally fall off his stool, but normally it is pretty quiet. A young woman laughing is big news.

Audrey's blonde ringlets bounce around her face like perfectly formed springs. "You English are so puritanical. What a crazy idea." She leans closer towards me, having spotted her swaying audience. "I have had seven lovers in the ten years I have been married. I'm sure my husband has lovers too." She takes a sip of her coffee before going on. "Here in France everyone does their own thing in their own corner."

At this stage I am feeling a little like Hugh Grant in *Four Weddings and a Funeral*. What a total lightweight I have been. I can't even pretend to have had an affair. I haven't even thought about it. In fact the closest I got was once very vaguely fancying the PE teacher at the children's school for about five seconds because he looked a bit like David Beckham, until he spoke and I realised he sounded like David Beckham too. I'm even vaguely trying to discourage one of my friends from having an affair. How dull am I?

"Are you having an affair now?" I ask her.

"*Bien sûr*," she replies, shrugging as casually as if I had asked if she was wearing matching underwear.

We are in the bar before school pick-up. Audrey suggested we go for a drink after our sons properly introduced us a few days ago. Her son is Charles, one of Edward's friends, the one who mistakenly thinks he is Spiderman. Although Calypso warned me Audrey is a serial seducer of other women's husbands, I am not worried – if she seduces my husband, it's going to annoy Cécile more than it will me. And anyway, it's hardly as if he's around much.

"Won't your husband mind?" I ask. "Who are you having an affair with?"

She laughs again. "I'm not planning on telling him, or you in fact," she replies in her flawless English, learnt from her British stepfather and a career in a British law firm in Paris. "And I'm sure he's up to his own thing. As Mark Twain said; 'A Frenchman's home is where another man's wife is.'"

"Listen, Sophie," she continues, patting my hand when she clocks my horrified expression, "you cut a French woman in half and what do you see?"

"Lots of cheese? A croissant? Probably not, as they never eat anything. A small list of do's and don'ts like 'You will wear matching underwear' and 'You will not drink more than one glass of wine with dinner'? I don't know, what do you see?"

"You see three words, embedded in our genes. And those three words are *liberté, égalité, fraternité*. And of those three, *liberté*, or freedom, is the most important. For any French woman, being married and then having affairs is asserting our right to be free."

"But why bother getting married if all you're going to do is sleep with other people?"

Audrey smiles at me indulgently. I notice that her teeth are incredibly white. Must be all that snogging.

"My dear English Sophie, marriage still has a very important place in society, it is the right structure to bring up your children in, and it is important to have a companion for life. But it gets boring. Dumas once said, 'The chain of wedlock is so heavy, it takes two to carry it, sometimes three.'"

I am trying very hard to digest and accept her arguments, but my puritanical English self is finding it difficult. Maybe we have got it all wrong, though; maybe infidelity *is* a way to keep your marriage alive, as Lucy says? After all, if everyone is off doing stuff "in their own corner", they are unlikely to get bored in their little corner at home.

"But what happens if you fall in love with the person you're in the corner with?" I ask, stirring my coffee slowly. There has to be a downside to this strategy.

"Oh, I fall in love with all of them, in a little way. But it passes, like a *petite infatuation*, and I am happy to go home. You have to remember that the family is very important and not to let the affairs ruin that. You just have to be grown-up about it. It's a little bit like *pain au chocolat*: something to enjoy now and again but not eat every day or you get sick. Not to mention fat."

"So you don't feel guilty?"

Audrey smiles: "Do you feel guilty if you enjoy some cheese now and again or a nice walk?"

"Well, it depends how much cheese, but in general, no."
"Then why should you feel guilty about enjoying another one of life's pleasures, sex and sensuality?"

She has a point, I suppose.

"And think of it this way," she continues. "If you are faithful to one man, you are being unfaithful to all the others."

It's an interesting concept.

"So having sex with someone who is not your husband is just

like eating a piece of cheese? And on top of that, a humanitarian act?"

"Exactly," she laughs, carefully applying a rather subtle pink Chanel lip-gloss at the same time. "You finally understood. I will make a French woman out of you yet. Come on, let's get the children."

As we walk out of the bar she flashes the drunkard a shiny smile and he promptly falls off his stool. It's a red-letter day at the Boujan bar: even the dog stops pacing to watch us go.

My husband may be off enjoying Cécile's seductive French accent and I may have a whole wine estate to run and a harvest to organise by September, but since I made my decision to stay in France I feel strangely calm. I feel as if although many things are beyond my control – for example, Nick's preference for Cécile and the fact that the vines are growing so quickly – and although I am struggling to keep up with everything I have to do, I am at least in charge of our life here.

There are times when all the hurt and anger wells up – when he phones the children for example – and I am reminded that he is not here with them, as he should be. But actually apart from that I am feeling quite mellow.

This Zen feeling may also have something to do with the fact that I am adding serene moves to my daily yoga routine. At the moment I am in a tree pose on my terrace, surveying my vines and staring hard at the tree opposite me at the edge of the field. My eyes are, as always, drawn to the beautiful château to my right, but if I stray from the tree I inevitably fall over, rather like the alcoholic in the Boujan bar.

I gaze at the landscape. If this were Provence, Cézanne would have painted it. I breathe in deeply while focusing on not toppling over. I can smell the thyme in the air; you could marinade a leg of lamb by waving it around on my terrace.

My body is so much more toned than it was when I still had a husband. OK so I have a way to go before I am Elle McPherson, but my infallible and yet to be copyrighted 'lose your husband and your midriff' diet is working a treat and I have been following Sarah's yoga routine every day with amazing results. Who would have thought yoga could be so effective at toning your muscles? Apart from the awful stomach one I am big into the Warrior Pose, where you stand like a warrior with your arms outstretched. An amazing way to work every muscle without moving. Then there is the bridge, which is fabulous for your buttocks and the most exhausting of all, the plank, where you are still and flat like a plank, balancing on your arms and toes. If I'm feeling really strong I ease my way down into chaturanga. There is no better way to tone your arms.

I am in a very good mood because tonight I am invited to my first ever dinner party in France, at Calypso's house. I am not quite sure what to wear, apart from perhaps a bulletproof vest – although I guess as it is a calm spring day, the old Gulf War Syndrome will be dormant.

It really is glorious at the moment, warm but not yet hot, and everything feels so fresh and new and fecund after all that rain we had in February. I am getting more and more into the work in the vineyards; there is something really satisfying about working in nature, and I think that is also contributing to my calm mood.

The kids are now eating lunch at school as I try to learn as fast as I can, as well as actually do the job I need to be doing.

Sometimes, when I think about the enormity of the task that awaits me, I do feel nervous. I am a woman who has been a wine drinker for as long as I can remember, but my expertise ends at choosing which bottle to buy at Sainsbury's. Lucy sent me a book to encourage me. It is called *The Complete Idiot's Guide to Growing Vines and Making Wine* – so thoughtful of someone to write it for me. This is now my bedside reading. I am learning about building a good trellis and the dangers of mildew – things I had never before encountered. And studying is all very good for the neural pathways too

We are now in March. If I were planting new vines, this would be the time to do it, but I have decided, as the new *châtelaine* around here, to delay all the planting plans until I actually have some money.

March is a relatively calm month for winemakers; the nasty pruning work is more or less done and there is a slight lull before the buds start to grow and you need to panic about something coming along and killing them. In mothering terms it is like the period of relative calm when your offspring is still a baby and you can happily plonk them down knowing they will not move, preceding the toddler stage when danger lurks around every corner....

The vines still look like small wooden chandeliers sticking out of the ground, but today the afternoon light is diffused and warm so it lights them up. Colette is busy dragging things in and out of the *cave*. She has made it very clear she is not interested in becoming friends with me by answering all my questions with a nod or a '*non*', which is fine; I have Audrey, the serial philanderer, and Calypso, the tie-dye queen. Calypso seems like good fun; shame about the husband trying to kill her, but then nobody's perfect.

I can't decide whether she's is incredibly posh and trying not to be or the other way round. She talks like Princess Anne and has that English public-school horsey manner about her but she looks like a hippy. I haven't asked her about the specifics of her background; although we have chatted a few times at the school gates and over coffee, I haven't told her the truth about Nick. In fact I haven't told anyone the truth about Nick.

It sounds like a bad book; *The Truth about Nick*. Here was a man who we all thought was solid and dependable, and it turns out he's a Viagra-taking faithless hound.

I haven't even told the children what has happened, but that will change when he comes out at the weekend. He has of course been calling them every day and explained his absence by blaming work. I hope they're going to be all right: I guess kids adapt quite easily. Sometimes when I kiss Emily goodnight she says she misses him, and then Charlotte overhears her and says she does too. I don't think she actually does miss him any less than Emily, but she's more practical than emotional, and I guess her reasoning is that if Nick's not there, there's no point in thinking about him too much. Poor Emily is the other way around.

I am dreading telling them. I remember my parents splitting up, even though I was so young. I can envisage my children's little faces dropping when we break the news, and it breaks my heart. I am not sure whether to be all mature about it and say it was a joint decision or just lay the blame where it belongs: in his over-zealous lap.

It is now three months since I found the bra. It feels like a lot longer. I could divide my life into pre-bra-in-bag and post-bra-in-bag. It is almost like two different mes. I feel like a different woman (there's another thing Nick and I have in common).

No, seriously, I *have* changed. I have gone through despair and horror and am coming out of it a stronger, more determined and (Sarah would say, most crucially) thinner person. At least that's the plan, and it had better work because there are several small people, two pets and a hell of a lot of vines relying on me.

"Mummy, mummy can we cycle to get some bread?" Emily yells up at me from the gravel path below. I ease myself out of the tree pose and walk to the edge of the terrace. The three of them are looking up at me expectantly. One of their favourite things is cycling to the village bakery and buying bread from the over-dressed baker's wife. Every time I see her I wonder what a woman who wears silver glittery leggings and matching boob tube to work at 7am can possibly get kitted out in when it's time to get dressed up? And how far away from the classical image of the French chic woman is it possible to get? Actually I would have to say that most of the women in the village veer towards the lesser chic end of the scale. The 'Baguette Ladies' as Calypso likes to call them; the gang that sit under the fading Dubonnet sign wearing pinafores and slippers. And some of the younger ones are clearly not following the latest fashion from Paris, but rather the latest in comfort clothing.

"I'll walk through the vines with you," I say and run downstairs, grabbing my fleece on the way. It is just after 5 o'clock and a lovely afternoon. I'm sure they will be fine but there is one road to cross to get to the baker's and it makes me uneasy

My phone rings. It's Sarah.

"Lucy got laid," she says breathlessly. "She and the preppy floppy-haired lodger finally went for it."

Apparently Lucy's plans for when Patrick went to Frankfurt a few weeks ago didn't work out as Joshua had to go back to the US to see his mother, who fell and broke her ankle (selfish woman). But now, eureka, we have take-off – literally.

"What happened?"

"Well, Patrick went out for dinner with some blokes last night. It was someone's birthday or something, and the kids were asleep and Lucy was in the kitchen wiping the table and she sensed that someone was there and she turned around and there he was, just staring at her. She looked at him and she knew that this was it and so she walked towards him and they kissed and then ripped each other's clothes off. She said it was just like that scene from *The Postman Always Rings Twice*."

"The what?"

"I don't know. Some film with Jack Nicholson. Anyway, apparently it was amazing. She told me it was at least as wonderful as she had imagined it would be, that it felt as if every one of her nerve endings came to life and she would start to levitate. She is so frigging ecstatic I had to hold the phone a metre from my ear so as not to be deafened by her shrieks. If she made that much noise when they were at it I'm surprised she didn't wake the kids."

"So she's happy? Not freaked out at all?"

"Yes, totally euphoric. I can't believe it, not an ounce of guilt. You'd think she was French."

"But where is it all going to end? What will happen if Perfect Patrick finds out?"

"Perfect no more you mean?" she says. "Who knows? Here's hoping he won't. Ignorance is bliss and all that."

"Wow, well lucky her. And how about Mr Enormous?"

"Can you believe I have yet to find out? The sexual tension is killing me; this has got to be the longest courtship I have ever had. But this weekend his family is away and we've arranged to spend the night together and if it doesn't happen then I can't see that it ever will. I am actually beginning to wonder if he has an impotency problem. I mean why has he not just done it? We've done pretty much everything else."

"I think it's quite romantic. And maybe he wants to be sure of you before he goes out for fully-fledged infidelity?"

"I think you might be right, he's testing my loyalty. And my discretion. How is everything with you?"

I look around me. "Actually it is fine, I feel strong and good and ready for the next phase of my life."

"Oh God, Soph, I am pleased. But there's no need to sound like an American self-help book."

"Very amusing. Nick is coming down soon and we will tell the children and then, well, I will carry on and hope an older version of Joshua or a younger version of Mr Enormous or whatever you call him comes my way."

"That's my girl," says Sarah. "Love you lots, and see you soon, just call me if you want me to come out again."

"Thanks, but I'm not sure I can stand any more yoga coaching," I laugh. "Bye sweetpea."

Wolfie follows me into the vines but shies away just as we walk onto M. de Sard's land. Yes, I know we're not supposed to be on it, but it's a lovely walk through the vines to the village and the ground is dry now so it's easy to cycle on.

Oh damn it. There is a man walking towards us. I can see from his elegant gait and height that it is not M. de Sard's irritating foreman. At least that's good news. The children are taking no chances though and pedal off rather quickly towards the village, leaving me to face the stranger alone. They have clearly already adopted the French attitude towards conflict.

If Nick were here, he would make one of his un-PC jokes or sayings about the French such as raise your right hand if you like the French, raise both hands if you are French, or what's the difference between toast and Frenchmen (you can make soldiers out of toast). "We're allowed to laugh at the French," he would always say if I told him I thought he was being bigoted. "They're like family."

I try to look casual as I saunter towards this particular Frenchman. What if it is the dreaded old M. de Sard himself? He might try to shoot me as well. But this man looks much younger than old M. de Sard. In fact, now that he is getting closer he looks like he might be what Sarah, Lucy and Carla would call a 'babe'.

Why oh why did I have to wear my tracksuit bottoms and faded Little Miss Bossy T-shirt and grubby fleece on the one day out of several thousand when a handsome stranger is walking across the deserted vineyards towards me?

"*Bonjour Madame*," he says as we meet. Help! I think. He really is gorgeous. His bright blue eyes are so luminous you can almost see the sky in them. His light brown and slightly curly hair makes him look a little like a Romantic Poet. He is much taller than me – probably around six foot three – but he is well built so doesn't look lanky. He is wearing what an English gentleman on an afternoon stroll would wear: dark-green cords, a beige cashmere jumper and a Barbour-style jacket. He looks to be around forty. There is the subtle trace of a rather expensive-smelling aftershave surrounding him that makes me want to get closer.

There's no denying it, this is your classic sexy older man. And he's in my vineyard. Actually, he's in M. de Sard's vineyard. But what the hell? – he might even be worth getting shot at for.

"*Bonjour Monsieur*," I respond. It's not a bad start. But then I do what I always do when I'm nervous. I start to gibber. Worse than that I start to gibber in incomprehensible French about the '*méchant monsieur*' who owns the vineyard and how he should watch out for him and his gun-toting foreman.

"We can speak English if you prefer," he says in an accent so sexily smooth I almost swoon at his feet. Pathetic woman. I am even blushing. How did I become such a walking cliché? I will not be moved by a smarmy Frenchman and his charming French manner.

"Oh, you speak English?" I say. There's no fooling *moi*.

"Yes, I was educated in England," he replies smiling down at me, eyes twinkling. "Have you lived here long?"

"Oh, just since the New Year. We bought Sainte Claire, over there," I say pointing in the general direction of our home.

"Yes, I know where it is. You say 'we'? Who is we – you and your husband?"

Of course my husband is no longer on the scene, but there is no need to let the handsome Frenchie know that, is there? Or is there?

"We did, yes, but sadly he had to go back to London. So I am here alone now," I smile.

Why did I tell him I am alone? What's wrong with me? I never flirt with anyone. I don't even ever fancy anyone. Quick, I think – mention the children to make amends.

"I mean I am here with the children. I, er we, erm". Come on Sophie, which is it to be? "We have three children."

The children! Shit. I suddenly remember why I am here. It would be just like them to get run over while I am chatting up a stonkingly sexy Frenchman.

"I'm so sorry," I say rushing off. "I have to run; the children are on their way to the village and I want to make sure they cross the road safely. It was lovely to meet you."

"*Enchanté*," he shouts after me. "*Madame*…. What is your name?"

"Sophie," I shout back, waving as I run. "My name is Sophie. Bye."

When I get to the bakery my heart is beating faster than it does after fourteen sun salutations. Is that because of the run or the smooth-talking Frenchman? Maybe a bit of both. Whatever else, I feel very hyper. And damn it! – I forgot to ask his name. Will I ever see him again?

"Mummy, Mummy, look what happened." The children drag me to the front of the bakery to show me. Someone has thrown a brick through the window. I can't believe it. This is meant to be a rural idyll, not downtown Brixton.

The bakery is dark. There are shards of glass covering the window display of baguettes and wicker baskets and some on the street outside. A few villagers have gathered and there is a lot of muttering. I look around to see if there is anyone I recognise so I can find out what has been going on. Why on earth would anyone want to throw a brick through the window of the Boujan bakery, even if they don't think much of their baguettes.

I spot Peter, the male 'wife', and his daughter Amelia and walk up to them.

"What happened?" I ask.

"There won't be any bread tonight," he responds and looks at me. "Not that you look like you'd eat any anyway. What happened to the voluptuous yummy mummy I was growing to love?" He takes hold of my hand and makes me do a twirl in front of him while whistling. "My, my you're quite the little vixen now aren't you? Even in your rather shabby gym kit. If I weren't as gay as a badger, as my friend Brad calls it, I might be interested myself. Have you been on some drastic diet?"

I nod. "Yes, I realised it was time to find my inner French woman before it was too late. But more to the point, what happened here?"

"Apparently the baker was having an affair with his wife's best friend. The wife caught them in the bakery covered in flour, kneading each other rather than the bread. Unseen, she ran back to her best friend's house, took all her clothes and burnt them in a bonfire." He leans closer to me. "Well, frankly, most of them needed burning. Anyway, then she packed her belongings and drove out of town in a rage, but not before she had put a brick through the window. A most unusual reaction really, considering infidelity is part of family life in France."

"My goodness, and I thought we had moved to a sleepy village in the middle of nowhere."

"Not a bit of it," says a man with a mop of grey hair standing next to us. He is carrying a copy of *Le Monde* and a book; I can just about make out the word Vichy in the title. He looks extremely intellectual. "I met a man in the bar here who claims to have invented the Internet."

Peter ignores him and the stranger moves on. "Well sweetie, it is in the middle of nowhere, but sleepy it ain't. Unless by sleepy you mean everyone is sleeping with everyone else."

"Everyone apart from me that is," I say, not without bitterness. "Having said that, I met a really handsome man just now."

Peter raises one eyebrow and looks at me questioningly. "Really?" he says. "Where?"

"In the vineyard, you know by the Château de Boujan."

"Name?"

"I forgot to ask. I could kick myself. But he was lovely. Very French, very, well, elegant really. And he smelt lovely. It's the first man I have been attracted to for years."

Peter tells Amelia to go and look for some fish in the fountain.

"And may I ask what your husband will think of your new vineyard friend?" he says when she's gone. "Should you ever happen to find him again that is? I was under the impression you were not in the market for any side salad, even with French vinaigrette."

At first I feel like I have a twig caught in my throat. I can't say anything. Then it all comes out. It pours out, in fact, more quickly than the water in the fountain the children are all mesmerised by in the square. I tell him everything, from finding the bra and to throwing Nick out to the Viagra incident (major eyebrow raise at that one) and the plan to tell the children this weekend.

I barely draw breath. It feels good to get it off my chest. But then I feel like a fool. "Oh God I'm sorry," I say. "I don't know why I told you all that, it's not as if I even know you. But once I started I just couldn't stop. I don't really have anyone to talk to here and, well…."

"A token girlfriend is better than no girlfriend at all?" he smiles, putting his arm around me. "Poor you, what a cad. How are you going to cope all alone? Will you stay?"

"Yes," I nod, scared to say any more in case I crumble again. His arm around me is almost making me cry, but I mustn't in front of the children. And the whole village come to that. They might think I threw the brick through the window and am regretting it. Or that I'm missing the baker's baguette….

"I am going to stay, I am going to make a go of the vineyard.

Heaven knows how, but I am determined not to be beaten by this."

"So you're going to make the wine alone?"

I suddenly realise how ridiculous this must seem. "Yes, well not totally alone. I have Colette. And a few books. And, well, lots of people do make wine."

Oh no, the eyebrow has shot up again; someone give this man some Botox. "Indeed, lots of people do. But most of them have more experience of the product than drinking it at dinner parties in Clapham. Have you any idea what it involves? I mean, I don't want to put you off, but I'm just injecting a dose of reality into your dream of becoming the next Château Lafitte."

I look at him blankly.

"You've never heard of it, have you?" He crosses his arms and faces me. "Oh. My. God. You want to be a wine maker and you have never heard of possibly the most famous, and certainly the most expensive, wine in the world. Sophie, I think you need to take a reality check. And you also need to keep an eye on that *vigneronne* of yours."

"Colette? Why?"

"Well, I'm not one to gossip," he begins, confirming just the opposite. "But let's just say she has an interesting past."

Before I can ask him any more, the children have all rushed over to tell us about the fish who live in the fountain. Apparently there are three of them. One husband and two wives.

"Sound like anyone we know?" quips Peter.

"At least I was the first wife," I retort.

The crowd outside the bakery has been dispersed by the

arrival of the police to investigate the crime scene. Not that any of the villagers are criminals – at least I don't think they are. But if there is no reason to get involved with the police then it's better not to, as Agnès my grumpy cleaning lady never tires of telling me. To the French, anyone in authority is there to make you pay tax, which you obviously have to avoid.

I say goodbye to Peter. "Good luck with Château Corkscrew," he calls after me. "Let me know if you need any grape-pickers come September. You do know you need to pick them, don't you? Or did you think the vines just give birth to small perfectly formed bottles of Chardonnay?"

The children and I walk towards home, I look across the vineyards in the hope that the handsome French stranger will reappear. No such luck. But Wolfie comes running towards us. As he runs it looks as if his tail is going round in a large circle behind him, almost in time with his eager steps. He is so happy to see us I feel floods of relief that we are not going. But I am worried about Peter's "reality check". It's clear I have a long way to go.

My worrying is interrupted by my mobile phone ringing.

"Hello darling, how are you coping?" It's my mother.

"I'm fine, thanks," I reply. At least I was until she called. Oh help, she's bound to want to interfere in some way. "How are you?"

"Oh very well, thank you. But I'm worried about you. I've been talking to friends and I think what you need is a holiday. This sort of thing is very traumatic. Can you get away from the vineyard?"

"Mother, I'm fine, thanks, really. I can't go anywhere. I've got to get things organised here. There's a lot to do, you know."

"I realise that, darling, but there's no point wearing yourself out. I have a plan, leave it with me."

"Please do not plan anything," I tell her. The last thing I need is my mother carting me off somewhere when I have a whole dictionary of wine-making to inwardly digest and make sense of. "I am coping, really, thanks anyway."

"Is that Granny?" says Emily, "Can I talk to her? I want to tell her about the brick."

I hand over the phone to my daughter. Charlotte, of course, immediately wants to do the same thing, so I have to distract her by promising she can chose my outfit for the dinner party.

She is thrilled. "Mummy, you're going to look like a princess," she says confidently, marching me up the stairs. "Do you still have your wedding dress?"

"I think a wedding dress might be a bit over the top for a dinner party," I say.

"Do you like dinner parties?" she asks.

"Sometimes," I say. "It all depends."

"On what?"

"On what they talk about really, or who is there, if they are fun or not."

"What do they talk about?"

I remember Nick complaining about dinner parties in Clapham. "Well a lot of people talk about commuting and nannies and schools," I say.

"What's computing?"

"Commuting; it is getting to and from work."

"That doesn't sound interesting, that's just about trains."

"You're right. But I hope as we're in France and we don't have to commute anywhere, or have nannies, they will talk about something else."

"I hope so too," says Charlotte as we walk into my bedroom and she makes a beeline for the wardrobe. "Otherwise you might fall asleep. Who's going to keep us?"

"I will get you ready for bed and then Agnès will come."

"Oh noooooo," wails Charlotte. "She's so grumpy. Please Mummy, do you have to go?"

At that moment half of me feels like doing what I always feel like doing when one of my children asks me for something. I want to give in. I want to hug her and tell her that no I don't have to go and see the relief and happiness in her lovely little face.

Then a rational voice comes into my head and tells me that my children will survive one evening with Agnès and that I need to get out, to make friends, to make a life here. It's all right for them, they're at school. If I don't go out I'll never meet anyone. I can't expect to make friends in the vineyard every day.

"I'm sorry, darling," I say. "I really want to go, and you can watch a film and then go to sleep, and she might be in a really good mood this evening."

"Who?" asks Edward, who has just come in, closely followed by Emily and my mobile phone. "Who might be in a good mood?"

"Agnès," Charlotte spits out. "Mummy is going out and Agnès is keeping us." She makes me sound like the most evil woman alive, or 'the worst mother in the world' as Edward calls me when I refuse him something that he wants.

I hold my breath waiting for them all to start wailing, squealing and shouting at me. They do. But I am not going to spend my life as a single parent held hostage to a lot of noise, so I shoo them all into the bath and start thinking about what to wear to dinner.

Charlotte will not be budged from either my wedding dress or the little black number that I wore on my first date with Nick. Just for fun I try it on. There is no way I will get it over my hips, is there? Oh my God, there is! But the zip will surely refuse to do up? Okay it's half-way up, but what happens next? I freeze out of fear of being stuck there like a contortionist, unable to get either in or out of the dress. This happened to Carla once in H&M in Oxford Street. In the end she had to get three sales assistants to wrench her out of the thing.

"They were all women," she complained. "Otherwise I might have bought the damned thing."

I might starve to death in my bedroom, unable to move or raise the alarm because the dress is too tight.

I keep going, rather gingerly. It seems to close smoothly. Yes! Maybe I will have to invest in a whole new wardrobe before buying the harvesting machinery I need? It's a tricky one; new barrels or new bras? Maybe I should have kept Cécile's. It would almost fit me now.

I look at myself in the mirror. I can't believe I can wear this dress again. Suddenly I feel reborn. And of course you can never go wrong with black. It seems ironic that every time I look at it

I am reminded of my first date with my then husband-to-be. Should I be in tears over this fact? Maybe, but being able to get the bloody thing on and done up has certainly staved off depression for now. I carefully take off the dress and carry on with my beautifying.

I rub a conditioning oil treatment into my hair. My arms are so tired from the endless downward dogs I've been doing along with the work in the vineyards, I can barely lift them to my head.

Next it's time for a face pack. I have bought a small sachet containing some wondrous mix from the pharmacy in the village. It only cost five euros so I'm not expecting miracles, but as I'm learning from my book about French women, the more time you spend pampering yourself and getting ready to go out, the more confident and attractive you feel. I rub the gunk all over my face; I look like a deranged ghost. I guess the plan is that once you take it off you look so much better you think the damn thing has worked.

I decide to take full advantage of my appearance to scare the children. I creep up the stairs to their bathroom and am about to jump in with a ghostly wail when I hear Emily's voice.

"Well, where is he then? He hasn't been here for a long time, and no one ever talks about him. That's what happens when people die. I saw it in a film."

"But if he had died, Mummy would have told us," says Charlotte. "And he has called us, lots of times."

"Not for two days," says Emily.

"If who died?" asked Edward. "I don't want anyone to die."

"Daddy silly," says Emily. "Don't you ever listen?"

Edward starts crying.

I run in and the girls both scream in horror. I have forgotten I look as dead as they think their father is.

"Edward, girls! Daddy is NOT dead, don't be silly," I say, leaning down to hug them.

"You look terrible," says Charlotte.

"Really bad," adds Emily.

"It's just a face pack to make my skin nicer, don't worry," I explain.

"So where is Daddy?"

I decide that half an hour before I am going out is not the time to tell them about Cécile and her strategically placed bra.

"He has had to work a lot but is coming out this weekend, so you'll see him then," I say cheerily. "Now come in, let's get into our jim-jams."

By the time they are ready for bed and settled in front of the video with Agnès in charge, I have about 15 minutes to get ready, but I do at least remember to wash my face pack off.

I arrive at Calypso's house at quarter past eight – politely late – carrying a bottle of wine and some flowers. Maybe this time next year I will be carrying one of my own bottles of wine. But suddenly that seems a long way away.

The door is flung open by a man wearing chinos and a pink shirt. He is blond, slightly balding, quite round-faced and friendly-looking. His body looks like it has undergone a lot of heavy-duty training.

"Hello, you must be Sophie. I'm Tim, Calypso's husband," he says grabbing my hand and shaking it vigorously. "Come in, come in, thanks so much for the wine, do give the flowers to Calypso, she'll be thrilled."

I follow him into the sitting room saying a silent prayer that there won't be a sandstorm this evening. I never did buy that bulletproof vest.

Calypso is sitting with another couple on a large cream sofa. There are drinks on the table in front of them and bowls of nuts and crisps. I am introduced to Robert, who then introduces his rather mousy wife Helen as his 'other half'. They were either both too busy to get changed or they are taking the shabby chic look to extremes.

"How long have you been here?" asks Robert, almost before Calypso has asked what I would like to drink. I have come to expect this. This is the first question any expat Brit in France will ask another expat. For some reason, there is a competition going on among them all as to who has been there the longest, speaks the best French, has the most French friends; in short, who has become the most French.

"Only three months," I say. I can see from the look of triumph in his eyes that Robert has won this particular round. Naturally I refuse to hand him victory by returning the question and carry on talking about myself.

"We moved here to make wine," I say. "We live at Sainte Claire, just across the vineyards the other side of the school."

"How interesting," says Helen, making it sound anything but. "Do you know a lot about wine?"

"Nothing at all," I say smiling. "But I'm willing to learn."

"You'll have your work cut out for you," Robert joins in.

"We've been here for over twenty years, and we're still learning."

At the casual drop of the 'twenty years' I am supposed to, according to a bit I read in one of my books about moving to France, say something along the lines of "How amazing, imagine, twenty years" as though he has completed a life sentence for some crime he didn't commit.

However, I am in a rebellious mood so don't flinch but respond with: "I know. I have to start right from the very beginning, but I'm hoping I will find some friendly wine-maker to point me in the right direction. Although it has to be said I've yet to meet any."

"Well, I think you might find things in *la France profonde* a little more complicated than in London," says Helen with a smirk that makes me want to punch her – and normally at dinner parties I'm a pretty non-violent person. Of course, I know it's not going to be easy to make wine alone and bring up the children, all in a foreign country with an administration system that is enough to send anyone off their head and a punishing tax regime. But how about just pretending I might make it for two minutes to make me feel better about my life? At least until I've had a glass of wine to cheer me up.

I am rapidly losing the will to live. A dinner party filled with what Bridget Jones so fittingly called 'smug marrieds' and chat about daily commutes and nannies seems exciting compared with this little soirée of smug expats.

Helen's 'other half' nods in agreement. "And as for friendly wine-makers, well they're few and far between," he adds, spitting out a piece of olive as he speaks.

Can this get any worse? If I want to watch people spitting out food, I'll just have dinner with my children.

"Did someone mention a friendly wine-maker?"

I recognise that voice. I leap up from my chair and am suddenly face to face with the man from the vineyard. I try not to look incredibly excited; after all I am not sixteen years old and this is not my first prom.

"Nice to see you again," I say as calmly as I can, stretching out my hand for him to shake. Being a smarmy Frenchman of course, he kisses it instead, without ever losing eye contact with me. Or rather, he 'kisses and misses' it, his lips hovering a few millimetres above the back of my hand. I will have to ask Audrey what this strange custom means and how it relates to 'corners'.

"Ah, so you know Jean-Claude de Sard?" says Tim.

Oh no. It's not possible. Please tell me I am dreaming. THIS is my evil neighbour? Only hours early I was slagging off this very same man to himself. Happily, the handsome Frog seems to have forgiven me and comes to my rescue.

"Sophie and I met today briefly in my vineyards," he says to Tim. I am amazed and more than impressed that he remembered my name. "But I think she has a bad impression of me, *n'est-ce pas?*" He turns back to face me.

"Ah, well, your foreman has forbidden us from walking across your vineyards and actually once tried to shoot me," I say, trying to ignore the seductive smell of his aftershave, which I recognise from earlier. "And he says that was on your orders, so I guess, well, no, my first impression was not good."

"And now?" he grins cheekily, "has it changed at all?"

I somehow stop myself from melting on the spot. "That depends," I say, "on whether or not you allow the children and me to walk across your vineyards."

Jean-Claude de Sard laughs. "It's a deal. And for the record, I never told him you couldn't walk across my land. But he does like to control the whole estate in just about every way."

Suddenly this dinner party is looking a whole lot more interesting. I can even make pleasant conversation with Mr and Mrs Smug-Francophiles without feeling irritated. We sit around drinking the champagne Jean-Claude has bought and chatting. Tim, Calypso's husband, who is just as posh as she is (or pretends to be), tells us tales of playing rugby for the Harlequins and life in the Army. He seems perfectly sane. I can't imagine him trying to shoot his wife, or anyone else for that matter. He is one of those classic 'Tim-nice-but-dim' types that the English middle classes are so good at producing. Not the gun-toting madman I imagined at all.

Dinner is lasagne and salad.

"Calypso only has two dinner-party menus," says Tim, laughing as he serves us. "The other one is shepherd's pie."

"Lucky I didn't come on a shepherd's pie night," says Helen. "I don't eat lamb."

I make a mental note to only cook lamb if I ever have a dinner party at Sainte Claire.

"So, Jean-Claude," says Helen's 'other half', "what do you think of all these English invading your country?"

Jean-Claude twirls his wine around in his glass and for a moment I wonder if he might take offence at the question. But he smiles his most disarming smile and says, "We are all invaders. It's just a question of when we came."

"But what about the effect on house prices?" asks Helen. "Aren't you angry that the English are driving up the prices, especially here in the south?"

"Is it the fault of the English that the French are selling at inflated prices?" he counters. Can nothing rattle this man? He is as smooth as a full-bodied Merlot and just as drinkable.

After dinner I carry some plates into the kitchen where Calypso is preparing sliced oranges with syrup for pudding.

"Thank you," I say. "It was delicious."

Calypso takes the plates from me. She is looking very pretty; her dark hair is tied up and she's wearing a pink tie-dye dress.

"Is everything all right with, you know?" I ask gesturing towards the dining room where Tim is sitting. "No more scares?"

Calypso smiles. "No, all fine thanks. It only happens about once a year. Our charismatic M. de Sard seems quite taken with you," she adds, changing the subject.

Rather annoyingly I blush.

"Oh, and it seems you're quite taken with him. Whatever will your husband say?"

"He doesn't really have a say any more," I begin. "He's been having an affair. I told him to go back to England."

"God, I wish my husband would have an affair. It's one of the main reasons I moved to France."

This was not the reaction I was expecting. Once again Calypso has turned my dramatic moment into something concerning herself. How typical is that?

"Why?" I ask. "It actually was quite a shock when I found out about Nick. I'm not sure I'd wish it on anyone."

Calypso looks astonished for a moment. "Oh, yes, I understand," she says. "I'm sorry, but things are just so irritating right now. One day I'll have to tell you about it. Meanwhile it looks like you may have found someone to console you?"

I smile. "Well, it is quite odd. Maybe it's the champagne, but I haven't felt this way for years. In fact, I thought I had stopped having these sorts of feelings, like they died in childbirth or something. But I feel like a sixteen-year-old."

"Maybe part of it is that until now you weren't really looking until your husband buggered off with someone else?"

Fair point.

"How is it all going anyway?" she continues. "How is Colette doing?"

"Great. Thanks for putting her in touch with me. I will need someone else too once it all gets busy, but heaven knows how I'll be able to afford it."

"Let me know if I can help with anything," she says. "I have harvested every year since we got here so know a bit about vineyards. And I like the work. There's something therapeutic about working the land, using your hands; it stops you thinking too much. Colette always says the best relief for stress is trellising – the mix of strength and precision needed, being outside in the fresh air, listening to the sounds of nature."

We go back to the dinner party carrying pudding and plates. Jean-Claude looks up and smiles as I walk into the room and for a split-second I feel like there is no one else there.

Sadly, that feeling is rudely interrupted by Robert, who is keen to tell me all about his latest property-rental venture, 'Pet Your Pets': holiday rentals where people can bring their pets.

"It's a huge niche market," he insists, leaning forward in that rather unstable way that people do when they've drunk more than their body weight, which for him wouldn't be too difficult – he's awfully scrawny.

"Never trust a man whose shoulders are smaller than yours," Carla always says. I couldn't agree more.

He talks about his venture as if he were talking about something that would really change the world, or a favourite child. I try to muster up some enthusiasm but find it difficult. This is more tedious than someone telling you the plot of their unpublished novel. And there's only so much I can contribute really; I can't imagine ever taking Daisy, the peacocks or Wolfie on holiday. The children are bad enough on their own.

"If you will allow me Sophie, I could walk you home across our vineyards." Jean-Claude de Sard is standing by my chair with his hand outstretched, waiting for me. I love the way he says 'our vineyards'. I wish Robert the best of luck, thank Calypso and Tim for a lovely evening, and within minutes am out in the starlit night with the world's most charming Frenchman.

"So how is the vineyard?" he begins. "All under control?"

"No, not at all under control," I tell him, sighing and looking up at the clear star-lit sky.

"What I need really is for someone to come in and wave a magic wand and make it all okay."

The moon is a delicate thin crescent – or a banana, as the

children would call it. I still can't get over how bright the stars are here compared with London

"I am basically going to have to run it alone," I carry on. "Nick, my husband, has gone back to London to… well, work and, another woman."

"I see. I am so sorry. What a fool he must be," he says looking at me. "But you will stay?"

"Yes, I am really trying to get to grips with it all, I have a helper, Colette, who is showing me the ropes. And I am reading a lot, learning about the wine-making process."

We are walking perfectly in time with each other even though his legs are much longer than mine. It feels very comfortable. And it is so nice to be outside in the clear air, away from the smug expats, listening to the gentle breeze and talking to someone who understands wine-making, unlike me.

"But to be honest I really haven't the first clue what I'm doing," I continue. "It could all be a total and utter disaster and we will all be homeless."

"There is only one thing you really need to know," he says, nodding towards the vines we are walking through. I hope it's not too complicated; I've drunk far too much red wine to remember anything technical. We stop by a vine and he gently caresses one of the leaves with his thin, elegant fingers.

"You have to know when to pick the grape," he says looking at me and smiling.

"When they're ripe?" I guess.

Jean-Claude smiles enigmatically.

"But how do you know when they're ripe?" I ask.

He laughs. "That, my dear little *vigneronne anglaise*, is the real question. But don't worry, I am here to help you."

Is this man too good to be true?

"To produce a good wine, you need to start with good grapes," he goes on. "And this you have. Your terroir is excellent, in fact better than mine, even though it is just next door. I know and love Sainte Claire, it used to belong to my grandparents, I practically grew up there."

"Really? How amazing."

"Yes, we were very sad when they sold it to the Grécos, but it was all part of an unpaid debt. Anyway, you don't need to worry, wines have been cultivated here in the region since the first century before Christ. It is the oldest wine-growing region in France. You are just continuing the tradition. There is nothing to fear."

We walk on and are home far too soon. He leads me up the steps of Sainte Claire. I feel like a teenage girl. What is the protocol for this? I mean, I am still married. Is he married? Oh help, I haven't even asked him that. Not that it seems to matter in France. And happily all my windows have shutters. The baker should have thought of that before he got in such a dough mix.

Or maybe I should ask him. I don't want to make enemies with my neighbour's wife, assuming there is one. But now might not be a good time to do so; if he says yes then there is no chance of a kiss, and if he says no it might look like I am hinting for more. Oh God, how do single people cope? It's all far too complicated.

We stop on the steps. He takes my hands in his. They feel

warm and comforting. I'm not sure if it's the effect of the wine, but I start swaying gently towards him as if I'm being drawn by a magnet. I try to remember if I flossed my teeth. Then I'm ashamed of myself. What a trollop. Talk about getting in touch with your inner French woman.

"Sophie, I really enjoyed this evening and normally I hate dinner parties," he says. Our faces are now less than two inches apart. "If you would allow me, I would love to take you out to lunch to talk about the vineyard and also get to know you better."

I gulp and nod. This is scary. I think I am about to kiss another man for the first time in almost ten years. What will it be like? Will I be struck down by lightning for adultery?

"Shall we say two weeks on Monday? I have to go to Aix until then to see my aunt."

I nod again and smile. "I would love that."

"Sophie!"

I hear my name being called but the voice is not coming from my soon-to-be – hopefully – French lover. It is coming from my front door.

"Oh, hi. Sorry to disturb. I managed to get an earlier flight and sent Agnès home."

It's my husband. Early as usual.

Rule 13

Sentimentality will cost you; never keep any evidence

The French Art of Having Affairs

I spring away from Jean-Claude de Sard as quickly as Daisy does from the children's leftover Weetabix when I catch her snacking. There is nothing like the sight of your husband when you're about to snog someone else to sober you up.

"This is Nick," I say to Jean-Claude. "My…." I'm not quite sure how to describe him, but Nick interrupts me.

"Soon to be ex-husband," he says confidently, stretching out his hand for Jean-Claude to shake. I am not sure how to react to this news. I certainly don't want to let Jean-Claude know I had no idea we were getting divorced until a few seconds ago.

"Yes, exactly," I add with more vigour than I feel. "He's here to see the children."

"*Bonsoir*, Nick," he says, shaking my husband's hand. I look at them together. Nick is shorter than Jean-Claude. The latter, though obviously a few years older, doesn't suffer in comparison. He is so very elegant, almost regal.

"Now if you will excuse us, I need to say goodbye to Sophie." He turns away from Nick and focuses his whole attention on me. I love the way he is doing that; it makes me feel like a princess. The Princess and the Frog – ha, that would make the girls laugh.

He takes my hands in his. He clearly isn't as bothered by the presence of my husband as I am.

"So, see you in a couple of weeks?" he asks, smiling.

"Yes," I nod. He kisses and misses my hand, nods to Nick and then saunters off back to his château.

Nick and I go inside. He looks tired but more or less the same. Cécile is clearly feeding him though; he seems to have put on some weight.

"Why are you here already?" I ask him. "You weren't meant to come until tomorrow."

"You look great. Soph," he says. "Really great. Wow – amazing in fact. How are you?"

"Fine, no thanks to you," I snap.

"You're wearing that dress," he adds. I don't react.

"You've even had your nails done. Christ, are you turning into a French woman?" he laughs. It's nice to hear that laugh again and his Irish accent, but I'm not about to forgive him. "And getting your hands on a Frenchman?"

"So I hear we're getting divorced?" I say.

"Yes," he says. "And it seems just in the nick of time," he adds, gesturing to the door. "You certainly haven't wasted any time making friends with the locals."

I think about defending myself but am suddenly too upset to even go into it all. Since when did we agree to a divorce? So instead I do what most of us do when we're hurt; I snipe at him.

"Well, as we're now officially getting divorced it's no longer anything to do with you, is it? And why are you here so early anyway?"

"Your mother asked me to come. She says she has arranged for you to go away for the weekend so she asked me to be here to take care of the kids. She says she sent you a text with all the details. Did you not get it?"

No I didn't. And bugger – I really don't want to go anywhere with my mother. Where is she taking me? Why does she insist on organising me as if I were still seven years old and just about to lose my gym kit? I'm now in my mid-thirties and have lost my husband; you don't get more grown up than that.

"Did you see the kids?"

"They were all asleep by the time I got here, but I looked in on them," he says. "It was grand to see them, really grand."

"They'll be pleased to see you. They thought you were dead," I say and then realise that may sound a bit harsh. But Nick, with his indomitable Irish sense of humour, finds it amusing.

"Dead? Is that what you told them?" he laughs. "Well, they'll wake up in the morning and meet a ghost. I'm knackered. I'll go to the spare room. Send them in when they wake up, will you? Night, Soph."

He walks upstairs and I go into the kitchen. My heart is beating hard. It was tough seeing him all happy and relaxed. I was rather hoping he might be hurt seeing me with Jean-Claude, or even better, consumed with jealousy, but he doesn't seem at all bothered. It's touching that he recognised the dress, though. I wonder if he still longs to take it off me. I guess not.

I make a cup of camomile tea and take it upstairs. I take out my phone and look for my mother's message.

"Darling," it reads. "Pack some nice things for a night away in smart hotel. Don't worry; I'm not coming with you. A car will collect you at 9am."

I can't imagine what she has arranged, but I send her a text back saying thank you. I suppose at least I won't need to stay here with Nick all weekend, which would be strange and strained to say the least. The temptation would be to read HIS messages, why didn't I think of that before? I could have sent one back to Cécile telling her to bugger off.

A break will be lovely; I am beginning to have a whole new level of respect for single parents. At that point when you've had enough and can't cope and just want to scream or at least say 'go and ask your father', you can't. There really is no one else to fall back on. And the thing about three children is that it is very rare that they're all happy; there is almost always someone needing something.

I take out a bag and think about what to pack. Something nice, she said. If I were a French woman, I would start with my underwear. I have yet to go shopping as the new slimline-ish Sophie so have to settle for the old stuff. I find some trousers I used to hate because they were so tight they gave me that very attractive camel-toe look, and I could barely sit down in them. I try them on. What joy – no camel. In fact, I can even do a downward dog in them. I will wear them with my pink cashmere jumper and brown leather boots for the journey. But what about the evening and the day after? I look through my wardrobe and conclude that I have absolutely nothing to wear. I could have told myself that without even looking – why did I even waste my time? My clothes were hardly likely to start reproducing overnight, creating new little chic outfits I might like to take with me to a luxury hotel that I don't even know the location of. The phrase 'familiarity breeds contempt' is doubly true when it comes to clothes.

As a last resort I pack some jeans and a couple of jumpers. And obviously that little black dress I can now fit into and have just worn. I have a relaxing bath and then get into bed. How odd it is, to be sleeping under the same roof as Nick again but in a separate room. Thankfully I don't have a desperate desire to go and pounce on him, so no change there. But it would be nice to just lie and chat to him.

Maybe that was the problem with our marriage; we were too much like pals. Isn't that what happens after several years of marriage, though? I mean, if you're not friends, then what else is there? I don't know a single couple that's been married for ten years and are still in it for the sex, or at least, the sex with each other.

I am woken by the children at around 6am. Emily and Charlotte are fighting about who can wear a certain pair of light purple leggings, which belong to Emily.

"You promised me last night you'd share them to me if I let you sleep with Johnny," she yells. Johnny is the name of her furry dog she bought with the £20 that Johnny Fray gave her. "And now you're saying no. You're just a big fat liar, liar pants of fire."

"Pants on fire," I correct her, "and share with." I roll over, wishing they didn't have an inbuilt alarm for 6am that only seems to work at weekends. But for once I have something that will distract them. And that something is on English time, so for him it is only 5am. How very satisfying.

"There's a surprise for you in the spare bedroom," I say. "Go and look."

All three rush into the spare bedroom, anxious to be the first to get there. I hear them say "Where is it?" and then Nick's voice yelling "Boo" and the shrieks of delight from the three of them.

"Daddy, Daddy," is all I hear, then Emily starts to weep. I get out of bed, pull on my dressing gown and go and see them. Nick is hugging Emily, who always gets very emotional, and the other two are on the bed.

"Morning," he says to me. "Are you ready for your trip?"

"Where are you going, Mummy?" says Charlotte. "And why did Daddy sleep in here?"

"He came in late and didn't want to wake me," I say. I had already prepared for that question. "And I'm not sure where I'm going, Granny has arranged it all."

"I know," says Emily between sobs. "Granny told me. It's called Some Trapeze and it's in France."

*

Three hours later a vast black Mercedes rolls up outside the door to take my very shabby bag and me to Some Trapeze – or St Tropez as it is more commonly known. I wave goodbye to the children and Nick, who are all standing on the steps of Sainte Claire looking gorgeous.

My heart always breaks a little whenever I leave them. But this time it is especially difficult, knowing that when I come back from this mystery jaunt Nick and I will have to tell them our news. I can't imagine how we begin. I mean, when is a good time to tell your children their parents are getting divorced?

The driver is French and either doesn't want to talk to me or really does misunderstand everything I say. So all I know about my magical mystery tour is that we are heading to St Tropez. I text my mother to get some more information but she just texts back "Enjoy yourself, it won't be a surprise if I tell you". So I decide the best thing is just to relax and enjoy the trip. There are worse ways to travel than in a black Merc with cream leather seats and little buttons that you can press to adjust their position. And there are worse destinations than St Tropez.

We whizz past a sign to Montpellier airport, which makes me think about those early trips Nick and I took here to look for a house. Was I being terribly stupid not to notice there was something wrong? Did I have an idea deep down there was someone else but just not want to face the fact? No, all I knew was that I was getting bored, but I put that down to a combination of a mid-life crisis and several years of marriage. I also thought things would improve between us; I guess I just never thought about how. And now it is all too late. Nick wants a divorce and I am going to St Tropez.

We pass a sign to Aix-en-Provence; that's where Jean-Claude said he was going. I have his mobile number now, I could text him to say hi, but that might seem a bit desperate. Whatever else happens at our lunch it will be nice to have someone to talk to. Do I want more? Am I ready for more? Maybe not, but it wouldn't do any harm to try to move on. What other option do I have?

I smile as I remember our walk home. I love the way he takes my hands in his; he has such strong hands. I wonder what his body is like. He is a bit older than me, probably around forty, but he does look in good shape. He told me he used to row at university and that he plays a lot of tennis now, when he isn't busy running his estates next to our house and in Limoux, a couple of hours away. He knows all there is to know about wine-making; he grew up in a wine-making family and now he runs the business himself.

He could become my wine guru – and maybe something else too? It would be a great way to learn French. And how many chances in life do you get to have a romance with a French aristo? I don't know for sure that he is one, but I did read somewhere that a de in front of your surname means you are aristocratic. I could become Madame Sophie de Sard. It has a certain ring to it.

I fall asleep daydreaming of a wedding in Boujan's church and wake up when we pull up to pay the toll at the entrance to St Tropez. So this is the place that made Nick fall in love with

France and brought us all here? Or rather the place with the girl on the beach he fell in love with.

We drive down a windy road into the town. It is very pretty; the light seems different here, more translucent. There are palm trees lining the streets, the houses are painted in pastel colours and in the distance the sea is shimmering. But I would still say the landscape around Sainte Claire is more dramatic and beautiful. Thankfully not many other people agree with me, which is why a vineyard down this way costs about five times as much as mine did.

We stop outside a hotel and the driver gets out to open my door. Almost immediately there is a man in uniform ready to take my shabby bag for me.

"Welcome to Byblos," he says smiling.

"Thank you," I smile back. But what the hell is Byblos and why am I here?

My driver gives me his mobile number and says he will be here should I need anything else. I try to ask him who sent him but he feigns incomprehension. I just can't imagine my mother would do all this; she doesn't have the money for a start. But then who? And how come she is in on it?

I walk to the reception, unsure what to do next. As soon as I get there a young woman wearing trendy jeans and a suede top approaches me.

"Madame Reed?"

"Yes," I reply.

"Welcome to Byblos, it is our pleasure to have you here, I am Chantal, the hotel's guest relations manager." She holds out a perfectly manicured hand for me to shake.

"Thank you. Can you please tell me what is going on? I haven't booked a room here but you seem to know all about me and I certainly can't afford it and…."

"Madame Reed," she interrupts me gently. "Please do not worry. I too have no idea who is behind this little gift for you but I can assure you that you will have a lovely time with us and there will be no bill to pay, it is all taken care of."

I sigh. Mainly with relief at not having to pay the bill. But I was also rather hoping she could tell me what was going on. What if it's some random psycho? Do I know any random psychos? Oh my God maybe it's Nick and he's going to pitch up too? But wouldn't it just have been easier to ask for my forgiveness at home? And if that is the case who on earth is looking after the children?

"Would you like to hear your itinerary?" smiles Chantal.

"I'd love to," I say.

"You are staying in the Riviera suite, which is Mick Jagger's favourite room here," she begins.

"Oh, I hope he won't mind," I joke.

"Oh no, he's not here," says Chantal, completely straight-faced. You've got to love the French for many things but not for their sense of humour. "I will take you there, where there is a light lunch waiting for you. After lunch a personal shopper from one of St Tropez's best shops, Riviera Chic, will come and escort you to the store, where you will choose any clothes you like."

My jaw is starting to drop. Is this woman for real? Where is her fairy godmother's wand?

"And I don't have to pay for the clothes?"

"Correct."

"And I get to keep them?"

Chantal laughs. "Yes, of course. May I continue?"

"Please. don't let me stop you."

"After your shopping you will be brought back here to the beauty centre. There you will have any treatments you feel like – for example, a pedicure and manicure, some waxing and a haircut, colour or whatever. You can spend a total of four hours there but then at 6pm you have a Balinese massage booked in your room. After that, I don't know any more!"

"It sounds too good to be true," I say. "And you really have no idea…?"

"None," she interrupts me. "Come on, you need to get going, you have a lot to do."

Chantal takes me to my room. I say room – it is more like a plush apartment, and I worry I might never find the loo. My little bag is sitting on the luggage rack in the bedroom, looking totally out of place. In my sitting room, which has a view onto the swimming pool outside from a huge window that takes up the whole wall, my lunch is waiting.

I walk over to the window. "You could actually jump from here into the pool," I say to Chantal. "Has anyone ever done that?"

"Yes, but we don't encourage it," she tells me in a rather stern voice. Do I look like the sort of madwoman who would jump into a swimming pool from a window before lunch? Maybe she thinks anyone with a bag as ugly as mine is a potential suicide.

"The personal shopper will be here in forty-five minutes," she says looking at her clipboard. "Please enjoy your lunch and your afternoon. With your permission I will book you a waxing, eyebrow threading, pedicure and manicure, some highlights and a cut and blow-dry in our salon?"

She's obviously clocked my unkempt state. I have no idea what eyebrow threading is, but at this point, who am I to argue?

"Yes please, sounds perfect, thank you so much," I say.

She leaves and I sit down to my light lunch of pumpkin and goat's cheese salad and warm brown bread rolls, and a glass of white wine. Am I dreaming? This morning I was a normal mother with nothing in particular to differentiate me from every other mother apart from the fact that I have three children and am about to get divorced, and now I am eating lunch in Mick Jagger's favourite room in St Tropez.

The personal shopper who arrives after half an hour is around sixty and fiercely smart in just about every way. The phrase perfectly turned out doesn't even begin to describe her. I look like I have just come from a church jumble sale by comparison. She speaks very good, very clipped English. She has a classic little brown bob and perfect skin. She is so thin I could fit her into one leg of my jeans. She is wearing what I can see from the buttons is a Chanel jacket and, I assume, designer jeans. She is a classic example of the 16/60 – a woman who looks 16 years old from the back but 60 from the front. I suppose at that age looking 16 from any angle at all is a good thing, but I find her a little disconcerting.

We leave my room and she leads me through a little

passageway, out of the hotel and across a road. I spot the boutique before we even go in. It is one of those shops I would never dare enter because a pair of socks would cost more than my annual clothing budget. But in we go. There are two sales assistants who welcome me smiling. On the background music I recognise Carla Bruni's soft voice.

"We've been so looking forward to this," says the shorter of the two, a young blonde girl with rosy cheeks and blue eyes. "We love to do makeovers."

"Let's start with your underwear," adds the other one, who is older and darker but probably still only about twenty-five years old. Has she got x-ray vision or can she guess the state of my smalls from my general look?

I feel like Julia Roberts in *Pretty Woman*, but with less hair. So who is my Richard Gere?

Isabelle, as the younger one is called, looks me up and down, has a brief discussion with the Chanel-clad personal shopper and scuttles off. Héloise, her sidekick, suggests we look around the store to see what they have and I can tell her what I like the look of.

What don't I like the look of? Where do I begin? Everything is gorgeous. This is where Madame Chanel comes in handy. She holds up a few items next to me, tells me what colours will suit me and what cut of clothes I should go for. Apparently the cut in the bias dress is a good look for me and the colour green works well with my complexion, for example. She does this brilliant trick of holding a piece of material in front of me and lifting it slowly up my legs to determine what length of skirt or dress will suit me best. My calves are quite chunky, so we settle on just below them.

Meanwhile Isabelle is back with some underwear. I am shown into a changing room and told to try on a bra and matching knickers (of course) made out of lace and satin. The colour is a gloriously rich deep purple, like something out of the film *Moulin Rouge*. I go into the changing room and undress. My own underwear seems like an extremely poor relation next to this ensemble even though I picked my least-faded set.

I put on the bra and knickers then look at myself in the mirror. Suddenly I understand why women spend fortunes on underwear. I am a different woman. The bra makes my mummy breasts look like sex-goddess breasts and the knickers have an amazing flattening effect on my stomach. I look at myself. For the first time in several years I feel really sexy.

"This light is for your husband," says Isabelle popping her head into the changing room. "And this," she says switching on another light that changes the ambiance into a diffused, rather more muted one, "is for your lover". These Frenchies; they think of everything.

"So this size is good for you," says Madame Chanel. "Try another three sets, you will need them."

"Need them for what?" I ask. Am I being sold into white-trade slavery? Aren't I a little old for that?

"Life," says Madame Chanel with a Gallic shrug.

Next come the clothes; two pairs of slim-fit cotton trousers, one in black, the other white, that make my legs look longer than I've ever seen, with cashmere jumpers to go with them, again black and white – all very Audrey Hepburn. These outfits are completed with a pair of black ballet pumps and a small black handbag. Then Madame Chanel gets me to try on a dress that I would never have picked out for myself but that looks incredible. It is made of thick white crinkle-effect cotton with silver lace stitching around the neck in a large V, joining more silver stitching that goes all the way to the stomach, creating a very sexy look. The dress is ankle-length and wide. The sleeves are wide too; the whole effect resembles a snow-angel. The edges are all lined with the thick silver stitching.

It's quite see-through and yet extremely classy. Madame Chanel suggests some flesh-coloured underwear to go underneath it and some white ballet pumps, which will of course also go with my other outfits. She then insists I try on a couple of skirts and shirts, as well as the most incredible pink cashmere cardigan that is almost the length of a coat but as light as a scarf.

I thank the girls and Madame Chanel escorts me back to the hotel. My clothes, she tells me, will be delivered to my room. Meanwhile she has been told to take me to the beauty spa, where again I am treated like a film star. I don't think I have spent four hours in a beauty spa in my entire life, but the time whizzes by. I can see now what all those 'ladies who lunch' are on. Why would you ever want to do anything but go shopping and get your nails done? Especially if someone else is paying for it.

The threading is extraordinary. I didn't even know my eyebrows were unruly until the beautician did one for me and showed me the difference. Now of course I am going to have find a 'threader' in Boujan – how likely is that? Or maybe I can just pounce on the new hairs and pluck them out as they grow back and keep this shape forever.

After the spa, the newly coiffed, manicured, waxed and threaded me is taken up to my room, where there a massage bed and a masseuse await me.

"Undress, please, and lie on your front," says the masseuse, an extremely delicate-looking Asian lady.

She puts a towel on top of me and then presses down firmly all over my body. After that she lifts the towel off my left leg and starts rubbing oil over my right foot and leg. It is an incredible feeling, being pampered like this. She pushes on pressure points on the sole of my foot and along the back of my leg. I feel my whole body relaxing beneath her touch, melting into the thick towel on the massage bed. Before I know it, I'm dozing off.

I wake up and realise I must have missed the other leg being massaged. She is now working on my back and neck; her hands feel incredibly strong. She runs her hands all the way down my spine, then up the sides of my body to my armpits and out along my arms. To my horror I gasp with pleasure. She repeats this several times, and each time I feel my body melting deeper into her oily hands. Then she moves her hands up along my spine, pushing gently as she goes. She massages my neck firmly and I feel all the tension of the past few weeks and months vanishing into them.

She moves down my spine again. I feel her reach the top of my buttocks. I am totally ashamed to admit that I start thinking how nice it would be if she went further down. She starts to gently rotate my buttocks so they move in time with her hands in a circular motion. For the first time in years I feel really turned on. This is ridiculous; I'm not a lesbian. I don't even much like sex with men, or at least I didn't when I was married. I need to snap out of this.

Maybe if I open my eyes and actually look at her I will come back to reality. This is a massage, not a porn film. All that pampering this morning has obviously sent me over the edge.

I lift my head out of the hole it has been jammed into throughout the massage and move it to one side, slowly opening my eyes and adjusting to the soft afternoon light.

And there, wearing nothing but a towelling robe and a big smile, is Johnny Fray.

Rule 14

Always maintain your dignity

The French Art of Having Affairs

I leap up from the massage table in shock. Then I remember that apart from some jasmine oil I am wearing nothing at all. Thank God for the waxing session earlier.

"Hey Cunningham, I didn't recognise you with your clothes off," grins Johnny.

"Johnny! What. On. Earth? Why are you here? What's going on?" I say grabbing a towel and wrapping it around me.

"Calm down, calm down," says England's answer to George Clooney. "Your mother called me."

"My mother? How?"

"We've been in touch on and off since that time we met in the pub. She told me what had happened with Nick. I would have come sooner but I was filming in Prague. Anyway, she said you needed a break to have your mind taken off things so I arranged all this." He motions around the room. "Have you had a good time?"

He smiles at me so sweetly and with such expectation, I want to fling my arms around him. But then my towel might fall off.

I smile back. "Johnny it's been amazing, every girl's dream, thank you. It really means a lot to me."

He puts his hands on my shoulders and looks at me intensely.

"You mean a lot to me, Cunningham, you're like family."

I blush, partly with shame when I remember how badly I treated him and partly because I am so touched.

"Now come on gal, we need to get dressed, we're going out on the town," he adds.

He really does look great; this film-star life obviously suits him. His hair is as wild and tousled as ever, his dark-blue eyes are fiery, as he takes his bathrobe off and puts his trousers and shirt on, I see that he has clearly been working out. I pretend I am not checking him out from where I'm sitting, although I am of course.

I go into my bathroom to get dressed. I opt for the white dress with flesh-coloured underwear and the white ballet pumps. Happily I remembered to pack my make-up and my hair still looks good from its pampering this afternoon. It's amazing what a difference a few highlights can make to a girl's confidence.

I look at myself in the mirror before I go to join Johnny. I look better than I have done for years, I conclude. I am not being bigheaded – after all, the bar wasn't set very high – but I do feel good.

Johnny is waiting with a bottle of champagne when I come

out. "You look great, Cunningham," he says pouring me a glass. "Cheers. Here's to old friends."

"Cheers," I say. The first sip of a glass of cold champagne is one of life's luxuries. It is lively and smooth, and makes me feel instantly relaxed. So far, on a scale of perfect days in my life, this really has to be up there.

"That was some massage," I say. "And I mean the part after the masseuse left."

Johnny laughs. "I had to play a gigolo in a film once and massaging was part of the package. Actually it was one of my favourite roles – not a bad one to do a bit of method acting for."

"I could tell," I smile.

"How are your lovely children?" he asks. Johnny was always such a traditional family man. It seems film stardom hasn't changed him. He has put us in separate bedrooms too. In fact this suite is big enough for at least three families.

"Great, thanks. We haven't told them yet, about us splitting up; I have that to look forward to when I get back tomorrow."

Suddenly the thought of tomorrow and going home seems utterly depressing. An ex-husband-to-be and a vineyard that needs running, wine that needs making, children who need telling Mummy and Daddy are no more and a cleaning lady who hates me.

"So you're definitely going to get divorced?"

I bite my lip and take another sip of champagne. Divorced; it's such a big word, a word I never thought would be associated with Nick and me.

"Yes, it looks that way. He showed up last night and told me,"

I sigh. "He's got this woman, Cécile. I think he must be in love with her."

"What a fool," says Johnny. "I would never have let you go. How do you think the kids will take it?"

"Badly I guess, who knows? I just don't know what to say to them, it's too awful."

Johnny moves onto the sofa next to me and puts his arm around me. "Don't worry Cunningham, it'll be all right. I'll look after you."

I almost start crying, but remember that I have just put some mascara on and do not want to spend the rest of the evening resembling a panda. But looking after is just what I need right now.

We finish off the champagne and then head down to Johnny's car and driver. As we walk through reception people look at us and whisper. I wonder if I have accidentally put my underwear on my head, until I remember that Johnny is now a huge film star and it's him they are all noticing. I strut along proudly next to him, imagining the headline in tomorrow's *Daily Mail*: 'Johnny Fray spotted with mystery blonde in St Tropez'. I hope that girl I hated at school, Claire Booth, reads it.

We get into the Mercedes and are whisked off towards the port. Johnny tells me we are going to a restaurant called Leï Mouscardins in the Tour du Portalet because it has the best views of the sea and also its own fishing boat, so the fish is always excellent.

"Seems you hang out in St Tropez a lot these days," I tease him.

Johnny laughs. "It's a long way from Leeds. But yes, one of the upsides to film stardom is that you get to come to the best places."

We are greeted like film stars, which of course one of us is, and shown to a table tucked away from the main room, with a magnificent view of the bobbing boats down below. After dinner Johnny suggests we skip pudding and instead grab an ice cream down by the port so we can go and ogle the yachts moored there.

It is chilly down by the water and Johnny lends me his jumper; it smells lovely, of some unidentified aftershave and also of him – a smell that still makes me go weak even if it has a hint of nicotine in it. He puts his arm around me and we wander along the port looking at the massive boats. Most of the owners are out and the crew members run around polishing and cleaning. The water splashes gently up against the boats.

We cross the road to an Italian-sounding ice-cream parlour. Johnny goes for vanilla, I am determined to try something exotic and opt for tiramisu, a creamy chocolatey and coffee mix.

"We can walk back to the hotel," he says. "There's just one more place I want to show you and it's in the hotel grounds. It's a nightclub called Les Caves du Roy. I have no idea who Roy was, but it's a place where you will often find George Clooney dancing on the tables."

"And what about Johnny Fray?"

"Only if you're an *extremely* lucky gal," he laughs.

I love the sound of his laugh. if Daisy Buchanan's laugh in *The Great Gatsby* sounds 'full of money', Johnny Fray's is full of mischief.

He takes my hand and leads me towards the nightclub. "Let's see if George is in."

We walk into Les Caves du Roy and the doorman greets Johnny like a long-lost brother. My eyes adjust slowly to the dim light; I can't remember when I was last in a nightclub.

"No sign of George," I shout to Johnny over the loud music, "I'll have to make do with you."

"Cheeky bugger," he mouths back and leads me to the bar, where he orders a bottle of champagne.

"Cheers, Cunningham. Whatever happens, we'll always have St Tropez," he says, smiling.

"You've been watching too many movies," I smile back, looking into those blue eyes.

The memory of that kiss comes flooding back. "It's lovely to see you," I say moving closer to him. Somewhere in the vague recesses of my brain there is a voice saying 'Hussy, last night you were sidling up to a French aristo and now look at you'. But I ignore it, and instead breathe in the scent of Johnny Fray, which makes my head spin even more than the champagne.

George Clooney may not be dancing on the tables, but by 2am I am. It is something I always wanted to do, and when better to do it than after several bottles of champagne in St Tropez with a film star? Johnny laughs and stops me from falling off several times.

"Thank God they don't allow the press in here, Cunningham, you'd be famous by the morning," he laughs as I fall into his arms after a spectacular twirl. "Come on gal, let's get you home."

We walk through the grounds of the hotel to our suite.

"Did you know," I say, as we pass the swimming pool, which is beautifully lit up, "that you can jump from the window of our room into the pool? Mick Jagger does it all the time."

"Maybe we'll try that one next time," says Johnny, "after we've invested in some life insurance."

He opens the door to our suite and takes me by the hand into his bedroom. We stand opposite each other. He puts his hands around my face and draws me closer to him. "Are you glad you came?" he asks.

I nod. My heart is racing, this is the first time I have been in a bedroom with any man except Nick for more years than I care to remember. What should I do? Etiquette dictates that I should say thank you for dinner and trot off to my bedroom, but I don't want to.

Slowly Johnny draws me into his arms and starts caressing my back, reminding me of the massage earlier. I put my arms around his neck and long for him to kiss me so that I can see if it is still as magical as it was all those years ago. He pulls himself away and looks at me smiling.

"After all these years," he says, "I've finally got you into bed."

"Not yet," I grin, not entirely soberly. I am taken over by a sudden rush of confidence and whisk my dress off before leaping under the covers. Johnny takes his shirt and trousers off and gets in next to me. I try to check out his body without being too unsubtle. I can see two of them, but they both look good to me.

I lie back in a haze of contentment. I am where millions of women across the world want to be: in bed with Johnny Fray.

Rule 15

Guilt is a wasted emotion

The French Art of Having Affairs

When I wake up I have no idea where I am. I try to open my eyes but it's too painful. I move my head – oooooowwwwww.

What happened to me? Did I get hit by a truck and end up in hospital? I feel terrible. But this bed feels too comfortable to be a hospital bed and the sheets are pure linen. Maybe I died and went to heaven?

I force one eye open. All I can see is a white ceiling. I turn my head slowly. Next to me in bed there is another person, someone with very thick, curly black hair. Oh shit. Now I remember – I threw myself into Johnny Fray's bed. But what happened after that? I look under the sheets to gauge my state of undress. I am still wearing my matching skin-tone underwear. I sneak a look at Johnny's tall, slender body. He is still wearing his boxer shorts.

Suddenly the theme tune to *Top Gun* comes blaring out from

somewhere. I sit up and look around me. What the hell is it? Then I see Johnny reach for his mobile phone and put it to his ear. I quickly hide under the sheet.

"Yep, thanks," I hear him say. "I'll be there in half an hour. What time is the flight? Okay, thanks, bye."

He leans back in bed. "Cunningham? Where the hell are you?"

"Here," I say, unable to show my face.

He burrows under the sheets to find me.

"Don't worry, your virtue is intact," he says softly.

"What happened?"

"You passed out."

"How classy," I say, blushing in my hiding place.

"After dancing on the tables in Les Caves du Roy for several hours. You put Clooney to shame."

"Oh God," I groan. "Sorry. I feel terrible."

Johnny slowly extricates me from the covers. I look at him through half-open eyes in the same way I look at my bank balance online: half-hopeful, half-terrified of what I will find. Will he be furious with me?

He is smiling. He bends down and kisses me on the lips. It's not a full snog, thank heavens – my breath must be worse than Wolfie's after he's been chewing a rotting rabbit. But it's a kiss somewhere between sexual and loving. I feel the blood race around my body. Did I really hear him say he had to go? I could weep.

He is leaning above me, looking down at me with such an intense expression in his eyes, I feel almost scared. Now he looks like Wolfie about to devour a rotting rabbit.

"Cunningham, I have to fly to Los Angeles, but I meant what I said last night. I'll look after you, gal."

"Thanks," I squeak.

He ruffles my hair and goes into the bathroom.

"Your car will be here at eleven to collect you," he says when he comes out of the shower. His hair is wet and even blacker than normal but still curly. He looks like a Greek God. I watch him get dressed with total fascination. He really is beautiful.

"I'll get them to send some breakfast up. Good luck with your task today, Cunningham." He is back over by the bed sitting next to me. "I don't envy you. I'll text you so you have my mobile number. Make sure you save it. Call or text me if you need anything at all. Love you, gal."

He kisses my forehead and walks out, leaving me feeling extremely alone. I touch his side of the bed; the imprint of his body is still there, and it is still warm.

I get up and throw his towelling robe on. There is just a hint of his aftershave on it. The doorbell rings and a man wheels in a table laden with fruit, an omelette, fresh orange juice and croissants. Around the plates are strewn rose petals. He pours me a green tea.

I hear my mobile phone ping. There is a message on it from a UK number.

"Have a nice breakfast, Cunningham. Miss you already.'

It's from Johnny. I save his number then look at his message again. It would be pretty easy to fall in love with this man, I conclude, as I text him back to say thank you.

We drive out of St Tropez; it seems unforgivably bright and sunny, even though I am wearing shades. In a small square a market is already set up for business; the fruits and vegetables look perfect, like marzipan sweets neatly packed in boxes. If I had more energy, or any energy, I would ask the driver to stop so I could take some home with me. Instead I recline the seat and sleep for most of the rest of the way home, my new clothes packed neatly away in their shopping bags next to me.

When I get there at around half past two, Nick and the children are just clearing away lunch. The children run to greet me. It is so lovely to see them, though I have only been away for a day.

"Did you bring us a present?" they all ask when they see all the shopping bags around me.

I feel like the world's worst mother, I am overcome with guilt. 'No, I was too busy shopping, being pampered, getting drunk, dancing on tables and falling in love with Johnny Fray to even think about you' is what flashes through my mind. How selfish can you get?

"I'm so sorry," I tell them, hugging them one by one, "I didn't have a chance to go shopping for presents. But I promise I will next time. How are you all?"

"Oh, is this going to be a regular trip then?" asks Nick, who has come out of the kitchen carrying a tea-towel.

"No, I mean, I don't know," I say, flustered. It feels very odd to be looking at my husband, even if we are estranged, knowing that just a few hours ago I was in bed with another man. "I would love a cup of tea," I say. "I'm parched."

We all walk into the kitchen.

"So who are all the presents for?" asks Charlotte.

"Actually, they are for me," I say.

"Why? Is it your birthday?" asks Edward.

"No," I smile, "but it felt like it."

"So where was the mystery trip to?" he asks.

"St Tropez, to a hotel called Byblos, I stayed in the Riviera Suite," I say, as if they will know what on earth that is. But I just love the sound of it.

"Wow, you've come up in the world," says Nick, looking at me and making that whistling noise he always makes when he's surprised. "I thought only film stars stayed there."

I go bright red and head towards the kettle.

"Oh, I get it," he says, putting down the tea-towel. "You were with a film star."

"Who, Mummy? Who were you with?" asks Charlotte, jumping up and down with excitement.

"I was with Johnny," I say.

"You saw Johnny Fray?" squeals Emily. "Did he ask after us?"

"He did," I say. "He was very keen to know how you all are and sends lots of love."

"Well, this is probably as good a time as any to tell them, eh?" Nick says angrily.

I glare at him. Why is he making this unpleasant? He's the one who wants a bloody divorce. He's the one who started hanging out with other people and even packing their underwear, or at least allowing their underwear to be packed, in his bag. But I can't say that in front of the children.

So why do I feel guilty? I mean, if he hadn't started shagging Cécile I would never have dreamt of going to St Tropez with a film star. Well, actually, I might have dreamt about it, but I would never have done it. Lucy would argue that dreaming about something is just the beginning and then it turns into the reality, so in effect you should feel guilty about dreaming too.

"It's like drugs," she says. "You start with marijuana and the next thing you know you're a crack-head."

She used to maintain she never had so much as a teeny weeny illicit little fantasy, but then she was married to Perfect Patrick. Or Less Than Perfect Patrick, as he became known after he started acting like a perfect bore, moping around the house doing nothing. And then of course she found Josh, the real thing and didn't even need to fantasise.

"Can we just talk about what it is we want to say alone for a minute?" I say under my breath.

"Sure," he responds. "Kids, will you take the leftovers to Frank and Lampard please?"

"Why?" they all say sulkily.

"Because I asked you to. Now come on, scram, and then come back here when you're done." He puts on his fake-scary face, which makes them all giggle and run out.

We are alone in the kitchen. My heart is racing because I feel so many emotions converging on me at once. The hangover isn't helping either; I feel weak from that, but more so from the thought of what we have to go through now.

Nick motions for me to sit down and sits opposite me.

"So, I think we can be grown-up about this, can't we?" he

begins.

I gulp. I feel like a naughty schoolgirl in front of the headmistress.

"I am happy to take the blame," he continues. "After all, it was all my fault. I didn't mean for it to happen, but it did."

"What you mean perhaps is that you didn't mean to get caught out?" I feel the nasty side of me coming out that often surfaces when I'm scared.

Nick sighs but doesn't have time to respond because our children have come running back into the kitchen with the news that Frank and Lampard are already eating.

"Right kids, sit down," says Nick. "Your mother and I need to talk to you."

Edward scrambles into my lap and I bury my face in the warm, soft space between his head and his shoulder. He squeals because it tickles. Charlotte and Emily sit on a chair each; Emily immediately puts her thumb in her mouth. I wait as expectantly as the children do for Nick to start speaking.

"Right," he begins. I imagine he is squeezing his toes. That's what he always does when he's nervous; he says it makes all your nerves go to your feet. "Your mother and I have decided – well, we thought it might be better if we lived apart for a bit."

There is silence.

"We still love you all very much," he goes on.

People always say that, I want to tell him, but then it is true.

"And we will both carry on looking after you. Just not at the same time. As much as before."

On a scale of speeches, it is hardly a classic, but at least he said it, which is more than I could have done.

And now it sinks in. Emily starts weeping first, closely followed by the other two. I try to console them. Charlotte is the first to speak.

"But why? Don't you love each other any more? Are you getting divorced? Amelia's parents got divorced and she had to move to Germany."

"No one is going to move to Germany," I reassure her. "We do love each other, of course we do and we always will. But somehow it's just not enough any more."

Emily is totally inconsolable. I would do anything to erase the pain on her little face. Even her cat's ears are wobbling with grief. Edward just clings into me, sobbing.

"Listen, kids, it really won't really make much difference to you. I was away during the week anyway and I will still come back at weekends and see you, and you can come to England and see me too," says Nick in his most jovial Irish voice.

"Of course it won't be the same," snaps Charlotte. "You'll be divorced. And anyway, why are you getting divorced if you still love each other?"

"Well, as your mother says, sometimes loving each other is not enough. And I have also, er, met someone else," he admits sheepishly.

"Who?" says Emily. "Who is she?"

"She is called Cécile, and you'll really like her," says Nick.

"No I won't," says Emily. "I'll hate her."

That's my girl.

"So will I," says Edward, extricating himself from my hug.

"I'm going to kill her with my Spiderman sword."

"That's not very nice," I say, taking the moral high ground and suddenly feeling rather saintly. "She might be a very nice girl." As if.

"Do you know her, Mummy?" asks Emily.

"No," I say. "But I am looking forward to meeting her. If Daddy likes her then she must be very special."

If Daddy likes her more than he likes us, is what I want to say, but I don't. I feel the anger and bitterness coming back. Best to end this here before I start yelling at him for hurting my children like this.

"Now who wants to come and look at the fish in the fountain?" I ask. No response. "And then when the bakery opens we'll buy some bread and some cakes for tea. Come on, last one on their bike is a rotten banana." I get up and chivvy them all along.

Nick grabs me as I go to walk out. "I suppose I'd better get to the airport. Sorry I can't come with you, it sounds lovely."

"That's fine," I say, looking at him. "You can be the rotten banana."

Anticipation is almost the best part

The French Art of Having Affairs

The buds are blooming; it is like the spring fairy has waved her magic wand over the vineyards. Suddenly the vines are no longer upside-down candelabras but vibrant green carriers of new life. The children and I are settling into a routine at home.

It is now the middle of April. One month has passed since the weekend we told them we were getting divorced. They are fine. It is extraordinary how adaptable children are, which is mainly an advantage since they get over things very quickly. But it can also be a disadvantage – if life is incredibly exciting or easy, they get used to that very quickly too. Some friends of ours moved back from the Middle East over a year ago and their children are still complaining about the lack of maid and driver in Streatham.

I walk through my vineyards; first the Syrah, then the Grenache, the Viognier and a small parcel of Cabernet Sauvignon, planted more than twenty-five years ago and potentially very valuable. They are all growing well, looking healthy and promising, rather like my children: Edward the blond like the Viognier, and the twins the two younger reds. But hopefully the vines will be a bit more profitable.

I love the vineyard with the Cabernet Sauvignon in it, and not just because it is the most valuable – it is the oldest and so looks the most established, and the views of the house and the surrounding mountains when you stand in the middle of it are gorgeous.

Somehow the ground is slightly raised and gives a 360-degree view of the graceful lines and colours of the landscape. It is also home to my favourite tree, a beautiful olive with an elegant, slightly twisted trunk and abundant branches with silver-green leaves. Often after dinner I walk and stand underneath it for a bit to contemplate the views around me.

From the sixteen hectares of vines I can produce just over 100,000 bottles of wine a year. The plan is to sell them at a cost price of around three euros a bottle. The cost of producing them is around one euro a bottle. Most of any profit will go back into the business, but even if I am left with a tiny bit of cash after the first harvest I will be happy – and extremely lucky, if all the articles I have read about the wine business are true.

It is the most lovely day; I stand for a moment just breathing in the air and looking around me. There is never a day that goes by when I don't appreciate the beauty of Sainte Claire. Looking at the elegant lines of the building and the mountains in the distance fills me with calm. The light today is particularly stunning: a translucent light filled with hope and warmth.

However low I get, there is something about this place that gives me hope – in part because the sun is often shining. Calypso always says that even if there is bad weather, it feels somehow as if it is trying to get better. Unlike England, which is always the other way around.

This morning I had a letter from Nick's lawyer. The divorce proceedings will be simple; neither of us is keen to spend money on lawyers that could go into the vineyard. I wonder how I will feel when the divorce actually comes through. Depressed? Liberated? Or maybe it will be a bit like losing your virginity or turning thirty – there'll be no discernible difference.

I have heard of people running riot minutes after their divorce comes through, dancing on tables and so on. I have been known to dance on tables, well one table, in St Tropez – but divorce hardly seems a reason to do so.

I can't quite believe how quickly it is happening. I never imagined Nick and I being divorced; it seems such an odd idea, and I don't think it's really hit me yet.

I take a deep breath and keep walking through the vineyards. Wolfie follows. I still have a lot of work to do, but things could be worse. The sun is shining, the children are at their lovely little school and oh, I see a familiar and handsome figure sauntering towards me.

I walk to meet Jean-Claude, who smiles broadly when he sees

me. It is nice to feel so welcome.

"I could have you shot for wandering over my vineyards," I joke.

"*Bonjour Madame*," he says, kissing me on both cheeks in that very Parisian way. I note with interest that I have been promoted from hand kissing and missing. I wonder what comes next. The anticipation is compelling and killing, at the same time.

He really is looking good. What is wrong with me at the moment? After years of not feeling remotely interested in sex or men I am suddenly experiencing lust. It's a feeling I haven't had for a long time and thought I hadn't missed. But now it's come back I realise how bland life was without it. Johnny is still in LA but happily there is someone else to stir my new-found feelings.

"How are the buds?" he asks.

"Beautiful," I say, blushing slightly. "Just look at them. Aren't they glorious?"

He looks at the buds and then a leaf, and then another. "*Mon dieu*," he mutters. "What have you sprayed them with?"

"Well, nothing yet. I was waiting for you to come back so I could borrow your tractor. Mine doesn't seem to want to start," I say. "Why?"

"You have a huge attack of mildew going on here, *ma chérie*. You could lose your entire crop. We need to act immediately."

"What does that mean?" I shriek. "Quick, what do we need to do?"

"Mildew is one of the most notorious vine diseases there is, it attacks everything. Look at the underside of this leaf; it is infested," he says, showing me a leaf that is grey on one side. He takes out his mobile phone from his pocket and dials a number. Then he barks some orders at someone; I understand very little except the words *tracteur* and *vite*.

"Right, where is Colette?" he asks.

"She only works one day a week now," I say, "I can't really afford to have her for more."

"Call her and tell her to come. The three of us will tackle the vines with handheld containers and my foreman will spray using the tractor."

I feel shaky; did he really say I could lose the entire crop? "Is everything going to be all right?" I ask him nervously. We're talking about thousands and thousands of pounds worth of vines here; vines that could eventually make 300,000 euros worth of wine.

"I think we have it just in time. Just pray it doesn't rain, and call Colette now," He rushes off to meet the tractor that is arriving from his fields.

I call Colette, who sounds as if she was asleep but says she will come straight away. Then I call Calypso and ask her if she could get the children from school.

"Problems with the vines, eh?" she asks me. How did she know?

Jean-Claude acts like an army general telling us all what to do. I am sent to spray the Syrah by hand with a contraption that looks like a diver's air canister; I march up and down the aisles of vines spraying the horrible smelling sulphur on them – apparently the only thing that can protect them from mildew. Jean-Claude is at the other end of the vineyard, the plan being that we meet in the middle. Colette is spraying the Sauvignon Blanc and the grumpy foreman in the tractor is in the Grenache field that Jean-Claude says is the most infected.

I walk as quickly as I can in my rubber boots. I am wearing rubber gloves to protect my hands from this poison that will, I hope, save my vines but makes everything it touches a livid blue. I stomp along from plant to plant, not daring to think what would have happened if my French knight and his gleaming green tractor had not shown up.

We must have been going an hour and a half or so before we meet in the middle of the field. Jean-Claude kisses me on both cheeks.

"There have to be some perks to the job," he smiles. "Come on, let's help Colette finish the Sauvignon Blanc."

I follow him through the vines, grateful and now even more taken with this elegant aristocrat from next door.

After my night in St Tropez, I thought Johnny might be the one, and indeed, every time he sends a text or calls, which is most days, I feel like jumping in the air. But looking at Jean-Claude I am no longer so sure. Maybe I should really get in touch with my inner French woman and have both. That would be one way to mark my impending divorce.

We find Colette, who is halfway through the Sauvignon Blanc vineyard, our biggest. When I thank her again for coming at such short notice, she nods and says *"C'est normal"*, which basically means anyone would have done the same, it is correct behaviour. One thing I have learnt after a few months in France is that you know you're in trouble in France when someone tells you *"C'est pas normal*".

We finish the vineyard after another half an hour and I offer everyone a cup of tea on the kitchen terrace in the afternoon sun. We take off our rubber gloves and sit down. Even Jacques the foreman joins us, although I suspect it is only so he can berate me on my ignorance of vines. I cut everyone a slice of a *quatre-quarts* cake I made yesterday.

"I love this terrace," says Jean-Claude. "My grandmother would always have meals here when she could, even in the winter if it was warm enough. Sometimes I thought I could smell her cooking from home."

I don't know if it's the relief of saving the crop or the sunshine or the fact that Jean-Claude has kissed me four times in the same afternoon, but I suddenly feel inexplicably happy. I smile at Colette, who gives me a rare smile back; she actually is very pretty when she smiles.

"Thank you so much," I say in French and then continue in a mixture of the two languages. "I feel very stupid and I can't thank you all enough for saving the day. I just hope there aren't any other nasty surprises around the corner."

"There are always surprises around the corner," says Jean-Claude smiling, "not all of them nasty. But you do need to watch out when it comes to fermentation. That is another potentially very dangerous juncture."

"Why?" I ask in English as Colette and her former father-in-law nip off to solve the problem with my tractor.

Jean-Claude leans closer to me and looks me in the eyes. I find I can't do anything but stare back at him and breathe in the smell of his aftershave, which is a relief after all that sulphur.

"Because fermentation takes place in two stages," he begins softly. "The first one happens immediately, and it is rapid, like a tumultuous love affair. The second one takes place in the spring the year after the first. Extreme heat or cold at any time can interrupt the fermentation and if it has to be re-started the quality of the wine is rarely good."

"Well, I'll be sure to be careful," I say slowly, partly because the way he said 'tumultuous love affair' has sent me into a tailspin, and partly because I had no idea fermentation could be so complicated. How will I ever cope? Trust Nick to run off and leave me with all this. He might just need to be here when it comes to harvest –it's his business too, in the sense that he also paid for it. We have still got to work all that out, but of course he's hardly in a position to demand anything.

The children arrive back with Calypso and her two kids. Colette comes back to join us; Jacques has taken the tractor home for further repairs. We chat and drink tea and listen to the happy sounds of the children tearing around the garden, playing cowboys and Indians. This is what I imagined life in the south of France would be like; sunshine, good friends and happy children. I feel at home.

Rule 17

Remember that nothing tastes as good as thin feels

The French Art of Having Affairs

Since the mildew incident more than three weeks ago, I have been studying my adopted industry with renewed vigour. For example, should anyone happen to ask me what fermentation is while I am standing in the supermarket queue, I will be able to tell them that fermentation is the process by which alcohol is created. It is a little like the process yeast goes through when it rises. Grape juice when left alone ferments naturally to 14 degrees of alcohol and then stops.

I would also be able to tell the, by now rather impressed, shopper that one should never lean over a vat when wine is fermenting in it because breathing in the carbon dioxide created during fermentation can be very dangerous. I have also learnt, among other things, that Château Latour is so famous because it is one of the five first growths in the 1885 classification of red wines.

But perhaps the most surprising thing I have learnt is that all grape juice is white. Amazing. So where does red wine come from you may ask? It becomes red after it comes into contact with the skin of black grapes, as red grapes are called. I have also learned some extraordinary names of grape varieties, like Inzolia, which sounds like a disease to me, and Nerello Mascalese, which could easily be an Italian shoe designer.

But while my knowledge of the wine business is improving, my finances are not. Nick pays me £2000 a month alimony but this has to cover all our costs: the vineyard and us. It is not enough. But he also pays the mortgage so I can't really complain and he can't really do any more.

*

Running a business in France is not as simple as just getting to know your product. You have endless amounts of bureaucratic hassle to deal with, and also the social security people just raid your bank account when they think it's time for you to pay some more of their astronomical social charges. My credit cards are maxed out, as I have had to pay half the bottling in advance on them. And of course I won't have a single bottle of wine ready to sell until early next year. I've stopped looking at my bank account as I can't bear to see the charges going out every time a standing order bounces, making the overdraft bigger every day.

On top of all this is the work running the vineyard, which is a full-time job for at least three people. I still have Colette once a week, but it's not nearly enough. I have given up yoga for the time being in favour of farm-work. It is early May there is so much more to be done than at the beginning of the year. I have never been so fit in my life from lugging vats around and trellising and weeding. I can see how Colette's arms are in such good shape.

"Charlotte, Emily, Edward, it's time to go to school now," I shout. The children have been Skype-ing Nick on my computer most mornings so they can keep in touch. He has been out to see them twice but it is becoming more expensive as summer gets closer, and we both agree we need to save as much money as possible to plough into the vineyard. It is still 30 per cent his business, which is fair enough as he is funding it.

There's still no sign of the children so I run upstairs to get them. "Am I imagining it?" I ask, "or did I ask you to come downstairs?" They all look up at me in a horribly guilty manner.

"What the hell have you done?" I demand. "Have you broken my computer?" I rush round to their side of the desk to see what is going on. And there on my computer screen is a woman with thick dark wavy hair and brown eyes wearing a pale pink suit. She looks very professional.

"I 'ave to go now," she says in a French accent. "*A bientot.* Here's Nick."

Nick comes into view but I switch him off. Very useful thing, Skype.

The children go downstairs and cycle to school without a

murmur. So that was Cécile. I suppose I would have to admit that she's attractive. And thin. Well, what did I expect? What did I imagine she would be like? I suppose I didn't want to imagine anything.

I stomp back though the vineyards in a foul mood. Stealing my husband is one thing, but to ingratiate herself with my children – gggggrrrr.

As I cross onto our lane, the postman comes bombing towards me in his van. He hands me the post, says *Bonjour Madame* and smiles before driving off.

I look through it; more admin and demands for money, plus an official-looking letter from England. I open it, hoping it won't be a tax demand or something equally horrid. It is another letter from the lawyer about the final details of the divorce that need sorting out.

I want to yell at someone, to tear the thing up, to kick and scream and shout and protest. The sight of Cécile talking to my children and the letter in my hand make the whole split so very final, so real, that there is just no way back.

My life, our life, as I knew it is now well and truly over. I have to move on, I need to go forward, but at the moment I just feel like weeping.

I sit down on my doorstep and read through the details of my broken marriage in stark black and white. The visitation rights (makes it sound like we're in a loony bin), my monthly allowance, how Christmas will work from now on (one year the kids are with me and then New Year with him, the following year the other way around). Oh, I am so looking forward to those Christmases alone while he and Cécile get to do the stockings and spend Christmas morning with my children on their bed peeling satsumas and wondering why Father Christmas always insists on putting a brazil nut in the stocking.

This isn't what I wanted, damn it. This isn't how the story was supposed to end.

Rule 18

Body hair is not an option

The French Art of Having Affairs

People always say that things come in threes. London buses, for example, or accidents. But I am still somewhat surprised as a third attractive man strolls into my life.

I get home from the school run with Audrey, who has come for coffee, to find a young man in jeans and a white T-shirt standing on my doorstep.

"Hmmm," I whisper to her. "Maybe he is part of a new 'get over your divorce' programme run by the local council. How very thoughtful of them."

As we approach he smiles and walks towards us. He has what you would call an inviting smile; broad and cheeky.

He looks like he is of Indian descent, with slightly wavy shoulder-length jet-black hair and dark eyes. He is wearing a dark-red and white checked shirt, which is just a tiny bit too tight and shows off a muscular torso. Is that on purpose, I wonder, or did it shrink in the wash? His jeans are black and held up with a black leather belt. He is just a bit taller than me. I would guess he is in his mid-twenties. He reminds me of a less bulked up version of Jacob from *Twilight*.

He holds out his hand. Audrey in typical French fashion kisses him immediately. They are shameless. Looking quite amused, he turns to me.

"Hello, I'm Kamal," he says. "I've come to work for you."

"What?" I say, shaking his outstretched hand. "Why? Doing what?"

"Well, looks like you need some help," he grins, nodding towards my un-weeded vineyards. I am trying to go as organic as I can right from the beginning, the aim being to go totally organic by year two or three. And the weeds love me for it. As does mildew.

I look at Kamal in dismay; much as I would love to have this young man sort out my weeds, it is just not possible.

"I would dearly love to employ you," I begin. "But I just can't afford to take anyone on at the moment."

"No worries," he says. "My salary is paid, I just need a roof over my head. I'm happy to plonk my sleeping bag down in the *cave* or a barn."

He points to his luggage: a rolled-up sleeping bag, a leather bag and what looks like a yoga mat in a thin black tubular cotton bag.

I sense Johnny Fray's involvement here. We have been in constant touch and he knows how frantic and broke I am.

"Who sent you?" I ask. "Where are you from?"

"What does it matter?" Audrey says in French, nudging me but never removing her gaze from Kamal.

"I'm from South Africa. My parents have vineyards close to Cape Town, I've worked with vines since I left school." He smiles. "I'm travelling around Europe for a year and want to get some experience of European vineyards."

"And who is paying you?"

"My employee would prefer to remain anonymous. That's what he told me to say." He gulps and colours slightly. "If it is a he that is."

How like Johnny to be mysterious. I suppose he knew I would say no because I've already rejected his offers of money. But this is different. I can at least pay Johnny back when I start selling the wine, I shouldn't think Kamal's salary is enormous, and if I don't have some time out of the vineyards to focus on how to sell the stuff, none of it will ever be sold. I would be a fool to say no to Kamal. And anyway, Audrey would never forgive me.

"Okay," I say, "you're on. You can live in the spare room until we get the wine-pickers' accommodation sorted out in the barn, which will be one of the jobs you can help me with. I'll show you to your room."

"So, is this your first time in France?" purrs Audrey, sidling up to him. How do French women manage to make such an innocuous question sound like an invitation to spend the afternoon naked in bed discussing *Justine* by the Marquis de Sade?

And another thing. Audrey is wearing jeans and a white T-shirt today, yet she looks incredibly chic. I guarantee you could put me in the same jeans and white T-shirt and I would look scruffy. What's that all about? Another of life's great mysteries, along with what is neutral pelvis and where do odd socks go?

I practically have to drag Audrey out of the spare room so Kamal can unpack in peace.

"You're here on another mission," I remind her. She is going to give my bathroom a makeover, or rather encourage me to continue my makeover by making sure I have the right products to turn me from frumpy to yummy mummy.

Unsurprisingly, nothing in my bathroom impresses her.

"Neutrogena, bah, what is this?" She picks up my moisturiser and eyes it with the same suspicion a turkey might view an invitation to a Christmas feast. I thought I had splashed out — normally I just use Sainsbury's own brand.

She rifles through my bathroom shelf, picking things up and reading the labels on the bottles. After a few minutes she turns to me.

"Is this all?" she asks looking around.

"Yes, why?"

"What do you use to cleanse your face?"

"Well, I have eye make-up remover, and then just water," I tell her.

"Water is not enough, you need a proper cleanser. And where is your exfoliator?"

"My what?"

Audrey sighs. "You should exfoliate at least twice a week; face and body. It removes all the dead skin cells, which if left on your skin create oxidants and are incredibly ageing."

"How do you know all this?"

"As a French woman, the *souci de soi* or personal grooming is something we are brought up with. Creams, lotions, potions, even vitamin supplements are indispensable allies in our battle to look better than all other French women."

"It sounds exhausting. I think I might just surrender here and now."

Audrey laughs. "It's not just about looking good you know. It's about feeling good about yourself too. The more care you take of yourself, the more self-esteem you have. And it really is not that exhausting, it is just a question of habit. Cleansing morning and night, exfoliating twice a week, a mask once a week and a facial once a month. Those are the basics. And you should read a lot. For example, you must get *Madame Figaro* every week. This week there was a wonderful article all about pubic hair."

"What about pubic hair?"

"How it is vanishing."

"Mine was fine last time I looked."

"No, it is no longer acceptable to walk around with a cat between your legs. You need to get it removed. Or at least most of it."

"Why? Says who? Who has the right to tell me what to do with my pubic hair? It's no one else's business."

Audrey shakes her head. "And it will continue to be no one else's business unless you do something about it. And the right is all yours. As the article said, it is your decision whether you want a forest, a formal garden or even *une éminence désertique*. I have gone for the latter and feel much better. But before we deal with your forest or lack of it, we need to go shopping for all the things you are missing."

"But I'm broke," I say. "I can't afford to go buying a lot of expensive creams."

I tell her about the situation with the vineyard and the money Nick is sending to keep us afloat. I am working night and day on the vines and cannot afford to hire any more help. Which also means I can't even think about earning money elsewhere. And who knows how Kamal will work out? Basically we have a very limited amount of cash until I start making money from selling wine. And that's assuming I can sell any wine at all.

Audrey listens in silence and then nods. "I had a client in Paris who was a wine-maker," she says. "He sold wine bonds up front to finance the first year's harvest. Basically he contacted all his friends and contacts and offered them a stake in the production: a certain amount of bottles for a certain amount of money."

"How does that work?"

"Well, how much were you thinking of selling the wine for?"

"Around £7 a bottle, with maybe some higher-quality more barrel-matured reds made from the Cabernet Sauvignon going for around £10 a bottle. The wholesale price would be around £3 per bottle."

Audrey does some mental arithmetic. "So if a case of 12 bottles of, say, the rosé would normally cost £84, the wine-bond holders will get it for £60 because they have paid up front for it. You will have to pay the shipping costs, of course, but you will still be making almost double per case than you would be if you sold it for the wholesale price, which makes a total of £36 per case."

"It's a great idea," I say. "But do you really think people will be interested?"

"That's up to you. You have to make them interested. Now, do you have a pen and paper? I want to make a list of products you need to buy. I think I had better come shopping with you, though, I dread to think what you might end up putting on your face otherwise."

We hear Kamal leave the spare room to go outside.

"He's cute eh?" says Audrey winking at me. "And the location is convenient."

"Don't be ridiculous," I say. "I'm not even divorced yet. I'm not ready to start a relationship with anyone, let alone someone ten years younger than me."

"I wasn't thinking of a relationship," she replies. "But you have to get under someone to get over someone."

When Audrey has gone I get together a list of potential clients and put all their email addresses in a group called 'wine bond'. I put old contacts on there, my mother's ex-husbands (they have to be of some use), friends, all the mums from school in London – heaven knows, most of them could do with a drink – and basically anyone else I can think of who might have an as yet undiscovered yearning to buy some wine from an unknown winemaker.

Once I have been through my whole address book I have fifty-two names on it. It's a start. Then I set about writing the email.

"Be among the first customers to sample this year's vintage

Sainte Claire," I begin. "This exclusive offer is only for friends and family. You can purchase wine bonds for the red, white and rosé wines. These bonds will translate to wine once it is bottled and ready. The cost will be £60 a case as opposed to £84, delivery to your home included."

As I write the last bit I say a silent prayer that none of the takers live in Scotland.

"Sign up for this exclusive wine bond and you could be drinking…." Help. I need a name for my wine. What should I call it? Château Sainte Claire? Bit dull. Château Sophie's Plonk? Not that appealing.

Just then my mobile phone peeps. It is a message from Jean-Claude.

'I see you have a new *vigneron*,' it reads. 'If I didn't know you prefer older men, I might be jealous, x'

I laugh and send him a message back, suggesting he come for dinner. I press send and almost simultaneously the name of my wine comes to me: The Arrogant Frog.

I am supposed to be cooking dinner but keep having to run upstairs to check my emails. At last at 6pm I have one response, from Johnny.

'Hey gal,' it reads, 'put me down for £2000. This is a great idea, will pass it on to some mates. Love ya'.

"Yipppppeeeeeee!" I yell so loudly that the children all come running upstairs. "We've sold our first wine." I am jumping around the room in a state of total excitement.

"Is that all?" says Charlotte, and they all trundle back downstairs.

Who would have thought that my computer, which was such a source of irritation earlier today, could bring me such joy?

And what a hero Johnny is. I email him immediately: "Thank you for everything," I write. "Love Cunningham xxx."

He emails back "Three xxx's? I might have to buy another £2k's worth! xxx"

Johnny's other godsend, Kamal, is already working away brilliantly and has got rid of the major weeds in the biggest vineyard. We're never going to get rid of all of them, but the big ones take the nourishment from the soil that we want going to the vine to create a juicy, flavoursome grape.

By the end of the week I will have Johnny's money in the bank, which will pay for wine labels. These of course have yet to be designed, and I still need to buy all sorts of tools still needed for the upcoming harvest. But as of now my vineyard is a business, which it wasn't a few hours ago. Because in a business you need customers, and now that I have one, I can imagine getting more. Even if Johnny is likely to be by far the most generous.

I feed the children before Jean-Claude shows up. I know the French are all for eating together as a family, but if I am going to get to know him better I need to give him my undivided attention.

"Is Jean-Claude your boyfriend like Cécile is Daddy's girlfriend?" asks Edward, mid-lasagne. "Are you going to kiss on the lips?"

"No," I say rather too loudly. "Of course not."

"Is Johnny your boyfriend?" asks Emily. "Did you kiss him on the lips?"

"No," I lie.

Johnny and Jean-Claude. Which one would I choose? According to Audrey, I should get on and decide if I'm going to get over Nick. But it is an impossible decision; they are so very different. Like Roquefort and Brie. Johnny being the Roquefort, of course, and Jean-Claude being the smooth, creamy Brie.

"You had better get a boyfriend," Emily interrupts my thoughts. "Otherwise you will be alone."

"Yes," nods Edward. "I've got a girlfriend."

"Have you?" I ask. "Is she French?"

"Yes," Charlotte butts in before he has time to answer. "She is. She's called Juliette and they are always in the playground together."

"We are not," screams Edward. "We are not." Then he runs out of the room. We clearly touched a sensitive subject here. I run after him to calm him down, giving Charlotte an old-fashioned stern look as I leave.

He agrees to come back with the promise of a sliced apple and some ice-cream.

Peace has been re-established when Kamal pokes his head around the kitchen door.

"Hiya. I'm just off to the local bar. Do you need anything from the village?" he asks.

He really is a lovely-looking boy with that thick wavy black hair that he is constantly running his fingers through, and his smooth skin. Sarah would love him.

"No thanks," I say. "Have fun."

"Oh, by the way, I do yoga in the mornings, so don't be surprised if you wake up to find me in a strange position on the terrace outside the kitchen," he adds.

"Mummy does yogo," says Edward.

"Do you?" asks Kamal. "Well why don't you join me? I used to teach back home. I've done it all my life."

"Thanks, I'd love to. What time?"

"Shall we say seven?"

"Perfect." I say, smiling. He smiles back and heads off. Am I imagining it, or did he wink? For goodness sake – he's practically closer to my children's age than mine. Roquefort, Brie and possibly a bit of *chèvre frais*?

"What's *chèvre frais*?" asks Charlotte.

Did I say that out loud? "Unaged goat's cheese. Would you like some?"

"No."

"Thank you." I add for her.

"Do you miss Daddy?" asks Emily, tweaking her cat's ears. "I do."

"Me too," say the others.

"I do," I say, and it's true. I've been so frantic lately, what with the vineyard together with washing, ironing, cooking, shopping and everything else that goes with looking after a family, that I have hardly had time to think about it. But when I do, I still feel a deep sadness that it ended like it did. Our relationship may not have been the most exciting thing ever, but there was nothing really that wrong with it. Well clearly there was, as Nick went off with Cécile.

But I'm determined to do well. If the business takes off, other things will follow, I'm sure. Talking of which, I wonder if I have had any more takers of my Arrogant Frog wine bond.

"Charlotte, you're in charge of clearing up," I say.

"Why is she always in charge?" groans Emily.

"She's not. But she is right now. I need to pop upstairs. You must all help put the dishes in the dishwasher. I'll be back in ten minutes."

I nip into my bedroom and have what I call a flash-shower: cold (very anti-ageing according to Audrey) and lasting less than a minute. I have a brief look at my pubes as I'm drying. Hmmmm. Maybe *Madame Figaro* has a point. It could be time to do some harvesting down there. I pull on my white trousers and black top from St Tropez. I put some make-up on and then go and check my messages. I have had three more responses, one from Sarah.

"Okay, put me down for £100, sweetpea. But more importantly – oh Soph, I am now well and truly gone. Mr Enormous is a god. We see each other about once a week, maybe twice in a good week, and it is literally the time with him that I am living for now. I am so addicted. Remember I told you about the first time? We went back to my place, got naked in bed and he turned to me, looked me deep in the eyes and said 'Are we really going to do this?' and I nodded and we went for it and it was like…. It was like coming home. He and I are just the MOST perfect fit. It was incredible. He filled me in a way no one has ever done. I don't mean just because of his enormous – you know, obviously that helps. But I feel so complete with him. It is totally out of this world (and I speak as a woman who has had many out of this world experiences). You know how normally you have sex and you think, well, this is all fine, and then there are some bits that are better than others and at some stages you actually find yourself wondering if the rain has stopped and you could hang the washing out? Well every damn time with Enormous is PURE ECTASY from start to finish. It is unbelievable. Of course the awful thing is I will never want to sleep with anyone else, and before you say 'I told you so'" – she was right, the words were forming in my mouth – "I KNOW it was stupid, but you know what? I wouldn't have missed these past few months for anything, even if I spend the rest of my life longing for a similar feeling again. Call me when you get a chance. How is the sexy Frenchman? How is the work coming along? Lucy, Carla and I are all keen to come out for the harvest."

There are two other acceptances. One of my mother's ex-husbands has agreed to buy three cases, one of each. I must tell her that her ex-husbands are of some use; she will be so pleased. Then there is a message from Carla, who orders ten cases.

"I'm so much better off since Peter and I got divorced," she writes. "I have a huge alimony settlement; I get to keep the house too. Added to which I can sleep with as many tennis coaches as I like without him bothering me about it. What's not to like?"

I run down he stairs shouting "I am a wine-making, wine-selling mummy, yiippeeeee!", straight into the arms of Jean-Claude.

"What a warm welcome," he says kissing me on both cheeks. "What have I done to deserve this?"

"Oh, so sorry," I bluster. "It's just that I have sold some wine and I got a bit over-excited."

"How have you sold some wine without even making any?" he asks, looking rather puzzled.

I explain about the wine bond.

"I see. Well, maybe I'll have to invest in some bonds myself."

"That would be lovely," I say, "but surely you have enough wine?"

He smiles. "It is always good to know what the competition is up to."

We walk into the kitchen, where Charlotte is taking full advantage of being in charge.

"No, Edward, I told you, in the dishwasher," she is saying. "Emily, bring me the drying-up cloth, please."

"Ah, a foreman in the making," says Jean-Claude. "She will come in useful for the family wine business. *Ca va, les enfants?*"

As is the custom in France, the children all come and kiss Jean-Claude hello. He speaks to them in French and they respond in French. I look at my beautiful bi-lingual children and am so proud of them. Jean-Claude strokes Emily's cat's ears, which makes her purr. They look angelic for once, and they have also done quite a good job of clearing up.

"Right. Now Emily will be in charge of bath time, and Edward," I say before he can start wailing about how unfair life is, "you will be in charge of choosing the DVD after the bath."

They all seem very happy with this arrangement and traipse off.

"I will be up in ten minutes to check on you," I say as they go.

Then I pour us both a glass of wine. It is a Viognier, the same white grape that I have, made by a Swiss lady who lives about half an hour away. It is more expensive than mine will be, retailing at just under £10. Jean-Claude and I both automatically swirl the glass to smell the aromas, a habit I have picked up not to look pretentious but to try to determine what actually makes one wine more agreeable to drink than another so I can try to do the same with mine.

We take a sip. "*Pas mal,*" says Jean-Claude. "Undertones of honey, a rich nose, and a clean finish."

I couldn't agree more – at least I think I couldn't agree more. I have another sip. Yes, now he's mentioned honey I can see what he means. It certainly tastes *good*. But I'm going to have to work on my tasting skills.

We sit down at the table that still has a few crumbs from the children's dinner on it. I automatically start to wipe them off into my hand. Jean-Claude takes hold of my wrist and looks at me.

"Relax," he says. "This is not a formal dinner, is it? I would rather talk to you than watch you clear up. Tell me about your wine. What are you going to call it?"

I smile as I remember the inspiration for the name. "The Arrogant Frog," I say.

Jean-Claude laughs and claps his hands. "I love it," he says. "And of course you need separate names for the red, white and rosé. Something like – let me think – Lily Pad White?"

"That's a great idea," I say. "Let me write that down." I grab a pen and paper. "What about the red?" I ask. "Tell you what. I'll go and check on the children and we'll see who has the best name by the time I get back."

I go upstairs and come back a few minutes later with the children. They all go into the sitting room and Edward tells me he chose *Spiderman Three* but Charlotte and Emily both said they would give him one of their Saturday sweets if they could watch *The Little Mermaid* instead. It frightens me how manipulative those girls can be; I reckon between them they could get anyone to do just about anything.

I walk back into the kitchen. Jean-Claude is doodling on the piece of paper. He has drawn a very arrogant-looking frog dressed a bit like Mr Fox in *The Tale of Jemima Puddleduck* (except for the beret) leaning against a bottle of wine.

"That's great," I say leaning over his shoulder. "And what about the name?"

"Ribet Red," he says.

"Brilliant. I can't beat that. In fact I hadn't even thought of one, sorry. But I will now turn my attention to the rosé while I put the spinach on."

"So what great English delicacies are you feeding me this evening? It will be the first time I have dined *à l'Anglaise* in this house."

"I am feeding you that famous English delicacy called *pommes dauphinoise*," I laugh. "And steak and spinach."

"Delicious. You really are a talented lady: wine-maker, mother, cook and marketing genius. You know, you have really done well with that name; it is funny, charming and above all memorable. The wine business is so competitive. I think nowadays 50 per cent of your success depends on how well you can market your wine."

"So the rosé…." I begin. "I think it should have the word pink in it, women love pink and I'm sure it is one of the reasons we all drink rosé."

"Agreed," says Jean-Claude.

"I guess I could just stay simple," I continue. "Sort of consolidate the brand by calling it Lily Pad Pink? What do you think?"

"I like it," he says. "Very good brand reinforcement."

"Great, that's that done. Now, how do you like your steak cooked?"

"*Saignant*, of course, like any French gentleman," he laughs. "I suppose you will have yours totally overcooked?"

I nod and put my steak in the pan first. "I have not yet gone native."

"Please never do," he smiles and looks me in the eye. "I like you the way you are."

I feel something like a fillip of joy in the pit of my stomach – or maybe I'm just very hungry.

The minute I serve the potatoes I notice they are undercooked. Damn. What with rushing every two minutes to see if I've sold any more wine, I didn't notice I was cooking them at too low a temperature. I apologise to Jean-Claude before he takes a bite and breaks his teeth on them.

"Oh, I prefer them undercooked," he says smoothly, taking a large mouthful of what is more or less raw potatoes in warm cream.

Is this the world's most charming man?

We eat and chat about village life, the school. Jean-Claude went to primary school here before being sent off to a Paris to complete his education, which he hated. He longed to come back to the sunshine, wide-open spaces, his English nanny and the vineyards of the Languedoc.

The Little Mermaid has swum away and the children come into the kitchen. I tell them to say goodnight to Jean-Claude.

They approach him individually and his face lights up.

"*Bonne nuit, ma puce*," he says to Charlotte and kisses her. He strokes Emily's hair and says the same to her. "*Bonne nuit, mon brave*," he says to Edward.

"Do you speak English?" Emily asks him.

"Yes, *bien sûr*," he laughs. "But you all speak French, *non?*"

They nod.

"Well, French is easier for me, because I am French," he goes on in his native tongue. "So, if you don't mind, we could all be French speakers together? And I will tell you stories about the mischief I got up to in this very house when I was your age."

He sounds so sexy. I mean he sounds sexy speaking English with a very slight French accent, but when he speaks French, the way those r's roll off the tongue, it's enough to make me want to kiss him goodnight too.

"You lived here?" says Charlotte. "How?"

"I didn't live here, but my grandmother did, and she was lovely. I used to visit her every day. Next time I come over, I will tell you a bedtime story in French that she used to tell me. How would that be?"

"Superb," says Emily, but she says it in French. She is also able to roll her r's. I'm hoping it's genetic but so far have not managed it.

"Okay, my little Frenchies, upstairs now and brush your teeth. I'll come up and put you to bed," I say. Miraculously they do as they are told. As they walk out, Jean-Claude lets out a long sigh.

"What is it?" I ask.

"Oh nothing, it's just, well, *quand on n'a pas d'enfants, on n'a pas d'enfants,*" he says, looking sad.

"But surely you could have children? There must be lots of women keen to marry a French aristo and bring little heirs into the world?"

He looks at me. "Maybe, but not many I'm keen to marry."

"Is that why you're not married yet?"

"You think I am too old to be single?" he laughs. "Of course you have a point. I am forty-one and I should be settled by now, as my mother keeps telling me."

"So why aren't you?"

He looks down at the floor, shuffles his feet slightly and takes a deep breath. "I was very much in love," he says in staccato tones, as if the words hurt him to say. "She was English, like you. We were together for many years. I thought we would get married and live happily ever after. It was not to be."

"Oh I'm so sorry," I say. "What did she die of?" I know it might be a rude question but I'm always desperate to know what people die of so I can avoid the same fate.

Jean-Claude looks surprised. "Oh she's not dead," he says and then adds. "It's worse than that."

"Worse than death? That must be bad."

"It is," says Jean-Claude, clenching his fist. "She ran off with my brother."

I pour him another glass of red wine. These French and their family feuds — you couldn't make them up.

"Ah, I see. Sorry to hear that. I can see that must be quite irritating."

"It was extremely irritating," he says, sipping his wine. "But maybe I will still get my revenge."

I can't quite decide whether or not he is joking.

"I'll be back in a few minutes," I say and go up to kiss the children goodnight.

"Hey baby," I say to Edward.

"Hey Mummy," he replies.

"Is Daddy coming tomorrow?" he asks.

"He is," I reply, sitting on the edge of his bed. "Are you excited?"

"Yes, I keep remembering all the things we used to do and missing him."

I feel like weeping. I hug him and tell him tomorrow he can do all sorts of things with him and that then soon they are going to England to be with him for a whole week.

"But then I'll miss you," says my darling little boy.

"I know, Ed, but I will be here, waiting to see you again. And you'll have your sisters with you."

"They're mean to me sometimes," he says.

I nod. "They're mean to me sometimes too, like when they fight, or won't go to bed. But mostly they're nice, aren't they?"

Edward thinks for a moment. "No," he says. "Mostly they're

mean."

I laugh. So does he.

"I love you, darling boy, sleep well."

"Love you Mummy," he says and turns over to hug his Spiderman bear. I go and kiss the girls.

"Have you brushed your teeth?" I ask, leaning over Emily to kiss her goodnight.

"Yes, smell," she says, breathing all over me.

"Smell me too," shouts Charlotte. I do and then kiss her goodnight.

As I walk back downstairs it strikes me that when my children are being sweet there really is nothing nicer. I suddenly feel very lucky, in spite of the divorce and the stress of running the vineyard, being constantly broke and having too much pubic hair. And what is more, there's a handsome Frenchman with slim hips and a penchant for undercooked potatoes waiting for me downstairs.

I resist the temptation to check my emails for more wine orders and join Jean-Claude in the sitting room, where he is looking through my books. I hope all the Jilly Coopers are upstairs. Actually, being French he probably wouldn't know who she is. He might think she is some Booker Prize winner. Which of course she ought to be.

"Coffee?" I ask.

"Yes, please," he says turning around. He really is very elegant – the way he moves and holds himself is just so, well, aristocratic. Actually, he reminds me a bit of Rupert Campbell-Black.

I nip to the kitchen and come back with two coffees. We sit

on the sofa. Suddenly I feel quite shy. If this were in England we would have had another glass of wine and things would have flowed more easily; we would have talked without inhibitions or possibly fallen on top of each other. But here in France one doesn't drink after dinner – it is just not seen as *normal*. So I sit soberly on the sofa sipping my coffee and wondering what is going to happen next.

We finish our coffee and chat a bit more about the vineyard and then Jean-Claude gets up to go. I watch him rather longingly, but that could be because I am feeling vulnerable and a bit lonely.

"Thank you for a lovely evening, Sophie," he says. "I hope to see you again very soon."

"It was a pleasure, thank you for all your help."

We walk to the door and he kisses me on both cheeks but very close to my lips. I tremble slightly.

"*Bonne nuit, ma petite vigneronne anglaise,*" he says gently, and then walks away.

As I head upstairs and set my alarm in good time for my yoga class in the morning, I reflect that it is not so bad getting divorced if you have three gorgeous men around to take your mind off things. Not so much a side-salad but a full-blown *tricolore*.

Rule 19

You are programmed to seduce

The French Art of Having Affairs

I check my emails before the yoga. There are no more messages, which makes me feel like weeping. It all started so well. But maybe people are thinking about it? I hope so. Because less than £3000 is not going to be enough to fund the harvest.

How do other people do this? Maybe they have a start-up capital. We have some money from selling the house, but it is still being decided how it is going to be split because of the divorce.

"Sophie?" Kamal is at the door to my office wearing tracksuit bottoms and a white T-shirt. He has tied his hair back. "Stop looking so worried. Remember your yoga practice begins even before you get to class," he says calmly. "See you on the terrace."

He's right – frazzled and stressed is no way to go into a yoga session. I breathe deeply in then out through my nose. I will just have to deal with the finances of the vineyard after my downward dogs.

On the terrace outside the kitchen I find Kamal sitting with his eyes closed, cross-legged on a blue yoga mat. In fact he is not cross-legged, I see on closer inspection: he has his feet on his thighs. I think it is what is called the lotus position. You could leave me in a room for several years with nothing else to do and I still don't think I would manage to do it. There is incense burning and a small brass elephant next to the incense. I clearly had it all wrong – I just dived into a pose whenever I had a chance. This is all very professional.

Kamal opens his eyes and looks at me. "Sit down in any comfortable cross-legged position," he begins. "We will start by centering ourselves. Bring your hands palms together in front of your heart. We are not praying; although you may have noticed the God Ganesh is with us, he is here more to create the right ambiance for our practice. Focus on your breath, try to make your in and out breaths equal in length."

I do as he says and begin to relax. His voice is lovely, his accent somewhere between Indian and Antipodean. After the centering we start the asanas, as he tells me they are called. I don't think I was even doing yoga before. This is so much harder. During the sun salutations (of which we do sixteen on each side) I even start lightly perspiring. After those we move into triangle and warrior poses.

"Do you mind if I adjust you?" says Kamal at one stage, looking at my triangle pose.

"Not at all," I say to the sky, as my head is upside down. He stands behind me and puts one hand on my buttock and the other on my outstretched arm.

"Take a deep breath," he tells me. I do as he says. "Good, now breathe out slowly."

As I breathe he pushes my buttocks and hips away from him and pulls my outstretched arm towards him. I find my body moving into a perfect triangle, I feel strong and invigorated, as well as slightly embarrassed. But I do begin to understand what it means to breathe into a pose, which all the websites I looked at tell you is essential. Kamal helps me with my sitting twists and forward bends too, gently easing me into position.

At one stage I sneak a look at him doing a seated forward bend. His head is resting on his knees, whereas I can barely reach my shins with my hands. Infuriating. I sigh and try to push myself further down.

"Yoga is not a competitive sport, Sophie," says Kamal, still with his head on his knees. How on earth did he know I was checking him out? "We all do what we do within our limitations and that is good enough."

At the end of the practice we have a relaxation, which is slightly interrupted by the children yelling at me because they couldn't find me. I thank Kamal.

"You're welcome, I practise most mornings; you are always welcome to come along."

"I ought to be paying you extra for the private lessons," I smile.

He shakes his head. "The gift of yoga is free," he says and then with a "*namaste*" he is off to get ready for work.

After breakfast the children and I drive to meet Nick at

Montpellier airport. I suppose to an outsider we must look like any normal happy family; three children excitedly trying to peek in through the arrival doors every time someone comes out to see if they can glimpse him. Their mother watching them and waiting for her loving husband.

Except this loving husband is arriving with his even more loving mistress. Oh yes, we're so mature now that we are all going to be jolly polite and act as if nothing is wrong at all. So instead of saying 'Hello, you must be Cécile, the bitch who stole my husband and broke up my family', I will shake her hand and say 'Nice to meet you', even though it's most certainly not. Okay, so I may have spent yesterday evening with a handsome French aristo and very nice it was too, and the week before getting drunk with a film star, but all that aside, poor Edward saying how much he missed Nick made me think that, if I could turn the clock back, I would much rather we were all together.

Dining with a French aristo and hanging out with Johnny is obviously just my extremely resourceful way of dealing as best I can with a bad situation. And I should be commended for making such an effort to adapt to the local culture of having affairs. Something my husband – sorry, soon-to-be ex-husband, obviously did before he even got here. Talk about forward-planning.

I may not be keen to meet his mistress, but I am looking forward to seeing what this vamp looks like in the flesh. Thank God I went on my 'Lose your husband and your love-handles' diet. I am wearing the black outfit from St Tropez; black for mourning my dead marriage, rather like Victoria Beckham when she showed up the day after the news about her husband and Rachel Loos broke wearing virginal white.

"There he is," shrieks Charlotte, running towards Nick. The others follow. I watch him from a discreet distance as he kneels down to scoop them all up and cover them with kisses. Then I turn my gaze to the woman at his side. Fuck! – she's thinner than me, and beautiful. Great. Stealing my husband may be forgivable, but being thinner and more beautiful than me is not.

She smiles at the children as Nick introduces them. She looks a little bit like a young Anna Wintour, with a perfect bob and lovely skin. She is extremely well-groomed in that way that French women are famous for. She is wearing jeans and loafers and a very pale pink silk shirt and blue and pink silk scarf. Her shoes and bag are clearly designer.

She seems a bit high maintenance for Nick – they look rather odd together I think. If you saw them at a party, you certainly wouldn't think they belonged together. Although I can see she has tried to smarten him up a bit; he has had a haircut and is wearing chinos and a Ralph Lauren polo shirt. Oh please! Since when does Nick wear fucking Ralph Lauren? He would only have heard of him if he played for Chelsea.

"Hi Soph," he says. He seems unsure of whether to kiss me hello or not, so does nothing.

"Er, this is Cécile," he adds, motioning to his mistress.

Cécile smiles and holds out her hand. I could be really immature and refuse to shake it, but I am Miss Mature so I shake the hand that has spent the last few months caressing my husband.

"Hello," she says, "it's good to meet you, Sophie."

"You too," I lie, forcing a smile. "Well, have fun you lot. I must dash, busy at the vineyard. See you here tomorrow evening at 7pm?"

"Yes, thanks a million Soph, saves us a lot of driving," says Nick smiling at me. "We'll call you from Uzès to say goodnight, won't we, kids?"

"Yes," shout the children jumping up and down. I kiss them goodbye.

'Don't like her too much and don't hold her hand and try to spill some food down her shirt,' I want to whisper to them, but of course I don't. Instead I leave the airport, not daring to glance back in case they are looking too happy.

As I drive towards the house I see Kamal running like a madman towards me. He is a different beast to the Zen yogi of this morning. What the hell is going on? At least I know the house isn't on fire; I can see it from here.

He pounces on my car like a wild animal, standing in front of it with both hands on the bonnet. I get out.

"What the hell are you doing? Lucky I was driving slowly, I could have killed you."

He is so out of breath, he can hardly speak.

"Kamal, calm down, what's going on?"

"Great news," he pants. "Fabulous news, quick, drive to the *cave*." He gets in the passenger seat.

"Kamal, have you finally lost the plot? Breathe," I tell him.

"I'm so excited," he says as I do as he says, "Okay, park here. Come on, let's go."

He leaps out of the car. I get out and follow him in. We walk right to the back of the *cave* where, until he fixed them yesterday, there were no lights. Inside there is an enormous steel vat with a ladder going up the outside.

"Follow me," says Kamal, climbing up it.

"I can't," I say.

He turns around. "What the hell do you mean, you can't?"

"I'm scared of heights." I tell him, feeling utterly pathetic.

He comes back down. "Okay, here's what we'll do. You go first, and I will go behind, and so there is no risk of you falling."

I must look horrified.

"And I won't look at your backside," he smiles.

Yeah, right.

"Can't you just tell me what's up there?"

"Sophie, if you want to be a wine-maker you're going to have to be able to climb up to the vats, that's just part of the job."

He has a point. I look up at the vat and feel the palms of my hands go clammy at the thought of going up there. I take a deep breath and put my foot on the first rung of the ladder. Then the second and third. I look back to make sure Kamal is there. He is at the bottom, grinning.

"I'm not climbing up until there's a bit more distance between us, I don't want to be accused of sexual harassment on a ladder. Now stop looking down and get moving up."

"For someone so young you're quite bossy," I tell him.

"It comes from being the oldest in a family of five."

I do as he says, gingerly climbing the ladder. When I get to the top he joins me. I am beyond nervous now. What if the ladder collapses under our joint weight?

"Kamal, what is all this about?" I ask, clinging to the vat. My knuckles are white.

"Close your eyes," he says.

"I might fall off."

"Just hold on and close your eyes. Pretend you're in that film *Titanic*," he laughs. I do as he says. I hear him move something. "Okay, open your eyes."

I do as he says. "Look in the vat," he urges. "What do you see?"

"Nothing, it's empty," I say. My eyes adjust to the light.

"Look again."

I do, and now I see what he's so excited about. The vat is not empty; it is full to the brim with deep, red wine.

"Kamal, that's great, but it's probably vinegar. It must have been here for years."

"No," he says, grabbing my arm, making me even more nervous. "That's just what I thought, but Sophie, it isn't vinegar, it's fully matured, deep, aromatic Cabernet Sauvignon. Sure we're going to have to blend it to make it really drinkable, but the fundamentals are there for about 2000 bottles of really top-end wine."

"Nooo." I almost fall off the ladder, happily towards the wine and not away from it

Kamal catches me.

"Wow, that's amazing," I say. "This could save us, assuming we can sell it that is. So what do we do next?"

"First we get you down from here and then we'll make a

plan," laughs Kamal, closing the lid and moving down the ladder. "But I reckon you could be talking about a retail value of say £15 a bottle, so wholesale £7 or so. In the worst case scenario, you could end up with around £14,000. But punters love aged Cabernet Sauvignon, it's one of the most popular grapes so you might be able to sell it retail. As soon as we have it blended and get some of it bottled we should get a sign up advertising wine-tasting and sales."

I get down to the bottom of the vat. Solid ground feels good.

"You're so sweet to be so enthusiastic about this," I say. "You've only been here a couple of days."

"Oh that's just me," says Kamal, patting the vat affectionately. "I always throw myself into things 100 per cent. My parents always taught us all there is no point otherwise."

We go into the house to look up some tips on blending Cabernet Sauvignon. Kamal has done a little bit of blending before but is nervous about the huge quantity we're talking about here.

It is hard to find anything concrete. I wonder if Jean-Claude could help, but from what he has told me they employ wine-makers to do the blending. I guess I could ask him if I can talk to the people he uses. I suggest this to Kamal.

"Don't worry," he says. "I'll call my parents and talk to our wine-makers at home about it. Can I use the phone please?"

"Of course," I say. "Here you sit at the desk and take notes, I'll go and look in the wine books I have downstairs."

That afternoon I have a sleep. This is my idea of ultimate luxury: to go up to bed after lunch, lie on the covers and listen to the sounds of nature while slowly dozing off, thinking about nothing in particular.

I am dreaming about bottles of wine when an almost deafening noise makes me sit bolt upright in bed. It sounds like the opening sequence to *Apocalypse Now* – only a thousand times louder than in the cinema. I run to my terrace and look outside. It is coming from behind the house. What is going on? Am I under attack? I can't see where the noise is coming from.

I run downstairs and out of the back door. On the far-away lawn, a blue helicopter with a white nose is landing. Out of it steps Johnny Fray carrying a large box. He puts his head down and runs towards the house as the helicopter's propeller slows down.

"Hi Cunningham," he smiles when he sees me. "I heard from your mother they were all away for the weekend and thought you might be a bit lonely. I brought dinner with me, and champagne."

"Lovely to see you," I smile. "You're a bit like the Milk Tray man aren't you? Jumping out of helicopters on lonely women's lawns."

It is lovely to see him; he looks good – more Heathcliff than Rochester, but anywhere between the two is fine with me. A date with a French aristo one night and a film star the next; how did my life suddenly get so exciting? I just hope the former doesn't show up tonight. This could all get very complicated. But I have in no way committed to either one or promised anyone anything. As things stand, I am soon to be single and keeping my options open.

"I thought I would come and claim those three kisses in

person," he says putting the box down and hugging me. "Let's put the champagne on ice."

"Yes, we have something to celebrate."

We go inside and I tell him all about the vat of wine. "Kamal is such a great find, Thanks so much. You've no idea what a difference he's made, even in just a couple of days. And he even teaches me yoga."

Johnny looks confused. "Who's Kamal?"

"The *vigneron* you sent me," I say. Has he gone senile since we met last? "You know, the Indian South African boy who is in Europe to learn about wine-making. He said you're paying his salary and he was here to help me."

"He said that?" Johnny looks even more confused.

"Well, no he didn't mention you by name, but he said someone was paying his wages who wanted to remain anonymous and I just automatically thought it was you, you've been so great about helping and…."

Johnny shakes his head and smiles. "It's not me, Cunningham, must be one of your other admirers."

"How very bizarre. I wonder who it is then," I say, taking the champagne and putting it in the fridge. "I just can't think who else would do that for me; I can't work out who else has the money and the imagination to do that sort of thing. It just seemed like such a 'you' gesture."

"Well, I promise it's not me," says Johnny, and I believe him; he's scarily honest.

We go for a walk in the afternoon sun. Johnny tells me all about the new film he is making in Prague and the other stars. It is so funny hearing about them all first-hand like this, hearing what their little habits and foibles are. You always assume they are somehow special and different, but of course they're just people. Once, when I was around nine years old and madly and utterly in love with some member of a boy band, my mother said to me one day, "You know, every morning, he gets up and goes to the loo, just like everybody else." I didn't believe her.

"You've really landed on your feet here, Cunningham," says Johnny, "it's a lovely place. So peaceful, so far removed from everything. You're happy aren't you? In spite of Nick and everything that's happened?"

"I am, yes, I mean, it's been tough at times and the children really miss him, but I love it here. Not a day goes by without me appreciating it. Even if it's bloody hard work."

"I envy you," says Johnny.

"Don't be ridiculous," I say. "You've got everything: fame, fortune, women in every country."

"Don't believe everything you read in the papers," he laughs. "No, but seriously, acting is quite a tough life too. I travel pretty much every week, I'm never in one place long enough to have a proper relationship, and the fame is pretty crap really when it comes down to it. It can be fun, of course, but basically the public puts you up there and they're just waiting for you to fall down with a bump, either with a bad film, or some sex scandal, or hopefully both."

"What, like trying to seduce a married drunken mother of three in St Tropez?"

He chuckles. "You really were rat-arsed Cunningham, I could

have had my wicked way with you."

"It would have been necrophilia," I smile.

"Well, I only brought the one bottle of champagne for this evening, as opposed to your habitual seven or eight," he says, smiling back at me. "Shall we try to stay just a tad more sober than last time?"

I nod and agree that would be a very good idea.

I take him on a tour of the vineyard, showing him my olive tree, the vines and the vat filled with the valuable Cabernet Sauvignon. I even brave the ladder again and stay relatively calm.

I'm amazed at how much I have learned in a few months; I sound quite knowledgeable. It is now early July; I have been a *vigneron* for almost seven months. I know things I would never have imagined I would ever need to know, like how to start a tractor or that a kilo of grapes makes a bottle of wine or that the *Guide Hachette des Vins de France* is the book to make it into if you're going to become the new Château Lafite.

The *Guide Hachette*, the wine-bible, is compiled by a huge team of wine experts who blind taste more than 30,000 wines from all over France. Only around 9,000 make it into the guide. The wines are rated with one (good), two (excellent) or three (exceptional) stars, or a wine can be awarded one of 450 *coups de Coeur*, which automatically means you're going to sell well, as wine merchants and consumers often buy wines purely on the basis of the guide.

We bump into Kamal in one of the vineyards, where he is working on the trellising. Not a flicker of recognition passes between the two men.

When we're out of earshot, Johnny leans close to me and says:

"Just for the record, if I was going to send some young stud to work for you, he certainly wouldn't be as fit as that. Are you sure it's not your mother's way of helping you get over Nick?"

"No, I think she thinks that's your job judging by the phone calls to you," I smile. "I just can't imagine who it can be, but I can't do without him now, although knowing it's not you makes me uncomfortable. But harvest is less than two months away and there is still masses to do. He will just have to stay with his anonymous donor, unless I can get him drunk one night and make him spill the beans."

"You'd probably pass out before he did," laughs Johnny. "Talking of which," he looks at his watch, "it's ten minutes past drinks deadline. Let's go and crack open the champagne. Shall we have a glass on that lovely outside terrace by the kitchen?"

I get the glasses and Johnny gets the champagne. "What are we drinking to?" I ask as he pours us both a glass.

"To a grand vintage, Cunningham. Here's to your successful wine business. And I have two grand in my back pocket for your wine bond. If that doesn't make you want to get into my trousers, nothing will," he grins.

I laugh and raise my glass. "Now you're talking. And here's to you, Johnny, even if you didn't send me Kamal, you have been a truly great friend."

"As I always say, life throws at you many things."

"But few true friends," I interrupt him. "One day you'll write a book with all your homespun wisdom."

"Oh, you mock me Cunningham, but I have been asked to."

"So why don't you?"

"I'm fucking dyslexic," he laughs. "How am I supposed to write a book?"

I nip inside to get some peanuts and olives to nibble on. When I get back Johnny tells me Nick called when I was gone.

"I told him you'd call him back," he says. "He sounded quite surprised to hear my voice."

"I bet he was," I say. "He probably thinks I waited to get rid of the kids and then sneaked you in here, like it's any of his business. But I need to call him. He said they would call to say goodnight."

"Go on, Cunningham, send them my love."

I call Nick's mobile and Charlotte answers. She says they are having a lovely time and asks to speak to Johnny. Then of course the others have to speak to Johnny too. He is lovely with them, asking them questions and chatting.

He hands me the phone; Edward is on the line.

"Hey baby," I say.

"Hey Mummy," he replies.

"How is everything?"

"Lovely. We're having so much fun. We played swords in the garden of the hotel and went for a walk and saw a big pig and now we're getting room service."

He chats on about their day then I say goodnight to him and the girls.

"Charlotte asked me to be her godfather," Johnny says laughing after I hang up. "She's got her head screwed on, that girl. She asked if I was rich and famous and I said 'quite' and then she said would I be her godfather and that it was very important to have rich godparents in case you ever need some money. Then the others asked if they could be my godchildren too. I agreed of course, I can't say no to them, they're adorable."

"Oh you don't know what you've taken on," I laugh. "Be very careful what you agree to."

"I'd like to take on more," says Johnny, suddenly looking very serious. He tops up our champagne. "You know, Cunningham, none of this success really means anything if you have no one to share it with. I'd like to settle down. I'm thirty-five now. It's time to find the person I'm going to spend the rest of my life with and start a family. Or even take on a family. Although I would like to experience having a baby – I mean, not personally, but being really intimate with a woman who is carrying my child; watching her progress, grow, become a mother, seeing the changes in her body. I bet you were really sexy when you were pregnant, Cunningham."

"I was quite, well, fat really," I say, embarrassed by the attention and also slightly scared as to where this might be leading. "I'm not sure it suited me, like it suits some women who just seem to get a neat little bump and not put on an ounce of weight anywhere else at all. Then they pop the baby out and slip right back into their skinny jeans. Hateful."

I am rambling on, partly because I'm nervous but I think in part to avoid what I guess is coming next. Although part of me longs to hear it.

He takes my hands in his and looks at me.

"Cunningham," he begins. "I just want you to know something. All this, you know, showing up here, St Tropez – it's not so I can get you into bed."

"It's not?" I'm not sure whether to be disappointed or relieved.

"No." He looks down at his feet and then back at me. "You see I've loved you since I was a boy. I've never stopped loving you. So I don't just want you for one night; I want you forever."

I look at him open-mouthed. "But you could have anyone," I say. "Why on earth would you want a married mother of three who is rapidly approaching her sell-by date?"

"Don't be daft," he says in his strong Yorkshire tones. "You're gorgeous. And your children are gorgeous; I'd look after them as if they were my own. And the thing is, for me now, it's so hard to trust people I meet. They might just want me for all the fame nonsense and the money. I knew you before all that; you wanted me before all that. I can trust you."

I can't think of anything to say. Johnny Fray wants to take on my children and me. He wants to look after us all. He wants to be with me forever. I feel dizzy.

"Cunningham, I really love you," he goes on. "I love your children and I would love to settle down here with you and bring them up as my own, maybe even have another baby."

"I don't know what to say," I gulp.

"Just think about it, will you?"

I nod.

"Good," he gets up. "I'll expect an answer after dinner. Only joking. But I am going to get it started; I have some delicacies from the best chefs in Prague to offer you. You just need to show me how to turn the oven on."

I leave him in the kitchen and think about what he just told me. I can't believe it. Does he really mean it? And is it what I want? How could anyone not want Johnny Fray? Maybe it is all just a bit too soon.

We eat outside. I light candles and lay the table on the terrace. The food is unfamiliar but it is nice to have something non-French for once. The French are very bad at that, I notice; for example, there are no Italian restaurants around. If you insist on eating pasta, they seem to be saying, cook it yourself.

We go easy on the red wine. After dinner Johnny says he has to go back to Prague; they're shooting first thing tomorrow morning. We talk about Lady Butterdish and the children and the wine-making process, but underneath it all is the unanswered question of whether or not we will end up together. It feels like a big step to me, but one I am quite prepared to think about.

We walk hand in hand to the helicopter. All through dinner I have been thinking, 'Do I want to spend the rest of my life with this man?' which kind of takes one's mind off one's Czech dumplings. But now he has basically proposed in all but the actual words, my mind is whirring round like the helicopter's blades.

When we get to the helicopter we stop, face to face. Johnny puts his hands on my hips.

"Bye, Cunningham," he says. Then he kisses me.

It is like small explosions are going off in all directions in my body. All the years melt away and I am catapulted back to Drake's almost fifteen years ago, when he is a young actor at RADA and there are no children and no divorce and no nothing: Just us, locked in a kiss that I never want to end. And this time there is no Lady Butterdish to interrupt us.

Eventually, though, it does end. When it does, Johnnny looks at me with such love in his eyes, I want to say 'yes' right then and there. But it's too big a decision and I respect him too much to go back on it. I have to be sure it's the right thing to do.

"Don't forget to think about it, eh Cunningham?" he says.

"Of course," I reply, nodding slowly and leaning closer towards him. We hug and then he kisses me on the forehead before walking to the helicopter.

When he gets there he turns around.

"You're still one hell of a kisser, Cunningham," he grins before going up the steps and closing the door behind him.

Rule 20

Always have a back-up

The French Art of Having Affairs

I collect the children from the airport the following day. Nick and Cécile look relaxed and happy and the children have all been bought new outfits. Emily has even taken off her cat's ears. In fact they look something from like a toothpaste advertisement. How annoying.

"Seems you had a perfect time," I say to Nick through gritted teeth (which, I tell myself, I need to have whitened).

"As it seems did you," he smiles back sarcastically.

"Yes, well, at least neither of us are still married," I retort under my breath.

"Actually we've only had the decree nisi," he retorts. "We're not actually divorced until the decree absolute comes through."

"Well, it can't come soon enough," I snipe. "Come on kids, we need to get home," I add and say goodbye to the happy couple.

They are full of news of the weekend in Uzès, a beautiful Renaissance town an hour from Montpellier in the direction of Provence.

"We stayed in a FIVE-STAR hotel," says Emily. "We even had our own room. And Edward didn't even wet the bed and anyway Cécile said it didn't matter if he did because the hotel staff would wash the sheets."

"And we had room service," adds Charlotte. "In the room."

"And Cécile's got an all-in-one," adds Edward helpfully. "I saw it."

"She's got long legs, like a giraffe," says Emily.

At this point I decide to put the radio on. Not even French pop can be worse than hearing how thin/rich/prone to wearing sexy underwear my soon to be ex-husband's mistress is.

Once we have eaten and I have put the kids to bed, I walk over to the *cave*. I find the place has a calming influence on me, especially now that there is a few thousand pounds worth of wine sitting in there. Kamal has been working on blending it and the last time I tasted it I was really impressed. It tasted berry-like and deep, with what they call in the trade a firm finish. Basically, it tasted like an expensive red wine.

Tomorrow the bottling lorry arrives and they will bottle it. We have to label it, but I have planned that as a job for us all next weekend. I just hope the kids don't compare their luxurious five-star stay in Uzès with their working weekend at home. Hopefully by then they will have forgotten all about Cécile and her all-in-one.

The cicadas are out in full force. They make an incessant buzzing noise caused by rubbing their legs together to attract a mate. And there are different levels of buzzing, rather like an orchestra warming up. From the hills I hear high-pitched buzzing, closer to me it is baritone, and over on the terrace there's a more chirruping noise. I adore the sound of them. It means heat and summer and home.

I love this place. I breathe in the sweet night air and look up at the bright stars. I love being this warm when it's dark; it makes me feel secure for some reason. Nick may think he has it all, but he is back in smelly old London, while I am here, in paradise.

I remember something Jean-Claude told me when we were walking through the vines one night. I commented on how luminous the stars are.

"I find them totally intoxicating," he told me. "There is a quote from the poet Racine who told his friends in the north of France that "our nights are like your days". That is how I think of the summer nights here."

I walk into the *cave*. Just as I am about to put the light on I see the beam from a torch by the large vat. I stop and watch it progress up the ladder. Why would Kamal not have put the light on? Maybe the bulb has gone? He really does work all hours. I flick the light switch and after a second or two the whole place is flooded with light.

"It's okay, Kamal," I say. "The light works."

As my eyes adjust to the bright light I see that it is not Kamal clambering up the ladder but Jean-Claude.

"Ah, Sophie, how are you?" He turns around to greet me and starts climbing down the ladder.

"Jean-Claude? What are you doing here?"

He saunters over and kisses me on either cheek. "I heard about your famous treasure and wanted to come and taste for myself," he says. "Great news, eh?"

"Yes," I say enthusiastically. "I've emailed all my wine-bond people again and told them they can get delivery of the cases of red within weeks. I have had orders for more than 1,000 bottles; this'll definitely tide us over until after the harvest. But you should have called me, I would have arranged for you to taste it...."

"Sophie," he interrupts me, grabbing my shoulders and pulling me towards him. "Let's go inside for a coffee."

The way he says it sounds like he doesn't mean coffee at all. Or does everything the French say just sound like they're talking about sex?

Is this what I want? How did I get to this point? Actually I think I do want it. But what about Johnny?

Well, I suppose if I'm going to make the right decision I might have to try them both on. Not that they are comparable to pairs of jeans, but how does one know otherwise? My sensible alter-ego would say I should just be alone for a while and see how I feel, but she's not here this evening.

We walk to the house and I make coffee. He watches me.

"Cheers then," I say raising my coffee cup. Jean-Claude finishes his coffee in one gulp and walks over to me. He takes the cup from my hands and puts it on the table. All the while he does this he smiles and looks at me with those bright blue eyes. I am not sure what he is up to but at least I no longer have to think about what I should do; I just follow his movements.

He leans over, takes both my hands and beckons for me to stand up. We are now standing opposite each other, very close. He put his hands on my shoulders.

"I seem to remember that last time we were this close, we were interrupted by your husband," he says looking down at me.

"Ex-husband," I correct him.

He raises an eyebrow. "Really?"

"Yes," I say, "the decree nisi came through a few days ago."

Jean-Claude draws me closer to him and leans his head forward until our noses are almost touching. I feel dizzy from being so close to him; his presence is intoxicating and there's that aftershave again.

"May I be the first one to kiss the former bride?" he asks.

I nod.

He touches my lips with his and puts his arms around me. Slowly our mouths open and we kiss. It occurs to me briefly that Nick and I stopped kissing a long time ago.

I put my arms around Jean-Claude's neck and pull him towards me. He is a very good kisser, but then what did I expect from a Frenchman? He is delicate but firm and very, very sexy. His tongue and mine play a game of getting to know each other, tentatively first and then with more confidence. I feel our bodies getting closer. I can feel what I assume is an erection pressing against me. This is all very unfamiliar. When you're married, sex is almost perfunctory. There is rarely romance involved – you never stand in the kitchen snogging like a couple of teenagers. Or at least not in my experience.

Jean-Claude moves his hands from my back to my buttocks

and pulls them closer to him. He starts to kiss my neck, which sends shivers of lust all through my body. I move my hands up to his head and run my fingers through his thick hair. It is when I feel him undoing my trousers that I suddenly realise that if I'm not careful, I could end up naked on the kitchen floor with a Frenchman. Not that there is anything wrong with that in itself, but a) one of the children might walk in, b) I'm not sure getting laid the same week as your decree nisi comes through is good for your sanity, c) I still haven't harvested my pubes to French standards, and d) It wasn't many hours ago I was kissing Johnny and I should really be taking things a bit more slowly.

Having said all that, I put my hands on his hips. Hmmm, I could certainly get used to this. These French do have a way of kissing that is so, well, French. I caress his body and come across something long and hard – wow, really long and hard. But that's a strange place for a…. Then I realise it is cold and made of glass.

I pull away from him. "Jean-Claude why are you carrying a bottle of wine?" I ask laughing. "Surely you don't get that desperate for a drink?" I pull the bottle out of his pocket and look at the label: *vinaigre de cidre*.

"Why do you have a bottle of vinegar in your pocket?"

Jean-Claude laughs. "Oh that, it's a present for you, from Provence."

"Thank you," I smile. "How sweet of you."

Somehow the bottle of vinegar has broken the kissing spell and what it was fast turning into.

"I must go," he says. "I promised to call my aunt at 9pm. Thank you for a perfect kiss. Can I take you out for dinner next week?"

"Of course."

I show him out and he walks off towards his château, but not before we have another massive snog outside the house. Then I run upstairs to watch him from my terrace. I love the way he walks; it's so graceful, almost feline.

When I get there, I see him talking to Kamal. I watch them chat for a bit then go in.

I walk into the kitchen and put the vinegar on the table. *Vinaigre de cidre de Bretagne*, reads the full label. Strange: I thought he said it came from Provence? Oh well, I suppose he could have bought it in Provence. It strikes me now that he seemed in a rather frenetic mood. And I still don't quite understand how we ended up snogging.

But I hope he comes back soon, and that he sees the children soon – they adore him, and I love watching them all speak French together. It makes me feel so... cosmopolitan. I can even understand most of what they're saying.

Jean-Claude is one of those people children just adore, I don't know what it is about him, but they seem to trust and like him. A few days ago when Charlotte fell off her bike on the way back from the village chemist, he arrived carrying her in his arms, her grazed knees bleeding and tears streaming down her little face. He walked into the kitchen where I was making dinner and she insisted he stay with her until I had done the nasty antiseptic thing and got the plaster on. I kept thinking about that sad thing he said the first night he came for dinner about not having children.

*

The morning after the French kiss, once I've done the school run and an hour's frenetic *cave*-organising, I meet Audrey at village chemist which is amazingly well stocked. I am told this is perfectly normal, because French women will tolerate nothing less. I am buying all the things she has told me I need. The list seems endless: night cream, eye cream, slimming cream, bust gel, hand cream, lip plumper, and so it goes on. It seems every part of my body needs an individual cream – even my feet.

"I hate diets," says Audrey. "I'd rather die. That's why I buy slimming creams."

"But surely a slimming cream can't work? How can a cream possibly make you thin?"

Audrey gives me an old-fashioned look. "You're so Anglo-Saxon," she tells me sternly.

In an effort to prove I am changing my Anglo-Saxon ways, I tell her briefly about my weekend.

"*Mon dieu!*" she exclaims. "You've been a busy girl. Good for you. This is a very French attitude; always have a back up. Men are notoriously unreliable so you need to have a reserve at all times. For example, I always carry two lip-glosses, just in case one runs out."

"I feel guilty all the time and a voice inside keeps telling me I have to make a choice between them," I protest.

"Can't you tell the voice to shut up? I mean it is a perfect situation; one lives next door and the other travels all the time. So when the film star is off filming you entertain yourself with the other."

I sigh. "Johnny would really not like that idea."

"Of course not, but he won't know."

"No, but I will," I say. "I just don't want to treat him like that, he's been so good to me, and we go back a long way. It's almost like fate has finally brought us together, although I wish it hadn't happened quite so quickly. I just don't feel ready yet."

"Stop being too serious about all this. Just enjoy the attention and have some fun, Sophie. You don't have to have either of them forever."

She's right of course. Why am I being so puritanical about this? Or as Audrey would say "Anglo-Saxon".

"What perfume do you wear?" she asks me, as she catches me looking at a bottle of Lily of the Valley.

"I wasn't actually going to buy it," I defend myself. "It's just that my grandmother used to wear it and I was very fond of her."

"A woman should have what I call a signature-scent," says Audrey. "I have been wearing Cuir de Russie by Chanel since my first boyfriend gave it to me when I was only 17. And I have been faithful to it ever since."

"Unlike to your boyfriends?"

"*Bien sûr*," she says. "Some things in life demand absolute fidelity. Perfume is essential. As Coco Chanel said; 'A woman who doesn't wear perfume has no future'."

While I am paying for my new stash of goodies, we see Calypso racing past the front door of the chemist on a bicycle, closely followed by Tim. I notice with some relief he doesn't have a gun with him.

We dash outside to see what happens, Calypso makes a beeline for the bakery, runs in and locks the door behind her. Tim is outside shouting and stamping his feet.

"It must be his old Gulf War Syndrome," I say to Audrey. "But it's not even windy."

Audrey looks perplexed. "Gulf War Syndrome? What is that?"

"Nothing you can use to make your thighs look thinner," I explain. "Calypso's husband was in the Gulf War and sometimes the wind reminds him of it and it sends him off his head and he tries to murder her."

"Aaah," says Audrey, "and I thought he was just trying to murder her because she's having a lesbian affair with Colette."

For some reason this news doesn't even surprise me.

Rule 21

The end of an affair is the beginning of another

The French Art of Having Affairs

"It's all over," Lucy weeps down the phone. "Josh is going back to the US. He's been offered a job there, one he can't turn down. Oh Soph, what am I going to do? He was the highlight of my day. The thing I most looked forward to doing was running my fingers through his hair and feeling his body on top of mine."

"When does he go?"

"Another three weeks. Another three weeks of heaven and then…."

"Then you can focus on your husband and children. Come on Luce, you knew this wasn't forever, affairs with young men never are. You had a great run of it, you got away with it, you should be happy. Take a Carla approach."

"What and find another young man? Don't be ridiculous."

"Noooo. I know Josh was a one-off. You're not as, whatever, as Carla. But just take it for what it was – great fun – and now get on with the rest of your life. Your ADULT life."

Lucy grunts.

"You could always write a book about it? An anonymous memoir; call it *Sex and the Married Woman* and write it under a pseudonym," I joke.

"That's a great idea," says Lucy, finally stopping sobbing. "My father always used to say those who can do and those who can't – well, they just write about it. At least that will take my mind off things. And I won't have to look far to find a publisher…."

I can almost hear her brain whirring.

"But I am going to miss him," she goes on. "And I won't ever be able to look at my kitchen table without remembering him."

"I know, I know, but you can relive all those moments together through your memoir."

"Good plan. Well it's a plan, which is more than I had. Gotta go: Antonia's just come in, she needs help with her homework."

I call Sarah to tell her about Lucy and ask her to keep an eye on her.

"How are you sweetpea?"

"I'm fine, thanks, gearing up for the harvest. Today I spent the morning in the vineyards. Bloody hell it's hot. It feels like the sun has sucked the countryside dry. The roots of the vines must stretch all the way to the centre of the earth to get moisture. This afternoon is dedicated to washing out barrels ready to put the wine into. How is Mr Enormous?"

"Enormous and I are still in a state of bliss. But I have decided to be mature about it all and take it for what it is."

"And what is it?"

"A rampant, gorgeous, sexy affair. His wife and he seem to have some kind of arrangement whereby she doesn't really care what he does during the week up in London, but his part of the deal is that he goes home at weekends, and he stays married to her."

"How very convenient for him. So where does that leave you?"

"Alone at weekends, I suppose. But also a free agent, free to do what I want, when I want, and also not be obliged to listen to some bloke snoring next to me. OK so sometimes I wish I could have him to myself, but as that's not going to happen I'm just going to have to be happy with what I can get."

"But Sarah, there's no future in it. What happens next? I mean where's the happy ending? Do you want to be a mistress all your life? Don't you want to be a wife?"

"I have been thinking a lot about this over the past few months. I've even started meditating to get a clearer picture of my life and where it's going. I have come to the conclusion that we are all, as women, conditioned to think that the way forward is marriage and kids. And I always thought I wanted that too. But you know there are other options, other ways to live. And being a mistress is one of them."

"But what happens when he gets too old to get it up, or he loses interest in you? Or you get too old to be a mistress. How many mistresses over 60 do you know? You could end up terribly lonely."

"Just because you're married doesn't mean you can't get lonely," says Sarah.

She has a point.

Rule 22

Personal grooming is your only religion

The French Art of Having Affairs

I am naked in front of my bathroom mirror. In front of me there are five bottles of creams. I start at the bottom with the foot cream. Onto my weary, vineyard-walking feet it goes, this pink peppermint concoction. Then I pick up the anti-cellulite cream. This has to go on in upward strokes on my thighs, buttock and, according to the instructions, 'other areas in need of attention'. This could be just about everywhere, but I focus on the most obvious bits.

Maybe as an experiment I should do one buttock but not the other, just to see if it makes any difference at all? But then who wants one buttock bigger than the other? Or even smaller than the other?

Next is the bust gel. I do as the instructions tell me and sweep it upwards towards my neck, I guess the idea being that your breasts miraculously go in an upwards direction as well. It's worth a try.

My phone rings while I am in the middle of this exercise. Hastily I wipe my hands on my buttocks, hoping they don't grow nipples. I run for the phone and almost kill myself falling over on my slippery peppermint-cream-covered feet.

"Hello?"

"Oh, hi there Soph, it's Nick. What you up to? You sound out of breath."

"Not much," I lie. "Just running for the phone. How about you?"

"Oh this and that," he replies. "How are the kids?"

"Asleep thankfully," I say, inching my way slowly back to the bathroom to grab a towel.

I feel slightly vulnerable talking to Nick in the nude. Especially now I have almost no pubic hair. Yes, I went to the beautician and I think there was a breakdown in communication because after a lot of pain and 40 euros there is now a Hitler moustache where my furry mound used to be.

"Today was just awful. Edward's girlfriend decided she was in love with Charles, typical French hussy, so he came home crying, saying his heart was broken in a thousand bits. Charlotte had some awful French grammar homework I had to try and help her with, but you know how much of an idea I have about French grammar, and as for the French poems they have to learn every week, oh my God, they are soooo difficult…."

I go on telling him about our day. It is lovely to be able to talk to someone about the children. Jean-Claude is great with them, as is Johnny, but talking to their father is somehow very different. It can be a lonely old job being a single parent.

"Anyway, sorry to go on, how is everything with you? You know we start the harvest in a few days, if you're bored you could always come and help?"

"I'd love to," says Nick. "And I love hearing about the kids. I really miss them. I even miss their bickering. We'll come out soon to see them, but I'm not sure I can make it to the harvest, Soph."

"Why not?"

"Well, that's what I rang to tell you. Cécile and I are getting married."

I am in shock but try not to sound like I care.

"Wow, that was quick. You don't hang around, do you?

"I could say the same about you," responds my ex-soon-to-be-Cécile's husband. "The decree absolute should be through by the end of August and we wanted to get married in September before the weather gets too bad. That's when the harvest is, right?"

This conversation has now become almost surreal. I am standing semi-naked in front of the mirror rubbing potions into my in-parts bald body and Nick is telling me he is getting married. Any minute now the mad hatter will appear and offer me a cup of tea. Or hopefully something stronger.

"The exact date will depend on the maturity of the grapes and the weather, but yes, normally it starts the last week of August and goes on until early September," I explain in a rather shaky voice. "And erm, congratulations," I add, although obviously I don't mean it.

"Thanks," says Nick. "I'm glad we're still friends."

"Yes, me too," I say. "Maybe I should get married too and we could have a double wedding, save on costs."

Nick laughs. "It's grand to hear you've not lost your sense of humour, Soph. And I meant to tell you, you looked great when we saw you in France, really fantastic."

You ain't seen nothing yet, I mouth to my Hitler moustache in the mirror.

"Thanks. I have finally got in touch with my inner French woman," I say. "It's been an expensive, and sometimes painful, encounter, but worth it."

"I love the look of your inner French woman Soph. She's grand."

"Well, must get on," I say quickly before I start enjoying his flattery. "I have nails to file and eyebrows to pluck. Thanks for calling to let me know. Bye."

I hang up and go back to my bust gel. I smother the cream vigorously upwards from the base of my breasts to my neck, the idea being that you don't rub down because that might increase the general gravity-induced desire one's body has to reach earth. Audrey was right. It does make you feel better.

The conversation with Nick has not exactly left me feeling overjoyed. This marriage thing. I mean it's one thing to run off with the French hussy, but why does he have to marry her? What if they have children? How will that affect our three? Will he be as keen to see them and take as much of an interest in them if he has a whole new family?

I walk carefully to bed and pull my nightie over my perfectly-pampered body.

Several hours later I am woken up by my phone ringing; it's Johnny, calling from Los Angeles.

"Hey Cunningham, how's things? Sorry to call so late but I just had to talk to you, gal."

"S'okay," I mumble. "You all right?"

"Yes, more than all right. Listen, I'm here with my agent who is friends with some bloke who has the most amazing vineyard for sale with a beautiful house and, hang on a minute 'how many hectares of vines?'" I hear him ask someone.

"Fifty hectares of vines. Well this bloke is selling it and he's in a rush because the tax man is after him and he's got to get the asset off his hands and well, Cunningham, you still awake?"

"I'm awake, go on."

"Well, you know what we talked about and all that, and well I've got to be in LA most of the year for the next three years, well I was thinking, maybe I should buy it and you and the kids could move out here and we could live there and you could run the vineyard and...."

I don't know what to say.

"Cunningham?"

"Johnny, I don't know what to say, I mean, it's a lovely idea, of course, but, well I have a life here, the children have a life here, they love it."

"They could love it here too, it's even sunnier, and everyone speaks English. Ed might even meet Spiderman!"

"Don't be silly, he's in New York," I tell him. "Johnny, I'm really happy you called, please let me think about it. I'm half awake and this is a big decision. I mean I've never even been to California."

"I understand, Cunningham, I was just so excited about it I had to call you. Let me try to email you some pictures later on. Sorry I woke you up. Love you, gal."

"Love you too," I say. I hang up. Seconds later there is a text message. 'Sleep well, Cunningham, miss you. LA is lonely without you.'

Johnny Fray: you couldn't make him up. Possibly the only young, successful and sexy film star to find LA a lonely place. I have to love him for that.

Rule 23

The hours cinq à sept are the most easily hidden

The French Art of Having Affairs

At 6am in the morning two weeks after the call from Johnny, Kamal knocks on my door with a cup of tea. There are worse sights to be greeted with first thing, though maybe not for him.

Today we start the harvest; weeks of frenetic picking, sorting and squashing grapes. Sarah and Lucy are coming to help, as are Peter and Phil, Calypso, Audrey, Jean-Claude and Colette, of course, who is full-time at the moment thanks to the income from the wine bonds and the Cabernet Sauvignon. Even Carla is leaving her various tennis coaches behind for a few days and coming over. So is my mother, who says she will take charge of the food. Quite what she has in store I dread to think – I remember Nick once said that eating my mother's home-cooked fare had made him appreciate in-flight meals.

With the money from the sales of the vat of Cabernet Sauvignon I have hired an additional two workers who will stay in the barn with Kamal. I have decided I'd better keep both Carla and Sarah (who is still a liability, even if Mr Enormous is her priority) in the house with me if Kamal is going to have any hope of sleeping through the night, although a lot of the nights we will spend picking grapes as the white ones need to be picked in the cool of the night air to avoid oxidation.

Lucy is less of a worry, but you never know with the stress of less than Perfect Patrick and her new-found libido. Especially now that Joshua has gone back home to his job and, we can only assume, a woman his own age.

I am nervous but also very excited about it; this is the most important time of the year for the vineyard – if the harvest is a success we go on for another year. If not, who knows what will happen to us and our life in France?

"Rise and shine, Madame Winemaker," says Kamal, opening the shutters. "It's the first day of your first harvest. You need to be among the vines, secateurs in hand, by half six. We'll give everyone a breakfast break around half nine."

"What did your last slave die of?" I moan, sitting up and taking the tea.

"Fancy a few sun salutations to get the blood flowing?"

"Very sweet of you, no thanks. How come you're so perky?"

"I love harvest time, it's just the best time of the year. Loads of hard work but great fun and the sense of achievement after weeks of labouring when you've got all the wine in the vats; it's just magical. See you out there."

I sip my tea and think about the day ahead. Today we have the new workers pitching up to work with Colette, Audrey and Calypso picking the syrah. The contingent from England arrive later on for two weeks, and friends from here will come and help as and when they can. The whole harvest will take around three weeks in total, at the end of which we will have a big party to celebrate – assuming there have been no major disasters.

I estimate I have around seven hundred vines, and each vine has maybe an average of five bunches of grapes that need to be picked. That means bending down around 3,500 times. Even if I divide that by the total number of pickers (ten), it is still a lot of bending over.

"Best get on with it then, gal," Johnny would say. He is back in LA but usually texts me during our night. I love waking up to his messages. I can see there's one on my mobile, which makes me leap out of bed and get dressed. I have told him I will think about his Californian plan, but right now, my mind is on the job in hand here.

"Good luck today, Cunningham," it reads. "Love you. Hi to the kids". The Frenchman is going to have to come up with more than a bottle of old vinegar to beat that.

Kamal is already in the vineyard when I get there. He hands me a large white plastic tub.

"This is to put the grapes in," he explains slowly. "And I mean put. You need to handle them gently; we've decided to start picking the Syrah today because it is on the cusp, as sweet as it is going to get on the vine before it starts to deteriorate. Also, the joy of handpicking is that you can manually sort the grapes. Don't put any that are not ripe enough or any rotten ones in the bucket. Tomorrow morning at 4am we start on the whites."

"Why so early?" A 6am start was bad enough.

"You'll thank me for making you pick when it's cooler. Not only will you be more comfortable but the wine will be better too. The grapes lose quality rapidly in the heat, so we will need to get as much picked by 9am as possible. As you know, some of the picking, especially of the whites, will happen at night. It's going to be a busy few weeks. We will be like soldiers on duty, sleeping as and when we can."

Colette joins us. I smell her cigarette long before I actually see her. Calypso is not far behind. Funny that.

"We'll rotate the jobs so we're not all bending down all day long," Kamal continues. "Someone needs to empty the filled tubs into the trailer and drive them to the *cave* ready for crushing. While there are just the four of us though we'll just focus on filling the first tubs."

The sun is already warm and my tummy is rumbling. Oh well, only another three hours until breakfast. But the vines are beautiful. I look down the edge of the vineyard. The outer vines bend in towards the line rather like the neck of a graceful giraffe.

"We'll work in pairs on either side of the vine," continues Kamal. "Calypso you work with Colette and I'll work with Sophie. I hope you've all got plenty of sunscreen on, and Sophie, you'll need a hat."

I nip back to the house for a hat and some sunscreen; it never occurred to me to put any on at half past six this morning. I notice that Colette and Calypso are well kitted out; they are clearly old hands at this harvesting game. The postman stops me just as I am on my way back to the vineyard. Among the usual junk mail and bank statements (what a waste of paper) is an official-looking large brown envelope. I know what it is before I even open it. The decree absolute. But of course I open it just to make sure. There it is in black and white; the marriage between Nicholas Reed and Sophie Reed (née Cunningham) is hereby declared null and void. I am no longer Mrs Reed. What the hell do I call myself? Cunningham I suppose, and single.

Once back in the vineyard I stand opposite Kamal, secateurs at the ready. I'm glad I have the harvest to focus on instead of my new single status. This is it; the first bunch of grapes of my first harvest of my first vintage. I take a deep breath and bend down.

'Snip'. The bunch falls into my hand. It feels heavier than I imagined it would. It sits in my palm like a beautiful statue, moist from the dew.

"Okay, Sophie, meditation time over," smiles Kamal. "Try to keep up with me so we reach the end of the row at the same time."

Kamal works more quickly than me. I find my normal efficiency is lost among the vines. I am clumsy and badly coordinated. I guess my body is getting used to the unfamiliar movements. Colette and Calypso are doing well. They seem to be able to talk as well as harvest, something I can't do – all my powers of concentration are focused on the task in hand, keeping up with Kamal without cutting my fingers, or dropping the grapes, or missing a bunch, or letting a rotten grape end up in the bucket for crushing.

At nine our workers show up. They are two Spanish boys called Rafael and Juan-Carlos from Barcelona, who are studying wine-making at university. Kamal shows them their accommodation, leaving me to overtake him for the first, and possibly only, time.

I am ashamed to admit that rather than worrying about the fact that I am a divorcee, I am more concerned with counting the seconds to breakfast, and not quite sure how I am going to keep this up for up to several weeks when three hours feels like a lifetime. My back is already aching and my fingers are clammy with grape juice and tired. It feels like the sun is focusing all its strength on one particular spot just between my left shoulder-blade and my neck. Soon it will bore a hole right through me.

I sneak a look at Calypso and Colette to see if they look in as much pain as I am. No, they are working away, happily chatting as if they were on an early-morning stroll. I have to stop being such a lightweight. After all, these are my vines and so if anyone should be enjoying the process of harvesting them it should be me.

"Breakfast!" calls Kamal after what seems like a hundred years. We lay down our secateurs, stretch our backs and walk towards the terrace, where he has coffee and croissants laid out on the marble table. Never has a croissant tasted so good. I wonder if eating two croissants is a deportable offence in France?

We sip our coffee and survey the vines.

"In three hours we have picked six rows," says Kamal. "There are 48 in total."

It seems an insurmountable number and that's just one of the vineyards, – three hectares out of a total of sixteen.

"Don't worry, Sophie," Kamal continues. "The first few days are always the toughest. Think of it as exercise, exercise that will make you money. Come on now, back to work."

I am rather reluctantly reunited with my secateurs that are sticky with grape juice. I rinse them off with some water from my water bottle.

"Mummy, can I have a go?" The children have woken up and Emily is keen to get involved. "We did this at school, I know how it works, and I didn't even cut myself."

Kamal beckons for her to join him and he shows her what to do. Maybe I could get all three of them working? I bet they could do a row per hour. Or would I be arrested for using child labour? Mind you, Rafael and Juan-Carlos don't look much older than my kids, even if their CVs say they are eighteen.

Emily though soon tires of the task and goes back to the house. It is late August and the last week of the school holidays. Next week is what the French call going back to school: la *rentrée*. This is an event that has just about the same significance as Christmas. Or possibly even more. Audrey has told me all about it. People spend weeks preparing for it, buying new school bags, organising themselves and discussing what their little ones will eat for their *goûter* or snack this school year. Needless to say, I have been preparing for the harvest so am not remotely organised, but maybe my mother can help when she arrives. And I am dreading trying to put them to bed at seven o'clock, when it is still sunny outside until 10 o'clock at night.

My picking is interrupted by a text message from Sarah: 'Boarding now, sweetpea,' it reads. 'Have terrible hangover so look dreadful, Lucy of course looks radiant.'

"No change there then," I text back sneakily, so Kamal won't notice, hoping I won't make my phone sticky with the grape juice. "See you this afternoon. Can't wait." This is a great day for them to get here; between them and the harvest I won't have any time to dwell on anything.

I get back to my picking. I am looking forward to seeing them all so much. It will be great to talk about everything that has happened; especially now we're divorced, Nick is getting married and I have to make a decision between two very eligible suitors and two very different lives. This is the kind of decision only your girlfriends can help you with.

Maybe Johnny will surprise me with a visit while they're here? I would love for them all to meet my famous film-star suitor. But I think he is filming in LA until the end of September.

They will be impressed with Jean-Claude, though. I have seen less of him recently as he's been in Aix a lot. Whenever I do see him, it is lovely, and since that first kiss we have repeated the experience about ten times. It's beginning to feel like the world's longest courtship. He says he wants to wait until my divorce is finalised. Maybe I should let him know about today's post.

I am young-ish, free and single for the first time in more than ten years. And actually I am ready to leap into bed with the frog, or Johnny, or even both. But I'm not sure I'm quite ready to commit to another full-on relationship, which is why Johnny's idea of the Californian vineyard rather worries me. I have asked him to wait until the harvest is over; it's not a decision I want to rush into.

"And if I you're going to end up with Johnny, then you might like to try a little piece of French side salad before you do," as Sarah helpfully pointed out on the phone the other day.

Talking of Sarah, she and Carla will probably be more impressed by Kamal than Jean-Claude. He is looking very sexy pruning opposite me, his brown arms toned and fit from all the work and yoga he does. For some reason he doesn't really appeal to me in that way – maybe because I already have my hands full with the others, or because he is around fifteen years younger than me. I am obviously far too young to have a toy-boy!

At lunch there is a feeling of wellbeing, almost bliss, as we all sit down to eat. We eat with the appetite one has after toiling outside all morning. The food is: Parma ham with melon and mountains of rustic bread courtesy of the baker, who I have found out is Colette's cousin (is there anyone in the village she isn't either related to or sleeping with?). We drink red wine.

"Not too much," warns Kamal. "We have an afternoon's work to get through."

I can see he was the eldest of five children. Bossy-boots.

"Surely we can have a little, tiny siesta?" I ask. "Even just a power-nap?"

"We go back to work at 2pm. How you spend your time is up to you," he replies.

I daren't even look at Calypso and Colette; I suppose they will be spending the time in some Sapphic love tryst. I can't say I'm jealous, I think I'd rather have a kip.

I can't wait for the girls to get here so I can tell them all about everything that is going on in this village. It's a wonder anyone in France ever gets any work done with all the sex they have to have and all the personal grooming they have to go through. I suppose one leads to another.

The latest from the bakery is that the wife has come back and seen off the best friend (now *sans culottes* after she burned all her clothes). The baker is apparently very happy, because the wife was always much handier around the bakery, if not the bedroom. I have to say the bread has improved since she came back. I guess he is now focusing on his job too, instead of working out how to organise the old *cinq à sept* with the mistress.

Trust the French to come up with a phrase to describe the time you spend with your lover. And it's such a perfect amount of time: two hours, neither too little nor too much. This truly is a country of seducers. And the funny thing is that they have such respect for the whole concept of seduction here; they treat it with the same reverence they approach a good wine or a Brie de Meaux, the best of bries.

It is true that since I got in touch with my inner French woman I have had a lot more offers of sex. The question is: which, if any, of those offers do I want to accept? I suppose I can accept them both. It doesn't tie me down to anything.

As if on cue, Jean-Claude appears. *"Bonjour mes amis,"* he says jovially and bows, taking off his Panama hat.

"Bonjour," we chorus back.

"Ah, Jean-Claude," says Kamal, standing up, "this is perfect timing. I propose a toast, on this, the first day of the harvest."

"A toast to what?" asks Calypso.

"I think it's time you shared our little secret with the rest of the class," says Kamal to Jean-Claude, who looks furious.

"What little secret is this Jean-Claude?" I ask.

He doesn't respond but just glares at Kamal, who answers on his behalf.

"I think you should know, now that the harvest is upon us, that Jean-Claude is the generous but anonymous benefactor who has been paying me to help you."

"Jean-Claude?" I leap up and throw my arms around him. "I can't believe it, I am so grateful. You saved my life, thank you, thank you."

Jean-Claude is dismissive. "It was nothing," he says, patting me on the arm rather like you would a pet dog, "really nothing. Just some neighbourly *amitié*, think nothing of it."

I look at him. How could I never even have suspected that he would be the one behind Kamal? I mean, he was my knight in shining green tractor when the mildew almost hit, and he has been supportive all the way through. I can't believe how I underestimated him.

"Jean-Claude, I am truly touched," I say, taking his hands. "Thank you again, really."

Before he has a chance to respond we hear the sound of a car horn beeping. A dark blue Citroen is making its way towards the house. It stops and Sarah jumps out. I run to her from the lunch-table to greet them.

"Hey scrawny, what the hell happened to you?" she laughs. "Don't they let you eat in France?"

"*Ciao bella*," Carla gets out of the car. "What a place, *che meraviglia*. It is wonderful."

"Hey darling." Two long limbs ease their way out of the hire car followed by a figure in a floaty dress. Lucy hugs me.

"It's so good to see you all," I say, almost crying with happiness.

My mother gets out and gives me a big hug.

"Sophie," she says beaming. "What a perfectly gorgeous place you have here. And you're so thin! What have you been doing? Running after Frenchmen?"

"Granny, granny!" we are interrupted by the children running to greet my mother.

Kamal and the other helpers follow. I notice with some disappointment that Jean-Claude has slunk off. I was looking forward to introducing them and finding out what the girls think of him. After the Kamal revelation I am more keen than ever. Especially now Johnny wants us to move to California. California or Boujan? For most people the choice would not be a tricky one, but then most people would probably not fall in love as deeply as I have with this place.

"This is Kamal, Calypso, Colette, Rafael and Juan-Carlos," I say as they approach. "This is my mother and Sarah, Carla and Lucy, my oldest and dearest friends."

"Less of the oldest," says Carla, holding her hand out towards Kamal and practically eating him up with her eyes. "Do you play tennis?" she purrs.

"Embarrassing," says Sarah to me under her breath. "She just gets worse."

Kamal smiles his best *namaste* smile and says hello to the rest of the guests, who manage to be a little less obvious about how gorgeous they think he is.

I can see the two Spanish boys blush as they shake Lucy's hand. She has that exquisite English-rose like quality about her that sends men mad, a kind of perfection that they only expect in porcelain dolls. I remember Lucy was even perfect when she was pregnant; she was one of those really annoying women unaffected by industrial weight gain, swollen ankles and water retention, rather like a superhero impervious to fire, bullets or any other calamity life throws at them. Lucy just grew a neat little bump that sat there, perfectly poised and firm, until a perfect little baby popped out and she popped back into her skinny jeans. It was almost enough to chuck her as a friend for, but she is the only one of the four of us who knows how to read a map.

"Come into the house," I say to them, leading them up the stairs. "Mummy, I put you in with the kids. You three will have to slum it between Edward's room and the spare room. And NO sneaking over to the barn in the middle of the night."

"As if," says Sarah. "I'm far too mature for that kind of behaviour these days."

We all look at her but feel the statement is too stupid to warrant any response.

Sarah and Carla, as predicted, are sticking close by Kamal. They maintain it is because they need Kamal to keep an eye on their picking technique. The fact is, Colette could easily do that, but neither of them is that way inclined.

Kamal goes off to take the trailer full of grapes to the *cave*.

"So," says Sarah, forgetting about her picking for a minute. "Tell me everything. How are you?"

"Well, considering my divorce came through this morning and my estranged ex-husband is getting married in two weeks' time, I'm in pretty good shape."

"He's marrying that woman?" Carla shrieks. "That French *puttana*? *Non é possibile*. Why?"

I sigh. "I really don't know. He must love her, I suppose. Oh, I know it's stupid, but this really means it's over, there's no going back. Nick and I are an item from the past. On September 15th he becomes Cécile's husband."

"But what about you, *cara mia*. I understand you have been very busy?"

I quickly stop feeling so sorry for myself and smile as I remember my kisses with Jean-Claude and Johnny. "I have actually, yes. Well, that is I have found two possibilities. One French, the other English."

"What she's not telling you," says Sarah, "is that one is a French aristo and the other a film star. I tell you girl, I am NOT feeling too sorry for you right now, even if Nick is marrying Miss Tiny-Tits."

"A film star? An aristo? *Porca miseria*," says Carla, "What the hell have I been doing all this time? And I still can't play tennis. Details please...."

"There's not much to tell really," I begin.

"People always say that when there is," interrupts Carla.

"She's slept with them both," laughs Sarah. "At the same time, *à la française*."

"*Bien sûr,*" I joke, cutting another bunch of grapes. I am finding it easier and easier to multi-task here; only a few hours ago I couldn't imagine chatting while harvesting, but I now feel quite comfortable. "Obviously now I'm in touch with my inner French woman, one man is not enough."

"Enough for what?" says a deep voice behind me. I drop my secateurs on the ground.

Jean-Claude is standing there beaming down at me. I introduce him to the girls, who stop picking and smile as he reaches through the vine to take their hands.

"How *charmant,*" says Carla, visibly swooning. "I have so missed continental European men. *Enchantée.* "

"Sophie has told me so much about you," says Sarah. "It's lovely to finally meet you. I gather you have been a bit of a knight in shining armour."

"Even more than I imagined," I add, giving Jean-Claude a hug. "I found out just before you got here that Jean-Claude is the mystery benefactor behind Kamal. Isn't that wonderful?"

Carla, Lucy and Sarah all nod. "Any friend of Kamal's is a friend of mine," says Sarah. "Where on earth did you find such a lovely young man?"

Jean-Claude looks at the ground for a split-second, reminding me fleetingly of the way Edward does the same whenever he has done something wrong. "That, my dear ladies, is my secret. Now if you'll excuse me, I am going to see if I can help him with the sorting."

"Very nice, very nice," says Carla as she watches him walk away. "Really Sophie, I'm impressed, he's sexy, and obviously adores you."

"Yes, I agree, a real hottie and sooooo French, good enough to eat," adds Sarah.

"However did you manage to seduce him? What's your secret?"

"It's all about matching underwear," I laugh. "Once you've cracked that you can seduce anyone."

Lucy is the only one who is not overjoyed with the presence of the hot frog, as Sarah immediately dubs him.

"What do you know about his past?" she asks. "He might be married for all you know, or have a terrible secret in his cellar."

"Yes, or maybe he has a trail of mistresses from here to Marseille," adds Carla.

"Don't judge everyone by your own standards Carla," says Sarah. I can see this is going to get ugly. "It is perfectly possible that the man has never been married because of some tragic saga or long-lost love."

"But you have to admit, he's too glamorous to be single and just wandering around the vineyards," says Carla.

"If you like older men," says Sarah, grinning at Kamal who has come back, and gently placing a bunch of grapes in the white bucket.

"He was in love with an Englishwoman," I say. "But his brother ran off with her."

"Oh poor thing," says Sarah. "These Englishwomen, you just can't trust them."

"I would rather blame the brother," says Lucy. "God my back hurts, how much longer do we have to do this?"

"Only another two weeks to go for you ladies," laughs Kamal returning with some empty buckets.

He seems to inspire them and they pick with renewed vigour.

"So what has happened with this Frenchman?" asks Carla. "Is he your lover?"

"No," I say, embarrassed to be talking about it in case Kamal overhears. "No, he's, well…."

"But you have snogged, I know you have, several times," says Sarah.

"Yes I remember you telling me about the first kiss," adds Lucy. "You said it was… hang on, it was a great quote, I even stole it for my book. You said it was 'like the first sip of champagne, utterly fresh, exciting and delicious.' That was it."

"You're writing a book?" asks Kamal who has come closer to help Lucy separate two vines. "What about?"

Lucy blushes slightly. "It's a kind of a memoir, about a love affair between a young man and an older woman."

Kamal grins at her.

"But really it's mainly fiction," she adds. "I mean I didn't… well, you know."

"What Lucy is saying, is that it's erotic fiction," says Sarah, gazing at Kamal before adding. "I did most of her research."

"Well, if you ever feel like researching any erotic non-fiction, let me know," says Kamal to Sarah and winks before wandering off to get the trailer.

Lucy and I make big eyes at each other in the manner of silly schoolgirls. Sarah looks like the cat that's got the cream as she watches him walk away. Carla looks like she's about to stab Sarah with her secateurs.

It's going to be a long harvest.

*

At dinner hardly anyone has the energy to speak, let alone flirt. We eat pasta and drink red wine and by 9pm we have all collapsed into our beds. I fall asleep within seconds and am woken by my phone ringing. I reach for it with closed eyes, assuming it must be Johnny from LA again, with some scheme or other.

"Johnny, it's the middle of the night, you are not good for my beauty sleep," I groan.

Silence.

"Hello?"

"Soph, it's Nick."

I sit up in bed and look at my clock.

"Nick, it's 3am. What are you doing? The kids are all asleep, why are you calling?"

He sighs. "You know, Soph, Cécile and I are getting married in less than two weeks' time."

"You called me at 3am to discuss your wedding plans?"

"No, not at all. I'm sorry, Soph, I just really needed to talk to you. I mean, we never really talked about the reality of us splitting up and me getting married and all that, and well, I just couldn't sleep and was lying here fretting and so just thought I would call and just…"

"Just what?"

"Well, just make sure this is what we really want. Make sure that we're sure this is the best thing. That there really is no chance for us to get back together."

Is he for real? I say nothing.

"I mean it's all happened so quickly, Soph," he goes on. "We had a life, a future, and I know I'm the one that messed it up, but is there really no chance for us?"

I am still speechless.

"Nick... this is all... too late," I manage finally.

"Is it though, Soph?" He has warmed to his subject. "Is it really too late? Do we want to throw everything away? Is it not worth trying again, for the kids, for us?"

"Nick, you're having pre-wedding nerves. Did you call your ex-girlfriend before we got married too?"

He laughs. "No. Soph, I am deadly serious."

"And so am I. Forget it Nick, you created this situation, it's all of your making."

"I know, I know, but that doesn't make it any easier for me."

"Easier for you? How the fuck do you think it's been for me? Coping alone and being dumped for a French woman with small breasts? But I have coped and I am trying to make a success of things and I think it's bloody selfish of you to phone and put a spanner in the works just as I am getting things together."

I feel tears coming on and I do not want to cry. I have already cried way too much over this man.

"And then there was the Viagra incident – just the icing on the cake of my total humiliation and hurt."

"She spiked my drink, Soph. It was meant to be a joke, only it backfired. I just want to talk about this, so we can be sure."

I turn on my bedside light. Is this what I want? I imagine Nick lying next to me. Do I want him back in my life? In my bed?

I take a deep breath.

"I'm hanging up now, Nick. This is what you wanted and you got it."

"When the gods want to punish you, they answer your prayers," he says quietly.

"Indeed," I say and hang up.

I throw some clothes on and go outside. There is no way I will ever sleep now. I hear noises coming from the Sauvignon Blanc vineyard. Kamal is there with the Spanish lads doing some night-harvesting.

"Give me secateurs," I growl.

"And good morning to you, too," he grins.

We work by the moonlight, which is so bright that our shadows and the shadows of the vines are thrown onto the ground. I remember Jean-Claude's quote about our nights being like the days up north. The cicadas are quieter but still chirpy. There is no wind. It is a still magical night and it has an immediately calming effect on me. Of course I have wanted Nick to call and beg to come back. It is only natural. We still have three children together and I want what is best for them. But too much has happened now for that to be an option. I would never be able to trust him again and, quite apart from that, I reflect as I look at my vineyard and over towards the Château de Boujan, I have finally moved on.

When I have finished my row of grapes, I tell Kamal I am going for a walk to stretch my legs. I walk over to Jean-Claude's château. It is now 5am. He is unlikely to be awake, but this can't wait any longer. I call his mobile and hope he has left it on.

A very groggy frog answers the phone.

"Oui?"

"Jean-Claude, it's me, Sophie. I'm sorry to disturb you, but I need to see you. I'm walking over to your house now, can you come downstairs and open the door please?"

"Yes, of course, are you okay?"

"Yes, never been better."

"But what is so urgent? Sophie, it's 5 o'clock in the morning."

"I know and I'm sorry about that but I just had to see you right away."

"Okay, okay, I am on my way."

I imagine him getting out of bed. What will he be wearing, I wonder? Does he sleep naked? Or does he have striped cotton pyjamas? These are all things I am prepared and eager to find out.

When I get to his house he is standing just inside the door with a white towel wrapped around his waist. I am relieved to see he is smiling as I walk up the steps.

"So, *ma petite vigneronne*, to what do I owe this surprising wake-up call?"

I walk up and stand opposite him. I breathe in his smell; a lavender eau de cologne mixed with something that is all him. I put my arms around his neck and kiss him. He is startled but then relaxes and kisses me back. He puts his arms around me and pulls me closer to him; I can feel him growing hard under his towel. I release myself to pull my T-shirt over my head and pull off my jeans. I don't go as far as my knickers and bra (matching, natch), but I do say a silent prayer that the Hitler moustache will be less obvious in this dawn light.

"*Mon dieu*," he says. "You're so beautiful."

I smile and kiss him again, and remove his towel. Luckily there are no neighbours to see us. I am loving the feel of his naked skin against mine and the anticipation of what is to come. I caress his shoulders, his back, his buttocks. He really is gorgeous, toned and firm.

He moves aside to close the door and then slowly removes my bra. He starts to circle my nipples with his tongue. This sends ripples of pleasure and lust throughout my whole body. I suddenly realise how very long it has been since I really wanted to be made love to; right now I could beg him to pin me down and just do it. But maybe that wouldn't be very ladylike? These French are a bit more romantic than your bog Irish.

He kneels down in front of me and removes my knickers. I run my fingers through his hair and hope he is not going to be too amazed by the lack of pubes. Bloody Audrey and her *Madame Figaro* articles. He doesn't flinch but starts to circle my clitoris with his tongue. Now I really am going to explode. I'm having that kind of combination between tickling and ecstatic sensation, I half want it to go on forever but part of me can take no more. I kneel down to join him and take his cock in my hand, enjoying my first touch of it, moving slowly up and down. It is what Sarah would call a porn-star cock. I can barely get my hand around it.

"May I take you to bed?" he says, grinning.

"You may indeed," I reply and go with him upstairs.

Rule 24

Fidelity is for other people

The French Art of Having Affairs

There is a click inside me, a sort of inexplicable and strange physical manifestation of Nick's wedding. I look at my watch but I know before I see the hands what the time is. It is just after 3pm and Nick will have just said his vows at Chelsea Registry Office. He is another woman's husband. Will he be faithful to her? Maybe as she's French she won't much mind. She'll be off doing her own thing in her own corner, as Audrey puts it.

I found Cécile's bra in Nick's bag less than eight months ago. Only nine months, but it seems like a different life. Nick's infidelity, him leaving, marrying Cécile, me shagging a French aristo and snogging a film star, me running a vineyard. How is it possible that all that has happened in less time than it does to carry a baby to term?

I am sorting the vines in the *cave*. The children sit outside in a circle. Charlotte is organising a quiz.

"Is it better to be Spiderman or to have a Ferrari?" she asks Edward.

"To have a Ferrari," says Edward.

"Right answer! Now, what is the nicest animal in the world?"

"Horses," says Edward.

"Wrong answer! Emily?"

"Sheeps?"

"That's the right answer," says the quizmaster. "Now, Edward, what is the best country in the world?"

"Is this the London question?" asks Edward. "I want the London question."

"I want gets nothing," says Charlotte.

"France?" asks Emily.

"Wrong! The right answer is England because there is daddy there and Granny."

"Granny's here," says Emily.

"Only for a holiday," snaps Charlotte. "Don't argue or you won't be allowed to play. Now, what is the best thing for you that you can eat?"

"Apples?" tries Edward.

"Wrong answer. Emily?"

"Is it drinking?"

"No, it's fruit."

"But apples are fruit," protests Edward but gets an old-fashioned look from his sister.

"Now what is the word we should be saying all the time?"

"I know, I know," says Edward. "Ketchup."

"Wrong! Emily?"

"Please and thank you."

"Is the correct answer. Well done Emily, you won."

"What do I win?"

Charlotte is lost for words for once. I can see tears welling up in Emily's eyes at the thought of winning for no reason.

"You win the right to come and help me clean the sorting machine," I tell her.

This has an immediate effect. My most expensive and newest piece of equipment is normally out of bounds. This miraculous piece of machinery sorts the grapes from the stems ready for the fermentation process. At the end of each day it needs careful cleaning, which I am doing with a hose and some cloths.

Emily now joins in. The quizmaster and her friend go off to find my mother.

"How are you darling?" I ask her.

"Fine, how are you?" she responds.

I laugh. "What a polite young lady you are," I say. "I was just wondering if you missed Daddy or if you're all right. I don't really get to talk to you very much."

It's strange, I feel almost shy with her. I am so rarely alone with my children; they are always a troop, a gang of three answering back and bickering. For once I am alone with my little Emily and I am able to hear how she feels about things without the others shouting her down.

"I do miss Daddy," she says. "I miss his jokes and him being here, but I'm used to it now."

She looks so serious, so brave; I want to cradle her in my arms but am worried I'll start crying. So instead I keep spraying the sorting machine.

"I know darling girl, I miss his jokes as well. But he'll come and see you soon."

He is due to come over after his honeymoon with the new Mrs Nick Reed to tell them about their wedding and take them back for the celebration party. They decided to keep the actual wedding very small.

"Will he come back and live with us? Or is he staying with Cécile?"

"He'll stay with Cécile," I say.

"Will you be lonely? Or will you marry someone else?" she asks, adjusting her cat's ears.

It's a good question. I think for a few seconds.

"I won't be lonely, I've got you. And for the moment, no, I don't think I will marry anyone else. Not just yet anyway."

I turn off the hose. "Well done," I say, "it's all clean and ready for another day's work tomorrow."

Emily puts down her cloth. "Good. Sleep well Mr Sorting Machine."

I join in the yoga session a few minutes late. Kamal has got Sarah and Carla doing sun salutations. He is directing their breathing, making sure it coincides with their movements. I find yoga relaxing even on my own but when you are being told what to do it is even more so. You just abandon yourself to your teacher and the only thing you need to focus on is doing the posture well, a big part of which is breathing in and out at the right time. It's amazing how connected your body and breath are, how your breath can actually help you get into positions you thought were impossible. Especially things like forwards bends, which we are working on now. We are sitting on the floor with our right leg bent and trying to lean over the other leg as far down as we can.

"Look," says Sarah excitedly, I can touch my knee with my nose."

"You have to have a very big nose to be able to do that," says Carla.

From the village I can hear the tannoy with the disembodied voice of the mayor's assistant announcing the arrival of the '*marchand de coquillages sur la place*'. I love that sound, though we only hear it here if the wind is coming from the south, which normally means bad weather will follow. On Thursday nights it announces that "*Chez Jojo est sur la place*", Chez Jojo being the red and cream pizza van from which we get delicious Margaritas every week, bringing them home and covering them in rocket to eat like sandwiches.

The wind here is remarkable; you notice it most when it doesn't blow, because it is almost constant, even if just as a pleasant breeze, as it often is. There is the *Tramontane* that comes from the north and brings clear skies, drying the vines and the land like a hair dryer, and the *Marin* that comes from the sea, bringing mist, clouds and rain but seldom any mud as the wind dries the ground in a day or so.

My forward bend and peaceful thoughts are interrupted by my mother running towards me shouting.

"Fire, fire, there's a fire in the vineyard. Come quickly, call the fire brigade!"

We all leap up and run towards my mother, who is frantically waving and motioning for us to follow her. She runs towards the Cabernet Sauvignon vineyard, where we see flames roaring. I immediately think of my favourite olive tree, which is ridiculous – I should be more worried about the vines and all that money going up in smoke.

We get there around the same time as the fire brigade; someone must have called them earlier. I see Jean-Claude showing them where to park and feel total relief. Once again he's come to my rescue.

Kamal has dragged the hose from the *cave* as close as he can get it and the rest of us work with the firemen to fill up buckets of water and throw on the flames.

Carla, Sarah, Lucy and I stand in a line passing water-filled buckets to Jean-Claude, who throws them on the burning part of the field. It helps a little, but the main fire control is being done by the gallons of water sprayed from the fire engine.

After about half an hour the fire eventually concedes defeat, like a dragon that has lost its battle for life.

We all stand there surveying the damage like Scarlett O'Hara in *Gone with the Wind*. My olive tree is fine – a little bit charred with some damaged branches, but it will survive. However, about a quarter of the vines are burnt to a cinder. I am cursing the fact that we hadn't yet picked them.

"Don't worry," says Kamal. "They will come back quickly. It could have been a lot worse."

My mother comes and puts her arm around me. "I'm sorry

sweetheart, but at least no one was hurt."

"Are you insured for this sort of thing?" asks Lucy.

"I don't know," I say, shaking my head, still unable to believe what has happened. But it's true that it could have been so much worse; the fire could even have reached the house with this wind and the dryness right now. But how on earth did it start and what can I do to make sure it doesn't happen again?

I look over towards the firemen and see Jean-Claude receiving treatment for burns. Poor man, he was here right at the beginning, he must have tried to stop it with his bare hands. He walks towards me when he catches me looking at him. I feel like running into his arms but don't want to make a spectacle of myself.

"I'm so grateful Jean-Claude. Thank God you were here. It could have been so much worse."

Instead of answering he just looks at me with pain and sadness in his eyes.

"Jean-Claude, what is it? What's the matter? Are you all right? Have you been badly hurt?"

He shakes his head. Oh my God, I think, it looks like he's about to cry.

"Jean-Claude, don't worry, it's over, everything's fine. We just need to find out what started the fire so we can avoid it happening again."

He puts his bandaged hands on my shoulders and looks me in the eye.

"I started it, Sophie," he says, before walking away.

Rule 25

The fantasy is often better than the reality

The French Art of Having Affairs

The harvest is almost over. There have been no major disasters since the fire and most of the grapes are safely in. The fermenting period is about to begin in earnest for the vines we have picked. But tonight it is party time.

I am still not feeling in much of a party mood after the fire and the discovery of Jean-Claude's betrayal, but I feel I owe it to all my helpers who have done a great job. Carla and Sarah, spurred on by a desire for Kamal's approval (and his body) have worked like Trojans. Colette and Calypso have been fabulous too, Calypso not working every day but whenever she's been able to.

Lucy has used her time as a manual labourer to think about how her memoir should end.

"I suppose a happy ending would be that my heroine slots

back into her old life without anyone noticing?"

We all nod in agreement.

"A book needs a satisfying ending," she goes on. "Is that satisfying enough?"

"Maybe the reader should be left with a hint that there is something more to come around the corner?" says Sarah.

"Is that realistic?" says Lucy.

"Yes!" we all shout at once. "Otherwise what's the point?"

The party is going to take place mainly outside, on and around the terrace by the kitchen. We have a band coming to play; some friends of Colette's who live towards the mountains and play anything you want to hear. I have given them a list of some songs I would like. She tells me they are in their late 50s but will play for free, so who am I to be ageist? And rather like Alice in Wonderland finds no point in a book without pictures, I see no point in a party without music.

Johnny has promised to come. He is in Paris filming and will be here by 8 o'clock. I haven't seen him since his last visit but we have been in touch constantly. I am really looking forward to seeing him. I thought I had made my decision, but I was clearly wrong.

I keep thinking about Jean-Claude. He came by with a letter the day after the fire. In it he explained what had happened.

"I just can't believe it," I told the girls after I'd read it. "It's the kind of thing you expect from an Agatha Christie novel, not the sort of thing you think will happen to you."

Basically the situation was this. Jean-Claude's brother, the one he fell out with over the English girl, had actually hired Kamal, who was unaware that he was being paid to spy, he just thought the brothers wanted to help me.

Alexandre, Jean-Claude's brother, was intent on getting hold of Sainte Claire as a way to gain forgiveness from Jean-Claude, because Jean-Claude had always loved the property and spent a lot of his childhood there with his grandmother.

For the boys it had always been a kind of haven, somewhere they could run to and get away from the endless socialising and arguing of their parents in the château.

Alexandre had tried to buy Sainte Claire before Nick and I did, he was the one who had made the lower offer, and he just couldn't raise the cash to match our bid. He didn't ever hear about it being for sale again during the time I was leaving.

He got Jean-Claude involved in the day-to-day working of the plan and told him to get as close to me as possible, because he is based in Aix, where he lives with their aunt, having split from Jean-Claude's English fiancée.

"It seemed like a good plan to begin with," Jean-Claude wrote. "I supposed a little part of me also wanted revenge on Englishwomen in general. But that night when I went to the *cave* to put vinegar in your Cabernet Sauvignon I realised I just couldn't go through with it. I had grown too fond of you. I wanted to tell you everything then and there but I was worried you wouldn't understand. We French have a very different attitude to family and love and land. I was convinced you would think I was a crazy person. So instead I tried to get Alexandre to stop. But by then he was on some kind of mission, he gets obsessive, like he did when he stole my fiancée. He said I had clearly lost my head to yet another English *salope* and needed saving from myself. I saw the fire as I was walking over to help with the harvest. Alexandre got one of the village boys to start it I'm sure. I got there as soon as I could to stop it and minimise the damage.

I don't expect you to forgive me, I have behaved abominably, but I just want you to know that you and the children are the best thing that ever happened to me. You gave me a whole new view on life, with no bitterness or ambition or feuds."

I have no idea where Mr Fox, as we have nicknamed him, is now. Probably sulking in his lair. Thank God the girls were all here to cushion the blow, although two betrayals in less than a year does seem slightly excessive. Could it be third time lucky with Johnny? Or maybe this is a sign that I should give up on men. I could always ask Calypso for some Sapphic tips.

Right now though I have to get ready for the party. It has been an exhausting few weeks.

The most important thing, of course, is to decide what to wear. It is still extremely warm. I need something sleeveless if I'm not going to end up in a sweaty heap. I opt for a pretty flowery pink strappy dress I picked up in Pézenas market for only 20 euros. It is cut on the bias, and the right length for me, if I go by the St Tropez method of measuring lengths.

Charlotte and Emily come into my bedroom. They are dressed in lovely pink and white polka-dot dresses my mother brought from London.

"You look gorgeous girls," I tell them. "Emily, is there any chance you could not wear your cat's ears for once?"

"No," she says.

Edward comes in wearing his Spiderman suit.

"You look stunning, Mummy," he says. Stunning is his new word; he uses it in most sentences.

"Thanks baby," I say, brushing my hair and adding a final touch of lip-gloss. "Let's go downstairs."

Kamal and the girls have done everything. The terrace looks lovely, lit up with fairy lights and lots of candles in brown paper bags. This is an old trick of Carla's: put some sand in a brown paper bag and then pop a candle in, and the effect is great while being so much cheaper than buying candleholders.

"We put the candles in," says Charlotte proudly.

"All of them," adds Emily.

"I did too," says Edward.

"No you didn't," snaps Charlotte, "you just got in the way."

A diversion is created by the band arriving in a battered old white Renault van. Simon and Ray, the singer and lead guitarist, who both greet me like a long-lost sister. Simon looks like he's rocked with a few girls in his time, he has a definite twinkle in his eye. Ray has an impressive moustache that reminds me of a character in that poem I often read to the children; *The Walrus and the Carpenter*. Ray surveys the terrace and at the stage we have created for them using wooden planks.

"Groovy," he says, looking anything but.

"Is that the Walrus?" whispers Edward to the girls, clearly thinking along the same lines as I am.

Emily tells him to be quiet. I send them off to help my mother, who is preparing some inedible eats for the guests.

I look around. I feel a real sense of achievement. The first harvest is over, the wine is bottled and ready to be sold with around £10,000 already pre-ordered thanks to my wine bonds and marketing drive to local restaurants and hotels. Of course there is a long way to go before the business is really stable, but it is a great beginning. My personal life may be all over the place, but the cicadas are chirping and I finally believe that Domaine Sainte Claire can be a success.

An hour later and the cicadas are drowned out by *Hotel California*. It's amazing how the proportions of a space change when it is filled with people, the noises of chatter, of glasses clinking, laughing and music. The crowd takes on a sort of life of its own. I am loving the buzz of my own party, of my friends bonding, eating, drinking. Is this how cicadas feel every evening? Is this why they are constantly chirping?

For the first time since Jean-Claude went from lover to villain I feel really relaxed and happy. That might also have something to do with the white wine, the fact that the stress of the harvest is over, and also the anticipation of Johnny showing up later on.

Kamal and Sarah are dancing; they look good together. It was only a matter of time. She is still seeing her CEO lover but obviously she does as she pleases when they're not together. Maybe I should behave a bit more like her. Why does it have to be all or nothing with me? If I had taken Audrey's advice and had a fling with Johnny at the same time as Jean-Claude, then I might not have been so heartbroken about the duplicitous frog. Being faithful has certainly never got me anywhere. I am beginning to think these French women are on to something.

"Is your friend Carla married?" Tim nice-but-dim is suddenly standing next to me.

"No, but you are," I smile.

He gives me a stern look.

"She's divorced," I go on. "But normally she goes for tennis coaches."

Tim's face lights up. "I used to teach tennis in the Army, we had marvellous facilities at Aldershot. Thanks, Sophie. Oh, great party by the way."

He skips off back to Carla to discuss forehand slices, or whatever it is tennis players talk about.

I go and sit next to Lucy, who has been entertaining the children by telling them short stories.

"Do you miss your kids?" I ask.

She smiles. "I know I should, but I'm having such a lovely time, to be honest I haven't really thought about them that much. I think I needed to get away for once. I really love it here, you've done a marvellous job, you know. You have so much to be proud of."

I feel close to tears. This is the kind of thing my mother should say but never does.

"Thanks Lucy, and thanks for all your help during the harvest."

"Oh, all that bending over, sweating and suffering in the scorching sun, you mean? I wouldn't have missed it for the world. Cheers, here's to you, Sainte Claire and your future together." She raises her glass.

"And you're okay about Josh?"

She twitches her nose, a little in the way Samantha from *Enchanted* does when she casts a spell. This is as close as Lucy will normally get to showing any emotions.

"I miss the excitement of him being there, and of course the sex. But the book is a good substitute."

"How are things with Patrick? I mean, are you….?"

"Having sex?" she interrupts. "Yes. Not much, but probably as often as most couples who have been married for almost 10 years. Of course it's not as much fun as sex with a young man who looks like a Calvin Klein model, but I am determined that my affair will not break up my marriage. I would never forgive myself. Are you OK, after the Mr Fox incident?"

I am about to answer when a loud, familiar sound drowns out our little party.

Of course it's Johnny and his chopper; why can't the man make a more subtle entrance? And being pathologically scared of heights, can I really marry a man who travels in a helicopter?

The locals look terrified; I think they assume anything loud with lights is going to be the taxman. I walk over the vineyard to meet him. I feel a little giddy and the walk does me good. It's amazing how much wine you find yourself downing as you stand around and chat. Without even meaning to I am slightly tipsy and feel the need to sober up. Nothing like the wind from the helicopter blades to do that; my breath is taken away as I get closer and see Johnny jumping down the steps towards me, doubling over to avoid the worst of the wind.

"Hey gal," he shouts and waves. When we get close, he puts his arms around me and I look up at him.

"Good to see you, Cunningham," he says, planting a kiss on my forehead.

"You too," I smile. "You certainly know how to make an entrance. They're expecting President Sarkozy down there."

"I hope they won't be too disappointed," he laughs. "Shall we?"

He extends his arm to me and we walk towards the rest of the party. I am grinning like the cat who got the cream as I arrive with my film-star friend. Carla, Lucy and Sarah are all jostling to be the first to greet him.

"We've heard so much about you," says Lucy.

"Did you really sleep with Scarlett Johansson?" asks Carla, shameless as always.

"Who's she?" laughs Johnny and puts his arms around my shoulder.

Sarah looks amazed. "God you really are gorgeous," she says, clearly refreshed with wine already. "Even more gorgeous than on telly."

I interrupt her before she embarrasses herself any more. "What would you like to drink, Johnny?"

"I suppose asking for a beer in a vineyard would be seen as very bad form?" he replies.

"Not at all." I go off to get him his beer, leaving him in the hands of my three friends.

In the kitchen my mother is preparing smoked-salmon blinis, sausage rolls and something that looks like guacamole.

"How are you?" I ask her as I walk over to the fridge.

"Alive," she says. "Alive and cooking." Then she collapses

with laughter. She was always very good at laughing at her own jokes, I suppose someone has to.

I go back and join Johnny. The girls see my return as a sign to push off and leave us alone.

We sit at the table and eat something indescribable containing avocado and red peppers, but which tastes great. I see Colette and Calypso dancing together. Tim and Carla look as if they've struck up a deep and meaningful discussion about tennis, so he's happy.

"You've got a lovely bunch of friends," says Johnny.

"I expect this isn't really the sort of party you're used to," I laugh.

"I hate all those parties," he smiles. "I'm much happier somewhere simple, with honest people around me. But sadly if I want to make a career out of films, that's where I have to be."

He pauses for a moment and takes my hands in his. "So Cunningham, have you thought any more about what we talked about? About moving out to California and running a vineyard there?"

I sigh. He has that sort of desperately expectant look the children have when they're asking me if they can go on a sleepover but they know the answer will be no. I hate to do this, but I can't move to California, I've only just got to grips with the vineyard here and it just feels, so, well, wrong.

I've been agonising over it since the fire. My first instinct after Jean-Claude's confession was just to pack up and go to California. For a while I was really set on it. But something just didn't feel right. I kept trying to convince myself it was right, telling myself how lucky I was to have Johnny and the offer of a vineyard and how everything would work out, but I didn't ever feel truly comfortable about it.

"I'm sorry Johnny," I tell him. "It's a lovely idea, but I just can't. For a start I love it here; I love the village, the life, even the smell of the earth and, of course, the people."

As I say that word I remember Jean-Claude and I feel like someone has just punched me.

"The kids are settled," I go on. "With everything they've been through I don't want to unsettle them again so soon. And you would hardly ever be there, what with your career and always travelling around. I can just imagine sitting in some Californian vineyard alone and feeling a long way from home."

I was worried the alcohol would make it more difficult to see what the way forward was but it has given me more clarity than I normally have. This job is clearly ideal for me.

Johnny takes a slug of his beer but doesn't speak.

"Johnny, I'm so sorry, you know how much I care about you. But I'm just not ready to uproot and move on."

"Okay, Cunningham. Well, is there any point in my being here?"

He is being what Edward calls 'grammatic'.

I smile. "I think there is. It's a great party and for once you don't have to fly off anywhere. Why don't you stay the night?"

He looks rather surprised. "Well, if you insist. OK gal, can I ask my pilot to join the party and kip down somewhere? And where are those beastly children?"

I watch him as he calls his pilot. He is so glamorous and

gorgeous, and without him in it, my life is far less interesting. But that doesn't mean I want to marry him and move to California. My heart is at Sainte Claire; there is no way I can just leave here now. Maybe I can convince him to stick around here a bit more.

"Johnny," I say when he gets off the phone. "I think you're amazing, and you, well, you wanting to be with me has made such a difference to me at what was the lowest point of my life, and self-esteem," I begin. "You really helped me through this time and I'll never forget that. Life throws at you many things…" I smile

"But very few friends," he finishes the sentence for me and smiles. "That's enough talking Cunningham, let's dance."

I get up and we move on to the makeshift dance-floor. The band is playing 'Sweet Home Alabama', it feels good to be moving. The kids spot Johnny and join us, Edward already dances like a boy, I mean he is a boy of course, but in that way that boys are all arms and legs jutting out. Johnny twirls the girls around and they squeal with delight. Emily has a great sense of rhythm, unlike her mother.

We dance on with them for another half hour or so, before my mother comes to take them off to bed, which she had promised to do. Johnny and I kiss them goodnight. They are exhausted and don't protest too much. On our way out of the house he takes my hand.

"I could get used to this Cunningham," he says. "Maybe we should think about a compromise?"

I smile and nod, touched but unsure of what to say. "Let's go and catch the end of the party," I say.

The band is playing 'You look beautiful tonight', Johnny takes me in his arms and we dance slowly. It feels good to be close to him, to feel his warmth and inhale his smell.

I see Carla and Tim dancing too out of the corner of my eye, as well as Kamal and Sarah. Lucy is chatting to one of the young Spanish grape-pickers, maybe she's plotting a sequel to her book. There is a full moon bathing the scene in diffused light. It is hard to imagine anything quite so idyllic. For some reason my mind flashes to Jean-Claude, I wonder if he's enjoying the moonlight, if he's alone and if he's thinking about us.

"A penny for your thoughts Gal?" asks Johnny, looking down at me with an expression filled with affection.

I have to move on from Mr Fox, there is nothing to be gained by dwelling on him. This is the new Sophie, independent and strong, ready to go it alone, and to take decisions that will be best for her. "I was wondering how difficult it would be to get a Hollywood star into bed?" I grin.

Rule 26:

Sex is just like any other sensual pleasure, be it eating or drinking: it is not to be taken too seriously

The French Art of Having Affairs

"Noooooooooooo!"

I think I can hear the scream, but am not even sure it is coming from me. It is as if my ears are blocked and my brain has frozen. In fact, nothing seems real. I am somehow removed from the scene in front of me, which is happening in slow motion.

I can do nothing to stop it. I run but I can't get there in time. The car brakes and there is a thud as it hits Edward and it skids to a halt, crashing into the fountain. My son is thrown through the air and lands on the other side of the road; the side he was trying to get to.

This is not a nightmare. I am awake. It has happened. My little boy is lying apparently lifeless on the ground; someone is phoning an ambulance. I am running towards Edward as fast as I can but petrified of what I will find there.

If only I hadn't gone back to see where Wolfie was, if only I hadn't stopped to send that text to Sarah, if only the children had been gripped by the television programme they were watching instead of deciding to go to the bakery, if only we had never moved to France… If only a million things.

I get to him and kneel down. He is lying as if asleep, with his arms by his head and his legs folded to one side. At least I made him wear his Spiderman helmet, although I think I can see a crack in it.

"Please let him be alive," I weep. "Please God, please, please."

I put my hand gently on his chest, he is warm; I think he is breathing, but I can't really tell. I long to scoop him up in my arms but remember you're not meant to move people.

"Is Edward all right?" Emily and Charlotte are next to me. Emily starts weeping when she sees her brother. I can't answer.

The ambulance arrives. Paramedics jump out like storm-troopers and surround my boy. A policewoman puts a blanket over my shoulders. In spite of the heat, I am shivering. There is a lot of activity on radios or walkie-talkies, I have no idea what is going on, I am desperate for any news at all but they are all busy. The girls cling to me watching it all.

"He has head and chest injuries," says the policewoman next to me after a briefing from one of the ambulance-men. "They are going to air-lift him to Montpellier. You can go with him."

"Will he be all right?"

"It is too early to tell, but children are stronger than we think. Is there anyone who can look after the girls while you are gone?"

I take my mobile phone out and call Calypso. There is no reply. I try Audrey, then remember she is away in Paris. I try Colette, Peter and even Agnès. No joy. Bloody hell. There is only one person left.

"I saw the helicopter," says Jean-Claude. "What is going on?

"Edward was hit by a car," I say quickly. "They are air-lifting him to hospital. I can't get hold of anyone else; could you please look after the girls for me?"

"I'm on my way."

Edward is being lifted carefully into a dark-blue plastic stretcher and strapped in. It is adult-size and his little body only takes up less than half of it. I am led to the ambulance and sit next to him. He is looking pale. I have one girl on each knee.

"I need you to be very brave," I say. "Edward needs me to come with him, I need to be there when he wakes up, so he won't be scared."

"Who will keep us?" asks Charlotte. "Please not Agnès."

"When will he wake up?" asks Emily.

"Not Agnès," I say, avoiding Emily's question. "Jean-Claude will take you home and I will be back as soon as I can. I'll call you as soon as we get to the hospital."

"Okay, Mummy," says Charlotte. "We will be brave."

Emily starts weeping hysterically. I try to console her but it's hopeless.

"We need to go," says the ambulance-man. "We have to get there as quickly as possible. The helicopter is waiting in a field up the road for us."

"Come on, *ma puce*," says Jean-Claude, who has abandoned his car in the middle of the road and is outside the ambulance. He coaxes Emily out and into his waiting arms.

"Thank you," I mouth to him as Charlotte joins them, the first contact we've had since he told me about the plot his brother cooked up. The door closes and the siren goes on.

"Hey baby," I say to Edward.

"Hey Mummy," I imagine him saying as I look at his little face, and I can't help but wonder if I will ever hear his voice again.

Three hours later I am sitting in a room in the Lapeyronie Hospital in Montpellier. Edward is being operated on for what they call a 'closed traumatic brain injury'. They are hoping there is only 'primary damage' to the brain, but are worried about a haemorrhage and potential secondary damage.

I have never felt so helpless in my life. I feel almost dead. I can just about manage to breathe . The coffee the nurse brought me is untouched. I clutch my mobile phone, as if that is going to give me any news.

I have spoken to Jean-Claude. He has fed and bathed the girls and will put them to bed in my bed. They will call to say goodnight. He is being wonderful. Maybe I have been a bit harsh on him, after all, it was his brother who was the real impetus behind the whole thing, and Jean-Claude actually saved the vineyard his dastardly sibling tried to burn to the ground.

I have texted Johnny to let him know what happened, he is back in LA so probably asleep. We had an amazing night; all the frustration and waiting of all those years finally over. I don't think we slept at all. We made love and laughed and talked and just enjoyed being with each other. But when it was time for him to go, neither of us was too upset. We were both happy it happened, but his life is in Hollywood in his world of films and glamour and glitz, however much he pretends to hate it. And my life is here.

"Soph." I hear a door open. I look up. I don't think I've ever been so happy to see anyone in my whole life. "Thank God I was in Paris when I got your call, and able to jump on a plane," says Nick.

I get up and throw my arms around him. For the first time since the accident I let myself cry, really cry. All the fear, the angst, the sorrow, it all comes out, and before long Nick's shirt is soaked. He strokes my hair and makes soothing noises. It feels good to be close to him again, good to breathe in his odour. A bit like coming home.

"No news yet?" he asks when I have calmed down.

I shake my head and go back to my plastic chair.

"How do the doctors seem?" says Nick, leaning against the wall.

"Great, they're all great. Oh Nick, I feel so, so… God, why wasn't I there?"

I start crying again.

"Shhh. There, there, Soph. You're not to blame. He was always cycling off when you told him not to, and you can't control everything all the time, especially with children. Come on now, you can't blame yourself."

"If this had happened on your watch, I'm not sure I'd be as nice about it," I say.

Nick smiles. "Well, there's no point in blaming you, is there? He's a lively young lad, you can't keep him on a harness."

"I wish I had," I sigh. "I really wish I had."

My phone rings: Jean-Claude with the girls.

"He's going to be fine," I hear myself saying to Emily. What's the point in giving her nightmares? He might well be fine; we have to be positive.

"You go to sleep and I'll talk to you in the morning. Daddy is with me, yes. I'm sure he'll come and see you too. Love you."

I say goodnight to Charlotte and thank Jean-Claude, who says he will sleep in the spare room.

"So the handsome Frenchie has moved in?" asks Nick.

"No, he was the only one around to take care of the girls. Everyone else seems to have left Boujan to celebrate the end of the harvest."

I haven't told Nick about Jean-Claude's betrayal. It's really none of his business.

"How are they?"

"Emily was hysterical, Charlotte was in control."

"*Plus ça change*," smiles Nick. "I miss them."

"They miss you too."

"I'll come back with you, after, when we know…" His voice trails off. "Shit, Soph, you realise how fucking insignificant everything else is when something like this happens."

I nod. I feel like my whole body has shut down, bar the tears, which keep pouring.

Nick walks over and puts his hand on my shoulder. "Come on, Soph, he'll be fine," he says in a shaky voice. "He's Spiderman, remember?"

I put my hand up to touch his and he squeezes my fingers in his. At that moment the door opens and Edward is wheeled in on a bed. I leap up, desperate to see him. He looks so tiny, surrounded by nurses and with tubes all over the place.

They put the bed in the middle of the room and smile at us. I look at them imploringly but they say nothing. They put a folder of papers at the bottom of his bed and tell us the surgeon will be here in a minute.

As soon as they've gone I lean over him.

"Hey baby," I say. "I love you."

"I love you too," says Nick, leaning over the other side of the bed. For a split-second I think he means me. When I glance up he is looking at me, which makes me blush. How could I be so stupid? Of course he means Edward. How egotistical can you get? And at a moment like this too?

The doctor comes in.

"*Bonjour*. Shall I speak in English?"

"Yes please," I say. "How is he? Please tell me he's okay, I just can't bear it."

"We think we have stopped any internal bleeding of the brain. But we won't know until he wakes up and his neural activity is back to normal. We will of course monitor him very closely. Your husband and you can stay the night here in his room; we will arrange for beds. It is important that he sees someone familiar when he wakes up."

"So, if there is no internal bleeding when he wakes up, he should be fine?" asks Nick.

"He's not paralysed or anything?"

"Thankfully there was no spinal injury, but there was a severe knock to his skull. If he had not been wearing his helmet he would be dead now."

I feel faint. I think about the times they have almost got away without wearing a helmet. Nick makes me sit down.

"We think he will be fine, that he will wake up and there will be no further consequences of the accident. But we have to be honest and tell you that there is a chance there will be."

"How much of a chance?" asks Nick. "I mean, can you give us a percentage please?"

Our surgeon smiles. "You are on the right side of 50 per cent, but I can't say any more than that. Please have something to eat, and get some rest. He's going to need you when he wakes up."

They bring in two beds and put them either side of Edward's bed. Nick goes down to the cafeteria to get some food for us. We share a cheese baguette and a small bottle of red wine. The alcohol calms me and I feel my body slowly starting to relax for the first time in hours.

"I'm scared," I say to Nick. "I'm so scared he's not going to be okay."

"He'll be fine, you heard the doctor: we're on the right side of 50 per cent."

"Yes, but that still means there's a 50 per cent chance things won't be okay."

"Actually, it means there's a less than 50 per cent chance, Miss Pessimist. Have another sip of wine, it'll do you good."

"It is doing me good, despite the fact that it's practically undrinkable."

"Well, why not see if you can get your Arrogant Frog in here? Never miss a business opportunity, that's what I say."

I smile.

"Oh, I almost got a laugh then," says Nick. "Let's see. Have you heard the one about the two Irishmen out drinking? One says to the other: 'I can never sneak into the house after I've been drinking. I've tried everything. I turn the headlights off before I go up the drive. I shut off the engine and coast into the garage. I take my shoes off and creep upstairs. I get undressed in the bathroom. I do everything, but then my wife still wakes up and yells at me for staying out late. His friend replies: 'Do what I do. I screech into the driveway, slam the front door, storm up the steps, throw my shoes into the closet, jump into bed, slap my wife's bottom and say, 'How about a blow job?' She always pretends she's asleep."

I can't help but laugh. "Oh the shame of it," I say. "That would have worked with me anyway."

"Why is it that wives go off sex?" says Nick.

"Has Cécile gone off sex already?" I ask, not really sure I want to know the answer.

"Well, let's just say she's not as gung-ho as she used to be, and you went right off it after the little man arrived."

We both look at our little man. He is breathing peacefully.

"I know, there's no excuse really. I was just always tired, and for some reason I think my libido died in childbirth." I pause before going on. "I just stopped fancying you really. I mean I loved you, but I lost that urge to rip your clothes off."

Nick looks down at the ground. "Yeah, well, I guess that's the difference between men and women. I never stopped fancying you."

"It seems so stupid," I say. "I mean there was nothing really wrong, was there? And who knows, maybe all the lust would have come back?"

He looks up at me. I look into those eyes I have looked into a million times. They are familiar but there is also something different about him. This is my Nick, but my Nick as I used to see him before the children were born. My Nick as a man, a lover, an attractive guy, not my Nick the husband, the worker, the person who irritates me with the way he sticks his knife in the butter. Finally, after all these years, I can see beyond all that.

"What's wrong, Soph? What are you thinking?"

Just the sound of his voice makes me feel weak. Fucking hell, this is ridiculous. I can't be in love with my ex-husband; he's married to someone else for God's sake. Maybe it's just the emotions of today. I have been sent over the edge with worry, angst and pain. This is just a manifestation of the fact that our son could have died today. It's the relief that he didn't, mixed with the continued panic that something might still be wrong.

"Soph," Nick puts his hand on my arm. "Talk to me. I know it's been a hell of a day, but what is it? You look strange."

"Good strange or bad strange?" I ask.

Nick laughs. "Just flipping strange. Although it's hardly

surprising after what's happened."

"It hasn't been the best of days, that's for sure. In fact I can safely say that it's been the worst day of my life."

Nick hugs me. I decide not to tell him about my feelings. He has just got married, for goodness sake. Why on earth would he be interested in me now?

Nick lends me a T-shirt to sleep in as I have nothing with me. We get into our separate beds. My mind is racing. Next to me lies my little boy and next to him my ex-husband, whom I now, inexplicably, find faintly attractive. I am convinced I won't sleep a wink but I must have dozed off because the next thing I know I hear a voice.

"Hey Mummy."

I sit up in bed. I think I must be dreaming, but then I look at him in the bright moonlight and his eyes are open and he is smiling.

"Hey baby," I say. "How are you?"

"Why are you sleeping in my bedroom?"

I look around in panic for any obvious signs of brain haemorrhaging. Will there be lights flashing? Should I call the doctor? But I have to keep him calm.

"Hey, little man," Nick has woken up. "You had a nasty bump on the head, I'm just going to get the doctor to make sure you're okay."

He puts on the bedside light and goes out.

"I'm hungry," says Edward.

"I love you," I say. "I love you so so so much."

"Why am I here?"

"You got run over."

"Phew, I didn't die," he says.

I want to squeeze him to me but am scared to disturb any of the tubes attached to him. I focus on not crying, I don't want to scare him.

The surgeon comes in and puts the main light on.

"*Ça va?*" he asks, looking into Edward's eyes with a small torch.

"*Oui,*" says Edward. "*J'ai faim.*"

"A good sign," smiles the surgeon. "We will get you some food, *jeune homme*. You had us all worried." He turns to me. "How long has he been awake?"

"A few minutes. Is he going to be okay?"

"Yes, it looks like he's fine Madame Reed, totally fine. He will need a lot of rest but there seems to be no sign of any untoward activity and if he's hungry it is a sign that all is well."

I have never felt so grateful to anyone in all my life. "Thank you," I say. "Thank you so very much."

We feed Edward a bowl of soup and some bread and cheese. He is still quite weak after the operation but I can see his strength returning with every mouthful. After his dinner he is tired and falls asleep quickly.

"Soph, stop looking at him as if he's never going to wake up," says Nick, smiling at me. "He's going to be fine, you heard the man."

"I know, I can't believe how lucky we are, when I think about the despair I was in a few hours ago. I would have given anything to have had the news we have now."

"So you're happy, Soph? In spite of everything?"

I blush when I remember my feelings for Nick last night. "Yes," I say, looking at Edward. "I'm extremely happy."

Rule 27

Know what you want from the affair before you pick your lover

The French Art of Having Affairs

"I did something truly terrible," I tell Audrey when she comes over for a cup of tea.

It is almost two weeks since the accident. Edward has been at home for two days. It is so lovely to have him back in his own bed. I was nervous driving him home from hospital, worried that any jolt might damage him, or that we would end up in a crash and back in hospital. It was like the feeling of vulnerablity when I left hospital with the twins, these two tiny people totally dependent on me; I was convinced every car on the road was going to crash into us.

I spent ten days in hospital, the doctors wanted to be completely sure everything was all right before they let us come home. Nick went to Sainte Claire to look after the girls. He left just before Edward and I got back, we met at the airport to say goodbye.

When we got back to the house, I was surprised to see Jean-Claude there, I thought Agnès was looking after the twins. He was playing *boules* with the girls along the track outside the *cave*, Jean-Claude was showing Emily how to aim the ball. Charlotte was laughing because Emily kept totally missing.

I stopped the car and got out; the girls came running towards me and hugged me. Then they spotted Edward. They were so happy to see their little brother I almost cried. I noticed Emily wasn't wearing her cat's ears.

"I lost them the day of the accident," she told me. "But Jean-Claude says they went to look after Edward to make sure he got better. And now he is better, we don't need them any more."

I looked up to acknowledge Jean-Claude but he had already slunk away, like a fox in the night.

Two days on and we are back in a routine; Edward is back at school, everyone is very impressed with his near-death experience and extremely happy to see him. I am feeling more settled than ever before, life feels good, it can't fail to when I remember how desperate I was by that hospital bedside. I have vowed I will never grumble or be grumpy about anything ever again, although I'm not sure it will last more than a week.

Talking of grumbling I have two weeks' of post to go through. I put the bank statement to one side and tackle the rest, there's only so much reality a girl can stand.

There are two letters from Jean-Claude, written in his beautiful sloping handwriting. The one just after the accident talks a lot about Edward and how he hopes all will be well. "I love him like my own son," he ends. The second letter was written after we had the all-clear; it is full of relief and hope for the future and more apologies. I sigh and put them back in their envelopes. Maybe I have been harsh, but after Nick's behaviour I can hardly be blamed for taking deception badly.

There is another letter that stands out as more interesting than the other usual dross. It is from the Guide Hachette. I take a deep breath. Of course I would love for it to be good news, but frankly I can stand just about any disappointment after what I've just been through.

I open the envelope and take out the letter; it's all in French but the message is clear: my Cabernet Sauvignon has been chosen as one of their *coups de Coeur* for 2012. Sainte Claire is on the wine-map of France. After only a year.

I look at the letter again in disbelief. I am longing to tell someone. Daisy the cat walks into the room, she's no use, she's never even heard of the *Guide Hachette*. I call Calypso who is thrilled.

"That's amazing news, we must celebrate, how about a picnic this weekend? Tim has gone off to London to see Carla but the kids and I are here."

They seem to have an open marriage since the party, which works for them. At least he hasn't tried to shoot her recently.

*

"I have done something truly dreadful," I tell Audrey who has come over for a cup of tea.

"I doubt that very much," she says, sipping her tea and refusing to eat any shortbread biscuits. Typical selfish French woman. How am I supposed to eat one if she won't? For some reason I think the calories I consume will have less of an effect if she eats one too; it's hardly rational, but then where does rationality fit in with women and food?

"What is it?" she asks.

I sigh. "At the hospital, just before he left, I put my bra in Nick's bag."

Audrey looks confused. "Why? Didn't you like it?"

"No, well, actually it wasn't one of my favourites. But the point was to cause him problems with Cécile. I thought, for some reason, that I wanted him back, and so I thought about how to get him back and thought I would try her method of strategically placed underwear."

"And has it worked?"

I finally give in to temptation and grab a biscuit. "Well, the thing is, I think my sudden desire to get my ex-husband back might have had something to do with Edward's accident and how stressed I was. The minute I got home and I saw Sainte Claire and the girls…"

"And Jean-Claude?" Audrey interrupts.

I blush. "No, not him! But I mean as soon as I got back to my home, I realised my life with Nick was really over. And I regretted putting my bra in his bag, and now I am thinking that I will have to call Cécile and tell her I put it there, or he just might end up divorced. Again."

Audrey laughs.

"It's not funny," I protest. "For the first time in my life I do something my inner French woman would be proud of and I feel wretched."

"You've done lots your inner French woman would be proud of," says Audrey, taking my hand. "You've lost at least ten kilos in a year, you now know how crucial exfoliators are, and you carry a lip gloss with you at all times."

I laugh, lean across the table towards her and reach out to hold her other hand. Despite her apparent aloofness, Audrey always manages to make me feel happy and is more affectionate than her cool exterior lets on.

"Are you two lesbians?" Charlotte is at the door.

We spring apart. "No, we're just friends," I splutter. "And anyway, how do you know what a lesbian is?"

"Calypso told Cloud, and she told us. I know what triplets is too," she goes on.

"Really? What is it?"

"It's when three people kiss on the lips. It happens a lot in New York. We saw it on that DVD you hid."

Audrey raises an eyebrow.

"Which DVD? Oh, you mean *Sex and the City*? You shouldn't be watching that. That's why I hid it."

"Oh Mummy," says Charlotte, walking out of the kitchen. "It's only sex."

"Now there's a girl who's in touch with her inner French woman," says Audrey admiringly.

Once she has gone I decide to do the grown-up thing and text Nick. Maybe it's not really the grown-up thing, but I can't face calling him.

"Sorry I left my bra in your bag," I write. "It was childish of me and wrong." Then I hit send. Almost immediately my mobile rings. It's Nick. And he's laughing.

"I haven't unpacked yet, but I will now! Soph, I'm flattered. Did you want me back, now?"

"No, I did not. I just had a minor blip, it was all the Edward thing, you know?"

"I understand. I am flattered you even considered it, though. Are the kids there? How is the little man? Can I talk to them?"

"He's fine, they're all fine. Emily's lost her cat's ears."

"Noooo! How can she hear anything? Amazing. I imagined she would be wearing them aged fifty. How is she coping?"

"Really well. She never even talks about them. It's incredible. I wasn't here when she lost them; it was while we were with Edward. Jean-Claude spun her some yarn about Edward needing them to look after him, and she fell for it."

"Is she the only one who has fallen for the handsome Frenchman?"

"Don't be ridiculous," I say. "He tried to burn the vineyard down. Well, his brother did."

I tell him the whole story.

"Well, you've got to admire that kind of passion. The French and their crazy sense of family values, I don't think they can help themselves. And it was a good effort of his to put the damn thing out."

"I don't want to talk about it," I say, and I don't. I pass the phone to the kids so Nick will stop bothering me about Jean-Claude.

I walk outside to breathe in the fresh air. It is now early October, and the weather is still gorgeous. That oppressive heat has gone and the days are comfortingly warm; it's the seasonal equivalent of a balmy evening in high summer.

I stand on the steps of Sainte Claire and survey my vineyards. Kamal, now a full-time employee, much to Sarah's delight, is pruning the Viognier. The frenetic action of the harvest is over and now we start steadily building up to next year's. But this time we have some money in the bank, sales are looking extremely promising, and I now know that mildew isn't some rather dodgy girl's name. With Kamal's help, next year's vintage could be even better.

I think forward to next year. By then we will have been here almost two years and this really will be our home. What do I want to achieve by then? I want the children to stay safe – that's the first question, as Charlotte would say. And I want the business to grow and prosper.

I hope I will stay in touch with my inner French woman enough to remain the shape I am now and always recognise the importance of carrying a lip-gloss.

I started the year off with one husband. Then I had two lovers, albeit briefly. Now I have neither husband, nor lover. Am I going to stay single? Should I re-think the Johnny option? No, I belong here. Although maybe there's no harm in rekindling an old flame, if he happens to be in the neighbourhood.

I look across at Château de Boujan. As I do so, Charlotte comes running out with the phone.

"It's Jean-Claude," she says. "I called him and asked him to come and play *boules*. He said I had to ask you, but it's all right isn't it, Mummy? He's so good at *boules*." She interrupts her own pleading to tell him to *attendez* before carrying on. "Please, Mummy? He says I have to ask you." She passes me the phone.

I take it, unsure of how to handle this. I'm not sure I'm ready to talk to him yet.

"Hello?"

"Sophie," I can hear him catching his breath. "I… Welcome home."

"Thank you," I say, trying to sound a lot calmer than I feel. My heart is racing. What's wrong with me? This is *boules* we're talking about for heaven's sake. Charlotte looks up at me with expectant eyes.

"I would truly love to join you and the children for *boules*," he goes on, rather tentatively.

"But I understand if you don't ever want to see me again. I tried to explain in my letters. I know how stupid I was. I have no excuses."

"No, you don't."

The other two have arrived and Charlotte explains what's going on. Edward does his 'cat from *Shrek*' face and Emily puts her hands together in prayer and does a little jig.

"Can I at least see you? I think maybe if you saw me, you would realise how sorry I am, and how I feel about you."

I look over at his château and imagine him pacing around his kitchen with the phone. I wonder if he's wearing my favourite aftershave. I also wonder if I can ever trust him again. I guess there's only one way to find out.

"Come on over," I say. "Girls against boys. But don't expect an easy ride."

The Sophie Cunningham

lose your husband and your midriff diet (and find your inner French woman)

Ingredients

One faithless husband (optional)
Time and dedication to do yoga
Lip-gloss (several shades)
Matching underwear (as above)
A string of lovers

Method – Yoga routine for trimming in preparation for la guerre

1. Set aside at least twenty minutes a day for your yoga routine; if you can only manage ten then reduce the amount of sun salutations. Remember to BREATHE throughout, only through the nose.

2. Start with sun salutations, do six on each side. There are

several versions of this, pick the one you are most comfortable with.

3. Next up the yoga sit-ups. Lie on the ground and lift your legs in the air. Make sure your stomach muscles are switched on. This is very important, not only is this part of the exercise, but it will ensure you don't damage your back. As slowly as you can, release your legs onto the floor. Do one for each year of your age. GET ON WITH IT!

4. Now go for the bridge. I love this one. I can FEEL my buttocks getting tighter with every second.

Lie down on the back. Bend your knees, bringing the soles of your feet parallel on the mat close to the buttocks. Lift your hips up towards the ceiling, one vertebrae at a time. Interlace your fingers behind your back and straighten your arms, pressing them down into the mat. Roll one shoulder under and then the other. Lift your hips as high as you can. Make sure your feet stay parallel and keep your chin tucked towards your chest. Hold for a count of twenty-five working up to fifty by adding five each time. If you're feeling extra strong then raise one leg at a time (both would be tricky) towards the ceiling, while keeping your hips level. Release your hands and come back down, again, one vertebrae at a time. Bring your knees into your chest and give yourself a hug.

5. The plank goes as follows: From downward dog (that's the one where you look like an upside-down V, bum in the air,

release the torso forward until the shoulders are over the wrists and the whole body is in one straight line. Just as if you are about to do a push-up.

Press your forearms and hands firmly down; don't let your chest sink, keep your neck in line with your back. Then slowly release your arms so that your whole body hovers about four inches above the ground. HOLD IT for a slow count of eight. Repeat.

6. Finish off the tough stuff with warrior pose. From downward dog, bring your right foot forward next to your right hand. Next turn on the ball of the left foot and drop the left heel to the floor with the toes turned out about 45 degrees from the heel.

Bend your right knee directly over the right ankle, so that your thigh is parallel to the floor. Make sure that your hips are facing the front. Lift your arms out to the side and raise them above your head. Bring your palms to touch and gaze up toward your thumbs, moving into a slight backbend. Hold for a count of fifty. Repeat on the left side.

7. Calm down with a tree pose: Stand up tall with your weight equally distributed on all four corners of your feet. Begin to shift your weight over to your right foot, slowly lifting your left foot off the floor. Bend your left knee, bringing the sole of your left foot high onto your inner right thigh. Press your foot into your thigh and your thigh back into your foot so they support each other. Keep hips squared. Focus on something

that doesn't move to help you balance. Repeat on your left foot.

8. Collapse on the floor for a good few minutes.

PS Look online if you can't work out a pose. You'll find lots of helpful images from every possible angle to help you out.

Acknowledgements

First and foremost a huge thank you to my lovely publisher Martin Rynja at Gibson Square, for his relentless commitment, hard work and belief in me. I would like to thank my girlfriends, to whom I have dedicated this book. They have all helped in so many ways; from inspiring me, letting me steal their jokes to listening to plot ideas and coming up with thoughts. A special thank you to Carla who put up with me endlessly tapping away on our yoga retreat, Noch and Justine for reading the early manuscript and Annika for providing so much material I can write another 20 novels, at least.

A huge thank you also to Jean-Claude Mas (no relation to the fictional Jean-Claude) who took time away from his own wine-making to teach me about it. I highly recommend you try his wines, especially the Arrogant Frog. Thank you JC, for years of excellent wines, fun and taking the time to explain mildew, among other things. Any mistakes in the wine-making parts of the novel are entirely mine.

I also owe a thank you to my agent Lizzy Kremer who gave me the idea for the novel; and to Rhonda Carrier for her excellent editing; and of course my mother Ella Fallgren and my French friend Jacques Kuhnlé for proofreading.

Finally a big thank you to Rupert, my husband and favourite editor, this is not really his kind of book, but I hope he likes it anyway.